The
Inportance
B^{of}eing
Maddison

The Inportance of Being *of* Maddison

Helen E Highton

Matador
9 Priory Business Park,
Wistow Road, Kibworth Beauchamp,
Leicestershire. LE8 0RX
Tel: 0116 279 2299
Email: books@troubador.co.uk
Web: www.troubador.co.uk/matador
Twitter: @matadorbooks

ISBN 978 1789010 077

British Library Cataloguing in Publication Data.
A catalogue record for this book is available from the British Library.

Printed and bound by CPI Group (UK) Ltd, Croydon, CR0 4YY
Typeset in 11pt Aldine by Troubador Publishing Ltd, Leicester, UK

Matador is an imprint of Troubador Publishing Ltd

For my mum, Katherine…
My brother Graham…
Sisters Caren, Georgie, and Bobbie…
And in memory of my dad, Ernie…

With all my love…
Always

Contents

Meet the McLarens
Maddison Elizabeth McLaren

Age:	7 yrs. (going on 70!)
Answers politely to:	sweetheart; princess; poppet; kiddo; Maddison; Maddie and Madds.
Answers impolitely to:	Medicine; Shortshanks; numbnuts; knob'ead; bird brain; foghorn and 'Oy'!

The youngest child of Liz and Joe, Maddie has grown up in a world of adults, and with an uncanny ability to hide in plain sight, she hears everything though understands little. So, having grabbed hold of the wrong end of the stick and with the absolute conviction that she knows what she's talking about, she runs with it with all the enthusiasm of an Olympic sprinter, repeating anything and everything she's overheard or misunderstood, at the least appropriate times.

Brimming with confidence and yet to grasp the concept of tact, Maddie's painfully honest observations leave Liz cringing with embarrassment while apologising profusely to anyone in her daughter's wake. She's eternally curious, fiercely self-willed, and unfortunately, fearless, and owing to her daily battles with big brother Robbie, has acquired a generous measure of resilience along with a crackin' right hook... which comes in handy when your name's Maddison and you have a significantly pronounced lisp.

She's also rather accident-prone and no stranger to causing complete chaos... but don't take my word for it... she's invited you to find out for yourself.

Elizabeth Jane McLaren

Age: 39 yrs.

Answers to: Liz; love; Elizabeth and MUM!

Liz is the mum; a role she takes very seriously. Well mannered; well spoken; intelligent with a twist of sarcasm, she chose to defer her entry to uni when she discovered she was pregnant with Rachel, but somehow never went back.

Pouring everything she had into the kids, she finds herself all too often wondering... *where did it all go wrong? What happened to my perfect family life? My perfect kids?* Oh, yes – Joe!

If only he wasn't so good-looking. Or funny. Or caring (in his own weird way). Or a brilliant dad (despite his appalling language). If only she didn't love him to bits... but she does...

So, bearing this handicap in mind, coupled with her determination to raise the kids in a happy, loving environment with strong and positive role models, she often feels like a solitary salmon, battling her way upstream while feeling completely ill-equipped to do so.

Joseph McLaren

Age: 44 yrs.
Answers to: pretty much anything for an easy life.

Joe's the dad; an alpha male, though he rarely gets to wear the trousers. Born in Liverpool and still a scouser at heart, he moved to Manchester when he was sixteen (to undertake an apprenticeship) and never moved back.

At aged nine his parents separated, and Joe, because he was awaiting a schoolboy trial for his favourite football team refused to go with his mother and siblings to live in Scotland, so remained with his womanising, alcoholic father who he now chooses to have nothing to do with.

Having had a tough upbringing he doesn't suffer fools lightly, and yes at times his language is 'colourful' to say the least, but with a heart of gold and incredibly good-looking, he's funny, caring, and despite all appearances, absolutely adores his wife and kids.

He's now a self-employed electrician but in the early days was a professional musician, touring up and down the country with his band, The Dragonflys. All he ever wants in life is to be left in peace to watch the football, or to sit in a chair long enough for the seat to become warm… but either Liz, or a certain young lady, puts paid to that.

Rachel Jane McLaren

Age: 21 yrs.

Answers to: Rachel or Rache.

Rachel's the eldest child and Maddie's big sister. She's in a serious relationship with Jonathon who she met while attending Liverpool University (and now shares a place with him) but with only a thirty-minute drive back to the family home, she sees her beloved family often.

Mature beyond her years, she's as beautiful as she is kind, and possibly the only living person to have never visualised strangling Maddison. Instead, 'Madds' provides Rachel with a constant source of love and admiration (largely of Maddie's boldness) and is a never-ending source of shocked amusement to her.

Robert (Robbie) John McLaren

Age: 19 yrs.

Answers to: Robbie; Rob; Softlad; Softshite; knob'ead, gobshite and Flash.

Robbie is the only son and 'piggy in the middle'. He's lazy, unmotivated, and most often moody. Supposedly at college with no idea as to what he wants to do, he smokes like a trooper and drinks like a fish, and with his swarthy good looks and 'can't be arsed' attitude, has no difficulty attracting members of the opposite sex and little desire to keep them.

He's the bane of Maddison's life (and vice versa) and having zero concept of how to behave around a seven-year-old, treats her on a par with everyone else (to the constant dismay of his mum). He has to be coerced into taking part in any family activities and will usually beat a hasty retreat to some quiet corner as soon as he's able…

Nanna

Age: 69 yrs (young).
Answers to: Nanna; Nan; Mum; Betty; Wicked
                    Witch of the West and The Grim Reaper.

Nanna's Liz's mum and a constant source of bemusement to her youngest grand-daughter, Maddison, who believes Nanna to be as scatty as a box of frogs – 'from the olden days' – with what appears to be her own special language (idioms), and at a trifling sixty-nine years of age, thinks she's 'probly the oldest person in the actual world!'. And maybe the stupidest, too? How can she not know what's a hashtag? Duh!

Having lost her husband (Grandad Ernie) just after

Maddie was born, Betty is now the most devoted mum and nan/nanna, which according to Joe means, 'she's always hangin' round like a bad smell!'

Nanna enjoys a 'We'll keep it our little secret, poppet' kind of relationship with Maddison, and with her son-in-law, Joe, she endures a typically good-humoured, love/hate relationship, where she most often gives as good as she gets.

Preface
12th December, 2015

"Mum."

"Not now, sweetheart."

"But, Mum!"

"Shush, Maddison. Can't you see I'm in the middle of reading?"

Course I can? I'm not blind?

"But, Mum, it'sth really inportant."

"Important – not, inportant. And how many times do I have to tell you, Maddie? It's rude to interrupt someone when they're reading."

Yeah, well, it's rude to interrupt someone when they're playing 'Gram Feft Auto', but honestly, last year when I said that out loud it was the closest I've come to actual flying. And so what if you have to be eighteen to play? It's not like the police come round to check. And, I still don't know what all the fuss was about cos what eggsacly is a badass niggle? I just heard the man off the game keep shouting it so I joined in shouting it, then next minute my mum burst into Robbie's bedroom and went absolutely mental. First; cos I'm not allowed in his bedroom under any circustances. Second; cos I'm not allowed to play on his egg box under any circustances. And third; if she ever hears me say anything like that again she's gonna wash my mouth out with – ooh? I nearly forgot?

"Mum, I bet your book'sth not as intrestin' as what I want to say."

"Is there ever anything as interesting as what you want to say, sweetheart?"

Erm? No, not really?

"And, it's very interesting, actually. It's by Oscar Wilde: *The Importance of Being Earnest*."

"The inportantsth of bein' – OOH? Isth it about Grandad?"

"Hahaha. No, Maddie. Earnest isn't a…"

"Did Osthcar Wilde know Grandad Ernie?"

"No, sweetheart. Earnest isn't a person, it's an adjective. It means to be seriously determined – a bit like you are now. So, what is it that's so important that it couldn't wait five minutes?"

"Oh, yeah. It'sth about my egg bo…"

"Get out, Maddison."

"Get out *with* a egg boxth for Christmasth or with—?"

"Out! Now!"

"But…"

"MADDISON – GO AWAY!"

Bugger.

Crappy Birthday to Me: Christmas Eve, 2015

Humph! I'm having a *rubbish* birthday! Mind you, it's rubbish anyway, having your birthday on Christmas Eve. And what does everyone mean – trust me to be awkward? How's it even my fault? It's not like I choosed what day to be born on. I don't think you can do that, can you? Don't you just come out when you're ready? But, if you could choose what day to be born on, I definitely wouldn't choose this.

Honestly, everyone's so busy doing Christmas stuff that hardly anyone 'cept my family remembers about my birthday, and I'm sure they only remember cos my mum reminds them about it every five minutes. I don't blame them though – even I forget to get eggcited about it and it's my flippin' birthday! And this year's been specially rubbish cos my best friend Matthew went to live in a Stralia in August so... hang on a sec... I'm just...

"No, I wasthn't a accident, Robbie! An' shut your big fat gob will you? You're ruinin' my flippin' birthday!"

"Yeh, well, you ruin every day for me, Shortshanks. Do one, will ya? You're doin' my swede in."

"Well, you're doin' my sthweed in."

What's a sweed?

"An' anyway, Robbie, how can I be a accident? You can't have a baby by accident. I saw a lady have one on *Coronation Street* one time, and I don't see how you can do THAT by..."

"Jeeze, Shortshanks, drop it, will ya? It was a joke, for fucksake."

"Well it wasthn't – AH! You said the *EFF* word!"

"*And?* Keep your voice down, fog'orn."

"I am not a FOGHORN! An' I'm tellin' my mum you said the– PUT ME DOWN, ROBBIE! I don't wanna go on top of the book shelf! *Muuuum*, Robbie'sth puttin' me on the..."

"For crying out loud, Maddison, what is it now? Put her down, Robbie. It's funny but you never hear Jamie Oliver's kids screaming in the background while he's trying to prepare the Christmas turkey."

"But Robbie'sth ruinin' my birthday! AN' HE SAID THE..."

"Stop shouting, sweetheart – I'm only here! Leave her alone, Robbie."

"*An'* he called me foghorn!"

"*Please*, Robbie? Can't you just be nice to her for once?"

"Course I can. It's not my fault she can't take a joke. She's so easy to wind up, Mum, I'm surprised she wasn't born with a friggin' handle."

"I thought I'd asked you not to say that word?"

"What, handle?"

"An' he said I wasth a accident."

"Robbie, why do you say things like that to her?"

"Cos she's a pain in the backside."

"She's a little girl and you're supposedly an adult!"

"Whatever – I'm goin' outside for a cig. An' she needs to learn to take a joke!"

"And you need to learn not to argue with a seven-year-old. And close the door after you, it's freezing."

"Jokesth are s'posed to be funny, aren't they, Mum?"

"They are, sweetheart. Come and give Mummy a hug. What else has he been saying?"

"Well, you know how he writed on my birthday card, 'Crappy seventh birthday, Maddithon. Oh, and, by the way, you're adopted'… Am I?"

"It's wrote, Maddie, not writed, and don't talk silly. Of course you're not adopted."

"But, he said my dad ordered me by accident, off eBay!"

"Take no notice of him sweetheart. You can't order babies on eBay – accident or not."

"Yesth, but, how come he'sth nearly twenty? An' Rache'sth twenty-one? An' I'm only just seven?"

"OH! Well? Umm? The thing is, your dad and I had

Rachel and Robbie when we were really young, so we decided to wait before having you, so that we'd have more time to enjoy you."

Enjoy me? I'm not a flippin' cheeseburger?

"O-kaaay. But, why've Robbie an' my dad got black hair and brown eyesth? An' you an' Rache've got brown hair and blue eyesth? An' I haven't got any of those?"

"No, but if you look at our family tree…"

Ooh? What family tree? I didn't know we HAD a family tree?

"Your dad's third-generation Italian, which is where Robbie and…"

I wonder which tree it is? There's loads in our back garden…

"And, even though I'm a brunette, my side of the family are predominantly blue-eyed blondes…"

I wonder if it's the big one in the corner? I've fell out that tree loads?

"So, you see, sweetheart. It all depends on your genes."

I'm deffo gonna have a climb of – WHAT?

"My jeansth?"

"Yes."

"MY ACTUAL JEANSTH?"

"Yes. Stop shouting! It depends on whose genes you share, and whether they belong to your dad or…"

How can I share my dad's jeans?

"So, Rache shares more of mine, and Robbie shares more of your dad's…"

"An' I don't share anyonesth jeansth costh I'm only seven?"

"Um? Age has nothing to do with it, sweetheart. It

depends on what you're born with."

Born with? Hahaha. Babies aren't born wearing jeans?

"So, just because you have blonde hair and green eyes, Maddie – what are you giggling at? Anyway, does that answer your question?"

What question? Oh, yes? Am I adopted? Erm? Not really? Imfact, I'm probly more comfused? But…

"Yup. Can I go now?"

"Yes, but – Maddie, come back, I haven't finished yet. Maddison!"

"What?"

"Never mind, *what*! You've got thirty-five minutes before bedtime – that's if you want me to read *The Night Before*…"

"But…"

"No arguing, Maddie. It's still not too late for me to phone Father Christmas."

"What – *really*? Father Christmasth'sth got a mobile?"

"Huh?"

"Well, doesthn't he start at the other side of the world first? So, surely, he must've set off by now? An' what if it goesth off when he'sth halfway down some-one'sth chimmley? It'll wake everyone up an' ruin their Christmasth. An' what if *everyone* decidesth to phone him tonight? He'll be so busy answerin' his phone he won't have enough time to deliver all the…"

"Never mind that, Maddie, just do as you're told! That's if you want any presents in the morning."

Course I want presents in the morning – I'm not the flippin' Grinch!

I'm *umbelievably* eggcited for tomorrow cos I've only asked Father Christmas for one present this year – well, one main present – and I think he will bring it cos I don't see how you can be on the naughty list when you've hardly been in trouble all year? Imfact, besides having a few little accidents, I can't actually remember being in trouble much at all. And all I've asked for's a egg box so...

"Ohmigod, Maddison – have you GLUED these antlers onto his head?"

Erm? Yes? But I didn't use loads. And Robbie said it was okay to put glue on dogs.

"What's wrong with you?"

Actually, now you mention it, I have got a bit of a tummy ache? But that's probly cos I ate Simon Eckersley's birthday present all in one go. But I had to – before anyone saw it and took it off me. And it's not easy eating a whole bucket of fizzy jelly—?

"Am I talking to myself, here, Maddison?"

I think you probly were?

"I said, what were you thinking?"

Well, I was thinking that he'd make a brilliant Rudolph, but now I'm thinking it's a good job I couldn't get the red nose to stick on proply, cos...

"Just wait until your dad hears about this."

"Wait till I 'ear about what, love?"

"Oh, Joe, thank God you're back. You'll never believe what she's done now."

"Hahahaha. Come 'ere boy! Did you do this, kiddo?"

"It's not funny, Joe. She's glued them on!"

"It's when she tries staplin' 'em, love, that's when

you wanna worry. Shame you couldn't find a red nose for him, princess. Then he'd really look the part."

"For God's sake, Joe – don't give her IDEAS!"

"'Ey, princess, I saw that miserable old bugger on the end 'ouse while I was out. He was sayin' about the other day, when you went carol singin' an'…"

Nooo… Shush, Dad!

"When she did WHAT? Sweetheart, when did you go carol singing without me?"

"Never mind that, Liz, d'you know what he said? He said, 'You scousers are all the bloody same.' I was made up, mind, cos I thought I'd lost my accent, but…"

Ooh? Good idea, Dad? Keep her talking long enough so she forgets about the carol singing. But, it's probly a waste of time cos it doesn't matter what anyone does in our family, my mum always finds out about it. She should be in the police or something. Or a spy! Or one of those weird men off the telly – the ones who knows what people are thinking – cos she nearly always knows that. Honestly, whenever she says 'Don't even THINK about it, Maddison!', I've already thought about it, and when she says 'And DON'T bother asking!', I've already breathed in to do it. Anyway, what was my dad saying? Oh, yeah…

"Mum, what'sth a Scousther?"

"A Scouser, sweetheart? A Scouser's somebody who was born in Liverpool. Remember when we watched Daddy's DVD—?"

"What deevy dee?"

"The one he got for his birthday and you said you couldn't understand what the man was…"

"Ooh! John Bishopsth?"

"LEGEND!"

"Shush, Joe. Yes, John Bishop. Well, he's a Scouser."

"*Really?* But, my dad doesthn't talk like that."

"No, but you can tell he still has a slight accent. Mostly, he just sounds…"

"Am I a Scousther, Mum?"

"No, you're a…"

"So, what are you? Costh, wasthn't you born near Manchester?"

"Sort off…"

"Your mum was born in the posh part, princess, that's why she's so…"

"Anyway! Back to the subject! When did you go carol singing without me, Maddie?"

Well, that didn't last long?

"Erm? *Yaaaaaaawn.* I'm proply tired now, actually. Can I go to bed, pleasthe?"

"'Ey? Did I just hear right, princess? You're askin' if you can go to bed early?"

"Yup! I'm *sooo* tired… *yaaawn*… I'm probly gonna fall asthleep even without a story."

"Sweetheart, where are you going? Maddie, come back."

"I can't, Mum."

"What do you mean, you *can't*? Maddison?"

"I just can't! *Yaaaawn.* Goodnight."

God's sakes? Now what am I s'posed to do? It's not even eight o'clock yet, and I'm wide-a-flippin-wake. Mind you, if it's true what my mum says about sugar making me hyper, then I'm hardly surprised. You wouldn't believe how many fizzy bottles I've ate today. But, least if I stay out the way she might forget about me going carol singing without her. And anyway, he started it – he definitely told me to bugger off first. And, I wouldn't mind but I was doing my very best singing! Anyway, I've lended my dad's – ooh? Someone's coming?

"Caught you! Hahaha. Why aren't you in bed, young lady? I thought you were *soooooo* tired?"

"I wasth, Mum… but then… I… *erm*… I waked up!"

"What's the matter, sweetheart? It's not like you to struggle for a ready-made excuse, plausible or otherwise."

That's cos I'm not usually trying to kick my dad's jeans under my bed while I'm talking. And, what's 'pausable or other wives'?

"Anyway, I thought you might like to know that Rache just rang. She said they didn't get stuck in the snow and they've arrived safely. It'll be weird, won't it? Our first Christmas without her."

"I know, Mum, I'll proply missth her. Why couldn't Robbie've gone insthead?"

"Well, I guess because he doesn't have a girlfriend whose parents live in Scotland. But, she'll be back the day after Boxing Day, sweetheart, so we'll see her then. Right, hop into bed and make yourself comfy. Have you had a nice birthday?"

Erm? Not really? Imfact, it's not even felt like my birthday, but…

"Yesth, thanksth."

It's nobody's fault, it's just… I've never had a actual birthday party before cos every year my friends are either not well, going to other people's houses for Christmas, or their mums' are too busy to bring them… so usually me and my family go out to the posh restaurant for my birthday dinner… but, cos Rache had to go to Scotland with Jonathon this morning we went out last night instead, so today's been a little bit…

"I'm so glad, sweetheart. Now, I know you said you're tired but I can't let you go to sleep on Christmas Eve without your special story, can I? So, are you ready?"

"Yup."

"Is Trevor ready?"

"Yup!"

Ooh! You've not met Trev yet, have you? Trev's my…

"'*Twas the night before Christmas, when all thro' the house… Not a creature was stirring, not even a* – are you listening, Maddison?"

"Coursthe, I'm listenin'. Carry on, pleasthe."

"Okay… *The stockings were hung by the chimney with care…*"

I wasn't really. I was trying to imagine how Father Christmas gets past the gas fire. But I'd best pay attention now, 'case she tries to catch me out – like when she reads the wrong words on purpose to check if I actually am listening. And, some of the time I am, but a lot of the time I'm – AH? Did she just say?

"Are you sure you're listening, Maddie? Because, I just said…"

"I know, Mum – it'sth, children snuggled in their

bedsth, not chip monksth!"

See what I mean? So, I've got to go now, cos I don't think Father Christmas's got a mobile but just in case he has. Merry nearly Christmas everybody and I'll see you all soon.

Goodnight!

The Egg Box Challenge:
New Year's Eve, 2015

"OY! Get out, shit-for-brains! I mean it Shortshanks, if I catch you in 'ere again…"

"I'm GOIN' – God'sth sakesth, Robbie! Stop pushin' me, idiot!"

"An' don't come back till you're old enough to make a brew!"

Ugh! I'm sick to deaf of him. I wish it was him what didn't live with us 'stead of Rache. All week he's been yelling stuff like that at me, which is actually quite rude, and why did he get a egg box for Christmas and I didn't? I'm not the one who comes home drunk in the middle of the night and puts pizza in the oven, then forgets all about it and goes to bed. He's done that two times this week and both times he didn't even wake up. Not even when the smoke alarm went off! Just, when my dad threw a jug of freezing cold water over him and dragged him out of bed. And, I don't see why I can't play on his egg box when he's not using it cos it's not like it runs out or anything? Ooh? My mum's talking to me…

"Sweetheart, did you put Robbie's mobile phone in your left-over chow mein last night?"

"Yup."

"Why? Why would you do that?"

Why? Well, first, cos he was skitting my lisp… asking me to pass him the 'thoy thauce', the 'thpring rollsth', and the 'thweet and thour thauce'… and then he videoed me trying to eat noodles with chop sticks and posted it on Facebook! It was *well* imbarrassing… so, I accidently dropped his phone down the toilet on purpose, but cos he was so cross I decided to fix it, and I've heard people say it loads of times before…

"Costh everyone knowsth fried rice getsth water out of…"

"Dried rice, sweetheart – not, fried rice!"

"Oh! Well, I didn't have any rice, so I put it in my noodlesth, instead."

"Maddison…"

"Well, *I* didn't know."

"Maybe, but – never mind, we'll discuss this later."

"Okay, but can I just disgussth somethin' now?"

"Is it important?"

"VERY inportant. It'sth somethin' what you said, so it must be."

Good one, Maddison!

"What did I say?"

"*Well…* remember on Christmasth day when I was completely upset costh Father Christmasth'd brought Robbie a egg boxth an' not me, an' I'd asked for one specially?"

"Brought him a what?"

"A egg boxth."

"Don't you mean an Xbox?"

Do I? Flippin' 'eck, Maddison, what a idiot?

"I do remember, Maddie, but in Father Christmas's defence, you did keep asking for an egg box…"

I did.

"And it was you who broke Robbie's old one."

It was. But, I didn't know they weren't supposed to get red hot then blow up cos nobody bothered telling me.

"Yeah, but, remember you said that if I wasth a good girl all year and didn't get into trouble once, or have any fightsth or accidentsth, an' if I did as I wasth told an' not just what I wanted?"

"I remember saying all of that, yes."

"That, if I did that for THE WHOLE YEAR, then he'd definitely bring me a egg– argh!"

Stop calling it a egg box, idiot?

"I mean a Xboxth, next Christmasth?"

"Yes, sweetheart. I did say that."

"An' did you mean it?"

"Well, I can't speak on behalf of Father Christmas, but I'm pretty sure that if you manage to maintain all of those conditions for the whole year, then he'll most certainly bring you an Xbox next Christmas."

"Promisthe?"

"Promise. Now, give Mummy a kiss."

YES! So, all I have to do is all that what my mum just said, and this time next year I'll have my very own egg– argh! Xbox, and I won't have to lend Robbie's without asking, again.

"So, doesth it start from tonight, Mum? After it'sth the new year?"

"Yes. So, does this mean I'm going to have a stress-free 2016, sweetheart?"

What's stress? Just say yes, Maddison…

"Yup!"

"Then, I shall really look forward to it. Now, do you think you could take your toys upstairs, please? I'm sure you don't want them getting trodden on this evening."

"O-*kaaay*…"

"Liz, love, I'm back! An' have you seen our Maddie anywhere?"

Uh? What have I done now? Quick – hide!

"Hi, Joe, yes, she's… well, she was here a second ago. Did you manage to get everything?"

"Yeh, except I couldn't find any o' that juice you wanted, oh, an' guess what? I nearly went three rounds with some knob'ead in the supermarket – but who kicks off over a bag of ice?"

"You had an argument over a bag of ice?"

"I know – unbelievable, 'ey? But, it was the last one in the freezer… an' I had my hand on it just about to pick it up when this guy made a grab for it. D'you know who I think it was, love? That Postlethwaite bloke. His daughter's in our Maddie's class at school…"

Lucy flippin' Postlethwaite? I can't stand her. Mind you, nobody can.

"So, he starts whinin' on about how he needs it for his cocktails an' I'm stood there thinkin' – if this nonce goes on for much longer we'll be arguin' over a bag o' bloody water! So, I turned round to walk off with it an' he shoved me! I couldn't believe it cos for a start off he looked like he couldn't knock the skin off a rice puddin'…"

"He shoved you? Really? How odd."

"I know! So, then he goes to call the manager over, so I said, 'While you're at it mate, tell him to call you an ambulance!'. Anyway, there's your ice, love. You're welcome."

"Joe! I wish you wouldn't behave like that. It's so indecorous."

"'*Ey?* If you're gonna 'ave a pop at me can you use words I've 'eard of?"

"Indecorous? Lacking in decorum? You should have just let him have it…"

"You what? Oh, you mean the *ice*? You're kiddin' me, right? You said not to bother comin' home without it."

"Yes, but only because you were making such a song and dance about paying for it. It's only ice, Joe – I didn't expect you to start a war over it!"

"Hahaha, it was hardly a war, love – he just flounced off! Anyway, that's me done for the day. Stick the kettle on, will you? I'm gaggin' for a – bloody 'ell, princess, what you doin' under there?"

"She's not under the table *again*, is she? Come on out! And how many times have I told you about listening in on other people's conversations?"

"Soz. Hey, Dad, guessth what? My mum'sth promisthed I can have a Xboxth next Christmasth."

"I said, if you managed to stay out of trouble for the whole year you could have an Xbox next Christmas, and hiding under the table isn't a very auspicious start."

Suspicious tart? What's she on about?

"I think we all know that's not happenin', princess, so I wouldn't get too excited."

"What d'you mean?"

"You? Stay outta trouble? You could cause an accident in a vacuum."

Isn't that what Nanna calls the Hoover? I wouldn't even fit in a Hoover, never mind cause a accident in one?

"An' while we're on the subject – how many days have you had your new bike, now?"

"Seven. Why?"

"Cos, I've nearly run over the bloody thing twice. I've told you not to leave it at the top o' the driveway, so go an' stick it in the shed where it belongs!"

But it's a flippin' nuisance getting it out the shed all the time? Why can't you just look where you're driving?

"Today, Maddie. An' look where you're goin'…"

"I AM LOOKIN' WHERE I'M GOIN'!"

"Oy – less of the attitude if you don't mind!"

God's sakes? I'm not a idiot? Stop telling me stuff what I already…

"WHAAH!"

"OH, FOR F— what did I just say, Maddie? An' you can pick all that ice up an' shove it back in the bag cos I'm not goin' out again!"

Humph! How's it my fault the shopping's ruined? It wasn't me what left it in the middle of the floor? And, if I hadn't turned round to say that I *was* looking where I was going I probly wouldn't have fell over it in the first place. Stupid grown-ups – I can't wait till I'm old enough not to get the blame for everything! Honestly, I'm hardly ever naughty but I'm always in trouble for something, and I wouldn't mind but it's hardly ever my fault. And even when it *is* my fault, it's not really… anyway, it's nearly time for the party so I'm gonna stay in my room and keep out of the way.

Oh, yeah, it's our New Year's Eve party tonight, and I can't help getting eggsited but that's usually when I get in the most trouble, and I'm doubly eggsited for tonight's party cos it's the first time I'm being allowed to stay up for all of it. I know. I've even learned the song and everything. *I wonder who old Lang is?* Then once it's turned midnight and 'Operation Xbox' starts, all I have to do is be good till next Christmas Eve and I'll have my very own Xbox… and really? How hard can it be?

***

"Dad! Daaaaad!"
"What? Hahaha. Who got you ready? Does your mum know you're dressed like that?"

"Yup! She said it'sth probly a good idea costh people won't be able to tell the difference between what'sth blood an' what'sth ketchup."

"True. Who did your face?"

"Me. Aren't the stitchesth cool?"

"*Very cool.* One sec, kiddo, I just 'eard the front door."

Ooh, more people? There's already quite a lot here, but – oh? It's just my dad's best friend.

"Hiyah, Larry, come in, mate."

"Cheers, Joe. Have you had a good – SHIT! You never said it was fancy dress? I didn't think you bothered with it anymore?"

"Don't worry, mate, we don't. Take no notice of our Maddie. You're not right in the 'ead, are you, princess?"

"I'm a zombie, Larry. Do I look scary?"

"Hahaha – terrifyin'! It's a shame you don't bother with the fancy dress anymore, Joe. It was a good laugh, that."

"Yeh, well, you've got our Maddie to thank for that."

Ugh? Not this again? Just cos when I was four and I was s'posed to be asleep in bed – not looking out of my bedroom window – and I saw a massive Spongebob Squarepants walk past our house so I sneaked out and followed him. And, I was having a brilliant time at the club till the police turned up and ruined it. And, just cos my mum and dad had to come and get me from the police station dressed up as – who's Wayne and Waynetta Slob? Well, them. My mum said we're never doing fancy dress again. Or was that the year I sneaked out to watch the fireworks and accidently got run over? That ended up being proply mental cos my mum jumped in the ambalance and forgot she was dressed like a nurse. And my dad wouldn't come with us cos they wouldn't wait for him to wash his make-up off *and* he was dressed like Marry Lyn Munrow. And, by the time he arrived in the taxi, my mum was having a nearly-fight with a very drunk man cos she wouldn't sew his head up in the waiting room. And…

"JOE, HAVE YOU SEEN – there you are, sweetheart! Thank God for that! I heard the front door go and couldn't see her anywhere, so – Hi, Larry – I thought she'd got out again."

"'Ey up, gorgeous, lookin' as sexy as ever. An' that's before I get the beer goggles on."

"Yes, well try to keep them off for as long as possible, hey, Larry. At least, until all the decent people have left. Now, sweetheart, remember what I…"

"I know, Mum! If I take so much asth ONE STEP outside the housthe tonight, it'sth on pain of actual deaf!"

"Death – yes! Now, come with me. Nanna's trying to teach everyone how to do Gangnam Style and she's got absolutely no idea!"

***

Well so far I'm having a fantastic time, and I can't believe it's nearly eleven o'clock at night and I'm still up! And, I specially can't believe I've only been shouted at three times. The first time for throwing peanuts in Nanna's mouth while she was asleep; the second time for being over-eggcited and showing off, and the third time for letting a whole bag of party poppers off in the downstairs toilet and blocking it up with all the streamers. And, I've been teaching everyone how to do 'Gang Man's Tile', '5 6 7 8' and 'The Macca Rainer', and I've eaten so many chicken nuggets with pickles on sticks that I feel like I'm gonna pop.

Anyway, my dad told me to find Robbie and remind him that Big Ben's coming at midnight, but I can't seem to find him anywhere. Robbie, that is… I haven't got a clue who Big Ben is. Probly someone from college? And I know I'm not s'posed to go outside but I don't think the back-garden counts? And that's where he'll probly be cos he's always out here doing smoking, so – *uh? Why's he in the greenhouse, though? He doesn't normally do gardening?*

"Robbie, my dad said – flippin' 'eck, it'sth smoky in here! What you doin'?"

"What's it look like, Frankenstein?"

"I'm not Frank Instine, I'm a zombie – duh! An' my dad said don't forget about Big Ben comin' at midnight."

"Er… right! Cheers for that."

"Who'sth Big Ben? Isth he someone from college?"

"WHAT? Hahahahahahaha. Hahahaha…"

"Stop laughin', idiot. What'sth so funny?"

"Nothin'! Do us a favour, will ya? You know that tin in the kitchen that's got all the chocolates in it? An' the biscuit tin, too? Bring 'em 'ere, will ya?"

"No. Get them yourself."

"I could, but you wouldn't want anythin' to happen to Suarez, would ya?"

"Don't call him that! His name'sth Trevor!"

Ooh! I still haven't told you about Trev, have I? Trev's my absolute…

"TREVOR! Hahahaha. Who the fuck calls a—?"

"Stop laughin', Robbie. What'sth wrong with you?"

"What's wrong with me? Have you looked in the mirror lately? I'm gettin' grief off a pint-sized zombie. Now, are you gonna get me the stuff or is TREVOR gonna—?"

"All right, put him down. I'll go an' get them."

***

Well, I've got no idea what's up with Robbie but he's acting proply weird. I brought him all the stuff what he asked for, so he just sat there stuffing his face with all the chocolates and biscuits and nearly laughed his actual head off! Anyway, it was freezing in the greenhouse so I came back inside, but not before he told me about Big Ben and how…

"Oy, numbnuts, what the bloody 'ell are you doin' up there? D'you wanna end up in 'ospital?"

"What d'you mean, Dad?"

"Get off the table. Now!"

"But…"

"Now! An' watch the food, will ya. No one's gonna touch it once you've had your hooves in it."

I've not got hoofs? I'm a girl, not a horse…

"But, I don't want to BE on the floor. Robbie'sth told me all about Big Ben, an' how…"

"What about Big Ben?"

"How he'sth a giant what getsth eggcited doin' the Okie Dokie an' accidently killsth children. I might die!"

"Don't talk rubbish. No one dies doing the Hokey – oh, for cryin' out bloody loud! You've stood in the soddin' cake!"

"No, I've not!"

"Really? So, what's that all over your shoe, 'ey? Scotch mist?"

Scotch – oh? How did that get there? And it might be cos, what's scotch missed when it's at home?

"Gimme your hand, Maddie."

"O-kaaaay."

Hmm? Seems like a awful waste of chocolate? I wonder? Would it be really disgusting if I licked it off my—?

"Oy! Stop fannyin' about an' get down. You've got three seconds. One!"

"But…"

"Two!"

"But…"

OHMIGOD? It's not cake?

"Three! Right!"

"DAD, IT'STH DOG POO!"

"DOG POO? WHAT THE—? Oy, numbnuts, stand still, will ya! Stop spreadin' it everywhere!"

"I CAN'T! I'm gonna do a SICK!"

"Oh, no, you're bloody well NOT! Where's your Mum? Stay there while I – LIZ, come here, love, you'll have to deal with this. This is your department."

Uh-oh? She's gonna go mental when she sees all

this. But it's not like there's tons of it? And if I'd known I had poo on my shoe then course I wouldn't have joined in with the 'Cha Cha Slide' – which wasn't at all easy with all that food in the way!

"My department? Why? What's the matter?"

"What's the matter? She's only gone an' trodden dog shit through the buffet!"

"Who has?"

"Who the bloody 'ell d'ya think? It's everywhere, Liz. An' I mean, everywhere."

"And why is that my department? You're in charge of dog poo, Joe, so if you'd done your job properly this morning there wouldn't have been anything left for her to…"

"Hang on a minute! How come it's my job to scoop up shit?"

"Because, you do the gardening."

"SO? You don't see Alan Titmarsh runnin' round with a shit shovel!"

"Stop swearing – and it's Titchmarsh."

"Well pardon fuckin' me! An' I told you this mornin' – it was frozen solid an' bringin' up half the lawn."

"So?"

"So, I left it."

"Well, it's clearly defrosted now. Where is she?"

"In there, on the table."

"ON the table? You left her on the—?"

"Yeh, an' if I were you, love, I'd hold my nose before I go in there – it *feckin' stinks*!"

"Thanks, but I'm sure it's not as bad as you're

making – OHMIGOD, MADDISON!"

"What?"

"What were you thinking?"

"I wasthn't."

"What made you scrape it on the tablecloth?"

"I didn't. I wasth doin' the 'Cha Cha Slide'. I slided to the left, then I slided to the…"

"Have you been outside after I specifically told you not to?"

"Yesth, but…"

"Keep still while I take your shoe off! *Eugh!* I don't believe this! You promised me on Trevor's life that you'd be a good girl tonight."

"I know, but…"

"Remember last New Year's Eve, Maddie? £76 for a taxi to A & E!"

"I know, but…"

"Two new fence panels and half the garden up in flames!"

"I know, but…"

"Who in their right mind glues five Catherine Wheels to the garden shed?"

"I know but, I didn't know you weren't meant to glue them. An' I wasthn't proply on fire."

"No, but your fingers were properly glued to my brûlée torch! And you know you're not allowed anywhere near fireworks. Or superglue. Or…"

"I know, but …"

"No more 'buts' Maddison. You're starting to sound like Vicky Pollard."

"But it'sth not *fair*. My dad told me to find Robbie an' tell him Big Ben'sth comin' at midnight, but I couldn't find him in the housthe so…"

"So, you went outside?"

"Yup! An' he wasth in the greenhousthe…"

"*The greenhouse?*"

"Yup! An' he told me to bring him the biscuit tin an' all the chocolatesth what nobody likesth – even the After Eightsth what Nanna left on the radiator an' melted! An' he said that if I told anyone where he wasth he'd seriously damage Trev."

"Oh, he did, did he?"

"Yesth – an' that'sth when I must've stood in poo! I couldn't see where I wasth goin' with all them tinsth in my face."

"*Those* tins! Was he drunk by any chance?"

"I don't think so costh he told me to make him a brew… but I told him I'm not allowed to touch anything what'sth got a plug on it – see, I *do* listen! So, then he said I might not live to be eight costh small people get kicked to deaf when Big Ben'sth doin' the Okie Dokie. Then, just laughed his head off… for agesth."

"*Strange?*"

"I know. Anyway, it stunk in there so I came back in. An' that'sth why I climbed on the table, so I wouldn't get killed by Big…"

"What do you mean, it stunk in there?"

"It smelled proply weird. But it was really smoky so I couldn't…"

"Smoky?"

"Yup. So, I couldn't see proply but it smelled a lot like… erm? Erm… just, weird."

"It's okay, sweetheart. I have a pretty good idea what it smelt of. JOE! JOOOOE!"

Uh-oh? What've I said now?

"Chill ya beans, love. What's up?"

"Let's see how chilled your beans are. M A R I J U A N A. Robbie. Greenhouse. Your department."

Why's margarine my dad's department?

"I'M GONNA SODDIN' WELL KILL HIM! I've told him about this till I'm blue in the face."

Blue? I've never seen my dad's face go blue before? Usually, it goes red or purple when he's shouting at me. And I know he goes mad at Robbie for smoking, even though it's allowed by the police, but he doesn't normally go this mad? Good news for me though. I bet I'm not even in the bad books anymore. Imfact, I bet I'm…

"Right, Maddie, I need to sort out this delightful mess you've made. So, you stay put! DO YOU HEAR ME?"

I'm not deaf?

"Because, it would be nice if we could all let the new year in together for once."

What does it mean, let the new year in? Is it waiting outside or something? And, why do we have to answer the door together? We don't normally do that? Imfact, I'm not even allowed to answer the door since I let Jehovah's Witness in – two of them, actually – but they said they had a really inportant message from God and I thought my mum'd be well cross if she missed

it. But, mostly I let them in cos they said Trev was –
OHMIGOD! TREV! Where is he? I can't let the new
year in without Trev. I can't do anything without him
and he'll be absolutely furious if he misses it. One sec…

"Nanna, have you seen Trev anywhere?"

"I haven't, poppet, but guess what? I've just passed
level fifteen on Candy Crush, and remember when I
accidently 'went live' on The Face Book on Boxing Day?
Well… I'm up to 11,116 likes! Isn't it exciting? And there
was me saying I didn't want a tablet for Christmas. I
can't remember what I did before I got it, hahahaha…"

What – really? Nanna's gone vinyl? But it's
absolutely *rubbish*?! It's just half a hour of her face right
up to the screen saying, 'Poppet, I've touched something
again. Can you make that funny dog come back on The
You Tube? Oh, never mind, Bradley Walsh is coming
on now'. Then the rest of the video's just twenty-nine
minutes of looking right up nanna's nose while she gets
all the questions wrong on *The Chase*. And, 11,116 likes
for not knowing how Facebook works? Umbelievable!
Ooh, Trev? I wonder where he is?

Well I've checked everywhere now but I can't find him.
I even asked everyone to help, 'cept Nanna, cos she's
so busy checking how many likes she's got on 'The
Facebook', that a bomb could go off and she'd probly
think it was a party popper. The only place I haven't
looked is the bathroom but I can't imagine what he'd be
doing in – Uh?

"Rache, why've you got your head in the toilet?"

"Go away… please… Madds… I've had a bit too much… Champagne… and I'm…"

"Isth Trev down there?"

I'm not sure he'd fit, actually?

"Gowaymaddsplease…"

"What? I can't tell what you're sayin', Rache. Are you okay?"

"Doilooklikeimokay?"

"Erm? Not really? But can I have a look, pleasthe? I can't find him anywhere…"

"Madds… gofindmum… andtellher… ohGod – BLEU-GH!"

Oh? This isn't good?

"Okay, Rache. Be back soon."

"Sweetheart, calm down! I know you're worried, but I can promise you Trevor hasn't been kidnapped – and definitely not by aliens."

"Then, where ISTH he? It'sth the only eggsthpla-nantion!"

"No, it isn't. Have you asked everybody? Your dad? Robbie? Rache?"

"Oh, yeah, I forgot to tell you, Mum. Rache'sth head'sth in the toilet… but what if the kidnappersth—?"

"Rache's, what?"

"Her head'sth in the toilet. I think she said she'sth drunk too much shampoo?"

"Is Jonathon with her?"

"Nope. He'sth gone off in a huff."

"Now you tell me! I need to go and check on her,

sweetheart, and we can look for Trevor when I get back. Deal?"

No chance! The kidnappers'll be miles away by then. They must've come in through the back garden? Time to imvestigate what's happened... 'cept it's pitch dark and my shoes're full of poo? Right! Where's my torch and wellies?

I'm glad the moon's proply out cos I couldn't find my torch anywhere, and I don't like carrots so I can't really see in the dark. Good job I found my wellies though, even if they are absolutely massive on me, cos it's proply slippy out here. But I'm sure I'll be fine if I stay on the path and be extra, extra careful. Ooh, I forgot to say. It turns out the family tree's not a actual tree it's a drawing of a tree, but, 'stead of having leafs on it's branches it has all the dead people what used to be in your – OHMIGOD? How did he get THERE? Trev's in the middle of the fishpond. THE ACTUAL FISHPOND!

I don't need three guesses to know who put him there. Robbie's dead when I get hold of him. I remember now. He said to leave Trev with him so I could carry all the tins and – AH! I can see where he's slided him across the ice. He must've done it when I was in the house. And what's my dad doing in the greenhouse? Whatever, I've not got time to find out...

"Don't worry, Trev, I'm comin' to resthcue you."

Concentrate, Maddison. Just take your time... and look where you're going... and be extra, extra – *ooh? I'm not sure this ice is completely safe?*

"Trev, I just have to be proply careful costh it'sth really really…"

Ooh? That was a big crack?

"… slippy, an' it'sth a little bit meltin' an'…"

Ohmigoodness? That didn't sound very good?

"Just a couple more stepsth and – phew! Aww, poor Trev. You feel abstholutely – WHAAAH! OHMIGOD! Heeeelp!"

"Hang on, Rob… Princess, is that –?"

"DAAD! HELP! I'M IN THE FISHPOND!"

"WHAT THE? Hahahah. What you doin' in there, kiddo? There's easier ways to clean your shoe."

"I'm not wearin' shoesth, I'm wearin' welliesth. Help me! I'm drownin'!"

"Are you bloody 'ell drownin' – it's three-foot deep, numbnuts – you'll freeze to death first. Hahaha…"

"Stop laughin' an' get me out!"

"What d'you think I'm try'na do? Hahahahaha. Have you seen this, Rob?"

"Seen it? I'm filmin' it! Shame it's so dark."

"I see you managed to keep Godzilla out the water."

"He'sth not Godzilla he'sth TREV! Get me out! IT'STH NOT FUNNY!"

"It is – an' you'll 'ave to walk towards me, kiddo…"

"But, I can't! I can't lift my legsth up costh my welliesth're full of…"

UH? What's that? Something's moving in my…

"WAAAAAAAH! GET IT OUT! GET IT OUT!"

"Get what out? Here, grab my – Jesus H Christ, it's feckin' *freezin'* in here!"

31

"GET IT OUT! There'sth a fish in my wellie!"

"Hahahaha. It's only a bloody fish. Calm down, will ya?"

"I DON'T LIKE IT!"

"Well if you'd keep still an' stop kickin' your legs all over the place I might stand half a – SHIT! SPUD, NO! Don't just stand there, Rob, get it off him, knob'ead!"

"What d'ya think I'm try'na – oh, for fuck's sake!"

Oh, dear? I didn't know dogs ate fish? I thought it was just cats what ate them?

"Joe, what's going on? I could hear all the yelling from upstairs!"

"Grab her, Liz – she's piss wet through, mind."

"OHMIGOD, MADDISON! I'm lost for words! What part of 'stay put' didn't you understand? Andwhatonearthwereyoudoinginthefishpondwhenyouweresupposedtobe…"

You don't sound very lost for words to me?

"Jeeze, love, take a breath, will ya? Oh, an' Spud's just took a chunk out the Krakken!"

Well that was a surprise and not at all how I planned, but the biggest surprise is – I'm not even in the most trouble? And I walked dog poo through the house, didn't once do as I was told, and killed a actual fish! The best fish, too – The Kraken!

It wasn't me what actually killed him, but my mum said that if I hadn't been so hysterical and kicked my wellie off – with The Kraken in it – or made so much racket that I woke Spud up – and he's had sleeping potion cos he's terrified of fireworks – then he'd definitely still be alive. But, I still can't see how it's my fault though? Anyway, what's left of him's in a bucket in the garden – The Kraken, not Spud – and my dad's promised he'll bury him in the morning.

"Bloody 'ell, Liz, what've we given birth to, 'ey? Look at the state of 'em."

"I know, I can't believe it, Joe. Isn't it supposed to get easier as they get older?"

"Not if tonight's anythin' to go by. Softlad's high as a kite – I've confiscated his stash so no doubt he'll be back to his miserable bloody self sometime soon."

"Did you tell him off?"

"I tried, love, but he was so monged out it was hard to keep a straight face. An' it's a waste o' time talkin' to him when he's like that – the light's on but no one's home."

"So, 'situation normal'?"

"Yeh! But Maddie, hahaha. I wish you'd seen her, love. I was pissin' my sides laughin'."

"I doubt I would have been. It's a good job you were there, Joe, or she could have drowned."

"Give over. I'll tell you what though, she managed to keep Godzilla out the water."

"Don't let her hear you calling him that. You know she doesn't like it."

No, she doesn't! HIS NAME'STH TREVOR!

"No kiddin', I had to prise him out her hand – an' I feel sorry for the poor bloke she ends up with cos with a grip like that she'll pull the bloody thing off!"

Pull what off?

"Joe, that's our baby you're talking about and you know how much she loves him. If anything ever happened to him, I don't know how we'd cope."

"WE? I think I'd cope just fine! Why can't she have a doll like a normal kid? Who carries a two-foot, plastic T-rex round with 'em everywhere? She's not wired up right!"

Yes, I am, and he's *not* two foots, he's fifty-one centymeters from his head to his tail. I measured! Meh!

"She does make me laugh though. She came bursting into the kitchen before; screaming on top note that there's a massive 'mergency – Trev's been kidnapped and we need to tell the police. Then as an afterthought, told me that Rache had drunk too much shampoo and had her head in the toilet. She meant champagne of course, which now seems to be mostly out of her system and all over the bathroom floor, and no prizes for guessing who'll be the one to clean up that?"

"What's goin' on there, by the way? It's not like our Rache to get shit-faced. In fact, I don't think I've ever seen her drunk? What happened to Johnny boy?"

"Hmm! Well you know it was their third anniversary tonight and Rache was convinced he was going to propose? Well, apparently his ex kept phoning; the one he knew from when he was a kid, the one with mental health problems… so Rache got a bit upset and said that if he was going to spend all night talking to her then he may as well go. So, he did."

"Bloody 'ell! So, one's pissed, one's stoned, and one's a fish-murderin' zombie?"

"In a nutshell, Joe, yes! Hashtag, proudparentsofthe-year? In fact, when you put it like that, are we the worst parents in the world?"

"Nah! All kids get up to that shit, love. It's just that ours do it right under our noses."

"I suppose so. Ooh, Joe, look! Let's get back to the party. The countdown's about to start. Come on you three – look lively!"

I can't believe I'm gonna start the new year smelling of fish poo but least I'm not in the hospital again, and…

"At least you've found Trevor, sweetheart. Mum, put your tablet down, it's almost midnight."

"What now, Elizabeth? But I'm just chatting to a really nice gentleman from Nigeria. He says I've won some…"

"Ohmigod! Remind me to talk to you about this later. Come on everybody, it's time for Big Ben."

Thank goodness for that – cos after all the trouble he's caused I thought he wasn't gonna bother coming.

Okay, so the plan is… I'm gonna join in at the top of my voice with 'Old Lang's Eyes', answer the front door to the new year then… hang on a sec…

"Isth it now, Mum? Do I? 4 – 3 – 2 – 1… HAPPY NEW YEAR!

Should old equatorsth be forgot, an' never brought to mine
Should older quaintnesth be forgot, for old lang'sth eyesth
FOR OLD LANG'STH EYESTH, MY DEAR;
FOR OLD LANG'STH EYESTH
WE'LL BREAK A CUP OF TIZER, YUP!
FOR THE SNAKESTH OFF OLD LANG'STH
EYESTH…"

Ohmigod. Can you believe I'm gonna be nine next year and I've only just finished being six? How weird's that? Anyway, I've got lots of dancing to do, so I'll see you tomorrow when Operation Xbox starts…

Happy New Year everyone and…

Goodnight!

Trevor McLaren

Age: 6 yrs (ish).

Answers to: Trevor, Trev, 'that bloody dinosaur', Suarez and Godzilla.

Trevor is Maddison's best friend in all the world. At just over two-foot tall, he's a very handsome T-rex; greyish-brown in colour, who goes everywhere with her… much to the consternation of her parents… and the school isn't very happy about it either!

Revolutions:
New Year's Day, 2016

I don't really get New Year's Day? I don't understand what all the fuss is? It's January, which is the worst month, cos it's the furthest away from next Christmas… and nobody gets any presents? And my mum spends all day conplaining that no one's helping her tidy up the mess from the party… and my dad spends all day conplaining about my mum conplaining that no one's helping her tidy up the mess from the party, and everyone 'cept me has a headache. And when grown-ups have a headache they just tell me to go away, shut up or be quiet! Imfact, the only good thing about this New Year's Day is, cos I've spent nearly all of Christmas showing Nanna how the Internet works, hardly any of my toys are broke. I know. It's never happened before. Usually, I've got nothing left to play with by Boxing Day, but…

"Maddie, are you in here, sweetheart? It's time for your – *good God*! It looks like a bomb's gone off in here. What on earth have you been doing?"

"Playin'."

"Playing what? Armageddon? You're going to have a really good tidy up once you've had your bath…"

AM I?

"… and there's a horrible smell in here."

"Isth it fish pond?"

"No, it smells like…"

"'Ey, Liz, 'ave you seen my jeans anywhere? I thought they were in the wash but – bloody 'ell, has someone farted in 'ere?"

"Don't you mean, has someone broken wind? And it's awful, isn't it? And look at the mess she's made."

"It's not that bad, love, but – jeeze, has she shit in her bin or somethin'?"

"She'd better not have! Will you find where it's coming from, Joe, while I plonk her in the bath? Come on madam… erm, the bathroom's this way. Now, do you think you can be trusted on your own for five minutes? Just, leave the bubble bath alone, try not to splash everywhere, and I'll be back in a minute to wash your hair."

Humph! I'm so flippin' cross! The tidy up police are nosying through my bedroom without my permission, and I can't do anything about it cos I'm stuck in the stupid bath! And there's not that much stuff that shouldn't be in there but – hmm? There's definitely some stuff

I don't want them to find. AH? I've just remembered? Ohmigod, I really need to stop them before they find out what's making the horrible smell but my mum hasn't even washed my hair yet, and…

"What'sth that, Trev? Just, wash it mysthelf? I could do, I s'thpose…"

And I'll be out miles quicker if I do? Now? Which one's the shampoo?

I'm not allowed to wash my own hair cos I don't do a very good job, but it's hardly a surprise when I've got this much. And nobody needs this much unless they're stuck at the top of a tower? But I'm not, so it's just a flippin' nuisance! And it's my hair so it should be up to me how I have it… but no matter how many times I've asked, my mum won't let me get it cut. And since I had a go myself – I'd hardly got started and now I'm not even allowed to look at scissors never mind touch them – but if she's happy to go to school every time I punch Carl Pilling for calling me Rapunzel or Elsa from *Frozen*, then fairy nuff.

Anyway, I've put tons of shampoo on and really really scrubbed it so it should be…

"Flippin' 'eck, Trev. I should've used thisth one costh it smellsth like proper strawberriesth. I wonder if that'sth why Rache drank it? Shall I have a taste of it mysthelf?"

Hmm? Well it does taste a bit like strawberries but mostly it tastes of… I'll just have another try, to be absolutely…

"MADDISON!"

"WHAAH!"

"What are you – STOP DRINKING SHAMPOO! For God's sake! And, would you care to explain to me why I've just found EIGHT SERVIETTES containing every single vegetable you've been given to eat – SINCE CHRISTMAS EVE – in a shoe-box under your bed?"

Not really…

"Ack! Ack! ACK!"

"It's no wonder your room smells like a methane— sweetheart? Ohmigod? Joe! QUICK! MADDIE'S CHOKING!"

Ohmigod, I was – and I'm *not* the stupidest person in the world, cos how was I s'posed to know my mum was gonna come bursting through the door like a howler from Harry Potter, right in the middle of my second taste of shampoo? And, she wasn't in the least bit bothered that I was choking to deaf *and* blowing actual bubbles out, cos she was miles more bothered about…

"You're unbelievable, Maddison!"

Umbelievable good? Or umbelievable–?

"How am I ever going to get these knots out of your hair? And you have a lot of explaining to do, young lady."

Well I probly just put a bit too much shampoo on my…

"Ignoring the vegetables for now!"

Oh, that?

"You can start by telling me why you're in possession of two Stanley Knives, a roll of Duck Tape and your dad's nail gun?"

Oh? Well I was trying to make a dream catcher like they did on Blue Peter but…

"At least fifty sachets – FIFTY SACHETS, MADDISON – of tomato ketchup?"

Well, the sign said help yourself…

"Turn around… and most puzzling… leave Trevor alone and stop fidgeting!"

"But, you're pulling my hair out. You're gonna give me a headache."

"And won't THAT be a turn up for the books?"

What books? I definitely haven't lended any of them?

"And, what's most puzzling is, I found this in your nurse's bag. Do you even know what—?"

"Liz, love, you'll never bloody believe this!"

Uh-oh?

"Remember last summer when I got that big contract – the rewiring job at the stables – an' on the first day I couldn't get the van started?"

"Yes. Didn't you accuse me of losing the jump leads?"

"Er… yeh, well, sorry about that… cos I've just burned my hand tryin' fish 'em out from be'ind her radiator. What the bloody 'ell d'you want with jump leads, numbnuts?"

Oh? Cos me and Trev used them to play Frank Instine and Draclia and we forgot to put them back. But I'm hardly gonna tell you that now. I'm not completely stupid.

"Erm?"

"Is that the best you can come up with? 'Erm'?"

"I don't know how they got there."

"Really? So, they magically made their way up the stairs an' into your bedroom, an' just 'appened to fall behind the radiator?"

"They must've."

"*Okay*... then d'you mind explainin' why you've got three pair o' my jeans in your wardrobe? I've been lookin' for 'em for a week now!"

Oh yeah? I'd forgot about them? And, I tried them on for ages but nothing at all happened to my hair...

"Honest to God, Liz. There's more of my work tools under her bed than there is in the bloody – why've you got that in your hand?!"

"Don't panic, Joe, it's not mine. I found it in her nurse's bag. I was just about to ask if she knew what it was."

"Thank Christ for that!"

"Sweetheart, do you know what this is?"

"YUP! A fermonitor."

"A what?"

"A fermonitor. I found it agesth ago. I used it for takin' my temperature to check if I wasth well enough to go to school, but nothin' happened so I think it'sth broke."

"You put it in your mouth?"

"Yesth? How elsthe can I measure my temperature?"

"I know how I'd measure your..."

"Shush, Joe. Where did you find it, Maddie?"

"In Rache'sth bin when she stayed at Halloween. She had loadsth so I didn't think she'd missth one. What you laughin' at, Dad?"

"You, ya daft melt! Try'na take your temperature with a..."

"She doesn't need to know that. Maddie, look at me when I'm talking to you."

Why? I don't hear with my eyes?

"For future reference, this is NOT something you put in your mouth. Do you understand?"

I'm not a idiot?

"Now Mummy needs to make breakfast, so I'd like you to go downstairs and wait in the kitchen and I'll tackle your hair after we've eaten. And don't move a muscle – do you hear me? Not one muscle!"

If I don't move a muscle, how am I s'posed to walk downstairs? Duh!

"Yup!"

"Good. Now I just need a quick word with your dad. Go on, off you pop. I can see you, young lady. Not that way. Downstairs! Good girl... OH! MY! GOD! Hahahahahaha..."

"I know, love. Jeeze! I nearly shit a brick when I saw that in your hand. I thought you were up the duff again."

"No, and it's negative, thank God, so we're not going to be grandparents yet but..."

"It's still covered in piss, though! Who takes their temperature with a pee stick?"

"I know. I don't know what to do with her? Maybe I should put her on a lead?"

Put me on a lead? I'm not a flippin' dog! And what's a peastick?

Whatever, I'm so cross with myself. I meant to throw the veggytables in the outside bin, but I was so busy having a happy Christmas that I forgot all about them. And, what's up with my mum and dad? They're always doing this; shouting at me for something, then soon as

I'm outside the room they burst out laughing. Anyway, I s'pose I'd best wait in the kitchen cos… *oh, flippin' 'eck? Not him.*

"HAHAHA. Holy shit, Shortshanks! What the fuck've ya done to your hair? You look like Amy Winehouse gone wrong. Let me take a pic."

"Don't you dare!"

"Too late. Cheers, knobchops! Eleven hours in an' I've got January sorted."

"STOP IT, ROBBIE!"

Not this again!

D'you know what he did for Christmas presents last year? He got one of those calendars made, the ones where you use your own photos and stuff, and he gave one to nearly everyone he knows. And d'you know what the pictures were of? Me. Having accidents. My dad nearly died laughing at October's when it was Rache's twenty-first birthday party and Nanna didn't know Cardy Breezers had booze in them… and I'd already drank three before my mum noticed. Ooh, talking about Rache… she doesn't look very well, actually?

"Are you two at it again? Please keep the noise down, guys. I'm not at all used to this hangover business and my head's absolutely pounding. Are you making coffee, Rob?"

"You're gonna need more than coffee, Rache. You look rough as a bear's arse. Why didn't ya just stay in bed?"

"Did you hear the racket up there? And besides, it's the annual 'Family Hall of Shame' meeting in a minute."

"So? You don't live 'ere anymore… an' even when ya did you never got a mention."

"True, but judging by all that yelling, it looks like someone's going to need all the support she can get."

Aww… I love Rache. She's the bestest big sister in the world. It's sad that I don't get to see her everyday, since she went to live in the universe city in Liverpool, but when I do see her she never shouts at me or tells me to get lost, or does anything horrid to Trev. Imfact, I think she's only been cross with me once and I did say I was sorry, but I thought it was a painting set not eyeshadows and make-up brushes, and least when she'd finished nearly crying she said it was a eggcellent picture of a Terror Dacktill… Hang on a sec…

"Rache, tell him! He'sth takin' picturesth of me again."

"Leave her, Rob, although you look pretty amazing, Madds."

"Thanksth. Are you better now?"

"Not especially, and sorry about last night, sweetie, not my finest moment. But hey, I think you'll have a worse headache than me by the time mum's got those tangles out. What did you do to it?"

"I washed it by myself."

"Oy, Shortshanks, was it you what grassed me up last night?"

"What'sth grassthed up?"

"Yes, Rob? What's the story with you last night? And no hangover this morning?"

"Nah!"

"This is a first. I don't recall seeing very much of you at all until midnight."

"That'sth costh he wasth smokin' in the greenhous-the an' eatin' chocolatesth. Fat pig!"

"Rob? Are you smoking green again? I thought you'd quit?"

Green? It wasn't green? It was definitely normal-coloured smoke?

"Yeh, well, I prefer it to booze… an' in future – zip it you, ya little shit!"

"Shut up, Robbie! What'sth that you're doin', Rache?"

"It's one of those quiz things, Which *Game of Thrones* character are you? One sec, Madds. Ooh, I like her. Melisandre – The Red Witch!"

"But, you're too pretty to be a witch. D'you think Rache'sth like Melisth Andrew, Robbie?"

"Is she the one who's always got 'er norks out? She's well fit, her!"

"Norks, Rob? Really?"

"Whatever… you look fuck all like 'er!"

"You should try it, Rob. I reckon you'd get Jon Snow. Or maybe, Robb Stark?"

"Can I try it, Rache?"

"There's no need, Madds, it's a no-brainer. One hundred per cent, Daenerys Stormborn. You've even got your own dragon, if you gave Trev a set of wings."

"No way's she Daenerys. She's Tyrion Lannister, all day, every day."

"Stop callin' me that, Robbie! I'm completely nor-mal sized for someone who'sth seven."

"Yeh! One o' the seven dwarves. You're deffo Dopey. Hi-hooooo!"

"I'm WARNIN' you, Robbie."

"Don't wind her up, Rob, you know what she's like."

Who's SHE? The cat's mother? I don't actually know what that means, but my mum says it all the time…

"Yeh. An Oompa-loompa from Charlie an' the – fuckin' 'ell Maddie! Watch what ya doin', knob'ead!"

"Don't call me knob'ead! I've WARNED you, Robbie! STOP IT!"

"THtop it! Hahaha. Don't ya like me takin' the piTH, MaddiTHon?"

"Leave her, Rob, she's only little. Come here, Madds, come and sit on my…"

"Or a Munchkin? What d'ya reckon, Rache? What's that song about the lollipop –?"

"Yeah, well, Robbie Blobby. You're like the Scarecrow costh you haven't got a brain."

"Yeh, well, leaTHt I can THpeak proply without THprayin' everyone with…"

"RIGHT! THAT'STH IT!"

"Don't be silly, Madds. Put it down."

"Yeh, put it down, Gollum…"

"SHUT YOUR STUPID FACE, YOU BIG FAT UGLY – AH! OHMIGOD?"

"Well done, dick'ead!"

"MADDISON!"

Oops! Three people just screamed my name all at the same time, and I didn't even know two of them were in the kitchen. It was a good shot though, and if Robbie hadn't ducked out the way I absolutely would've knocked his head off with the apple and we'd still have a kitchen window. I wonder how much one costs? Cos I'm not getting any pocket money till it's paid for, apparently. Thank goodness it wasn't the big one or I'd be in real trouble?

Anyway, my dad's fixed it enough that the wind's stopped blowing in the kitchen so we can ventually have our breakfast... and I love New Year's Day breakfast cos it's like normal Sunday breakfast mixed with stuff left over from the party... so it's just a shame my mum has to ruin it by going on about revolutions the whole time I'm eating it.

Revolutions are a waste of time if you ask me. It's just a bunch of stuff I have to promise to do for the whole year, but I've usually forgot what it is by teatime, and according to my mum... oops! She's started talking. I'd best pay attention.

"... and no phones at the table, Robbie. Okay, who wants to go first? Joe? Rache? Robbie? Anybody?"

Am I imvisible all of a sudden? How come nobody ever asks me? Well, if I am imvisible there's no need for me to stay here listening to this rubbish. I'm going upstairs to watch *Kung Fu Panda* and...

"Come back, Maddison!"

Humph? Seems I'm not imvisible, after all?

"Okay then, if nobody wants to volunteer, I will – and I'll begin with Maddie."

Ohmigod! I swear on Trev's life, the only thing I'm actually allowed to do is breathe… and even then I have to do it quietly. How am I ever gonna get a Xbox now? I'm sure my mum's done this on purpose cos I can't possibly do all of this? I'll never remember to look at people when they're talking; look where I'm going; watch what I'm doing; listen to what I'm being told; do what I've just been told; stop talking so much; stop shouting completely and absolutely NO SWEARING! I'm not allowed to touch anything with a plug; anything to do with water; anything what can cause fire; anything with sharp edges; anything what's not mine; anything what IS mine but my mum's decided I'm not allowed to play with. Pick up my mess but don't pick my nose; don't answer the door, the phone, or anyone one back… and I can't remember anything after that cos I was too busy thinking how funny Trev looked with a chocolatey Claire in his mouth to even bother listening.

I don't think I want to be in this family any more. I think I might actually prefer it in the orphanage. They're always saying about sending me there, so I may as well go now and save myself the – hang on a sec. I think my mum's talking to me again.

"Maddison! That's three times I've asked you now…"

Oh, please don't let it be, 'What did I just say?' Cos I've got absolutely no idea?

"I said, do you think you can manage all of that?"

"All what? Oh, my revolutionsth? Yup!"

"So, you're going to at least eat some vegetables?"

I don't remember saying that, but…

"Yup."

"And you're going to do as you're told for the whole year?"

That's a awful long time? I can't see that happening, but…

"Yup."

"And…"

"Liz, love, can I just stop you there? I've been sat 'ere so long my arse cheeks've gone to sleep."

"I thought I 'eard 'em snorin', Dad!"

"HAHAHAHAHAHA…"

"Quiet, Maddison. And, will you two please lead by example?"

"Yeh, but… our poor Rache doesn't wanna be sat 'ere listenin' to all this – look at her – she's the colour o' boiled shite! Tell you what, I'll take it from here. You go an' put one of your Downton-whatsit DVDs on an' you can do the dishes when it's finished."

"Or, you could do them?"

"I could, or I could shampoo the dog shit out the carpet."

"Really? Would you? I scrubbed it last night with disinfectant but…"

"Anythin' for you, my little Fuhrer. Right, you miserable set o' reprobates – time to earn your keep. Rob, you're in charge of binnin' the empties."

"WHY ME? I wasn't even drinkin'!"

"You sure you wanna remind me about that, Softlad? Move it! Now!"

"This is bullshit… what colour bin do they go in?"

"Brown! Rache, you're in charge of combin' out mop'ead."

"For God's sake, Dad. It'll take me all day!"

"*And?* Your mum spent 'alf the night chiselin' dried puke off the side of the bog after you'd thrown your ring up everywhere, so now it's evens."

"Okay, but I'm billing someone for my detangling spray. It costs a fortune, that stuff."

"Yeh, well, you can join the back of the queue, love. There's a window to pay for first."

"Dad, what about usth? What can me an' Trev do?"

"Well, my little princess. In a few hours time when Rache's straightened out your wig, you an' Godzilla can do whatever the bloody 'ell ya want, cos let's face it, you will anyway."

Yey… something I can do! Hmm? I wonder if this is a good time to ask?

"Mum, can I just asthk a questhtion?"

"That depends on what it is."

"It'sth about my Xth…"

"No, you can't, Maddison, and at this rate, there's no way Father Christmas will bring you one, I can tell you that for nothing!"

"But, why? What have I done?"

"What have you done? *Where do I start?*"

Hmm? It's probly a good time for you to go now cos this could take ages…

"You've broken a window, for one. Your bedroom needs fumigating. The Krakken's dead!"

"But that wasth *before* midnight!"

"It still counts! There's more contraband in your bedroom than on Blackbeard's ship. Half your dad's work tools are under your bed. And to top it all off, your hair's a tangled mess! And if I have to – are you listening, Maddison?"

Not really, but I probly should be if I want to get a Xbox next Christmas, and I really really do. But a whole year of not getting in trouble? I'm not sure I can…

"MADDISON!"

Humph. See you soon, everyone… and Happy New Year's Day…

Goodbye!

The Trouble with Parties

"Mum, pleasthe can I come out my room?"

"How many more times, Maddison? No!"

"But, *pleasthe*?"

"No! And don't look at me like that – you're your own worst enemy!"

No, I'm not? Lucy Postlethwaite's my own worst enemy?

"I've told you, you can come out of your room when you're sorry."

"But I AM sorry."

"Well, you don't look very sorry to me!"

How does that even look? I bet I could Google it?

"Well, can I least lend your tablet?"

"No, you can't lend my tablet – or borrow it. You can sit quietly and think about what you've done."

"But I don't *want* to think about what I've done. I'm too sorry to think about what I've done. An' if you let me have your tablet it won't take me *two minutesth* to look…"

"Maddison, shut up! One more word, and that'll be your third strike today."

"THIRD? What'sth the other two?"

"SHUT UP!"

Honestly, this is so umfair! I've been completely good as gold since New Year's Day – even at school my mum hasn't had to go and see my teacher once – then I have one tiny little accident, and I know I've made a little bit of a mess, but you can easy get paint off clothes and people and dogs… and how is it even my fault? Why didn't anyone tell me they'd painted Robbie's bedroom? I know they wanted it to be a surprise for him when he gets home from Hamster's Dam tomorrow, but it didn't have to be a surprise for me! And I just thought it was the normal sticky on his window sill from where he spills everything. And how am I s'posed to know what paint smells like? And yelling at me that I'm not s'posed to be in there in the first place is hardly helping. And now, just cos of this, I'm not allowed to go to Simon Eckersley's birthday party this afternoon! I know! My mum's so unreasoningable.

"And, I don't know why you're looking so badly done to, Maddison, because it's going to take a whole gallon of turps to remove this paint from everything. And, don't think you're going to get around your dad this time because he's absolutely livid! I just hope for your sake that he's calmed down by the time he gets back and doesn't still want to string you up by your…"

"What'sth a gallon?"

"Really, Maddison? Out of everything I just said, that's what you're concerned about? Honestly, I'd get more satisfaction if I was talking to the wall."

So would I, actually…

"I don't know what's taking him so long, but if I were you I'd be as quiet as a mouse when he gets back – he said, if he hears so much as a peep out of you for the rest of the day, then he won't be responsible for his actions."

Meh!

I'm so cross I don't know where to start. First; mice aren't quiet, which is how we know there's one in the loft. Second; if I was at Simon Eckersley's party where I'm s'posed to be, my dad couldn't possibly hear a peep from me. And third; is that a actual thing? Not being responsible for your actions? Cos if it is, I'm gonna say it every morning even before I wake up, and that way I'll never be in trouble again. Anyway, I'm mostly cross cos my mum's comfyskated Trev… and he's not *covered* in mangolian paint… he's got some on his head, some on his body, some on his arms… oh, and some on his legs, but…

I wouldn't mind but Robbie's bedroom's the only place where I can see Simon's house from, so I was only watching for his mum coming to pick me up for the party. And I didn't imvite Spud to climb up on the window sill with me – he just did it! And we only had a little jump on Robbie's bed. My mum was completely eggzaggerating when she said it looked like a centypeed with size twelve feet'd been running all over his – ooh? I think my dad's back? I'll just open my door a bit and listen to what he's saying, and if he sounds in a better mood I'll ask about going to the party. My dad never stays grumpy for very long so...

"Joe, is everything ok? You've been gone ages – I was genuinely starting to worry."

"Yeah, love, everythin's fine..."

Brilliant. I'll just let him take his coat off then I'll...

"But, you're never gonna believe this!"

Oh?

"I drove into the car park, right, an' it was completely empty – not a single car in sight – so I parked in a space by the door, I was in there less than five minutes, came out, an' there's some smug twat stickin' a..."

"JOE!"

"Sorry, some smart-arse stickin' a ticket on my windscreen – said I was parked in a disabled bay an' unless I could produce my badge, the ticket stands. An' you know me, love, when have I ever parked in one o' them? I don't even park in the kiddie..."

"One of *those*, and it does seem a tad extreme, if the car park was empty?"

"It was. An' unless they were expectin' a sudden rush o' – anyway, I tried reasonin' with him but..."

"What did you say?"

"I told him if he didn't take it back, HE'd be fuckin' disabled."

"You didn't? Ohmigod! You didn't really say that, did you?"

"Yeh, why? You should've 'eard the way he was talkin' to me, Liz. He really pissed me off an' I wasn't in the best o' moods to begin with. You know those blokes who couldn't punch their way out of a paper bag, but give 'em a badge an' a uniform an' they think they're fuckin' 'itler?"

"JOE!"

Who's Itler?

"Anyway, I ripped the ticket off the windscreen an' told him to shove it as far as he could reach. So, then he starts wavin' his camera at me like a right nonce; quotin' some parkin' violation shite an' gobbin' off about photographic evidence, so I…"

"I don't think I want to hear this."

I do, Dad… carry on.

"So, I opens the boot to put the paint an' stuff in, but d'you remember that massive brolly we borrowed off your mum before Christmas? When it was pissin' down an' we took Maddie to see the reindeers? Well, it was still in there. In the meantime, Softlad's makin' a beeline for me, an' as I lifted the brolly out the boot I must've pressed the button or somethin' cos the bloody thing went off in his face! Fuckin' hilarious!"

"Oh, thank God for that. Not that that's not bad enough, but I thought you were going to say that you'd hit him."

"Oh, I did that all right, but only in self defence. An' it was only a tap, mind, but the soft bugger dropped like a sack o' shit! The coppers saw it clear as day on the CCTV, so it was…"

"THE POLICE?"

"Calm down, love – they saw the brolly go off an' him swing first, so they slapped me on the wrist for brandishin' a mildly dangerous weapon… somethin' like that? I wasn't payin' too much attention to be honest cos I was busy thinkin' that I'd better not miss the match. Anyway, it's all sorted now. I've got seven days to pay the fine an' produce my licence down the station and I'm back in time for kick-off. Are you stickin' the kettle on, love? I'm spittin' feathers 'ere."

"So, nothing much happened then? Just, another uneventful day in the McLaren household? FOR GOD'S SAKE, JOE! You go out for TURPS and PAINT and come back with a PARKING FINE and a CRIMINAL RECORD!"

"Friggin' 'ell, love – don't get ya knickers in a twist! What is it? Wrong time o' the month?"

"WHAAT?"

Uh? Is my mum a weird wolf? I'm sure it's weird wolfs what go mental at the wrong time of the month?

"All right, love – calm down! I was only 'avin a…"

"CALM DOWN? I'LL SHOW YOU CALM DOWN! Maddison, put your dress back on; you're going to the party! NOW!"

WHAT?

Well, this is a surprise. Funny thing is, I'm not even sure if I want to go to the party now. And not just cos it's started already or cos I'm scared of missing something, but besides one leg, I'm mostly covered in mangolian paint. Two times I breathed in to ask my mum if she'd clean it off me but she looked so cross that I just breathed back out, and when I tried to wash it off myself she yelled at me, 'Don't be ridiclious, Maddison. You can't remove gloss with soap!' How am I supposed to know that? I'm only flippin' seven.

So, now I've got to go to Simon's party looking like a mangolian-coloured idiot. And that's a other thing? Why can't I go to parties dressed how I want? Why do I always have to go dressed how my mum wants? I feel proply stupid in this party dress, specially now it's rock-hard from all the paint – and fancy buying me party shoes what're at least two sizes too big! Why can't she just buy me ones what fit? Why do I always have to grow into them? And, usually by the time I *have* growed into them they're almost completely destroyed cos it's took me all that time to learn to walk in them…

"Straighten your face, Maddison, you're going like that, whether you like it or not."

"*But, Mum…*"

"Never mind '*but Mum*'! You're lucky to be going at – where are you going NOW?"

"To get Trev. He'sth imvited to the…"

"He's in the garage, soaking in a bucket of turps…"

HE'S WHAT?

"… so, say goodbye to your dad, Maddison, and I'll see YOU, Joe, when I get back!"

★★★

Flippin' 'eck. I can't remember the last time my mum

was this cross? And she definitely didn't take her time cos that's the quickest I've ever walked anywhere! And I was so busy trying to keep my shoes on that I missed most of what she was saying… something about behaving myself? But, I do that anyway? Anyway, she proply threw Simon's present at him, shoved me through the front door, then stomped off up the path like a actual mad woman. But, least I'm at the party now…

"Happy Birthday, Simon."

"Thanks, Maddie, but, where've you been? We've already played musical statues and all the food's nearly gone. And – how come you're covered in paint?"

"Well, I had a tiny little accident and got some paint everywhere so my mum wasthn't gonna let me come, but then my dad got in trouble with the police so she changed her mind again. I think she'sth turned into a weird wolf or something? Anyway, sorry your present'sth a bit rubbish. I told her you don't like jigsawsth but she just egnored me."

"It's okay. Where's Trev?"

"The weird wolf'sth comfyskated him. He'sth in the garage soakin' in a bucket of twerpsth."

"Twerps?"

"I know. I don't know what it isth either. Anyway, what did you get for your birthday?"

"Lots of things really. My favourite present's a radio control helicopter, but my mum's took it off me."

"How come?"

"Cos I flew it into her head by accident, and it got stuck in her hair."

"Isth that all? It'sth a bit mean taking it off you just for that when it's your flippin' birthday!"

"I know. AND she's invited Carl and he's already strangled two people!"

"*Really?*"

"Yes! And he's made Alliah cry for wearing glasses and stuck two fingers up at my mum, and don't go mad, Maddie, but he's ate all the chicken nuggets. He – where're you going?"

"I'm just gonna say hello to everyone, that'sth all."

"Promise? You're not gonna fight him, are you?"

"Coursthe not!"

I'm not! I'm just gonna say hello…

★★★

"Right! Have you calmed down now, Maddison?"

Not really – and why's she asking me if I've calmed down? What about Carl?

"Yesth, but HE started it, Simon'ths mum!"

"Yes, well, I'm sure he regrets that now – no, Carl, not like that! Lean forward and keep pinching it and I promise you it'll eventually stop bleeding… Really, Maddison, that's not very ladylike behaviour. Now, no more fighting, okay? I don't want to have to send you home."

Humph! What's ladylike behaviour? And I don't know why I'm the one she's saying it to cos Carl definitely tried to strangle me first. And, how it's worse, using my ponytail to do it? Strangling's strangling, no matter what you use? And, I only choked him half to deaf cos I was waiting for him to promise he'd stop spoiling Simon's party. And, if he'd promised that, 'stead of promising he was gonna melt Trev next time he sees him, then I absolutely wouldn't've burst his nose. And it's not bleeding that much – big baby!

Humph. I wish I'd not bothered coming to the stupid party now…

"Okay, Kids, everyone gather round."

Actually, I think I'm just gonna go home. I'm starving hungry and the food's all gone so – OHMIGOD! CAKE! *Okay, I might stay a little bit longer?*

"Are we all ready to sing 'Happy Birthday'? Yes? Okay, everybody, after…"

"HAPPY BIRTHDAY TO YOU. YOU LIVE IN THE ZOO. WITH THE ELEPHANTSTH AND THE MONKEEEEEEEEEYSTH, AN' YOU SMELL LIKE DOG P…"

"Thank you, Maddison! I've never heard that version before, or anyone sing with quite so much gusto. They ought to rechristen you 'Maddie Blessed'."

"*Aww…* thanksth Simon'sth mum!"

What a lovely thing to say. Jesus was blessed and so were the angels. She must really like me. Imfact, I might stop saying 'Simon Flippin' Eckersley'?

"Okay, sunshine, time to blow out your candles. Big breath and after three, 1 – 2 – 3."

Whoosh!

"Hurray! Well done Simon. That'sth– uh?"

That's weird? The candles have come back on fire?

"I wonder how that happened, sunshine? Try it again… After three… 1 – 2 – 3."

Whoosh!

"Hurray! Well done Sime… UH?"

They've come back on again? He's obviously not blowing hard enough… and it's all right for everyone else cos they've had loads of party food already, but I'm absolutely starving and I want some cake…

"Okay, sunshine. Let's see if the birthday boy can blow them out this time. So, big breath and after…"

Let's not! Some of us are starving to deaf here, and if it's up to Simon, we'll be here all day…

WHOOOOOOOOOOOOOOOSSSSSHHHHH!

"YESTH! HURRAAY!"

"MADDISON!"

"WHAT?"

They're out NOW, aren't they?

★★★

Humph. How was I s'posed to know they're magic candles? Who's ever heard of them? And I did not gob all over the cake, I just blew extra hard that's all… and it's not my fault everyone's so fussy that now they won't eat any of it… which probly eggsplains why I feel a bit sick though… cos I've ate tons.

I ate most of it while I was watching Mr Majestic, and I'm still not sure what he was meant to be cos aren't clowns s'posed to be funny? But, even though he looked like a clown and was dressed like a clown, he wasn't very funny at all. Imfact, he was proply, proply grumpy.

First, he made a bunny pop out of his hat, and birds fly out of his sleeves, and flags come out of his mouth... and a tiny bottle of booze fell out his coat pocket but I don't think we were s'posed to see that. And, every time I asked if it's allowed to keep bunnies in hats or birds in sleeves he didn't bother to answer – just egnored me and carried on doing magic.

Then he got a puppet out of a box and pretended to make it talk, but no one could understand anything it said! 'Cept, maybe when it kept saying 'Ee choir Addison' – which we think was s'posed to be, 'Be quiet, Maddison' – but every time I asked it, it just said it again! And it kept calling Simon, Shimon, and Michael, Ichael – then Carl threw a cushion at it while it was singing 'Hahee Girthday' and its actual head fell off! I know! It was so funny but Mr Majestic didn't think so... and I don't care what Simon's mum said, he definitely did tell Carl to 'huck off!'.

Anyway, after Simon's mum paid him some extra money so he wouldn't go home, he made us all balloon animals. I don't know why he didn't just do that in the first place cos he was brilliant. He made unicorns and giraffes and my Nemo fish was awesome, but Simon's was the best – a crocodile what came undone and turned into a actual sword! So, then everyone's animals came undone and turned into swords and we had a massive big swordfight, and that's when Mr Majestic ventually went home – and in a massive great huff too!

Anyway, I've definitely had too much cake and fizzy pop – well, I'm not allowed them at home cos too much sugar makes me hyper, apparently, but no one's here to stop me so I've ate and drank loads!

Hmm? I think I'll go upstairs and put my head in the toilet like Rache did, cos I really don't want to do a sick on Simon's mum's carpet.

★★★

"Maddison, where ARE you? Everybody's waiting to play pass the parcel."

Ooh? Pass the parcel? I definitely don't want to miss that? And I've been here ages now and nothing at all's happened. And it's really boring just looking down the toilet when I could be at the party…

"I'm upstairsth in the toilet, Simon'sth mum! Pleasthe don't start without me."

They'd better not cos I've already missed musical statues and – uh? Where's the flippin' stairs gone? They were definitely here when I came up them? Ah, there they are…

"Hurry up, Maddison!"

"I am!"

"Everybody's waiting to start!"

"*I know!*"

"COME ON!"

God's sakes, I'm going as fast as I…

"WHOAAAA! Ow! Ow! Ow! Ow! Ow! OW!

Flippin' 'eck, that wasth a surpristhe!"

Why's everyone screaming? Haven't they ever seen someone fall downstairs before? And – *uh-oh* – BLEU-UUUGH!

★★★

Stupid slippy carpet! Stupid, too big shoes! And who's so stupid they keep a goldfish at the bottom of the stairs? People fall down them all the time, don't they? I know I do... so, isn't that just asking for trouble? And no one cared at all that I banged my head on every stair on the way down, or that I did a massive sick when I got to the bottom – they were all too busy screaming, 'I'm not touching it – someone put it back in the bowl!' – to even bother noticing. And, I'm not saying anything – BUT? The last time I saw Webster he seemed perfekly happy to me. Imfact, he seemed so happy, he was actually dancing on the carpet. So, it wasn't me knocking him out of his bowl what killed him, it's cos no one'd touch him to put him back in, and by the time Simon's mum'd found something to scoop him up with, he wasn't dancing any more. Poor fish...

Anyway, my mum's gonna be here any minute now, and I hope she's in a better mood than she was before. But, if she's not... Hmm? I could run away, I s'pose. 'Cept, I've got a really bad headache and I don't think I'll get very far covered in mangolian paint and party sick... but worse of all, I haven't got Trev. I hope he's not in a specially bad mood when I get back cos I don't think he's gonna be very happy at spending the afternoon in a bucket of twerps, 'stead of coming with me to the party. Whatever, I'm not running away without him, so, good luck, Maddison…

Ohmigod! If I thought I was walking quickly on the way to the party, then I'm nearly flying on the way back – and my mum hasn't spoke a word! Not one word! That's never happened before? The only thing I *do* know is that I'm never going to any more parties, and I only know that cos I heard her scream it in Simon's mum's face. And, she's proply squeezing my hand too, but I'm too scared to tell her it's hurting. Least, she'll have to let go of it to open the front door. I hope so, cos it's actually turning…

"Get in, Maddison."

What? Still no shouting? Mind you, she hasn't shut the front door proply ye…

"WHAT'S WRONG WITH YOU?"

Well, my hand's really hurting if you must know.

"What goes on inside that head of yours?"

Ah? They're two different colours? One hand's normal coloured and the other hand's—?

"We're only in January – you've been to two parties and killed two fish!"

Ooh? That's what my hands look like? One fish, two fish, RED fish, BLUE fish?

"ARE YOU EVEN LISTENING TO ME, MAD-DIE?"

"What? *Coursthe* I'm listenin'."

The whole street's probly listenin?

"SO, WHAT HAVE YOU GOT TO SAY FOR YOURSELF?"

Erm? I don't know? What have I got to – OOH?

"Actually, Mum, I'm not responsthible for my own actionsth!"

★★★

Some words of a vice. Turns out you're *always* responsible for your own actions, and never let your mum get paint off you when she's in a really bad mood. Honestly, she took half my skin off *and* called me a cereal killer, and when I asked 'how can you kill cormflakes?' she very nearly eggsploded! She's calmed down a little bit now, but...

"Maddison! Bath!"

But, why? You've just got all the paint off me? Why do I have to go in the—?

"Today, please!"

"*Noooo.* Can't I just—?"

"NO! And when you come out we're going to make a list of everything you have to pay for. The kitchen window; the paint; a goldfish..."

Rachel's tangle spray... blah blah blah.

"...and any more messing from you and I swear to God you'll go straight to the orphanage."

What, again?

"And before you ask, this does NOT bode well for you getting an Xbox next Christmas."

I wasn't gonna ask, I'm not completely stupid? But, seeing as you've mentioned it...

"But why? I didn't fall down the stairsth on purposthe, an' Carl definitely…"

"WHY? Have you seen the state of Robbie's bedroom? I've had to wash everything! The bedding; the curtains; the carpet; THE DOG!"

Stop shouting…

"And money doesn't grow on trees! Have you any idea how much paint costs?"

Not really? 'bout a pound?

"So, this is your last warning, Maddie. One more…"

"Liz, love, can you come downstairs a minute?"

"I'm busy, Joe, what is it?"

"Can you just come down, love?"

"Whatever it is, can't you deal with it?"

"Er… not really."

"Why not?"

"Cos, there's a clown at the front door."

"A *what*?"

"A clown…"

"A CLOWN?"

"Yeh – said his name's Mr Majestic, or summat? Wants to know if…"

How the flippin' 'eck did he find out where I live?

"A CLOWN? AT THE FRONT DOOR?"

"Bloody 'ell, Liz – yes! A clown. He wants to know if our Maddie knows anythin' about…"

"Maddison, why is there a clown at my front door?"

Uh-oh? Quiet voice? Now I'm really in trouble…

"I'll ask you again, Maddison. Why is there a clown at my front door?"

God's sakes – I'm gonna have to go now, soz, but it's probly best anyway. I'm sure you've heard enough shouting for one day, and there's probly gonna be quite a lot of it when my mum finds out that I've...

"Well, Maddison?"

Soz, I'll have to tell you next time... see you soon, everyone.

Goodbye!

Everybody Loves Pizza

Well, thank goodness for that. After four whole weeks of being stuck in the house – 'cept for when I had to go to school of course – I'm finally not grounded.

First, I was only grounded for two weeks… oh yeah, turns out Mr Majestic was quite cross about me letting his bunny go in Simon's back garden, and seeing as we couldn't find Mr Hop anywhere, that's a other thing my mum's wrote on the, 'Things Maddison has to pay for' list. But then it snowed, and I mean *proply* snowed… and I was so upset at missing it that my mum ventually gived in and said if I promised to behave myself I could go out to play. So I did, and I did *everything* I was told. I kept my gloves on, didn't eat snow, and didn't throw snowballs at windows, people or cars, and 'stead of joining in with everyone else I stayed on the front garden all by myself and concentrated on building the world's best snowman.

Olaf was awesome. He had the orangest carrot for his nose and two pasher fruits for his eyes and Grandad Ernie's old hat and scarf for his clothes – imfact, he was so good my mum said she'd be out to take a picture of him in a minute but he didn't last that long umfortunately.

Robbie came home from college – saw Olaf – picked up his whole head and threw it at me! Right in my face! I couldn't breathe it hit me so hard, but that's 'No eggscuse, Maddison! You're grounded for a other two weeks!'… and I couldn't even pretend I didn't say it cos it was on the video.

Oh yeah, my mum'd decided to make a video of my snowman 'stead of just taking a picture of him. It's still on her phone actually, and it's well funny. Imfact… hang on a sec. I'm gonna find her phone and watch it again…

'Okay, let's go outside and – Oops! Sorry, Spud, I didn't see you there. Let's go outside and see what a clever little girl Maddie's been. And she made him all by herself you know. There she is, tongue sticking out and – oh, and there's Robbie home from…'

'ROBBIE, DON'T YOU FLIPPIN' WELL…'

'STRIKE! Dwarf down… Hahahahahaha… hahaha…'

'WHAT DID YOU DO THAT FOR? YOU FRIGGIN' FUCKIN' IDIOT!'

'MADDISON! OHMIGOD! GET INSIDE! NOW!'

And that's why I got grounded for a other two weeks.

Anyway, cos I've been as good as gold ever since, and tonight's a special night, me, my mum and dad are going out for pizza. D'you know which special night it is? Shall I give you a clue? It's when you get flowers or chocolates or a teddy bear – or if you're my mum, a ironing bin. Well, that's what my dad got her last year and she didn't talk to him for nearly a week. But, she seems happy this year with her new curly tongues and my dad loves his new football deevy dees – oh, yeah, have you guessed what it is yet? It's Valentime's Day!

I'm not sure what time we're going but it must be nearly time now, so I'm just gonna ask my dad cos he's always ready first when it's anything to do with food…

"…I thought you said you liked this girl, Rob? So, what's she done to deserve this?"

"You're not funny, Dad. Stop takin' the piss!"

"I'm not takin' the piss. An' I was only askin' in case we have to tell the paramedics. Food poisonin's a bastard."

"Give it a rest, will ya."

"I'm just sayin', for someone who can't cook a frozen pizza without settin' the house on fire, it seems a bit risky cookin' for someone you wanna impress."

"Well I'm not cookin' frozen pizza so problem solved!"

"All right, Heston, keep ya bloody wig on! So, what's she like then, this… has she got a name?"

"No, Dad, her parents couldn't be arsed thinkin' of one. Course she's got a name."

"Well? Are you gonna tell me, or do I 'ave to guess?"

"Knock yourself out."

"I'll knock you out, you cheeky shit! I'd have more joy talkin' to Rumple-friggin'-stiltskin."

"Rumple who? Who the feck's he?"

"You've never heard o' Rumplestiltskin? I used to read it to our Maddie…"

He did… and *The Three Billy Goats Gruff* and *Hansel and Gretel*…

"God's sakesth, Robbie, how can you not know who Rumblestiltskinsth isth?"

"Ey up, princess, who rattled your cage?"

"No one, Dad. Don't you know anythin', Robbie? Rumblestiltskin'sth a mean imp what stealsth a girl then stealsth her baby, an' he won't give it back till she'sth guessthed his name."

"HA! Sounds like a right paedo, if you ask me."

"What'sth a pea-doh?"

"Never you mind, princess."

"Isth it rude?"

"Nah, it's not rude, it's just – do us a favour, kiddo, go'n get the flowers out the car, will ya? They're for your mum, if she ever comes downstairs again. They're on the front seat, there's a good girl."

You're not getting rid of me that easy? I'll just listen from the front porch instead. Oh, and… message to Maddison: find out, what's a pea-doh?

"Jeeze, Rob, I dodged a bullet there…"

"JOE, IS MY PASHMINA ON THE COFFEE TABLE?"

"D'YOU MEAN THIS SCARF THING, LOVE?"

"Yes. I thought I'd left it…"

"JESUS, MARY 'n' JOSEPH! What the fuck've you done to your hair?"

"Thanks, Joe – not quite the reaction I was hoping for, and the curls will drop a bit."

"I should bloody well hope so – I'm kiddin', love!"

"You don't like it, do you?"

"If I say yeh, will it get us out the house any quicker? I'm bloody starvin' 'ere!"

"Well, I like it!"

"Good, cos my stomach thinks my throat's been cut. I can't wait another two hours."

"Don't exaggerate! It doesn't take me that long to straighten my hair."

"Not far off! D'you know, son, there's been times I've sat here waitin' so long, I've had to go back up for another bloody shave! Anyway, where's our Maddie with those—?"

Ooh? The flowers?

"Are these what you – flippin' 'eck, Mum! What'sth happened to all your hair?"

Humph! Me and my big mouth? What about my dad's? He's the one what said she looked like Harbo Marks, whoever she is? Anyway, he's ventually managed to comvince her that she looks lovely, so it looks like we're ready to go…

"Okay, Softlad, we'll be back about nine, so try not to burn the house down, 'ey? Er? You can leave that 'ere, princess."

"BUT…"

"He's not comin', an' that's my final word!"

★★★

"Good evening, madam. Table for three?"

"*ROOOOOOARRRRRRRRRRR!*"

"Yes, thank you. Sweetheart, take Trevor out of the nice lady's face."

He's hardly in her face? We're not that tall? And, three? Do they make triangle tables?

"Follow me, madam… Will this do? So, here are your menus. The salad bar works on a 'help yourself' basis, and I'll be back in a minute to take your…"

"I know what I want now, nice lady. Can I tell her, Mum? Pleasthe?"

"Actually, we all know what we want, so we're ready to order now, if that's okay?"

"Of course, madam. Can I take your drinks order first? What would you like?"

"I'd like…"

"CANIHAVEACHOCOLATEMILKSHAKE-PLEASTHEMUM?"

"Shush, Maddie! One chocolate milkshake, a large salted caramel latte, and you, Joe?"

"Well, if you're only 'avin' coffee, love, will you drive home an' I'll 'ave a pint?"

"I suppose so. And a lager, please."

"So, that's one chocolate milkshake, one salted caramel latte, large, and one pint of lager. Any starters?"

"We'll just have the salad bowl, please."

Salad? I'm not a flippin' rabbit?

"Large or small?"

"Small, please. And for my main, could I have the fettucini Alfredo? Lasagne for you, Joe?"

"Yeh, an' d'you do chips, love?"

"We do, sir. One portion of fries. And for the little lady?"

Who's the little—? Oh me!

"Can I have a massthive meat feastht pleasthe, without ham but loadsth of pepper only?"

"Sweetheart, you'll never manage a large one. Can you make that a—?"

"I WILL eat a large one. Honestht!"

"You won't. Can you please make that a small—?"

"But, I WILL!"

"Okay! But you'll get nothing else to eat until it's gone."

"*Okaaaaay.*"

"So, that's one salad bowl; small. One fettucini Alfredo. One lasagne with a side of fries and one large meat feast, no ham but extra pepperoni. Here's your salad bowl – do help yourself, and I'll be along with your drinks in a couple of minutes. Is there anything else I can help you with?"

Ooh, I know?

"Yesth – what'sth a PEA-DOH?"

God's sakes, how can I be trying to imbarrass my mum on purpose? I don't even know what a pea-doh is? I thought it was like Play-doh, but different. And my dad didn't say anything, just legged it with the salad bowl, so, I still don't know what one is. Anyway – ooh, the lady's back…

"Sorry for the delay, madam. The barista was on his break."

"No worries… my husband's not back from the salad bar yet."

"Scusthe me, nice lady. What'sth a—?"

"Don't you dare, Maddison!"

"But, what'sth a—?"

"SHUT UP!"

Grumpy dragon. I only want to ask, what's a barrister?

"Is there a queue at the salad bar? My husband's been an awfully – oh, he's here now."

AH! He is and ohmigod? I think he's just broke the world's record for how much salad you can fit in a bowl? He's even used cumcuber round the edge to make the bowl bigger, and his shirt pocket's full of tomatoes…

"'Ey, love, check this out! Ta-dah! An' that's not all…"

"Sit. Down. Now."

"What's up with your face? She said, help yourself?"

"Yes, but she didn't mean to the entire contents! Well, I hope you enjoy eating it."

"Shit. I never thought o' that."

"For God's sake, Joe, everybody's looking. I expect Maddison to embarrass me when we're out but…"

"DO YOU, MUM?"

"Shush, sweetheart. Why, Joe? You don't even like salad!"

Stupid Dad! The lady's been two times now to ask if we're ready for our pizza, but my mum said we're not allowed to eat anything till all the salad's gone. I've managed to hide some green stuff by pretending to drop my fork under the table, but I can't keep on doing it or my mum'll get...

"Sweetheart, what ARE you doing under there?"

Sticking cumcuber to the underneath of the table if you must know...

"Erm? I'm just gettin' my fork."

"Well, hurry up about it. Enjoying that, Joe?"

"Fuck off!"

"Hey! And watch your language in front of Maddie!"

"Be'ave, she can't hear me."

"You'd be surprised at what she hears, Joe."

You would, and I wonder if cerely floats? Cos if it doesn't, I could probly flush some down the toilet? Good thinking, Maddison...

"Mum, I need a wee!"

"What, again?"

"Yesth. Can I – Ow!"

"Was that your noggin', princess?"

"Yesth."

"Well, be more careful next time. You nearly spilled my ale!"

"Soz... Mum, when I come back *pleasthe* can I have my pizztha?"

"I suppose so. It's not your fault your dad's an idiot."

"It'sth not, isth it, Mum?"

"No, sweetheart. Okay, but hurry up back. And, if you're not back in two minutes, I'll be coming to – ooh!

What's that on my leg? It feels very cold and – CUCUM-BER? Where on earth did that come from? Maddison, do you know anything about – Maddie, come back!"

***

Well, this isn't good. And not just cos I didn't come back or cos she's probly found the rest of the cumcuber by now, but you'll never believe what Trev's done. So, we went to the toilet and I told him not to do it, but he did it anyway, and now my mum's gonna go mental when she finds out. Stupid boss-lady. Why can't she wait till after I've ate my pepper only pizza before she snitches on me? I'm sure she doesn't have to tell her right this minute cos it's not like anyone died or anything... *well...*

"Excuse me, madam. I'm sorry to disturb you, but there's been an incident."

***

Well... we're back in the car again, and it seems like we've only just got out. My dad's in disgrace cos of the salad, I'm in disgrace cos of the cumcuber, and Trev's in disgrace cos he spied under a toilet door and made a old lady scream. But, fancy having a nearly heart attack at that? I'd love it if I was sitting on the toilet and a T-rex's head popped underneath the door – and he didn't roar that loud! Anyway, we're nearly home now, so least I don't have to listen to my mum keep going on about it...

"Come on, love, have a sense of humour, will ya? All

I said was, if you're gonna shit yourself at least you were in the right place."

"You think I have no sense of humour, Joe? I married you, for God's sake! How much more of a sense of humour do I need? And – Joe? Is it me or is it getting really foggy all of a sudden?"

"It's gettin' really – SHIT! STOP THE CAR!"

"What, *here*? But, we're very nearly – OHMIGOD!"

Hmm? That's quite a lot of smoke coming out of our kitchen window?

"Gimme the keys – QUICK!"

I hope my house isn't on fire?

"HERE, JOE, RUN! Hold this, sweetheart, and stay in the car. Mummy'll come and get you when it's safe."

Mmmm, pizza? And no way am I staying in the car – I've got toys in there!

"Come on, Trev, let'sth see what'sth– OH?"

"FOR FUCK SAKE, ROB, EVEN THE BLOODY DOG's COUGHIN'!"

Hmm? That's a awful lot of shouting? And the smoke's making me cough, too? I think I'll stay here in the front porch and eat my pizza before I… *mmmm, pepper only…*

"Open all the windows, will ya, love. Well, Softlad?"

"Well what? I had music on so…"

"WHAT – SO LOUD YOU COULDN'T SMELL SMOKE?"

"I was kinda – you know – busy!"

"BUSY? HOW BUSY D'YOU 'AVE TO BE NOT TO NOTICE THE HOUSE IS ON F – where's your T-shirt?"

"It's hardly on fire, Dad. It's just a bit of smoke, that's all."

"AH! Now, I get it! Too busy gettin' your end away, were ya?"

"Jeeze, Dad, I wasn't gettin' my 'end away' – it's not the seventies!"

"Watch it, smart arse. An' look at the state o' the bloody oven. What was it meant to be, anyway?"

"Joe, that's all the downstairs' windows opened, and whatever it was, it's cremated now. I think forensics would be hard-pushed to identify those remains."

"Sorry, Mum – it was a pizza, but I guess fresh ones don't take as long to cook as…"

"Fuckin' 'ell, birdbrain! Didn't you read the instructions?"

"Leave him, Joe, there's no real damage done. Let's all take a deep breath and…"

"A deep breath? You'll be bloody lucky! You'll need a fuckin' oxygen mask for that."

"Oh yes, hahaha – and will you please stop swearing? I'll go and open the upstairs' windows, and someone tell Maddie that it's okay to come…"

"Ohmigod, Robbie Blobby! What the flippin' 'eck'sth THAT?"

"Knob off, Shortshanks!"

"Oy! Don't speak to her like that. It's not her fault you're an absolute knob!"

"It'sth *not* my fault he'sth a abstholute knob, isth it, Dad?"

"Er… it's probably best if you don't say that, princess,

specially not in front of your mum. Right, Softlad, take this oventray outside an' don't come back till all the burnt shit's gone."

"*Fucksake…*"

Phew. Least most of the smoke's disappeared now. And my dad seems to have mostly finished shouting. I hope this doesn't mean it's my turn now? When my mum remembers about the…

"Joe, look who I found upstairs!"

Who's THAT?

"The poor girl was too scared to come down, what with all the shouting. This is Joe, Robbie's dad."

Hahaha. She looks absolutely ridiclious.

"And this is his little sister Maddison. Say hello, Maddie."

"Are you s'thposed to look like that?"

"Shush, sweetheart."

"Wasth you born like that or did it just fall off?"

"I'm sorry, I don't know what you mean. Did what fall off?"

"Your eyebrowsth. Isth it normal to just have one?"

"ONE? OHMI– I need a mirror! WHERE's MY BAG?"

Well, it turns out she didn't mean to have one eyebrow cos the other one was on Robbie's pillow. I know? How weird's that? Apparently, it wiped off when she was having a lie down before. But, who goes for a lie down in someone's bed when they've imvited you round for dinner? She's not Goldilocks? And she can't have been that tired cos it's not even nine o' clock?

It's weird that, isn't it? Drawing eyebrows on your face? I didn't know people did that. I knew they did lipstick and stuff cos I've watched my mum and Rache doing it, but… anyway, I decided to have a go on mine to see what I'd look like. I couldn't find any actual make-up to use but it still looks fantastic, and when I've finished listening to what they're saying, I'm gonna show my mum…

"What's your name again, love?"

"It's – sorry, has anyone seen Robbie?"

"He's outside, havin' a ciggie. Liz, tell our Rob – sorry, what was it again?"

"Oh, Chardonnay."

"No, I mean your name, love, not what you're drinkin'."

"That is my name. I know, it's awful, isn't it? Can you believe, my mum named me after her favourite drink?"

Hahaha. If my mum and dad did that, I'd be called Coffee or Stella!

"It's not that bad, love."

"It – there you are, Robbie! Where've you been?"

"Scrapin' all the burnt shit off the oventray an' 'avin' a fag. You've met The Addams Family, then."

"I hope you're not including me in that, Robbie?"

"Nah, Mum – you're sound. It's just the rest o'…"

"'Ey Rob, *Chardonnay* was just sayin'…"

"Don't start, Dad – she really 'ates her name, so no takin' the Mick."

"Why don't you change it then, love? You can do it by deed poll, you know. Cheap as chips."

"I know. I'm going to when I'm… *er… er… er…*"

Flippin' 'eck? She sounds like me?

"Spit it out, love. When you're what?"

"When I'm… *er… er… er…*"

She really does sound like me?

"When I'm… when I'm sixteen…"

What? No way?

"Flippin' 'eck, Shardyneigh! Are you *really* only–?"

"OHMIGOD, MADDISON! WHAT THE HELL HAVE YOU DONE TO YOUR FACE?"

God's sakes! How am I s'posed to know what a pernament marker pen is? And who's Scott Tracy, when he's at home? I'm sure it *does* come off? But, so what if I have to go to school tomorrow looking like one of Thunderbirds? It's not that bad! Not as bad as being fifteen?

I don't know what's so bad about fifteen but whatever it is, I've never seen a person's face go that white before – Robbie looked like Casper the actual ghost – and my mum'd probly drived Shardyneigh halfway home before he'd started to look normal-coloured again. Course, I've been sent to my room till she gets back, but no one ever checks, so…

"Listen, son, I'm not havin' a go cos no way did she look fifteen, but you might wanna be a bit more careful the next time you go gettin' an 'ardon. You'll be twenty in a few weeks."

A nardon? What's one of them?

"I know, but what am I s'posed to do? Ask for ID?"

"I dunno, son, but rather that, than landin' in jail."

Wow? Nardons must be well dangerous, if you can go to actual jail?

"I can't believe she was only fifteen. Thank Christ you came back when you did!"

"Yeh, well, you can thank our Maddie for that…"

Ooh?

"…if she hadn't scared the livin' shit outta some poor old biddy on the crapper, we'd still be there now."

It wasn't me, it was Trev!

"Hahaha. She's off 'er 'ead, that one."

"Oh, yeh, Rob – guess what else she did? Only asked the waitress if she knew what a bloody paedo is? You shoulda seen your mum's face. Hahahaha. An' now we know the answer, son… *Fifteen, for fuck's sake!"*

"Don't joke about it, Dad, it's not funny."

"You're right, but your mum'll be back any minute, so I'm laughin' while I can."

"She's got Scott Tracy to sort out first so – shit! Is that the car? D'you fancy gettin' out of 'ere, Dad, before she kicks off? My 'ead's battered enough as it is."

"Sounds like a plan, son…"

What about me? Don't leave me on my own with the dragon?

"…we'll have a quick pint, then bring her back a Chinese."

"Haven't you just been out for a meal?"

"Yeh, but your mum never got to eat hers thanks to…"

"Joe? Robbie? MADDISON!"

"Come on, son, out the back way. We'll cut across the fields an'…"

No! Come back, you two.

"Get down, Spud! Where is everyone?"

Well my dad and Robbie have legged it out the patio doors and I'm hiding in the coat cupboard, trying to decide if now's a good time to ask if I can have a fire distinguisher in my bedroom but it's probly not a good idea at the moment…

"What do you think, hey, Spud? Some Valentine's Day, huh?"

"WOOF!"

"Woof to you, too. What's that you're eating?"

Hmm? Well, she doesn't seem like she's in too much of a bad—?

"PIZZA? Maddison, why's Spud eating pizza? Did you just eat the pepperoni again? What have I told you about that? COME ON! STOP HIDING! Do you know where she is, Spud?"

"WOOF! WOOF! WOOF!"

"Come on, Maddie, I need to get the marker pen off your face. Spud, where's Maddie? Where is she, boy? Show me…"

No! Go 'way, Spud! You're gonna give me away…

"Where is she, boy?"

"WOOF! WOOF!"

Stop sniffing at the cupboard, you stupid dog!

"WOOF! WOOF! WOOF!"

Don't scratch it – Oh, no!

"Well, what have we got here? Good boy, Spud. Move it, Maddison, NOW!"

Oh, well, time to get half my skin scrubbed off again.

Happy Valentime's Day, everyone! See you all soon and…

Goodnight!

Old People

"Mum, what did they mean when they said they'd rather you didn't bring me?"

"I don't know, sweetheart. Well, I do, but…"

"Don't they like me?"

"Of course, they like you, Maddie. They'd just prefer it if you didn't come, that's all."

"But, why? Why don't they want me to come?"

"Have you forgotten about the last christening you went to?"

I didn't even know I'd been to a christening?

"You completely ruined the service…"

DID I?

"… by repeatedly asking the vicar if he'd hurry up and do Trev next…"

Oh, THAT was a christening?

"Then, you upset Auntie Ailish, by announcing to

everyone that her baby looked like Gollum."

"But, it did! An' I thought it wasth a actual Gollum costh she kept calling it 'my preciousth'. An' Robbie callsth me Gollum, an' you don't get upsthet."

"That's not the point. And do you remember saying, 'Finn's not a name, it's part of a fish, idiot!'?"

"Well, it IS."

"Then you dipped Trevor in the chocolate fountain and used Finn's antique christening blanket to wipe it off!"

I didn't dip Trev in the fountain, I dropped him there by accident, and I didn't think anyone'd mind me using that scabby old…

"So, I'm thinking, maybe that's why they'd rather we didn't bring you?"

Oh?

Sometimes I really don't like grown-ups. I mean, it's not that I specially want to go to the christening, not since I remembered what one is, it's just… I'm not being mean but I don't want to stay at Nanna's. I love Nanna to bits but her house smells like cabbage and fish. And all she ever talks about is who's not feeling very well, who's had a operation and who's died. And, I wouldn't mind if I knew who she was talking about, but I haven't got a clue who any of them is. And none of my toys are there so I am not…

"Sweetheart, stop sulking and move out of the way, please. I just need to put these socks in your – WHAT's ALL THIS? Put it back now!"

"But, I won't have anything to do."

"Put it back! And you can put these DVDs back too. For the love of God, Maddie; how many more times?"

"What?"

"It's pardon, not what; and you're not watching *Ted*! I know it's about a teddy bear but it's not meant for – OHMIGOD! *Fifty Shades of Grey*? Where did you get THIS?"

"It'sth Rache'sth. I heard her tell Robbie it'sth hilariousth so I thought me an' Nanna could watch it."

"Well, think again!"

Think what again? And why d'you have to shout so much? I'm surprised you don't run out of voice.

"What else is in here? You can put that back! And that! And – I've been looking everywhere for this, Maddie. What could you possibly want with an aromatherapy candle set? There're twelve candles in here and you're only going for one night!"

Humph? Why does my mum always have to spoil my fun? She's took all my packing out and put her own boring stuff back in, and now that she's took the smelly candles out, I'm gonna have to spend the whole time breathing in cabbage and fish. And, I'm gonna have absolutely nothing to do now, so…

"Right, Maddie, that's everything. Now, hurry up and get in the car."

***

Nanna only lives ten minutes away but that's a long time when your mum's giving you millions of 'structions. No asking for cakes and biscuits every five minutes. No jumping on the bed or doing summer-salts on the couch.

No telling Nanna you're allowed stuff you're not. And no – UH? Am I seeing things?

"Hold this, sweetheart, while I get your bag out of the boot. And I've told Nanna that you don't like cocoa so please don't pour anything else in her plants. And don't flush anything down the toilet that's not meant to be…"

"Mum, why'sth Nanna'sth feet stickin' out the kitchen window?"

"Nanna's, what?"

"Nanna'sth feet. They're…"

"Ohmigod, what's she doing? Come on, sweetheart. MUM? ARE YOU OKAY?"

"Oh, hello, Elizabeth, I didn't hear you coming. Don't look so alarmed, dear, I do this all the time."

Really? Why doesn't she just use the front door like a normal person?

"Are you stuck, Nanna?"

"Hello, poppet, I didn't see you there."

Well, you wouldn't when you're hanging upside down like Batman?

"I forgot my key again, Elizabeth."

"Again? You mean you make a habit of this? Why don't you keep a spare in the garden?"

"Now, where's the fun in that? See, I'm fine! Go to the front door and I'll let you in."

I'd much rather climb in the window but…

"Come on, sweetheart – and don't you even think about doing that. It's very dangerous."

Too late… Hmm? I wonder what kind of cake Nanna's got?

"Come on in, poppet. Are you coming in, Elizabeth?"

I hope it's chocolate?

"I'm sorry, but I can't stop, Mum. We're running late as it is."

Or Swiss roll?

"Now, be a good girl for Nanna, sweetheart, and I'll see you Sunday night. Here's her bag, Mum. Maddie, give Mummy a great big kiss. MWAH! I'll miss you so much, sweetheart."

Or chocolate brownies?

"Don't be silly, Elizabeth! Have a lovely time at the christening and give my regards to the McLarens. And don't worry about Maddie, she'll be fine, won't you, poppet? We're going to have so much fun. Wave goodbye to Mummy."

"Bye, Mum! BYE!"

I wish she'd hurry up and go. It's so windy out here, it's making my eyes proply water…

"Awww… don't cry, poppet."

I'm not? Oh, cos my eyes are watering?

"Mummy'll be back before you know it."

"I know, Nanna, I'm just so sad she'sth gone without me… Nanna, d'you know what my mum doesth to cheer me up every time I'm sad? She givesth me cake."

★★★

Well, Nanna wasn't born yesterday – duh! Like I didn't know that? So, 'stead, she gave me a cup of tea with a baldy-gary biscuit then said we're going out for a surprise. But it's not a very good surprise when it's outside and it's too cold to snow. I know? Who's ever heard of that? But, Nanna said so… Mind you, Nanna's said lots of things that haven't been true? Cos, I've gone cross-eyed millions of times when it's been windy and my eyes haven't stuck like that, and I've swallowed loads of bubble gum and my heart hasn't stopped yet, and if I have got a apple tree growing inside me cos I swallowed all the pips, then I'm sure I'd be able to notice it by now?

Anyway, I don't even like ducks – but even if I did, I can't really see anything cos my eyes won't stop watering – and so far, all they've done is quack at me and tried to pinch the food… and the extra-quacky duck bit my actual finger… so I threw the bag of food at it to shoo it away from me, and the park man shouted at me for being dangerous! Like I was the one going round biting people! Oh, and, guess what I learned today – swans've got legs! I thought they just bobbed on the water like my rubber ducky but they don't, they can walk and everything, and they're proper massive when they stand up.

Ugh! How much longer? I'm freezing cold, my nose won't stop running, and soon I won't be able to feel my feet. I hope Nanna wasn't talking about this when she said we're gonna have so much fun, cos this isn't fun in the slightest?

"Poppet, come away from the edge. If you fall in, I'm not going after you. Anyway, five more minutes then we'll have to go."

"Aw, that'sth such a shame, Nanna. Nanna, have you seen my finger where the duck bited it? It'sth really sore… an' d'you know what my mum buysth me when a duck bitesth me? Mc…"

"Nice try, poppet, but you'll have to get up a lot earlier in the morning if you want to get past me."

I don't want to get past you? I want chicken nuggets and a cheeseburger?

"If I didn't know better, I'd think you were trying to pull the wool over my eyes…"

What wool? I haven't got any wool. I wish I did, actually. Least I could knit myself a…

"… and when you're as long in the tooth as I am, it's not quite so easy to get taken for a ride."

Uh? Are we going on the bus now?

"Doesth that mean we *can* go to McDonald'sth or we—?"

"It means, I'll think about it – but don't count your chickens before they've hatched."

WHAT? I'm just gonna pretend she didn't talk…

I do that quite a lot with Nanna. Like the other day when my brother did his driving test and accidently drived on the pavement – which you're not allowed to do apparently – and he was cheesed off cos he didn't pass, so d'you know what she said to cheer him up? She said, 'Never mind, luvvie! You can't make a omelette without breaking a few eggs!' How's that s'posed to cheer someone up? But that's not the worst thing she's said this week.

Two days ago she was telling my mum about the farmer's field behind her house, the one he keeps his horsie in, and how he's sold it to some people so they can build houses on it, and when my mum asked her if she was sure, she said 'Absolutely, Elizabeth! I heard it straight from the horse's mouth!'. Horses can't talk! And if they could they'd be asking for carrots or hay, not talking to Nanna 'bout building houses!

Anyway, Nanna thought about us going to McDonald's, then decided that we weren't – three miles is not too far to walk for a cheeseburger – so we ended up going to the Weather's Spoon instead. I was a bit disappointed it was just a pub and not somewhere what had massive spoons floating in the sky, but least it was warm and they sold cheeseburgers. The only trouble was, I didn't get to eat much of mine, cos just as I was eating it Nanna said she's got a 'surprise number two' for me later, and I laughed so much it mostly went down the wrong hole. I can't believe she doesn't know what a number two is? And it's so funny when she says it, I don't want to tell her in case she stops. Anyway, we came home after that cos her feet were aching, her back was killing her, and she wanted to have forty winks…

Forty winks is what old people call 'having a sleep in the day'. They don't go to actual bed or anything – just sleep in the chair with their mouth wide open then wake up and say they haven't been asleep – but can you do snoring when you're awake? I don't think you can, can you? Whatever, so, after forty winks she woke up and put *Countdown* on what she'd recorded at Christmas? I know. How weird's that? Then she fell asleep again, but this time for a thousand winks, then woke up and told me off for making a mess in the kitchen, but it wasn't my fault I was starving cos my dinner went down the wrong hole, and now I think she's ready to go back out?

Least, she's umplugging everything out the walls to save 'lectricity, which is what she usually does before she goes anywhere, but she leaves half the lights on so burglars think she's in… which doesn't make any sense?

"Hurry up, poppet! Leave Trevor alone and put your coat on or we'll miss the start."

AH? Fancy telling ME to hurry up? I'm not the one what's been asleep all afternoon?

"Are you ready for your surprise number two, poppet?"

She must be saying this on purpose? How can she not know?

"Is it a really BIG 'surpristhe number two', Nanna?"

"Huge – you won't know what hit you! What are you laughing at, Poppet?"

OHMIGOD! Hahahahahaha. This is the funniest thing ever!

★★★

BINGO! Flippin' BINGO?

First, I thought it was gonna be brilliant cos of the adverts on telly, cos there's always glitter and streamers eggsploding everywhere and I'm sure I've seen a talking fox in a purple suit? But, there's nothing like that here? Just loads of old ladies talking 'bout hips and hospital and bowels? And, I'm not in the least bit interested in how many poos I've had in a week, so why would I be intrested in someone else's? And I'm s'posed to sit here and say nothing while Barry the bingo man calls a load of numbers out over the micra phone, and if he says one what's on my piece of paper I have to cross it off. And, that's it! Honest to God, I'd rather Nanna did throw a huge number two at me – *and* I got told off for drawing a rabbit on my first set of numbers…

"Okay, ladies, it's eyes down… twenty pounds your line; fifty pounds, your full house."

"Isth it now, Nanna?"

"Yes."

"Quiet down the front please."

Quiet yourself, mister. I've never done this before.

"And, your first number is… three and seven, it's thirty-seven. Two little ducks, twenty-two."

QUACK! QUACK!

"HAHAHAHAHA…"

"Shush, poppet."

"Why'sth everyone quackin', Nanna?"

"Quiet down the front please."

Don't tell me to be quiet. They're the ones quacking.

"One and nine…"

"I got bit by a duck today, didn't I, Nanna?"

"Shush, Maddie!"

"Again, can we have quiet down the front, please… One and nine, nineteen. Two and seven, twenty-seven. Five and three, fifty-three. Six and four, sixty-four. Doctor's orders, number nine."

"Why'ths doctorsth orderths—?"

"Quiet down the front – *please*."

I'm gonna proper kung fu kick him if he doesn't stop picking on me.

"Those wonderful legs – e-*leven!*"

Phwe-phwew!

"Na—?"

"Don't ask!"

"On its own, the number two…"

Ooh? I know this one?

"QUACK! QUACK! QUACK! QUACK! QUACK! QUACK!"

"Maddison!"

"*What?*"

"Quiet down the front!"

"Ugh! But, I thought we were s'thposed to quack for – this is too comfusthing!"

"Eight and six, eighty-six. Dinner for two…"

Dinner for two?

"It's sixty-nine!"

"Nanna, why'sth—?"

HOUSE!

Well, now I'm even more comfused? What I don't understand is, why's it okay for all the old people to shout and quack and whistle, and not me? Honestly, Nanna's best friend – a massive fat lady called Mavis – screamed 'house' for no reason, and nobody yelled at her to be 'Quiet down the front'! 'Stead they shouted stuff out and really loud too, telling her she's a jammy bugger or if she fell down the toilet she'd come out smelling like roses… and that's a big fat lie cos I actually fell down Nanna's toilet when I was little and I definitely didn't come out smelling like that. Anyway, it's over now thank goodness, cos I don't think I could stand a other…

"And, it's eyes down for your full house."

WHAT?

"And your first number is – knock at the door…"

KNOCK! KNOCK!

"It's number four."

They're all mental?

"Two and four, twenty-four."

Duck knock? No?

"Top of the shop: blind ninety."

Why's Top Shop in bingo?

"Five and nine, the Brighton line."

Why?

"Seven and six, was she worth it?"

Who?

"Two fat ladies, eighty-eight."

"You're fat, aren't you, Mavisth?"

"MADDISON!"

"Well, she *isth!*"

"QUIET DOWN THE FRONT!"

"You be quiet! Tell him, Nanna."

And, if you don't mind, it's quiet PLEASE? Where's your flippin' manners?

"All the sixes."

CLICKETY CLICK.

This is ridiclious? How much longer? Bingo's just mental old women clicking and knocking and quacking and…

"Six and two…"

Clickety quack? No? Why not? I don't understand? I'M BORED!

"It's the number sixty-two. Four and three, forty-three. Almost there, it's eighty-nine. Thkit at my lithp, it'sth theventy…"

AH? How dare he?

"OY, MISTER BINGO MAN!"

"MADDISON, SIT DOWN!"

"Yes, young lady… SIT DOWN! Now, where was I? Oh yes. Thkit at my lithp, it'sth theventy-thixth…"

Right, that's it! I've had enough of him. It's bad enough that he keeps telling me to be quiet, never mind being mean and making a holy show of me…

"Come on, Trev! CHAAAAAAARGE!"

★★★

Nanna's never been asked to leave the bingo before. Apparently, no one has. Not ever. She said Barry was quite scared when I ran at him with Trev, but I didn't mean to trip up the step and knock all the bingo balls flying; that bit was a actual accident. Anyway, Nanna can go back to bingo if she wants, but…

"Honestly, Maddison. I'll never be able to show my face in there again."

"But, he started it."

"He didn't start anything – he says that every week. That's what bingo callers say for the number seventy-six."

Every week? He says the same thing every week? How boring's that?

"Bingo'sth stupid! I never want to go again."

"Well, you're in luck there because you've been banned. Banned! From Bingo! And if they can't find the number eighty-eight ball, they'll be billing me for a new set."

"Is that the two fat ladiesth ball, Nanna?"

"Yes. And I can't believe you said that to Mavis. She has a thyroid problem."

She's still proply fat though.

"What am I going to do with you now?"

"Erm? Why don't we get a deevy dee?"

"A DVD? I'm not entirely sure you deserve it… but if it'll keep you occupied…"

"It will keep me – what did you say, Nanna? Ocky pied? An' besidesth, if I've not got a deevy dee to watch I'll probly just keep takin' an' talkin' an'…"

"Yes! And you could talk the hind legs of a donkey!"

WHAT? I could talk so much a donkey's legs'd fall off? How?

"Okay, we'll stop off at the supermarket and…"

"Thanksth, Nanna. There'sth a dead good film I want to watch, actually. It'sth called *Ted*! I bet you'll love it."

"What's it about? Because, the last film you said I'd love gave me horrific nightmares."

"Really? *King Kong*'sth not scary?"

"No, but all those giant spiders, cannibals and man-eating worms were. It was horrible!"

"Well, this one'sth definitely not horrible. It'sth about a cute teddy bear called Ted. It'sth got a picture of him on the front an' everything. My mum definitely said I can watch it."

"You said that about *King Kong*! Well, if it's about a

teddy bear, I don't see the harm. Come on, we'll have a movie night instead."

"Yesth! An' can we get cockporn asthwell?"

"I beg your pardon? It's pop corn – and don't push your luck, poppet. You may think I'm a few clowns short of a circus…"

WHAT? I've never thought that in my life?

"…but, you'd be barking up the wrong tree."

I give in. She's absolutely mental!

★★★

I wish Nanna'd hurry up. She's been on the phone the whole time since we got back. First to Mavis, where she just kept saying sorry, then to Barry to ask if they've found the two fat ladies ball yet, and now someone's phoned up to ask Nanna if she – actually, I don't know what's going on? I can't work it out?

"She *didn't*… she *didn't*… she did! And, it just popped out? Well, that'll teach her to try to move the washing machine on her own… I bet it is! Has she got some Anusol? No… no… I had some once… yes, *Loose Women*. They said it works miracles on puffy eyes… no, not really… so, more of a plum than a bunch of grapes? I bet she can't. Tell her to sit on a rubber ring… I haven't, no… True, but there's never a good time, is there? And, how long is the coach trip? Two hours? Alfie Boe? Ooh, well, tell her if it hasn't popped back up by then, then I'm definitely interested. Okay… yes… bye… bye… bye… or Preparation H! Yes… yes… bye… bye… he thought she said what?"

Ohmigod, just put the flippin' phone down?

"Emma Royds? Hahaha. Typical man…"

I'm so comfused? I think what's happened is… someone called Emma Royds off *Loose Women*'s moved her washing machine which's made her eyes go puffy and one's popped out… so, now she can't go to watch Alfie Bow on a coach, least not till it's popped back in again… but you can still see with one eye though? Unless it's proply popped out and it's dangling on her face?

"Okay, well, give her my regards. Yes… bye… bye… bye. Right, poppet, are you ready to watch the film? Because, it's getting late and…"

WHAT? I've been ready for hours! Imfact, I've already pressed pause twice! Well, I'm not pressing it again… and I'm sure Nanna will enjoy *Ted* as much as she enjoyed *Paddington*, but if she doesn't, or if she's still a bit cross by the time it's finished, I'll just give her the two fat ladies ball back from the bingo and she can hardly still be cross with me then. Good plan, Maddison.

"Be careful with your drink, poppet. I don't want it going everywhere."

"I am bein' careful…"

It's just too disgusting to drink. Have you ever drinked oval team? Apparently, it's Nanna's favourite…

"See, Nanna, I said Ted wasth cute, didn't I?"

"You did, poppet. Hey, just imagine if you went to sleep one night, and when you awoke in the morning, Trevor was alive…"

What d'you mean, IF?

"Although, that would be slightly terrifying…"

Uh? That's weird? How come Ted's suddenly all growed up?

"Poppet, why's Ted drinking beer?"

I'm not really sure, but – Ohmigod? What's he doing NOW?

"Goodness gracious ME! Maddison Elizabeth Mc-Laren…"

Flippin' 'eck, she sounds like the actual teachers.

"I do *not* believe your mum said that you could watch this!"

But, I didn't know it was gonna be like THIS? Ted's smoking his head off and won't stop saying the Eff word!

"Just wait till I tell your…"

"Ohmigod, Nanna – look! I mean – can you actually believe it?"

"Believe what?"

"Look what I just found!"

"MADDISON!"

Humph! Well, she didn't believe it but she could've least said thank you 'stead of threatening to phone my mum. *Some people are so umgrapeful?* Anyway, she's put this programme on the telly while she's gone to tell Barry that the number eighty-eight ball's magically turning up, but why doesn't she just watch what's on the actual telly? Why does she record everything then watch it miles later? I've never actually seen this programme before but I'm sure they don't wear Christmas hats all of the time?

"Right, poppet. Barry seems happy enough, thank goodness… now come on, it's bedtime."

"But Nanna, I *love* this programme. What'sth it called, again?"

"*University Challenge.*"

"Yup – Universsthally challenged. I watch it every single night!"

"Oh really? Because, it's not on every single night. It's no wonder your dad calls you Little Miss Drag-it-out. And, it's no good looking like butter wouldn't melt in your mouth, poppet…"

Butter wouldn't melt in my mouth? What does that even mean? The only kind of person I can think of where butter wouldn't melt in their mouth's a dead person? And, I'm definitely not a…

"Oh, Maddison! Why is my yucca plant drowning in Ovaltine?"

Flippin' 'eck, has it not sinked in yet?

"Right – that's it – I'm phoning your Mum! Honestly, you're enough to try the patience of a saint."

NO! Do something quick…

"Hahaha. Not again, poppet? How many times is this now? Get up off the floor and stop pretending to be dead – you've had more resurrections than Madonna! And it gets very boring after a while…"

Well, so does getting shouted at!

"You'll get bored before I will, poppet, and corpses don't blink, remember!"

They don't talk either, so I've got to pretend to be dead for quite a long time now so I'll talk to you a other time, okay?

"I can see you breathing, Maddison."

God's sakes… see you all soon, everyone…
Goodnight!

Happy Mother's Day!

I'm so eggcited I can't hardly wait. Imfact, I'm going in again. I've been in three times already but she just keeps telling me to come back in a hour, but it must be a hour since the last time she told me to go away? Whatever…

"Mum."

"*NotagainMaddison…*"

"Are you awake yet?"

"*Nosweetheart… comebackinanhour.*"

"What, again?"

"Maddie, it's twenty past six in the morning. It's still dark outside. Go back to bed, please!"

"Well, shall I come back when it'sth light?"

"Yes. Now let Mummy go back to sleep. She's really, *really… zzzz…*"

God's sakes! How can she sleep when she's got presents to open? If she doesn't wake up soon, I might

106

have accidently opened them myself. I wonder what time it gets light? Come on Mr Sun, WAKE UP!

Ooh? It must've heard me thinking cos I'm sure it's getting lighter? It is!

"Come on, Trev – hey, Trev, why don't you give her a great big kiss to wake her up? That usually worksth."

Aww, she looks dead cute, all snuggled under the duvet with just the top of her head poking out. I'll just let Trev give her a tiny little kiss on the nose and…

"WHAAAH!"

"WHATTHEFUCK?"

"HAPPY MOTHER'STH DAY, MUM!"

"BLOODY 'ELL, PRINCESS! What time is it, love?"

"Six thirty-seven, Joe. Go back to sleep."

"Go back to sleep? I've just nearly had an 'eart attack! Feel my chest. It's goin' like the clappers."

"I know, Joe, mine too, and before you ask, no, you can't feel it. It's Mother's Day, not Father's. Sweetheart, I've asked you before not to do that. As lovely as Trevor's kisses are, opening your eyes to a T-rex millimetres from your face is genuinely alarming!"

"Soz. Are you ready to open your presentsth now, Mum?"

"I guess…"

"Yesth! I'll just go an' get them…"

She's gonna LOVE these. I bought them all by myself with my own money. Well, Nanna gave me ten pounds in case my dad forgot it was Mother's Day, and my dad gave me ten pounds not to tell my mum that he had, then he took me to the supermarket last night just before it was closing… and it was all my own idea. I didn't even bother asking my mum what she wanted this year, cos she always says the 'xact same thing; 'I'd just like one day where I don't have to shout, Maddison!' – *boring* – so I choosed them by myself. And, I wrapped them myself, too. Come on, Trev. Present time…

"Dad, isth your phone ready to take picturesth of my mum openin' her presentsth?"

"You bet, princess. Now remember, Liz, I can't take any credit for this. It was all her own work."

"Well, aren't you a little angel? Now, which one should I open first? What about this one? It feels very unusual… and I love the wrapping paper. Didn't you use a lot of Sellotape? I wonder what it can…"

"Just rip the flippin' paper!"

"*Sweetheart*… I was only saying what a good job you've – Oh? Um? What a surprise? It is a block of butter, isn't it? I… er… I don't know what to say."

"There's a bloody first! Smile for the camera, love. Perfect!"

"Let me see, Dad."

I like that picture but she looks a bit comfused. Oh yeah? Course, idiot?

"Mum, you've done it wrong. You're s'thposed to open them in order."

"What's the order, sweetheart?"

"I don't know. I think you're s'thposed to open this one first."

I think this one's the cross ants? YUP! Definitely cross ants…

"I wonder if this will be as big a surprise as – Oh, croissants! My favourite! Now it all makes sense. How sweet, Maddie – literally!"

"D'you like your surpristhe, Mum?"

"I do, sweetheart, but where did you hide them? Near your radiator, by any chance?"

"Yup! How did you guessth?"

"Mummy knows everything... Joe, would you do me a favour, please? Would you put the butter in the fridge before it melts all over the bed? Sweetheart, which one should I open next? This one? I wonder what this can be. It feels quite heavy and..."

Stop talking and open it! It'll have gone off by the time you've finished guessing.

"Well, you really did spoil me, didn't you? I must be the luckiest mum in the world. A whole block of butter; an *extraordinarily* large jar of jam; six croissants; a box of chocolates; three Happy Meal toys and a Mr Potato Head."

"YUP!"

"So, love, was it worth bein' woken up at – Oy, numbnuts, put the lid back on the jam! Now you lie back an' play with your Mr Potato Head, an' we'll be back in a minute with your brekkie. Come on, princess... Er, I'll carry the pressies if you don't mind."

"But, I do mind. I want to carry them."

"Well, you're not so give 'em 'ere."

"But, it'sth just jam an' crossth antsth. I can carry them."

"OY! Look where your goin' an' give 'em 'ere."

"NO! They're my presentsth so I want to –WHOA-AAAAAAAA!"

God's sakes? Not again?

"You okay down there, princess? If I had a quid for every time you've fallen down the stairs, I'd be rich as bloody Croesus."

"YUP! It'sth okay, everyone… I'm all right… nothin'-'sth broke… I'm abstholutely…"

Woof! Woof! Woof! Woof!

"JOE, WHAT'S GOING ON OUT THERE?"

"Nothin', love. You carry on playin' with your Mister Potato Head!"

"*Fucksake*… what's with all the noise? Keep it down, will ya? Some of us are try'na sleep."

"Go go back to bed, son. It's just Maddie's gone arse over tit down the stairs…"

"What, again? *Retard!* Tell 'er to fall quietly next time."

"Like that's gonna – OH, FOR F— look at the state o' the bloody carpet! There's jam everywhere!"

It's not everywhere? It's definitely somewhere, but not everywhere?

"An' it's all up the walls, too!"

It can't all *be up the walls cos there's definitely some on me and Trev.*

"I see you managed to keep hold o' Godzilla while you were bouncin' down the stairs, Maddie… Go on, Spud, bugger off!"

Oh? And there's quite a lot on Spud, too. Imfact, it's all over his paws.

"I dunno how you managed it but congratulations

on redecoratin' the whole bloody staircase with jam!"

Aww, Spud's all eggcited, and I think he likes jam cos he doesn't normally lick the walls.

"DON'T LET HIM EAT IT, MADDIE!"

"Why? Aren't dogsth s'thposed to eat jam?"

"No… an' grab hold of him before he runs through the house with – MADDIE, I SAID GRAB HOLD OF HIM BEFORE – Jesus Christ, DO I HAVE TO DO EVERYTHIN' MYSELF?"

★★★

Don't grown-ups get puffed-out easy? By the time my dad'd catched Spud he was so puffed out he had to have a really long sit down. Mind you, Spud's got four legs and my dad's only got two, and playing chase's Spud's favourite game. I'm not kidding – he chases after *everything* – he even tries to jump in the sky after birds! It's cos half of him's a Collie dog and the other half's a Beagle and they're both fruit loops apparently, but he's proply cute and funny and I love him to absolute bits… even though he is sometimes the most disobediance dog in the world.

Anyway, we've ventually finished making my mum's Mother's Day breakfast and I've even picked some daffydills out the garden for her too, so I really hope she likes them…

"Doesthn't it look smashin', Mum? Sorry the crossth antsth are a bit squashed but that'sth what I landed on when I fell down the stairsth."

"It looks lovely, sweetheart, and these daffodils smell gorgeous. Where did you get them?"

"Out the garden."

"But, we haven't got any daffodils in the garden?"

No, but…

"Hurry up, Mum! You have to eat it all, before it getsth cold. It'sth a good job I got such a massthive jam, isthn't it? Or there probly wouldn't have been enough left for your crossth antsth."

"It is, sweetheart, although I don't think your dad would agree."

"No, he bloody wouldn't!"

"I'm sorry, sweetheart, but I can't eat six croissants, so will you both eat some?"

"Go on then, love, I'll – 'ey, what's that on your right one?"

"My right one?"

"That! There! That green thing on your…"

"Whaaaaaaah! Get it off me, Joe! Aaaaaaagh!"

So, that's where he went?

"Calm down, love. It's only a bloody caterpillar."

"GET IT OFF ME! *GET IT OFF ME!*"

"Don't you like catty pillowsth, Mum? I put him on your flower specially."

"Aaagh! NO! Get it away from me! You know I hate creepy crawlies, Maddie."

"But he'sth not even a little bit creepy? He'sth all fluffy and cute, aren't you, Colin?"

"Liz, keep still, will ya? You're spillin' your brekkie all over the duvet."

"Just move it, Joe – put it back where it came from. Where did it come from, Maddie?"

"Erm? Look, Mum! Most of your cup of tea'sth…"

"Don't change the subject, Maddison. Where did it come from?"

"*Well…*"

Well, this isn't 'xactly how I imagined Mother's Day to be. I've been to say sorry to the man next door for picking flowers out his garden, and I've been in the bath to wash the jam out my hair, and now I'm in the living room waiting for my mum and dad to… actually, how long does it take to wash orange juice out of duvets? And jam off carpets? And wallpaper? And dogs? Whatever, if I haven't made any more mess by the time they've finished cleaning everywhere, then we're going to eat chocolates and play Mr Potato Head. I hope they've not forgot about me? I can hear them laughing so I'll just go and check…

"… so *that's* what I was laughin' at last night, Liz. I kept picturin' your face when you opened the butter. Hahahaha…"

"Quiet, Joe, or she'll hear you. I know it's a little unorthodox, but it was really sweet."

"Yeh, as was the whole bloody house! Spud was covered in it."

"Where is he?"

"I've chucked him in with our Rob to dry off – an' he's still hungover, the knob!"

"*Still?* But, his birthday was on Friday?"

"Yeh, well, he was neckin' all them Jaegerbombs. D'you want me to get him up, love?"

"God, no – don't poke the beast! The longer he sleeps, the less they can argue."

"True. Okay, let's get this over with… Mr Potato Head… Jeeze!"

"I loved Mr Potato Head when I was little. I'm really looking forward to it."

"I loved it when I was a kid, Liz, but I'm forty-friggin'-four. I don't wanna spend 'alf the day rearrangin' a pissin' potato!"

"Don't be such a spoilsport, Joe… or shall I rearrange your face instead? Hahaha…"

"Thanks a bunch! What's wrong with my face?"

"It's okay, I suppose, but you're no George Clooney."

"Piss off!"

"You do remind me of somebody though."

"Not this again. For fuck's sake, Liz, don't you ever get bored?"

"Nope! Hmm? It's on the tip of my tongue?"

"Yeh, well, you can bloody well keep it there."

"What's his name again?"

Ooh – I know! I've heard this story loads and it's proply funny…

It was in the olden days – I think my mum said 1994? Anyway, my mum was seventeen and at her college party and there was a actual band on stage, and at the time there was a song what had just gone to number one on the radio, and when the band started singing it, their singer sounded so much like the man what sang it, that everyone thought it was him. Anyway, when the band finished my mum went to ask him for a naughtograph and he asked her out for a date, and for three whole days my mum thought she was going out with Marty Pillow from Wetwetwet! I've seen him on the video and my dad looks a tiny bit like him, but…

"Three whole days, Joe! You even let me promise Adele I could get her a backstage pass."

"Yeh, well, I couldn't believe you were so gullible. I mean, why the fuck would Wet Wet Wet be playin' at a school disco?"

"It wasn't a school, it was a college, and I didn't know about things back then."

"You weren't *that* naïve… especially when you told me you were nineteen. I only found out when your mum asked me why I hadn't come to your eighteenth! I nearly shit a brick!"

"Okay, but in my defence, you were unbelievably hot…"

"Stop takin' the piss."

"I'm not – *well, I am* – but you were dreamy and you really made me laugh. Of course, that was before I discovered you were a foul-mouthed idiot… hahaha!"

"FUCK YOU VERY MUCH!"

"And you know I thought you wouldn't be interested in me if you knew how young I was. Anyway, courtesy of our little baby we've got chocolates to scoff and potatoes to disfigure. It'll be a laugh, Joe – and it's Mother's Day, remember."

"It's Mother's Day every friggin' day. Okay, mein little fuhrer. Anythin' for you."

I knew my mum liked Mr Potato Head cos she said so at Christmas when she was talking to my dad about their favourite toys when they were little. See! I do listen! And she's proper laughed her head off, too, but that could be cos she's drunk quite a lot of Bay Leaves?

Robbie came downstairs about a hour ago; plopped a bottle on the table; said Happy Mother's Day; why can't we live in a bungalow? Which bright spark let Spud in his bedroom when he was p.i.s.s. wet through? – I spelled it so it doesn't count – and thanks to me and Spud, he's still knackered so he's going back to bed. Least I made a effort, even if I did make a mess. And Rache phoned from her holidays in Scotland to say Happy Mother's Day; did her card come in the post? And she's coming home for Easter in a couple of weeks with Jonathon, so she'll give her her present then. I'm glad my mum's having a nice Mother's – ooh? Knock at the door. It must be Nanna?

Can you believe Nanna told my mum I'd been good as gold the whole time she minded me? She didn't say *anything* about me watching *Ted*, getting thrown out of bingo, or about the two fat ladies ball what I accidently borrowed. Apparently, it's our little secret, but we've got quite a few of them already... like last week when she picked me up from school and had to go and see my teacher cos I'd got a massive 'See Me' on my St. Patrick's Day story. Stupid Mrs Jolley – I'd already told her it wasn't my fault so I don't know what she wanted to see Nanna for, cos it was Robbie what told me Cunny Lingus is somewhere in Eyeland…

"Bloody 'ell, Betty – you've only just walked through the door an' your talkin' about death. Give it a rest will ya?"

"Anyway, Elizabeth, the funeral's this Friday – eleven o'clock at the church."

"And, who is it again, Mum?"

"Barbra Davis. You met her when you had that Saturday job at…"

"WHAT? I had that Saturday job when I was sixteen! No, I don't want to go to the funeral of some woman I met twenty-four years ago! I wouldn't know her if I fell over her!"

"Well, you could hardly fall over the poor woman now, Elizabeth – she's dead!"

"Nanna, open your flippin' presentsth."

"I am doing, poppet. And, I only mentioned it, Elizabeth, in case you – oh? Thank you. What is it?"

"It'sth a iPod, Nanna."

"An eye pod?"

"Yup, it'sth for listenin' to music."

"An EYE pod? Shouldn't it be called an ear pod then?"

"Not a EYE pod… a i Pod."

"Oh, I see. It's very small, isn't it? Where are the speakers?"

Ohmigod? Don't you know anything, Nanna?

"There are no speakers, Mum, that's the whole point – you use headphones, instead."

"I see. But, what if I don't like what's on it?"

"There isn't anything on it. You download your favourite…"

"Download? What's that when it's at home?"

Not again? I wish people'd stop buying Nanna presents what she doesn't know what to do with. She still doesn't know how to work her tablet proply yet and now she's got a iPod!

"Maddie'll show you how it works, won't you, sweetheart? So, all you need to do, Mum, is write down a list of your favourite songs and…"

"OOH – MALTESERS! Thank you, poppet. We'll share these later."

Least she knows how to work them.

★★★

God's sakes – I've never heard of any of these? 'Be-Bop-A-Lula'? That's not English. 'Do Wah Diddy Diddy'? Neither's that. 'Da Doo Ron Ron'? 'Boom Bang-A-Bang'? 'Chirpy Chirpy Cheep Cheep'? She's making these up! I only know 'Crazy Frog' and 'Gang Man's Tile' so how am I s'posed to know if it's the right one? Humph. It's not fair that I have to do everything – I'm gonna tell Robbie it's his turn. Nobody ever asks him to do stuff cos he's so grumpy, but I don't care how grumpy he is…

BANG!

"Robbie, my mum said you have to – *eeeeeuw*. What'sth all that?"

"Come in, Shortshanks."

"I *am* in."

"I was bein' sarcastic – an' watch the wall, dick'ead, you're gonna put an' 'ole in it. Don't you ever knock?"

"Not usually. What'sth up with Spud?"

"Dunno? He started actin' all weird then barfed everywhere. Go'n tell Mum, will ya?"

"Hahaha! Look, Robbie, he'sth proply smilin'. Say cheesthe, Spud! Haha…"

"He's not smilin', Shortshanks, that's his – I'm-gonna-do-a-shit face! Quick, help me get him out before he drops his arse all over my – OH, FOR FUCK'S SAKE!"

"MUUUUUUUM!"

***

Everyone's quite cross with me at the minute – but I didn't make Spud eat the jam so how's it even my fault? The mergency vet said dogs aren't s'posed to eat any amount of jam, never mind that much…

Anyway, my dad's finished cleaning all the dire rear out the car and my mum's finished cleaning it off Robbie's carpet, and Nanna's done the stairs, so now we're s'posed to be going out for our dinner but no one's really hungry. I hope this hasn't ruined my mum's Mother's Day.

Ooh, I know what'll cheer her up?

Stupid iPod! I can never get it to go in this player thing proply. Now turn it up full blast, Maddison, and…

"Who's put this shite on?"

"It'sth my mum'sth favourite, isthn't it, Mum? She lovesth…"

"I don't give a monkey's uncle whose favourite it is – turn it off! My 'ead's bangin' enough!"

"But, it'sth Mother'sth Day…"

"You've got three seconds, Maddie, then never mind feelin' it in your bloody fingers, you'll feel all ten o' my toes up your backside, won't she, Godzilla?"

"Okay… Let go of him, I'll turn it off! Tell him, Mum."

"Joe, I was just going to dance with you then."

"Like hell you were!"

"But, it's Mother's Day."

"So? You're not my bloody mother."

"Speaking of which, have you phoned her yet?"

"Nah. I never know what to say to 'er."

"You could start with 'Happy Mother's Day' and go from there."

"Then what? Thanks for buggerin' off back to Scotland when I was nine an' leavin' me with a knob'ead of a…"

"Maddie, sweetheart, would you like to go and find Nanna and ask her to wash the chocolate off your face?"

I didn't know I had chocolate on my face? And I'd like to stay and listen actually, cos no one ever talks about Nanna and Grandad McLaren…

"O-kaaay."

I'll just listen from behind the door instead.

"I'm not phonin' her, Liz. I'm not bein' a hypocrite."

A hippogriff?

"I know, Joe, and I respect that, but there are two sides to every story, and your dad wasn't an easy man to live with."

"No, he wasn't. He was a bad-tempered, womanisin' piss'ead, so not easy to live with, especially when you're only nine."

"But, you refused to go with your mum because you didn't want to leave Liverpool, so…"

"Yeh, Liverpool. Footy was my life back then, an' I'd been spotted by one o' the scouts, remember. An' if my arse'ole of a dad hadn't been too pissed to take me to the trials, who knows what would've happened? Plus, I didn't wanna leave my mates to go an' live in a country I'd barely 'eard of. I honestly thought they spoke a different language in Scotland cos I never understood a word my gramps said."

Awwwww? My poor dad?

"An' I was nine, Liz. I wouldn't let our Maddie decide which brand o' ketchup she prefers, never mind somethin' that'll affect her for the rest of her bloody life. But, if it makes you feel any better, I'll send her a text. Anyway, I don't wanna talk about it."

"Come on, Trev. Let'sth hug him to deaf."

"Ey up, princess… *whoa*… watch my family jewels. What's that in aid of?"

"Nothin'! Just, we love you to the moon, that'sth all."

"Well… er… cheers, princess. I love you to the moon, too."

"An' Trev?"

"An' Godzilla. Now, how's about we get a takeaway then do somethin' Mother's Day-like? What d'you fancy, Liz?"

"Besides you?"

"Hahaha. Good answer."

Please say something what I like?

"Okay, Joe, how about, we'll get a takeaway and watch the second half of the football, and after we've eaten we could either play charades or watch Harry Potter? What do you think?"

★★★

And that's what we did! Liverpool won 4–1; I had chicken noodles with porn crackers, and then we started playing charades – but, have you heard of a film called *Snatch*? I haven't, but soon as my dad started miming it my mum chucked her shoe at him and said it was time to watch Harry Potter – *The Prisoner from Azkaban* – and just at the bit where Buckbeak turns up, so did Rache!

She was playing a surprise when she phoned my mum before cos she was actually in the car on her way home. She said she couldn't not see my mum on Mother's Day, so after my mum'd finished crying and jumping round the living room cos they're going to the theatre to watch some *Hairspray*? No idea? She put the deevy dees on from when me, Robbie and Rache were little and cried again. Anyway, I have to go to bed now cos my mum thinks I've got school in the morning, but least Rache's gonna read me a story…

"Are you sure about this, Madds? It's not exactly what I had in mind."

"Yesth. My mum alwaysth readsth me *Draclia* when I've been good."

"You're always good Madds, you're just… what

122

about Snow White? Or Cinder—?"

"No! Soz, Rache. Pleasthe will you read me *Draclia*? I…"

"'Ey, Shortshanks…"

"Get out, Robbie!"

"Suit yourself. I just thought I'd let you know you're up shit creek."

AM I? What's shit greek when it's at home?

"Somethin' about a letter from school?"

Oh?

"Mum just found it in your schoolbag."

OH?

"Somethin' about…"

I know what it's about. I just wasn't gonna…

"MADDISON! Any idea when you were going to let me know that you need a leprechaun costume for school tomorrow? Apparently, everyone else's were in weeks ago!"

I wasn't gonna let you know? I don't want to BE a stupid lepra corn.

"So, now I have to spend the rest of my Mother's Day trying to come up with something leprechaun-like for the morning! THANK YOU VERY MUCH!"

"Madds, what are you like? I'd better go and help, Mum. Why don't you want to be a leprechaun, sweetie?"

"Costh it'sth *stupid*… an' Robbie'll only – OOH, RACHE! Do *you* know where'boutsth Cunny Lingusth is? Costh, I've – UH? Not again? Rache, come back!"

God's sakes, am I ever gonna learn the answer to that? I mean, it's not in my atlas or on my globe, and everytime I ask someone they either burst out laughing and run away or say I'm on detention! Least I can hear them laughing their heads' off downstairs, so...

I really hope my mum's had a nice day and that my little accident didn't spoil it too much. It's umbelieveable how – ooh? Someone's coming?

"Sweetheart, I'm sorry for shouting, but you know how I hate leaving things till the last minute. Anyway, I've come to say that in spite of having to clean the house from top to bottom twice and cancel our dinner reservation in favour of takeway, I've had a really lovely Mother's Day. I genuinely appreciate the thought you put into your presents..."

"But, what about my lepra corn costhtume? Aren't you crossth?"

"Don't worry – Rache is in her element. She's looking for Robbie's old Kermit The Frog tunic, so don't be surprised if you have a..."

"'Ey up, trouble... Liz, love, can you come downstairs? Our Rache's gone all Stella McCartney an' there's shit flyin' everywhere. Come an' sort her out, will ya?"

"I'll be down in a minute, Joe. Now, sweetheart... *please* don't ask anyone else whereabouts cunny lingus is because I can promise you that there's no such place. Robbie was winding you up, just for a change. So, you lie back and go to sleep – apparently, you have a big day tomorrow..."

Not really, cos I'm definitely gonna have a sore throat and a headache in the morning.

"Okay, Mum. Happy Mother'sth Day... Mum, can I just check somethin'? Doesth Spud eatin' jam count about my Xth—?"

"Goodnight, Maddison!"

"O-*kaaaay*!"

Happy Mother's Day, everyone!

Goodnight!

Jesus and Chocolate

"Hahaha. You're so funny, sweetheart. Whatever made you ask that?"

"Becausthe *Mary Poppinsth* is alwaysth on telly, an' *Chitty Chitty Bang Bang*'sth alwaysth on telly, an' *Night at The Mustheum* wasth on yesterday so…"

"No, sweetheart, I can assure you – Dick Van Dyke isn't Jesus!"

"Then, why'sth he alwaysth on telly at Easter?"

"I don't know. Ask your dad."

"I did – *yesterday* – but he just told me to be quiet costh he wasth watchin' the snooker. Then while the man wasth puttin' all the ballsth back in the triangle thing he said he didn't know anythin' 'bout Jesusth, but if I wanted to see a real messtheyer, I should watch Ronnyo Thullivan… an' then he told me to go away costh I wasth doin' his head in."

"That wasn't very nice of him!"

I know, and I don't know why? All I was saying was what's the point of snooker? Cos no one ever looks like they're enjoying it, imfact they all look completely fed up. Mind you, I'd look fed up if I spent all that time putting the balls down the holes then soon as I'd managed to do it, someone put them all back on the table and I had to start again.

"Right, sweetheart, you stay here while your dad and I hide your eggs, and I'll give you a shout when we're done."

Ohmigod! Ohmigod! OHMIGOD!

After my birthday and Christmas… which is really just one extra-long day where I have a tiny little sleep in the middle, today's my favourite day of the year. *Ooh? What about Halloween?* After Halloween, too.

I'm not sure what Easter's about cos it's actually quite comfusing. Mrs Jolley said it's because of Jesus dying… and I know it's something to do with snooker and the *Mary Poppins* man's always on telly, but mostly it seems to do with my favourite thing in the world besides Trev – chocolate!

I don't understand what chocolate's got to do with Jesus, though? I don't think they ate chocolate in The Bible? I'm sure it was just bread and fishes. And, isn't it s'posed to be sad when someone dies? So, it's a bit tight calling it *Good* Friday. It should be Sad Friday or Bad Friday? And I'm sure I was listening proply when Mrs Jolley said that two days after Jesus died he got up and went for a walk – but that's inpossible! Even if you're completely bored, you can't change your mind halfway through being dead.

Unless you're a ghost? Or Draclia? Or a – Ohmigod? I think Jesus might've been a zombie! I'm definitely gonna find out more about him after I've found my Easter eggs, and if he is a zombie I might start going to actual church.

I wonder if they've finished hiding them yet? Unless I've got hundreds? I'll just go and check…

"… the audacity to ask if the Easter Bunny might bring her an Easter Xbox! Can you believe that, Joe? Hahaha… shall I give her a shout now?"

"Nah, love, let's leave 'er for a few minutes, 'ey? Enjoy the peace and quiet before all hell breaks loose."

"Don't be cruel – you know how egg-sited she gets."

"Bloody 'ell, Liz, did you just crack a yolk then?"

"I did, and it was most egg-cellent. I'm going to get her, Joe. It doesn't do to let her get dangerously excited."

I'm not sure I've ever been dangerously excited before?

"Ooh, quick, Trev, she'sth…"

"Erm – who's 'she'? The cat's mother?"

I still don't know what that means?

"Soz, Mum. How many Easter eggsth have I got?"

"Don't you mean, how many Easter eggs have I got please? Now, remember, Maddie, keep away from the…"

"Howmanyeasthtereggsthhaveigot, pleasthe?"

"I said…"

"Have I got more than ten?"

"Maddie, let me finish. Keep away from the fishpond and – come back, Maddison! Keep away from the fishpond and watch where you tread."

"Right! Got it!"

One's near the fishpond and one's in the shed…

★★★

Fantastic! I've just found seven whole Easter eggs and I've still got ones off Nanna and Rache to come, but my mum was telling fibs when she said there was one in the shed, cos the only thing I found in there was a massive big spider, and…

"Sweetheart, leave your Easter eggs and come and eat your breakfast."

But, these are my breakfast?

"Look, Maddie, I've even drawn a funny face on the shell for you."

God's sakes? Not chucky eggs? I hate chucky eggs!

"But, can't I just have a Easter egg for my–?"

"You know the rules, Maddie. You're not having any chocolate until you've eaten something sensible."

How can food be sensible?

"But, I don't like chucky eggsth!"

"I don't care, Maddison, just eat it."

"Well, can I just eat the white bit, pleasthe?"

"Ohmigod. Why does everything have to be a battle with you? No! You can eat all of it!"

"But, I *can't* – it'sth *horrid*! I only said I like them so I can bash the shell in, but the actual egg'sth revoltin'. What if I–?"

Ooh? I know? Good plan, Maddison…

"Mum, look! I've finished! Can I bash the shell in now?"

"Close your mouth, sweetheart, I don't need to see your tonsils, and yes, you can. Where did it go so quickly?"

"I ate it like they do in the jungle. Like when they eat cockleroachesth and kangaroosth…"

"Okay, well, I guess you must have eaten it because you wouldn't have been so stupid as to feed it to Spud, would you?"

"Coursthe not – I'm not a idiot! So, can I have my Easter eggsth now, pleasthe?"

"Yes, after you're dressed. I don't want you getting chocolate on your clean dressing gown."

"Okay… Mum, d'you remember when I wasth little an' you used to read me storiesth about the ten commandersth?"

"'The Ten Commandments'? Yes. From *The Children's Bible*?"

"Yup. Have we still got it?"

"Yes, it's in the back room on one of the bookshelves. Would you like me to get it for you?"

"Yup. I just wanna check somethin'."

"Really? I must say, I'm very impressed that you're asking to read The Bible on Easter Sunday, sweetheart. That's unusually reverent of you."

"UH?"

★★★

I don't know what revernant means but I wanted to check if Jesus was a zombie and what happened to him after he got up, but before I got to that story I saw the one about Moses and the Ten Commanders so I started reading it and… I thought the stories in The Bible were s'posed to be true? But, it says Moses climbed to the top of a mountain to write the commanders – they're the police rules like don't tell lies, don't steal anything, don't kill people, normal stuff really – then it said, and you're never gonna believe this, it said he wrote them on TWO TABLETS! I know! That's absolute rubbish! No way did they have tablets in Jesus's days cos they didn't even have 'lectricity! Then, it said he talked to a bush – and not just a normal bush either – one what was on fire! Then, he parted the red – well, that's a load of old rubbish cos the sea's blue, not red. Then, his walking stick turned into a snake and – flippin' 'eck? Jack and the Beanstalk's truer than this and that's about a actual giant? I wonder if my favourite story in The Bible's true? It better had be…

Okay, so, Jehovah told Noah that it was gonna pour down for forty days and nights – ooh? He must have been the weatherman? So, he told Noah to build a enormous ark for him and his sons, who were called Shem, Ham and – HAM? You can't call a baby Ham? That's just mean! Anyway, he told Noah to put all his family on the ark aswell as two of every kind of – UH? This can't be true either. I mean… I need to ask my mum…

"Mum… MUM… MUUUUUU…"

"She's not in, princess, she's gone to get the Wicked Witch o' the West…"

Yes! Nanna's comin'! I hope she's got me a good egg and not one what tastes like it's gone off?

"She said she won't be long cos she wants to get back

before Rache an' loverboy turn up."

"Okay. Well, can you ansthwer my question then?"

"Depends 'ow long it's gonna take – the snooker's startin' in a minute."

"So, you know how in The Bible, how Noah built a massthive big boat an' put two of every kind of animal in it – which is abstholutely inpossthible, costh I saw the size of a elephant when we went to the Safari Park two yearsth ago, and you couldn't hardly fit two of them on a boat. Or hippopotahorsesth. Or rhinoserusthessth. An' what'sth them massthive big thingsth what lionsth eat?"

"Buffaloes, an' move it on, princess, I get the drift."

"Well how come when it landed an' someone opened the doorsth? How come there wasthn't just a massthive pile of bonesth and two big, fat, smiley lionsth? Costh, remember when we had Fluffy, an' he wasth actually Fluffy the third – costh I kept leaving his cage open an' Spud likesth chasin' hamstersth? Well, how come they didn't just eat each—?"

"Can I just stop you there, princess. I have no idea how your mum wants me to answer this question, plus, the snooker's startin' now, so why don't you ram some more chocolate down ya kisser an' you can ask her when she gets back?"

"But, I haven't finished yet. What about the dino-saursth? Is that how come they got egg-stinked? Costh, Noah forgot to put them on the boat? Costh, what kind of idiot forgetsth dinosaursth but remembersth waspsth and cockleroachesth?"

"Dunno, princess, ask your mum. Anyway, Ronnie's comin' on now, so either sit down an' shut up, or…"

"Bye!"

I will ask her – and about Moses – and what about Samson and Delightful? Cos if that's not true then next time I ask if I can get my hair cut I'll tell her that it won't make me rubbish at kung fu!

I'll just finish my Easter egg and uh? Where's it gone? I could of swored I left it on the couch? God's sakes… I hope Spud hasn't eaten it cos dogs are definitely not supposed to eat chocolate, and I know that cos of what happened the last time he ate it and my dad missed most of the Cup Final cos they didn't have a telly in the vets. And, he's only just finished swearing 'bout how much it cost when Spud ate all the jam on Mother's Day? Actually, I'd best find him to check if he's all right…

BANG!

"Robbie, isth Spud—?"

"SHIT! Come in, why don't ya!"

"I *am* in, idiot! Why d'you alwaysth say that?"

"It's called sarcasm – an' no, he's not, so bugger off!"

"What you doin' under the coversth? An' why'sth your face bright red? Are you not well, Robbie? D'you want me to get you some more tissuesth costh you've nearly used all…"

"DON'T TOUCH 'EM! An' by the way, aren't you s'posed to say thanks when someone gets you an Easter egg?"

"I have said thank you."

"Not to me, you 'aven't."

"But, you didn't get me one."

"Says who? You just 'aven't found it."

"You've got me a egg? Really? Where isth it?"

"In the garden – *kind of.*"

"But, I looked everywhere."

Ooh? 'Cept, in the bins?

"I think I know where you've hided it. Back in a minute. An' if you see Spud, an' he'sth actin' weird again – never mind. Hope you get better soon!"

Altogether, we've got four bins and I've fell in three of them. I don't like falling in bins, specially on Sundays when they're full, but I don't have a choice if people keep putting Trev in them. Hmm? First, I have to find something to stand on? I can't wait till I'm tall enough to reach everything. Ooh? That'll do. Now, which one?

"Ip dip dip, my blue – blue! Isth it in the blue one, Trev? Nope! Ip dip – I can't be bothered sayin' it again. Let'sth look in the green one. Yesth! What d'you think, Trev? It looksth like a real Easter egg but – euw, it proply stinksth in here. I can't reach it, Trev. See if you can hook it on your tail. We've never been in thisth bin before, have we? That'sth it... nearly. Just a little bit more and..."

"BOO!"

"WHAAH! ROBBIE, YOU STUPID IDIOT! GET ME OUT OF HERE – IT STINKSTH!"

"Hahahahaha. Smile for the camera, Shortshanks. An' that's April!"

"GET ME OUT OF HERE NOW!"

"You didn't say, 'I'm a Celebrity'!"

"I'm NOT a celebrity, an' I'm COVERED in PIZ-ZTHA!"

"Keep your voice down, fog'orn. D'you want dad to…"

"Oy, Softlad! What the bloody 'ell's goin' on ere?"

"Dad, get me out! I'm in the green – *Hello!*"

"Is this your doin', Softlad?"

"Yup! He pushed me in!"

"No, I bloody never! I said boo, an' she…"

"For christ's sake, Rob. If brains were dynamite, you wouldn't 'ave enough to blow a bloody candle out. An' what you gorpin' at?"

"You! Look at the back o' your jeans. It looks like you've shit yourself."

"*Shit myself?* What d'ya? OH, FOR FUCK'S SAKE!"

So that's where my Easter egg went?

"Scuse my French, princess, but where the bloody hell did ya leave THAT?"

Ohmigod! Who's so stupid to sit on a Easter egg and not even notice? And, it's not just all over his jeans it's completely melted in the sofa, too. So, now we've got to hurry up and fix everything before my mum comes home and sees all the mess, cos she'll go mental if she finds out I fell in the bin while my dad was watching snooker 'stead of watching me. Ooh? I think I can hear the car? I can… won't be a minute…

"Dad, quick, here'sth my…"

"WHAT THE – have you only got 'alf a brain? I told you to get changed so's your mum wouldn't notice!"

"I know, but…"

"Just stay out the way, d'you 'ear me?"

"YUP!"

"Well go on then, scram! Before she – Hiyah, love!"

"Joe, can you – why aren't you wearing any trousers? And why's the sofa cushion crooked?"

"Shittin' Nora! It's like livin' with Sherlock bastard 'olmes!"

Who's shitting Nora?

"Elizabeth, dear, what should I do with – JOSEPH! That's a brave choice for Easter Sunday."

Ooh? That's a other good story. Joseph and his amazing techly-covered dream boat…

"Elizabeth, what shall I do with Maddie's—?"

"NANNA!"

"Oy, birdbrain! What 'appened to stayin' out the way?"

"Maddie, who said you could get changed? And I don't know what you think you're doing dressed like that!"

"I'm bein' Jesusth, Mum. Jesusth wasth a zombie."

"Don't be ridiculous – Jesus wasn't a zombie – and where's your pretty dress?"

Well…

"What's been going on? I've been gone half an hour and I come back to a semi-naked husband and a cast member from The Walking Dead. Well, Joe?"

"I sat on one of her eggs, that's all."

"Yeah, Mum – an' I fell in the bin!"

"All right, mouth!"

"Don't call her that, Joe. You fell in the bin? How? Never mind, I don't think I want to know. Where are your jeans, Joe?"

"In the wash."

"Did you check your pockets?"

"Er?"

"Of course, you didn't! And the sofa cushion – is that covered in chocolate too? Pass it here and I'll put a wash on now. And will you *please* go and put some trousers on? Rachel and Jonathon should be here soon and I don't want them traumatised… Come with me, Maddie, and you are *not* wearing that on Easter Sunday. It's positively sacreligious!"

It's what? And why can't I wear my zombie dress on Easter day? It's well nicer than the one I was wearing before I fell in the bin, and…

"Typical! Look at this, sweetheart. I'm going to kill him."

"Who, Jesusth?"

"See what I have to put up with? Tissues, in both – Maddie, why's your dressing gown in the washing machine? It was clean on this morning!"

AH? I completely forgot about that…

"Erm? I spilled…"

"And did you check your pockets?"

"YUP! DEFINITELY! There'sth abstholutely NOTHIN' in my – NO! You don't need to…"

"What's this, Maddison?"

"Erm?"

"So, you ate it like they do in the jungle, did you?"

Uh-oh? But I've told you a million times already – I don't like chucky eggs!

"It must've fell in there by accident."

"Really? And I'm supposed to believe that, am I?"

Well, if I'm supposed to believe that Moses talked to a bush what was on fire, then I don't see why not?

"Euw – gross! There's egg yolk everywhere! Right, follow me young lady. And Jesus wasn't a zombie because there's no such thing. I don't know where you get such rubbish. And, while I'm on the subject…"

Blah blah blah blah blah… and there is such a thing as zombies cos I just read about it. It's called lepra sea, which is when bits of you fall off, and d'you know who else has bits of them what falls off? Zomb…

"Are you listening, Maddie? I said, stay in your room until Rachel arrives and don't make a mess!"

***

God I'm bored! I'm bored of being in my room, and I'm bored of thinking how it's naughty to tell lies, and I'm bored of reading not true stories in The Bible. I mean, how's it even possible to walk on water – unless it's ice, of course? But, I'm pozzytive they didn't have ice in The Bible, cos I'm sure it was always sunny. And how did he make water into wine? Or feed millions of people with fishfinger butties? Did Jesus go to Hogwarts or something? Come on, Rache, where are you? I wish she'd hurry up cos my mum's always in a good mood when Rache's home… but, least I've got lots of Easter eggs to eat while I'm waiting.

I wonder if I can fit a whole half of one in my mouth? I bet I can cos chocolate's ridicliously melty… Hmm? There's a bit more than I thought but – AH? Someone's coming?

"Sweetheart, Rache and– MADDISON! For God's sake, how much chocolate have you got in there?"

Erm? I can't really talk right now, but, quite a lot actually.

"Look at the state of you. And what's this all over the carpet? I thought I told you not to make a mess?"

Uh-oh?

"GRASS? Why's your carpet covered in grass? And, are those leaves, Maddie? What on earth have you been doing in here? Building an indoor forest?"

Not eggsacly.

"I can't leave you on your own for five minutes. Anyway, Rache is – is that a branch poking out from under your bed?"

"No, Mum, don't…"

"WAAAH! WHAT THE HELL, MADDISON? GET THAT OUT OF THE HOUSE – NOW!"

"But, he'sth my friend. I've made a den for him an' everythin'!"

"I don't care – you're not keeping a spider in your bedroom! Put it out of the windoooow – GET IT AWAY FROM ME!"

"Poor Inthy Winthy…"

"Never mind *'Poor Incy Wincy'*. Right, close the window and come on! Rache is here and she has an announcement to make. Thank God I've got one normal daughter."

I wonder what it is? I hope it's something good and not like her last 'nouncement when she said she was going to the Universe city...

"Hahahahaha. Happy Easter, Madds. I'd give you a kiss but have you seen your face?"

Lots of times, yes?

"Sweetheart, let me wipe some of the chocolate off. Honestly, Rache, I caught her trying to ram..."

"NO! Not the hanky!"

How is it even allowed? To wash someone's face with spit?

"Keep still, Maddie! A whole half of a..."

"Yo, Rache... what's all that shoutin', Mum? Sounded like someone was bein' murdered."

"Somebody nearly was, weren't they, Maddison? Can you believe she had a spider the size of a goddamn tarantula under her bed – *on purpose!* And there's half of Nottingham Forest under there, too."

"What, the football team? Hahaha."

"No, Robbie, although I'm sure they'd make less mess. Honestly, there's so much greenery on her carpet, it'd be easier to mow it, than hoover!"

"Madds, what are you like? Anyway, now that everyone's here, Jon and I have something we want to say."

"Shit, love – you're not up the duff, are ya?"

"No Dad, I'm not 'up the duff' as you so delightfully put it, I'm..."

★★★

Well, this is turning out to be the worstest Easter ever… and not just cos my mum's made me throw Incy Wincy out the window *or* cos she said I've got about as much chance of getting a Xbox for Christmas as I have of going to the actual moon… but I can definitely smell sprouts cooking; she's comfyskated my Easter eggs cos they'll spoil my dinner apparently, and Rache's getting married in October! I know? How awful's that? And worser still – I have to be a prizemaid and I don't even know what one of them is? And my mum's so busy talking 'bout the wedding that she's hardly listened to anything I've said, so I still don't know if The Bible's true. But I think not cos I just read the first bit of the grown-ups Bible where it says about God making the world in six days and nights, and it doesn't mention anything about dinosaurs, and dinosaurs definitely lived on the world before people did cos it says so in *Jurassic Park*. Oh, well? Least she didn't know about these…

I wonder how many Mini Eggs it'd take to *actually* spoil my dinner? Imfact, I wonder what's the world's record for how many I can fit in my mouth? I bet it's about fifteen?

"Six. Seven. Eight. Hahaha. Look, Trev! I can't hardly talk. Nine…"

"Sweetheart, your dinner will be – MADDISON! Right, that's it! Hand over your chocolate now, before you choke to death, you stupid child."

I'm not gonna choke to deaf? I know how to eat chocolate?

"And you'd better be hungry because your dinner will be on the table in five minutes."

"Why? Have we run out of platesth?"

My dad always says that, and it's well funny…

"HAHAHAHA-Ack! Ack! ACK! ACK!"

"Honestly, if you'd been my firstborn you most definitely would've been my – *Sweetheart?* Ohmigod, Joe, Maddie's choking! HURRY UP! I'M NOT…"

"All right! *Friggin' 'ell* – I'm try'na watch the bloody snooker, 'ere! Shift out the way, love."

"Be careful, Joe – watch her ribs!"

"I know what I'm doin', Liz, it's not my first time remember. Brace yourself, kiddo."

HACK!

Phew? But what a waste of Mini Eggs? And why's my whole family staring at me?

"How many times 'ave I done this now, Liz? Given 'er the Heimlich—?"

"SWEETHEART… are you okay? You gave me the fright of my life!"

"Madds, are you okay, sweetie?"

"Goodness me, poppet, you were blue as a Smurf!"

"Hahahaha. How many did ya manage, knob'ead?"

"Right, stop fannyin' about an' be'ave yourself! I'd like to see some o' the snooker today."

"Soz, Dad. I didn't mean to nearly choke to deaf."

Flippin' 'eck? I'll definitely wait till my mouth's got a bit bigger before…

"OHMIGOD! THE DINNER!"

★★★

My dad's done that Hamlick manoover quite a few times to me now, which is actually better magic than Jesus did, cos one time he did it a piece of Rache's old Fuzzy Felt came flying out of me, and nobody knew it was in me to begin with.

And imagine that? It only took nine Mini Eggs to spoil my dinner. It spoiled everyone's actually, and not just cos the sprouts went mushy, the gravy boiled over and the Yorkshire pudding went completely burnt, but while everyone was busy watching me choke to deaf, Spud ran off with the chicken! But it wasn't me what left it out on the table so I don't see how it's my...

"Honestly, Maddie, if I find out this was all part of some elaborate scheme of yours – who ordered the Hawaiian? Pass that to Jonathon, please – to get out of eating your vegetables – Rache, I think this is yours – and believe me, Maddie, I will – Joe, Robbie, those are your Mexican Hot and Spicy – I'm going to get every single takeaway menu we have in the house – there's your tuna and red onion, Mum – and throw them all in the – OOH! WEDDING MENUS!"

Thank goodness for that. I thought she was never gonna stop talking. And, even though I've not had chance to check yet, I don't think I've broke the world's record for eating Mini-Eggs-all-in-one-go, but, I'm sure my mum's just broke the record for talking to the most amount of people in one sentence. And, maybe Rache getting married's not such a bad thing? For starters, it's stopped my mum from going on and on and on, and so far, no one's even noticed that I've switched the telly over from the…

"OY! What the 'ell's happened to my snooker?"

"Yeh – knob off, Shortshanks! We're not watchin' Shitty Shitty Bang Bang again."

"It'sth not called Shitty Shitty…"

"MADDISON!"

"What?"

"What do you mean, what?! It's Easter Sunday and you're seven years old…"

"Yeh, Princess. Don't say Shitty Shitty Bang Bang!"

I never said bang bang?

"I don't know about you, Joe, but I think somebody could do with an early night!"

Noooooooooooo. Quick. Change the subject, Maddison…

"Robbie, are you better now?"

"Excuse me – don't interrupt me while I'm talking, Maddie – and what do you mean, better? Are you ill, Robbie?"

"Nah! Just ignore 'er."

"Yesth you wasth! You wasth in bed before, all out of breath with a bright red face, an' there wasth loadsth of soggy tissuesth on your…"

"Shut it, Shortshanks!"

"Hahahahahaha. Sounds like someone was caught 'avin' a Thomas the Tank!"

How can you have a Thomas the Tank? Thomas is a train?

"Thanks for that, Dad… an' you, you, poison dwarf – just wait till I get 'old of you! I'm gonna…"

Oops! I've got to run now, soz…

"Pick on someone your own size, Robbie... MUM! TELL HIM!"

"Robbie, leave her alone and – don't you dare throw that, Maddison!"

Happy Jesus and Chocolate Day everybody!

Goodbye!

The Big Four O

"Now remember, princess, whatever you do, don't mention the…"

How many more times, Dad? I know how to keep a secret…

"I won't – promisthe! Pleeeeasthe can we go in now?"

"Okay, kiddo, but…"

BANG!

"HAPPY BIRTHDAY, MUM!"

"Oy, numbnuts! Watch the bloody wall."

"It's a good job I was already awake, sweetheart… is there any damage, Joe?"

"Nah! Nothin' since the last hole, love. Why can't you open the door like a normal person, 'ey, Maddie? Why d'you have to burst through everywhere like a bloody wreckin' ball? Every wall in the 'ouse has had an 'ole in it, thanks to you!"

"Soz, I was just eggcited for tonight. Are you eggcited

for tonight, Mu—?"

"Oy, mouth! Put a sock in it, will ya?"

"Joe? What was that for?"

"Er? Nothin', love. Just – anyway, Happy Birthday! The big four O, 'ey? An' you don't look a day over…"

"What time is it, Joe?"

"I was givin' you a compliment there, an' it's half eight. I couldn't hold her any longer, sorry. It's been murder tryin' to keep her quiet this last couple of hours."

"Have you been up since half six?"

"Yeh… I only got up for a pee but then I 'eard somethin' downstairs, didn't I, princess? Bloody Houdini there – standin' on one of the brekkie stools tryin' to get the dead bolt off the back door."

"Maddie, you know you're not allowed to do that!"

"Yeah, but I wasthn't after hedgehogsth thisth time."

"I don't care what you were after, you're not allowed out of the house while we're still in bed!"

"But there wasth a kitten on the…"

"Jeeze, Liz, 'ow d'you cope with this all day? She never stops for breath, does she?"

I am here, you know? And I do stop for breath else I'd be dead.

"… yap yap bloody yap – an' she's got an answer for everythin'! Anyway, love, how does it feel to be forty?"

"Well, I've only been awake ten minutes, but…"

"Mum, you know now you're proply old, you won't die, will you? I don't want you to EVER die."

"Sweetheart, forty isn't old…"

It flippin' well is? Ooh? I wonder if she smells of cabbage yet?

"… but I have no plans to die in the foreseeable—

what are you doing, you strange child? Stop sniffing me, it tickles! Hahahaha…"

Maddison reporting: no cabbagy smell yet! Phew.

"Trev wantsth to say happy birthday. He'sth nearly as eggcited as me about your p…"

"PRINCESS!"

"WHAT? Oh, the…"

"So, Joe, what's the plan for today? I know we're going out…"

"Ooh! Ooh! Can I tell you, Mum? We're not doin' presentsth now… we're gonna do them later at th— OW! What did you do that for, Dad?"

"Sorry, princess, my foot slipped."

No, it didn't!

"Well, love, I thought the best way I could spoil you is to take madam out for a few hours. That way, you can have the mornin' to yourself."

"Really?"

"Yesth, Mum! My dad'sth takin' me to the club to help…"

"SO, WHAT D'YOU THINK, LOVE? Does that sound like a plan?"

"Are you all right, Joe? Why do you keep randomly shouting? Is there something going on?"

"Flippin' 'eck, Mum, how did you *noooo*… I want to stay with my mum!"

"Hahaha. Aww, Joe, don't drag her out. She's not that loud."

"Drag her? I'll string her up by her bloody ankles if she doesn't dial it down. An' no love, there's nothin' goin' on. She's just doin' my 'ead in, that's all!"

"Okay, then, yes. That sounds wonderful."

"I'll even run you a bath – see, don't say I never spoil ya. Happy Birthday, gorgeous."

Eeeeeeuw? Stop kissing?

"Come on, you – mouth almighty! Leave your mum in peace."

I can't believe my dad dragged me out while I was in the middle of talking, and I never even *said* the word party. Anyway, my mum thinks she's going out for a meal with Rache and Jonathon tonight but she's not, cos instead we're doing a surprise party for her. I know. And the best bit is – my dad's band are playing!

I've never seen them play before cos my dad stopped doing it just after I was born, but that's how come I found out about the party. I know I'm not s'posed to play with his phone but I accidently did. And I know I'm not s'posed to read his messages but I accidently did. And I saw one off Larry what said about… hang on a sec… I think we're going now…

"Liz, we're off."

"Aww, thanks, Joe. I can't remember the last time I had a proper soak."

"You're welcome, love. Come on, princess, let's go to the park."

"THE PARK? But I thought we were goin' to the – Ow! You're pullin' my arm out!"

"I'll keep her out as long as I can, love. See ya later! Wave to your mum, princess."

"BYE, MUM!"

"Right, she's gone. For Chrissake, Maddie?"

"What?"

"WHAT? *'Course I can keep a secret, Dad!'* I'm warnin' you, princess, if you spoil your mum's surprise tonight you'll be the first kid in space – an I'll bloody well launch you there myself! Now, get in the car an' we're gonna play a little game called, 'Let's see how long you can 'old your breath for'? An' you're goin' first!"

I'm not playing that. I'm not stupid.

Anyway, we're going to the club now so the band can set all the instraments up for tonight. I've met Larry millions of times cos he's my dad's best friend, but I've never met Gary or Dave before, so it's gonna be brilliant...

***

"OY! What have I just told you, Maddie? Stop pissin' about with those drumsticks an' get off the bloody stage!"

"But I'm bored. Can I least have a go on the tambreen?"

"No, you can't! Here, take this next door an' get yourself some sweets..."

Ooh? Two pounds?

"An' come straight back. D'you hear me?"

"YUP!"

Brilliant! But, I need a wee first? I wonder where the toilet is? I think this is the – Oh? The door's stuck? Never mind, I'll just go in these ones instead...

"Eeeeuw, Trev, sniff up! It abstholutely stinksth in – OOH! A MACHINE!"

Hmm? I think it's bubble gum? Whatever, it says banana or strawberry flavour.

"Which shall we pick, Trev? Banana? Really? I wasth gonna pick strawberry, but – Uh? It'sth ate the money but it hasn't spat any bubbly out! What, Trev? Maybe, if I bash it? Well, it might work I s'thpose... nope... nothin' seemsth to be happenin'? I'll just try one more time and – OH MY GOODNESSTH! I didn't eggspect *that* would happen, did you, Trev? And I only wanted one."

Well, I can't let them go to waste now?

"Flippin' 'eck, Trev, why do they make the wrapper so hard to get off? Anyone'd think they didn't want you to eat them."

Ooh, at last? Hmm? It's a bit weird? Imfact...

"Eeeeeeuw! That tastesth flippin' disgusthtin'! Let'sth try a other one."

If this is what grown-up's bubbly tastes like it's no wonder they hardly ever chew it cos it's absolutely...

"Okay, Gaz, I'm gonna check in 'ere. You check the car park, Dave!"

Ohmigod, my dad's coming. I'm gonna get in so much trouble cos I'm absolutely not allowed to eat bubbly but this is nearly inpossible to swallow? Imfact...

"There you are, princess! What the bloody 'ell are you doin' in the – Er? What's goin' on?"

"Nothinthsgoinon."

"Nothin'? Then how come the floor's covered in – what's that in your mouth?"

Flippin' 'eck? How are you s'posed to swallow this stupid thing?

"Open your mouth, Maddie! Now, Maddiso—OH,

FOR F— CRYIN' OUT BLOODY LOUD!"

"What?"

"SPIT IT OUT!"

There's no need to shout? And I was gonna do that anyway cos it's the worsest bubbly I've ever tasted...

"I need eyes in the back o' my 'ead, with you! Panic over, lads, I've found 'er!"

"Where was she, Joe?"

"In the gents – SIT THERE, AN' BEHAVE – an' you're never gonna believe this! You know that money I gave her for sweets – she's only gone an' knackered the johnny machine up, thinkin' it was chewy!"

"HAHAHA..."

"I'm glad you're laughin', Larry. They're all over the bog floor if ya fancy a freebie, but you'll have to make do with strawberry cos she's had a go at most o' the banana."

I have, but only cos I was trying to find one what tasted nice – which was none of them – and now I've got a absolutely *horrid* taste in my mouth. Whatever, we're going to McDonalds after my dad's finished practising, and surely he can't be that much longer?

"'Ey, Calamity Jane, don't let ya dad see ya standin' on there, or he'll flip his lid again."

"What'sth it called again, Larry?"

"A drum riser. It's to the lift the drums up off the floor so the cymbals don't deafen ya dad."

"An' why'sth this big one got a hole in the front of it? Isth it broke?"

"No, it's meant to be like that, kid. It helps it sound better."

"Hahaha. Look, Larry. I can fit my whole…"

"Oy, birdbrain! Get your noggin' out the bass drum, will ya, an' grab Godzilla – that's us done!"

Thank goodness for that.

"See ya later lads – really lookin' forward to it. Right, trouble, tell me where've we been?"

Trouble? What have I done now?

"Erm… The park?"

"Yeh. An' what did we do at the park?"

"Went on the swingsth?"

"An' what did you fall off?"

"The monkey barsth."

"Good. We have to make it realistic. Now remember, not a word to your mum."

***

"Hello, you two, have you had a nice time?"

Not in the slightest! I can't believe my dad didn't take me to McDonalds. Four whole hours I had to sit there for, with nothing to eat and no one to play with, listening to him saying '1 – 2' down the micra phone every two minutes – and how can I have made him take twice as long as usual? I'm not even in the band? But, least I'm home now, so my mum'll make me some dinner…

"Did you missth me, Mum?"

"I did actually. It was eerily quiet for a Saturday."

"Was four hours long enough, love? I kept 'er out as long as I could. We went to the park, didn't we, princess? Then Maccy D's."

No, we didn't!

"I thought so. I can smell banana milkshake from here."

"But, I've not had a…"

"PRINCESS, TELL YA MUM WHAT YOU FELL OFF AT THE SWINGS!"

"Joe, why are you shouting again?"

"Sorry, love. I didn't know I was."

"I can't remember, Dad? What wasth it you said I fell—?"

"HAVE YOU HAD A NICE DAY, LOVE?"

"Yes. And, remind me to book you an appointment at the doctors. I think your ears might need syringing."

"OOH? Wasth it the monkey barsth, Dad? Mum, you know tonight? Do I HAVE to wear my party dressth costh – nooooo. Dad, put me down!"

★★★

Humph! Guess where I've been all afternoon – in prison! Not actual prison but… what's a more on? Cos, I'm one apparently, and if my mum hasn't guessed about the party by now, then she's one too. But it's really hard to remember not to say anything all of the time. Anyway, Jonathon and Rache are here now, so it's nearly time for me to pretend to go to Nanna's.

Nanna's pretend minding me while they go out for the pretend meal – see, it's not easy – but really, we're going to the club early to be there for the surprise. And I'm completely starving now. My dad told my mum that we'd been to McDonald's so she wouldn't let me have anything to eat in case it spoiled my dinner – and Nanna *hasn't* spent all day cooking something nice for me cos she's spent most of it at the flippin' hairdressers.

Least I got to pick my own clothes for the party tonight and – ooh? My dad's shouting me. I think it's time to go. It's *so* eggciting. Have I said that already?

★★★

"Right, princess, I'll be back in an hour. So, sit there – don't touch anythin' – an' be a good girl for your nan! An' keep an eye on her, will you, Betty? I've already had an earful from the steward cos she's buggered up the johnny machine."

"I have looked after her before, Joe!"

"You have, haven't you, Nanna? Bye, Dad! Nanna, where'sth Robbie?"

"He's in the conserva… in the big glass building at the back. He's putting up the photo gallery now that the caterers have gone."

Ooh? Food?

"Can I go an' help him?"

"Of course, poppet, I'll just be out in the beer garden, putting up balloons."

Right? Where's the flippin' – Ooh? That's a good idea? I didn't notice they had curtains on the stage before. Now my mum won't be able to guess about the band playing cos she can't see any of the instraments…

"What you up to, Shortshanks? You're not bringin' that to the party, are ya?"

"If you mean Trev, then course I am. Is this all the food, Robbie?"

This looks rubbish? Where's all the hot stuff?

"Dunno, an' you never answered my question. What you up to?"

Where's all the chicken nuggets and pizza?

"Oy, I'm talkin' to you, knobchops! Tell Nan I'll be in the sports bar if she needs me. Smell ya later."

"Okay, bye. Flippin' 'eck, Trev, there'sth nothin' here what I like? 'Cept, maybe those sausage-roll thingsth but – eeeeuw, what'sth THAT?"

It looks like a massive fish, covered in lemons and cumcuber?

"Look, Trev, it'sth got a actual eye. Eeeeuw, I'm not eating any of that! I'll just try some of these sausage-roll thingsth…"

If I can reach them? If this stupid cumcuber fish wasn't in the way? I'll just move it a bit and…

"I can't reach, Trev. See if you can move it with your tail. That'sth it. Just a little bit more… and a little bit more to the – just be careful of the edge of the table costh it'sth very close to – OHMIGOD! Did you *see* that, Trev? How did that happen?"

Honest to god, it just cattypulted right up in the air all by itself, then did a summer-salt and landed upside-down on the floor.

"God'sth sakesth Trev – it'sth gone everywhere! What are we gonna do? What'sth that? We should scoop it up and hide it? But, where? *Really?* That'sth a brilliant idea, actually. No one'll ever look in there and – ooh. An' we can have a little play with stuff at the same time. But, then we need to get clean costh we abstholutely whiff of fish!"

"Roaaaar! Okay, Maddithon. Whatever you say. An' don't forget the sausage rollsth."

★★★

Well, that's that hided! And while I was hiding it I found the best imvention in the world. It's for when you want to cut sausage rolls into perfeck slices, and it's proply…

"Poppet, are you in here?"

"Yup! I'm just gettin' mysthelf…"

"Oh, good Lord – not again? Well, it's too late now; your mum and dad have just arrived. Come on… this way… Shhhhhhh! Lights out everyone and absolute silence… and that includes you, poppet."

Oh, dear? I can hear my mum from here and she sounds quite grumpy, actually.

"YOU'VE GOT TO BE KIDDING ME, JOE! HERE? But it's my fortieth birthday, for God's sake! I don't WANT a pie and pea supper! I can't believe you forgot to book the restaurant. You're absolutely – I'm so sorry about this, Rache – USELESS! We could have…"

"SURPRISE!"

"WHAAA!"

"SURPRISTHE, MUM!"

"Oh, my! Oh, my *goodness*…"

"Did you guessth, Mum?"

"No… not at all… I'm… I'm, sweetheart, why have you got your zombie dress on? Oh, my! I can't believe this. Did you do this, Joe? Did I really just say you were useless?"

Why's she crying?

"Don't you like it, Mum?"

"I love it, sweetheart! It's wonderful!"

This is so confusing cos, is it normal to cry when you're happy? My mum's only been here a few minutes but she's already cried so much that her manscara's run all down her face. It looks fantastic actually, like me, when I'm being a zombie, but she looks so different that even my dad mistaked her for a lady called Alice Cooper. And I don't know who Alice Cooper is but she must be a right weirdo if that's how she looks? Anyway, Rache's just been to help fix my mum's face back to normal so now we're gonna show her the photo garrely, but I don't know what's so good about it? It's just loads of imbarrassing photos of her from when she was little, and…

"Sweetheart, come here!"

Not again? I don't want to spend all night being intra juiced to people? It's boring and imbarrassing, and if one more person says…

"This is my youngest, Maddison. Say hello, sweetheart… Robbie! Over here!"

"Oh, Liz, what a beautiful little girl… and don't you look like your mum?"

Argh! I think I'm gonna do my first murder. Or, I

could just spray her with my fizzy pop?

"What's up, Mum? Oy, knob'ead! Stop shakin' that bottle, will ya? D'you want it goin' everywhere?"

That was the idea, Robbie Blobby… Never mind, I'm going for a slide…

★★★

Well, my mum loved her photo garrely so she cried at that. And every time someone new turned up she cried at that. Then my dad did a speech and she cried at that. Imfact, she's spent so much time crying she's hardly noticed me, which is why so far I've found a fifty pence, a twenty pence, and a weird thing what looks like a pen but smells like cough sweets…

"Sweetheart, come out from under there and say hello to my friend, Adele."

Ugh! Not a other person I have to be intra juiced to? I thought this was s'posed to be a party? How am I s'posed to have fun if I have to keep saying Hell—?

"OH? *Adele*? But, isthn't that a girl'sth name?"

"Shut up, sweetheart. We used to go to school together, didn't we, Ad—?"

"Really? She looksth milesth older than you…"

"Maddison! For God's sake, stop being so rude."

I'm not being rude? I'm telling the truth? And stop intra juicing me to people then.

"It's okay, Liz. She's not exactly wrong."

"Rubbish, Adele! You look fantastic!"

No, she doesn't? She looks like a nearly old man?

"And what's that you're hiding behind your back, sweetheart? Show me, Maddie. I'll count to – an E-CIG? Where on earth did you find that?"

"Under the table. But, I couldn't find how to make it write and it tasted abstholutely revoltin'."

"Good! Have you seen your dad anywhere?"

"Yup! He wasth talkin' to the food man. Come on, Mum, I'll show you."

"He'll be so pleased to see you, Adele. If it wasn't for the obvious, I'm sure he'd have preferred – OH?"

"I don't give a flyin' fuck! I'm not payin' sixty quid for an invisible bloody salmon!"

Oops?

"Mister McLaren, will you please calm down. I can *assure* you that when we left before, there was a whole dressed salmon adorning the buffet table."

"Where the fuck's it gone then? I s'pose it jumped off the table an' legged it?"

It did, sort of?

"I have no idea, and can you please temper your language."

"I'll temper my bloody language when you knock it off the – 'Ey up, princess, I didn't see you there. I don't suppose you know anythin' about this, do ya?"

"No, Dad."

Sorry for telling lies, Jesus, but I can't afford to pay all that money for a stupid cumcuber fish.

"Well, bugger me! If it isn't my favourite drinkin' buddy back from the Orient? How are ya, love? Give us an 'ug! I wasn't sure you'd be able to make it."

"Hey, you! Still as charming as ever, I see. Hahaha…"

"Yeh… sorry about that, but the cheeky sod's try'na charge me sixty quid for an AWOL salmon. He must think I'm wet be'ind the ears. Anyway, how long's it been? It must be at least ten years."

"I got transferred in 2006, so, yes."

"Give over – ten years, 'ey? So, 'ow was it in 'ong Kong? Looks like you enjoyed the food, love. You've put on a bit o' timber since I last saw ya."

"Well, I've had three failed relationships out there, Joe, and you know me – I've always been a comfort eater."

"Yeh, but, how much comfort did ya need?"

"JOE!"

"Be'ave, Liz, she's knows my sense o' humour. 'Ey, Dell, it's a good job you came out the closet when you did, cos you wouldn't bloody fit in one now!"

"Hahahahaha. I've really missed you, Joe. I could always rely on you to…"

"Mum, what'sth a closthet?"

"A closet's another name for a wardrobe, sweetheart."

A wardrobe? Really? Why's she come out of a – Ohmigod? Is Onkong in Narnia?

I have heard of Adele cos she's Rache's fairy godmother and she was my mum's best friend since imfant school – she was even at the party where my mum and dad met and was proply best friends with him, too… but then she got sent to work in Onkong, before I was even born, to live with a lady called Lesby–Anne, but now they've fell out so she's come back to – ooh? I wonder if she knows Aslan?

"Princess, grab my pint off the table an' bring it

backstage will ya? An' don't let your mum see. Cheers, kiddo."

"Yup!"

I think it's nearly time for the band? I'm really looking forward to watching them cos my dad's miles better at singing than I thought he was, and he's way better at the guitar when it's actually plugged in, too. I don't think my mum's guessed about them playing cos the curtains are still closed on the stage but – oops! Try not to spill it, Maddison – you're doing a really good job so far. Just a few more steps and…

"WHO THE FUCK'S DONE THIS? There's sausage roll all over my bastard strings!"

OH? I'd forgot about my 'perfeck-sausage-slices' imvention?

"I dunno, Joe, but someone's been fuckin' about with my bass too. The strings're loose as a wizard's – 'Ey? Where's my tuner gone? I coulda swore I left it on my amp?"

Tuna? What, more fish?

"Shittin' hell – what's 'appened to my keyboard? It's sticky as a pickpocket's fingers?"

It sounds like Goldilocks and the three bears but with swearing?

"What about you, Larry, lad? Your drums okay?"

"Yeh, all seems fine here, Gaz. There's a bit of a weird smell like, but…"

"Yeh, I can smell somethin'? Have you dropped your arse, Dave?"

"Don't go lookin' at me!"

"Well, someone 'as. An' where's our Maddie with my pint? My throat's as dry as a nun's…"

"It'sth here, Dad."

"Cheers, princess. I don't s'pose you know anythin' about – OY! Come back 'ere, you!"

No chance – I don't want killing yet! I haven't even watched the band! I'll probly own up when they've finished. Or tomorrow? Or, maybe they won't remember at all if it goes brilliant? Hmm? I need to find somewhere to stand…

"It's been murder trying to keep it a secret, Mum."

"I can imagine, Rache… and I can't tell you how relieved I am now that I know he's been rehearsing. He's been disappearing that often of late, I was beginning to think he was having an affair."

"Don't be daft, mum, he idolises you – Madds, get down, sweetie."

"Maddie, get down! You're not standing on the table – you'll see just as well if you come around here and stand with me."

"LADIES AND GENTLEMEN! Will you please put your hands together, for the first time in seven years, it's, 'The Dragonflys'!"

"Good evenin'! Thanks everyone for comin'. Okay, so, we're here tonight to celebrate my gorgeous wife's 'big four O', so I thought we'd kick things off with this one, love. Take it away, Gaz – GAZ ON KEYS, EVERYONE!"

"Ohmigod, Rache, I can't believe he's going to sing this. He wrote it as a joke after I'd said… never mind…"

"Recognise it, love? I wrote this for our first anniversary, remember? It's called, 'She Goes Down like a Cherry Liqueur'…"

HAHAHAHA!

"What doesth it mean, Mum? Goesth down like a—?"

"Nothing, sweetheart."

It can't mean nothing? Nothing means nothing?

"This one's for you, babe. An' it goes somethin'… like… this…

Let me tell you what I know about the girl next door
In the daytime she's an angel, in the nightime she's…
hahaha
The way she makes me feel, I couldn't love her anymore…
Introducin' MISTER LARRY POPALOPADUS
ON DRUMS, EVERYONE!"

What, WHO?

"A – 1 2 3"

"Cos, when she wakes up in the mornin', she goes down like a– WHATTHEFUCK?"

OHMIGOD?

"STOP – WHAT THE?"

"'Ey, Joe, lad? What's all that pink stuff slidin' down ya back?"

Run, Maddison…

"SALMON? WHO THE BLOODY 'ELL's DONE THIS?"

***

God's sakes! How was I s'posed to know the cumcuber fish'd come flying out the hole in the front of Larry's bass drum soon as he started playing it, then hit my dad on the back and slide all the way down his legs? Anyone'd think it was still alive! And Larry, Gary and Dave laughed so much they had to stop playing. But, I'm not really sure what happened after that cos I legged it and hid in the toilets, and I only came out cos I heard Nanna say, 'If we don't find her within the next minute, I'm calling the police'!

Anyway, everyone loved the band, specially the song about Alice – *Ah? Is that who Alice Cooper is?* But, I didn't really get to hear that one cos just when it started Nanna told me to stand in the beer garden with her… and I don't know how much fresh air old people need but there was definitely more inside the club cos everyone outside was smoking. But it was brilliant, right, cos one minute we were standing there talking, then next minute everyone yelled 'Alice! Alice! Who the f.u.k. is Alice?' – all at the 'xact same time! I spelled it so it doesn't count, but how funny's that? I'm deffo gonna ask my dad to teach me that next time he's had booze, cos he usually says yes to everything…

"Sweetheart, come on. The taxi's waiting!"

So, besides getting in trouble for a couple of little things I've had a smashing time tonight, and least I don't have to remember about the secret anymore, even though I was brilliant at keeping it. I am gonna pretend to be asleep in the taxi though, 'case anyone wants to shout at me, but they seem to have forgot to be cross cos everyone's had such a good time…

"Joe, can you budge over a bit? You stink to high heaven."

"Sorry, love, but I did tell you to go in the other taxi. An' look at her. She's fast-a-bloody-sleep!"

"I'm not surprised. Did you see her dancing to 'New York, New York'? I can't find her shoe, anywhere."

"I know. She nearly took your mum's 'ead off with it!"

"And, did you know she was going to burp 'Happy Birthday' down the microphone?"

"Did I bollocks! She told me she wanted to sing!"

"I don't know how she does that? I'd be sick if I tried to do it."

"I know. An' then when she started doin' armpit farts – jeeze! Gaz an' Dave've never met her before – they thought she was funny as fuck. It's okay, love, she's asleep."

She's not.

"You should've heard her try'na say Popalopadus, Liz. Larry was killin' himself laughin'!"

"Well, it is a mouth-full. It's Greek, isn't it?"

"Yeh. An' Larry's not even his real name, remember. It's Stefanos."

Ohmigod? Imagine being called Stefanos Popple Octopus?

"Oh, yes, I'd forgotten. Why do you call him Larry, again?"

"It was after that guy who used to do *The Generation Game* back in the eighties – Larry Grayson. We were in school an' he was the last one in class, so the teacher yelled at him to 'Shut that door' an' he's been Larry ever since."

"Oh, yes – that was his catchphrase! Hahaha. Kids, huh? So, Stefanos Popalopadus? I bet Maddie'd have fun saying that."

Stefanos Popple Octopus? She's not even gonna try.

"Anyway, I was sayin' – so, Larry starts tellin' 'em some o' the things she's got up to, an' when he said about the time she glued the Catherine wheels to the shed an' set 'alf the garden on fire, they were full-on cryin'! I told 'em they could 'ave her for a week; see if they're still laughin' then. Oh, an' I forgot to tell you, love. You know when you thought she'd had a banana milkshake this afternoon? Well…"

***

I had to pretend to wake up then cos my mum shouted comdom so loud she nearly broke the taxi windows. Anyway, I'm s'posed to be in bed now but I'm not in the least bit tired, and I really want some of the cake what's left over from the party. So, I'm just gonna tiptoe past my mum and dad's bedroom and – Ooh? What's going on?

"Joe, pack it in! Hahahaha. I'm tired and I've had too much to drink."

"No worries, love. You don't have to be awake for it."

"YOU CHEEKY… *get off!*"

Are they fighting?

"Come on, love. You're not gonna let this go to waste, are ya?"

"Ohmigod, Joe! Is that a gun in your pocket or are you just—?"

A GUN? My Dad's got a GUN?

"It is, an' it's fully loaded."

It's got bullets in it, too? Ohmigod?

"An' he's very pleased to see you…"

Who is? AH? Is there a murderer in my mum and dad's bedroom?

"An' he's gonna give you a bloody good seein' to…"

Oh no, he's not?

BANG!

"DON'T WORRY, MUM, I'LL SAVE…"

"BLOODY 'ELL, MADDIE…"

Oh? Definitely not a murderer?

"… LEARN TO SODDIN' WELL KNOCK, WILL YA?"

"Don't shout at her, Joe. Go back to bed please, sweetheart, and I'll be in in a minute."

"Sweet'eart? More like, the human contraceptive."

"Humph! Come on, Trev, let'sth go. Goodnight, Mum."

"Goodnight, sweetheart."

"Goodnight, Dad."

"It was till you burst in!"

Message to Maddison: find out, what's a humour contraseptic?

See you all soon everybody…

Goodnight!

We're Going to The Zoo

"Jeeze, Liz, have you got somethin' against me havin' a day off or what? If it's not the garden centre it's B&Q or – what's that place where they do the meatballs, again?"

"IKEA, and I don't care, Joe, just hurry up and make your mind up, because we're going somewhere today, whether you like it or not."

Yeah, Dad, hurry up and make your mind up. I don't know what about though? I only came downstairs to ask how can a bank have a holiday? But, this is miles more intresting …

"You're not gonna give it a rest, are ya? What's the choices again?"

"Safari park or zoo. Which is it?"

Ooh? Ooh? Please say the zoo. Please say the zoo. Please say the – or the safari park, actually? But I've never been to the zoo before…

"Come on, love – that's like askin' me if I'd rather be shot or stabbed."

"Is it? How?"

"Cos either way it'll be a bloody nightmare. I said last time we took her to the safari park – never again! Two hours trapped in a bakin' hot car with her screechin' down my ear."

"She was only five years old, Joe, and there were monkeys on the car. What did you expect?"

"I didn't expect those little bastards to spray shit everywhere an' rip half the fuckin' car to bits. I wouldn't be surprised if they had shares in Halfords."

"Who? The monkeys?"

"Nah! The safari park, ya daft melt! Two new wipers; a wing mirror, an' I had to replace the rubber seal round the windscreen."

"Yes, but this time we'll check she hasn't smeared banana all over the car. You have to admit, that was exceedingly enterprising for a five-year-old."

"It was exceedin'ly fuckin' annoyin'! It took me half a day to get all the dried baboon shit an' baked banana off it – in fact, that's made my mind up – we're goin' to the zoo."

Yes! And I'd completely forgot about that. Thank you, Robbie, it did work!

"What time d'ya wanna set off?"

"Ten-ish? We'll leave it till the last minute before telling her or she'll be insufferable."

"Won't she bloody just. Where is she?"

"Upstairs, tidying her bedroom."

Erm? She's not actually. She's outside the door. Very, very eggcited and…

"Mum, pleasthe can I wear my zombie dressth to the zoo?"

***

"INDICATE, YA COCK! I'm not a fuckin' mind reader!"

"For God's sake, Joe, just park here – I don't care how far we have to walk."

I'd forgot what my dad's like when we're in the car. Honest to God, he's moaned 'bout everything. He's moaned 'bout the traffic; 'bout people's driving; 'bout the queue at the petrol station; 'bout having to pay to put water in the engine and air in the wheels, and he nearly had a heart attack when he saw how much it cost to get in the car park. But, mostly he's moaned 'bout me. But, I have not got a voice like a foghorn, and I only asked a few times if we were nearly there yet.

Anyway, least we're here now, even if this queue is taking ages…

"Oy, princess, watch my bloody feet, will ya? That's the third time you've stood on 'em an' we've only been out the car five minutes."

Then, let go of my hand!

"How many, sir?"

"Two adults an' one child, please."

"That'll be fifty-seven pounds and…"

"HOW MUCH? FIFTY-SEVEN QUID?! I only

wanna go for the day, love. I didn't ask to buy the fuckin'…"

"JOE! Move out of the way! I'm really sorry, how much did you say it was?"

"Fifty-seven pounds, and would you like a souvenir guide?"

"No, she bloody wouldn't!"

Flippin' 'eck. They've been arguing for ages now. Does it really matter which way we go? Surely, anywhere's better than standing in the actual entrance. Least, there's peacocks here, but who comes to the zoo to see peacocks? Imfact, I'm not sure they even belong in the zoo cos they're – Ohmigod! How did it do THAT?

"Dad, let go of my hand! I want to look at the peacock. Look at what it just did."

"Oh, aye! All right, princess, but keep where I can… *bye then.*"

"Hey, Trev, look at all it'sth feathersth. It looksth like there'sth loadsth of eyesth stuck on them, doesthn't it? I wonder if they're glued on? Shall we imvestigate?"

Actually, do peacocks bite? I can't imagine they do, or they wouldn't be allowed to just walk round, would they?

"Shall we try'n stroke it, Trev? Yesth? Okay, you go first seein' as it wasth your idea."

It's a little bit scary close up but Trev's a eggceptionly brave dinosaur.

"Trev, I think it likesth you. Mum! Look! We're strokin' the…"

"Maddie, come away!"

"It'sth okay. It likesth usth."

"Really? Because, I'm pretty sure it's displaying aggressive behaviour."

Gressive behaviour?

"And, I don't think it appreciates being poked with Trevor."

"He'sth not pokin' it. He'sth strokin' it."

"Maddie, do as you're told and come away."

"But, it likesth us!"

"Come away. Right, that's enough! Give me your haaaaaaaaaaaaaaaaaa…"

"Flippin' 'eck!"

"Hahahaha. Go on, love, put ya foot down! Look at 'er go, princess. Hahaha…"

"Aaaaagh! Stop laughing, you two. IT's NOT F— aaaaaagh!"

It flippin' well was! And I didn't even know my mum could actually run. But, least my dad's cheered up now. Imfact, he was still laughing when she tiptoed out the toilets yelling 'Has it gone yet?'. But honestly, I don't think I'd scream that much if I was being chased by a actual lion – and who knew peacocks could run that fast? Besides Jonnie Peacock, of course? Hahaha. I've just thought. It's a shame it's not allowed to have a real peacock chasing you at the Lympics cos I think my mum'd win a gold medal, too.

Anyway, she's finally got her breath back so we're going to see some proper animals now. Apparently, the chinpamzees are just round this corner so we're going to see them first…

"Sweetheart, look."

"Can I run on, Mum? Pleasthe?"

"Yes, but stay where we can see you."

God's sakes? I hope they're not gonna say that all flippin' – Ohmigod, what's THAT?

"Dad, come quick! What'sth up with it'sth BUM?"

I think it's got a giant Babybel cheese stuck to it?

"Pipe down, princess… an' that's a fiver you owe me, Liz. I said all she'd be interested in's shit, piss, arses an' snot."

"She's not *just* interested in…"

"Why'sth it got a giant cheesthe stuck to itsth bum?"

"Stop shouting, sweetheart, and it hasn't got a…"

"Hahahahahahaha. Look at that one over there, Mum! It'sth throwin' POO!"

"You were sayin', Liz?"

"Okay, don't gloat…"

"LOOK AT THEM TWO, MUM…"

"It's *those* two, Maddie, and will you stop shouting!"

"I'm not shoutin', I'm – are they fightin'?"

"Ohmigod, Joe."

"WHAT ARE THEY DOIN'?"

"'Ey, princess, d'you fancy an ice cream?"

Uh? That's weird? I haven't even asked for one yet?

"Erm? Coursthe…"

"Come on, then. What flavour?"

"Erm? Chocolate? Dad, why're we walkin' so fast? I haven't finished watchin' the chinpamzeesth yet."

"Chimps are borin', princess, why don't you look at the zebras instead? Aren't they interestin'?"

Intresting? What's intresting about a stripy horse? All it does is eat grass and get eaten by—UH? Hang on a minute? Now, *that's* intresting?

"We can't buy her an ice cream everytime she asks an awkward question, Joe, or she's going to go home morbidly obese."

"I know, but, what d'you want me to do, love?"

This is proply weird? I've counted three times now and... I'll just count again...

"Just tell her the truth in an age-appropriate way."

Yup? It's definitely right?

"What d'ya mean, an age app—?"

"Dad, why'sth that zebra got five legsth?"

"Five? *Oh, shit!* Hahahaha. D'you wanna take this one, love? In an age-appropriate way?"

"Did you say you wanted chocolate, sweetheart?"

I said, 'why's that zebra got five legs?' But chocolate's fine.

It's all a bit weird, actually? I usually have to ask and ask and ask for a ice cream and even then I don't always get one, but this time I didn't ask, and – I can't believe my dad was more intrested in hundreds and thousands than a zebra what's got five legs? Specially, when one wasn't even proply touching the floor? Anyway, my ice cream was scrummy, and even though I ate it as fast as I could, it hardly gave me brain-freeze at all. The reason I ate it so fast's cos next we're going to see the llamas.

I'm specially eggcited at seeing the llamas, imfact, I've been looking forward to seeing them the most all day. My mum said they're at the end, down here somewhere? Past these weird pink birds what stand on one – Flamencoes – that's what they're called. And this massive field of grass what's got tigers in it, apparently? And all these boring ones what mostly look the same, 'cept with different kinds of horns. And, oh my goodness?

"Mum, what'sth THAT?"

"What's what, sweetheart? Oh, that? That's an ostrich."

"A nostrich?"

"Yes, they're amongst the biggest birds on the planet. In fact, are they the biggest, Joe?"

"What the bloody 'ell are you askin' me, for?"

"It'sth massthive isn't it, Mum? Can it fly?"

"I don't know, sweetheart. Can ostriches fly, Joe?"

"What am I now – an ostrich expert? How should I know?"

"There's no need to be like that! Sorry, sweetheart, I don't know, but I wouldn't think so."

I can't believe the size of its eyelashes. It looks like Rache when she's going out, and – UH?

"Mum, why'sth it'sth legsth on back to front?"

"Oh, yes, look at that, Joe. Its legs are on back to front. Why is that?"

"Do I look like David Attenborough? I 'aven't got a bloody clue!"

"Okay, I was only asking. There's no need to be so— Maddie, stop waving Trevor at it."

Why? It likes him?

"I don't know much about 'em, love, but I know they can be nasty buggers if they're provoked."

"And would waving a dinosaur in its face qualify? Maddie, please stop waving Trevor at the ostrich."

"Oy! Do as your mum said an' stop wavin' Godzilla at it."

"I'm not waving him – Trev'sth talkin'! He'sth asking the nosthtrich if it can – OHMIGOD!"

You STUPID dinosaur…

"Nooooo! TREV'STH JUMPED IN WITH THE NOSTRICHESTH!"

"Ohmigod, Joe – you'll have to climb in and get him!"

"What, ME? Get in THERE? With THAT? NO fuckin' chance!"

"GET HIM BACK, DAD! *PLEEEEEEEASTHE!*"

"Please don't cry, sweetheart. JOE?"

"Come off it, Liz – why can't we find one o' the keepers to get it?"

"BUT DAD… what if the nostrich eatsth Trev?"

"Yes, Joe, what if it eats him?"

"Fuck that! What if it eats ME? Have you seen the size o' the beak on it?"

"DAD! *PLEEEEEEASTHE!*"

"Don't cry, sweetheart, you'll make yourself sick."

"Oh, for f— okay, princess. The things I do for you!"

"Thank you, Joe. I'd go myself but I'm wearing a skirt."

"Like fuck, you would! You were shit-scared of a bloody peacock! Right, wish me luck – I'm goin' in!"

"Be careful!"

"Cheers for that, love. I was gonna punch it on the beak but – okay, nice birdy – stay there. I just wanna get the – WHOA! Did you see that? Cheeky bugger – get away! Here, Maddie – catch!"

"TREV! Thank *goodnessth* you're okay. Thanksth, Dad!"

"You're welcome, princess – WHOA! Go on, Big Bird, piss off back to Sesame Street."

Hmm? The nostrich seems to really like my dad? Imfact, it won't leave him alone…

"Dad, hurry up an' climb back over!"

"I'm tryin', princess, when I can get past this bloody thing. WHOA!"

"Dad, it'sth tryin' to…"

"I know exactly what it's – OW! YOU CHEEKY BASTARD!"

Oh, dear! I'd best keep tight hold of Trev from now on, cos if he falls in with any other animals it'll be me what goes in to get him. But, it can't have hurt that much? Anyway, we're nearly at my favourite animals now.

I can't wait to see the llamas. I've been dying to see a real one ever since I first saw *Doctor Dolittle*, which's one of my top ten favourite films of all time and…

"Well, we're here, sweetheart, although I don't quite understand your fascination with them?"

UH? What's that? That's not a proper llama?

"Where'sth it'sth other head?"

"What do you mean, it's other head? How many heads do you think llamas have?"

"Two?"

"*Two?* Why on earth would you – Oh, sweetheart! Hahaha. Are you thinking of the Pushmi-pullyu?"

"The, what?"

"The Pushmi-pullyu from *Doctor Dolittle*? Because, it's not real, sweetheart."

"WHAT?"

God's sakes – I can't believe I've waited all day to see that! Stupid Doctor Dolittle. I'm so disappointed cos it's absolutely rubbish – like a sheep gone wrong – and if my dad doesn't stop laughing at me, I'm gonna proply…

"'Ey, princess, d'you wanna see the Hippogryffs after this? Or, the Unicorns?"

"Not funny!"

"Poor thing, Joe. I can't believe she thought the 'Pushmi-pullyu' was real."

"An' I can't believe she's spent all day yammerin' on about friggin' llamas an' now she won't even look at the bloody things. Oy, princess, we've walked miles for this so look at it!"

No!

"Look, kiddo, it's quite cute when you get up close, an' at least it hasn't got a beak."

So? It hasn't got two heads either?

"Why couldn't you have dropped Godzilla in 'ere, 'ey? Hello, mate, what's your name? It's really friendly, Maddie, come an' stroke it."

NO!

"It's got a funny little face, 'asn't it, Liz? We should get one for at home, save me mowin' the lawn every five – Whatthefuck? Did you see that? It just spat in my bloody face!"

It did WHAT?

"Oh, Joe, hahahahahaha. Ohmigod, hahahahahaha. They do that, apparently."

Now, I doubly don't like Doctor Dolittle. Fancy making me miss that!

"Cheers for that, love – you coulda warned me! Have you got any tissues in your – stop laughin', it's not that bloody funny."

"Hahahahahaha… you're not looking at what I'm looking at, Joe."

Eeeeeuw? That's absolutely disgusting? Imfact it's probly a good job they don't have two heads, if that's how they behave?

"Remember that scene from *There's Something About Mary*? Where Cameron Diaz mistakes Ben Stiller's 'you know what' for hair gel? Well, you look like that!"

I wish my dad'd stop being grumpy and I hope this isn't the last time we go to the zoo, specially since he's said no to every single animal I've asked for. No, you can't have a meerkat, Maddison… no, you can't have a hippopotahorse, Maddison… and, 'Can you bloody 'ell have a crocodile – I don't care if it would fit 'dead easy under your bed'! It's probly a good job about the crocodile though cos it'd probly keep me awake all night, ticking. Anyway, I've decided not to believe everything I see on telly cos mostly it's just – MONKEYS!

I love monkeys. I've asked a million times if I can have one but they say no every time, and I absolutely would look after it…

"Thisth isth the one I wasth tellin' you about, Mum. *Pleasthe* can I have one?"

"Listen to this, Joe, it's so cute. What kind of monkeys are they, sweetheart?"

"Copperchinosth... duh!"

"Hahaha. She means capuchin."

"I know what she means, Liz, I'm not a total idiot."

"Aren't they cute, Dad? An' people do keep them in the housthe costh Rossth off Friendsth had one called– hahahahaha. What'sth that? A red thing'sth just popped out!"

"Jesus H Christ! Is there anywhere safe 'ere? If they're not flingin' shit at each other, they're shaggin' each other's brains out!"

"I know, but we can't just keep feeding her, Joe. Say something."

"Like what? An' look at the size of his boner. No wonder he's made up with himself."

"HAHAHAHA. HE WON'T STOP PLAYIN' WITH IT!"

"Yes, sweetheart..."

"What'sth them little blue thingsth, Mum?"

"It's *those* blue things, and, um..."

"Chicken nuggets, everyone?"

"Absolutely, Joe!"

"After you, my dear."

But, I'm not even hungry?

I might be imagining it, but it seems like every time I ask a animal question they force me to eat more food?

Honestly, I could hardly eat my chicken nuggets cos I was still full from when I asked why was the little buffalo giving the big one a piggyback? Hmm? It's probly best not to ask any more animal questions cos I don't think I can eat anything else? 'Cept, there's a question I really wanted to ask about the next animal we're going to see. I've watched a video on YouTube about them and if it's true, well… I s'pose I'll just have to find out for myself?

"Dad, pleasthe can I have a piggyback? My feet're killin'."

"Go on, Joe, give her a piggyback. She's only got little legs."

I've got normal size legs, thank you very much?

"And, Joe, look on the bright side – have you ever seen a randy penguin? So, once we get there you can sit down and relax."

I know quite a lot about penguins cos I've watched tons of programmes on telly about them, but the question I wanted to ask is – okay, one-time Robbie was in his bedroom and he was laughing so loud that I went in to see, and he was hysterical watching penguin fails on YouTube. He told me there's a island on the specific ocean… I think? Or was it the other one? Anyway, he said millions of penguins live there, and every day airoplanes fly over, and when the penguins watch them they tip-over backwards and can't get up. So, there's a person whose actual job it is to stand them all back up again. How brilliant's that? And, I really want to be a penguin stander-upper when I leave school, which is why I want to find out if it's true.

"Okay, p-p-p-p-princess. We're at the p-p-p-p-penguins. Time to dismount."

Uh? Why's he talking like that?

"Aren't they funny, Joe? The way they walk – it's comical."

"I know. What are they, love? Birds?"

"I don't think so. I think they're mammals."

"But they've got feathers, 'aven't they? Do mammals 'ave feathers?"

"No, so they must be birds. Fancy me not knowing that."

"An' there was me thinkin' you knew everythin'."

"I don't profess to know *everything*, Joe, but since we've decided that they are birds, do you think we ought to take a step back? We haven't had much luck today where they're concerned."

"Good point, love. Like you said, she's safe enough 'round the penguins... let's have a sit down."

"I'm sure she'll be fine on her own for a minute. And, she can't go anywhere without passing us. And, I *can* see her from here. And..."

"Liz, love, have a minute an' chill. 'Ere, swap seats. I'll keep my eye on her."

"Okay, Trev, the plan isth... I'm gonna throw my shoe as hard as I can, right over that onesth head, an' if it doesth tip-over over backwardsth, we can start making plansth to be penguin stander-uppersth when we leave school. An' the zoo man'll stand it back up again, no problem. Imfact, he probly doesth it all the time. So, are you ready, Trev? Yesth? Okay. Ready. Steady."

"It's lovely and peaceful here, isn't it, Joe?"

"It's lovely an' peaceful anywhere that's ten feet away from – WHATTHEFUCK?"

"WHAT? Is Maddie okay?"

"She is, but I'm not sure about the poor bloody penguin!"

Oh, dear. That didn't go at all like I planned.

"Do you think it's dead, Joe? WHAT POSSESSED YOU, MADDISON?"

"Nah, it's in shock, that's all. WHAT THE BLOODY 'ELL WERE YOU THINKIN', NUMBNUTS?"

"The keeper's been a while though. Who does this, Maddison? Who knocks a penguin out with their shoe?"

Me, apparently?

"I'm sure it'll be fine, love, once it stands up. For chrissake, Maddie, you're not safe let loose!"

"I'm sorry. I didn't mean to do it."

"What do you mean, you didn't mean to do it? You can't accidently throw your shoe at a penguin!"

You can, if it's further away than it looks...

"But, I'd NEVER hurt a penguin on purposthe."

I wouldn't! It was s'posed to fly over its head, not hit it in the face. I'm so upset...

"Here we go, Liz. Here come the waterworks."

"Stop crying, Maddison! It's the penguin that ought to be crying! Come on, we're going home."

"But, I've only got one shoe."

"Tough!"

***

Well, when I'd ventually stopped crying and my mum and dad'd finished yelling at me, I told them proply what happened... and even though they were still cross, my mum said she was relieved to know that I'm not a cycle-path? No idea? And my dad said that I'm forgived about the penguin, but the next time I go to the zoo I'll be old enough to drive myself. Humph. Least, I won't have to listen to him yelling all the way home though. Honestly, he's so flippin' grumpy. Just cos he has to sit on his bum where the nostrich pecked him and he's got a massive headache cos I've never stopped shouting, apparently...

"Who taught you to drive? Stevie bloody Wonder?"

"So, sweetheart, what did you think of the zoo?"

"Look at this pillock 'ere, Liz. GET OFF YOUR BLOODY PHONE!"

Hmm? Lots of things really? I thought peacocks are fast runners and flamencos are ridiclious. Llamas are disappointing and *eggstremely* rude. Some zebras have five legs but most zebras have four. Monkeys like throwing poo. Buffaloes like giving piggybacks. Nostriches have got fantastic eyelashes and 'Penguins aren't skittles, young lady!' – but they do fall over really easy. Oh, and...

"Isthn't elephant'sth poo *massthive*?"

"Told ya, Liz! Don't forget that fiver you owe me. Look at this idiot, 'ere! GET OUT THE MIDDLE LANE: PRICK!"

"Sweetheart, would you like to listen to music on Mummy's phone?"

"Yup!"

Anything's better than listening to this?

"There you go. Make sure you push the headphones in tight, Maddie. Can you hear me?"

"WHAT?"

Ooh? I love this song? Imfact, it's the first song I learned all the right words to…

"DOOBIE DOO… YOU CAN DIE… LA LA LA LA LA LA LA LA LA… Oo Oo Oo… STEAL THAT GIRL… WATCH HER SCREAM… KILLIN' THE – OY! MUM, TELL HIM! He'sth pulled the head'sth phone out my earsth without lookin'!"

"Joe, what did you do that for? She was enjoying herself then."

"AND? I'm try'na concentrate, 'ere! Seems like every knob'ead an' his dog's out drivin' today!"

Humph? I'm gonna count blue cars instead?

"One. Two. THREE-FOUR! Five. Six. SEVERN! HAHAHA. That'sth what the man saysth on *Strickly Come…*"

"Oy, mouth – button it, will ya? OH, FOR F— what's happenin' NOW?"

Are we stopping? Surely, we can't be home already?

"I think there's been an accident, Joe."

"You're kiddin'? Oh, for – that's all we bloody need! Stick the traffic news on, love."

"*… closed at junction 23 of the M6 due to an overturned*

lorry. Motorists are being advised to avoid the area where at all possible, as all vehicles are being diverted off the motorway, with long delays to be expected. And on the A580..."

"OH, FOR CRYIN' OUT BLOODY LOUD!"

Hmm? You might want to go now cos out of everything there is in the world, the thing what makes my dad the most crossest is being in the car when it's not actually moving...

"Brilliant! All we need now is for it to start pissin' down, an'..."

See what I mean? And that's before I tell him I need a wee...

"Didn't I tell you it'd be a bloody nightmare, Liz?"

See you soon everybody...

"Erm... Dad. Promisthe you won't be crossth, but..."

Goodbye!

New People

Wow it's hot! It's hotter than it was yesterday, and yesterday was so hot my dad actually changed colour. I'm not kidding, he went to work normal coloured and came home brown. AND he missed all the fun cos new people came to live next door.

It was funny cos when I got home from school and saw the back door was open I thought Mrs Collins'd come back from the Pearly Gates, so I went in to say hello and ask if she had any good biscuits, but it wasn't Mrs Collins it was new people, lying on the kitchen table, and they looked dead surprised when I walked in. Anyway, cos I've only just told my mum about that, she's gone to say hello and sorry both at the same time, but I wish she'd hurry up cos...

"Dad!"

"Not again, princess. You're in an' out like a fiddler's

elbow. What is it this time?"

"There'sth no clouds."

"And? What time's your next weather report?"

"*No...* my mum said I can have the paddlin' pool out when there'sth no cloudsth. An' there'sth no cloudsth!"

"That's kind of her seein' as it's muggins 'ere has to put the bloody thing up."

"Let'sth do it now, Dad. Me an' Trev'll help. We've already got it out the..."

"Er, before I do anythin', kiddo, I'll talk to the organ grinder, not the monkey."

"ARE WE GETTIN' A MONKEY?"

"Are we bloody 'ell gettin' a monkey. We've got you, 'aven't we?"

"Not funny. She'sth been in there *agesth*. How much longer will she be?"

"Dunno, kiddo. How long's a piece o' string?"

Uh? What a stupid thing to say? Depends how long it actually is?

"But, if you hadn't flounced in yesterday, uninvited an' unannounced..."

"Have you seen the new people, Dad?"

"Nah. I'm not interested as long as they're quiet."

"What? Like Mrsth Collinsth? She wasth quiet, wasthn't she?"

Specially the last time I saw her – right before she went to live in the Pearly Gates...

I loved Mrs Collins. She was really really old but she cooked the bestest biscuits and she mostly just cooked them for me. And I loved listening to her stories about the olden days. Stuff like, how she was fifteen before she saw a actual pineapple and how you only got one egg in the war. Anyway, one day I went in to see her and she was fast asleep on the chair, which was weird cos she normally jumped out her skin when I walked in yelling, 'Have you got any biscuits'? Anyway, after a bit I poked her with her walking stick but she didn't wake up. So, then I screamed BOO but she still didn't wake up. So, then I tried to open her eyes for her but she *still* didn't wake up... so, then I went to get my mum.

It was all very weird, actually? Cos I didn't know there was such a thing as a mergency pizza, but when my mum came back from Mrs Collins's she was crying and said we needed to go out for one now... and by the time we got back, Mrs Collins'd gone. I didn't even get a chance to say goodbye. And I do really miss her so I hope she likes living in the Pearly Gates, but they're in a Stralia and that's on the other side of the – ooh? My mum's back...

"Sorry I was gone so long. Sweetheart, why are you wearing your swimming costume?"

"There'sth no cloudsth."

"And your swimming goggles?"

"There'sth no cloudsth!"

"I can see that, but it'll take your dad at least an hour to fill the pool. Besides, we need to go to the supermarket..."

But, we only went yesterday?

"So, go and put your shorts on while I have a quick word with your dad. And close the door after you,

Maddie – little pigs have big ears!"

No, they don't? And I can hear just the same with it shut. Hmm? I wonder what's going on?

"Whatever it is, Liz, I'm not interested."

"Well, you'd better start being interested because I've invited them to the barbecue…"

"What bloody barbecue? It's news to me!"

Me too… fantastic.

"It's such a lovely day, I thought we could invite them over and get to know them."

"I don't wanna get to know 'em – an' is there anythin' else you've volunteered me for, besides sortin' out the paddlin' pool, goin' shoppin' an' doin' a friggin' barby?"

"Well, I might have mentioned something about you being an electrician and that you'd be happy to fix their bathroom light. Mike can't get it to work and it's definitely not the…"

"Who the fuck's Mike? An' he can shit in the dark for all I care, love. It's my day off!"

"Don't be such a killjoy – they're actually really nice. Mike works in computers and Wendy has a beauty salon in the…"

"I'm made up for 'em, Liz. Is it just them, or 'ave they got kids?"

"No, no kiddies yet."

"Good! Give 'em our Maddie for a day an' she'll put 'em off."

"I know. Wendy said they were just about to christen the kitchen table when she burst through the door and asked if they had any good biscuits, and Wendy was so surprised, she panicked and said, 'Don't you look like Daenerys from *Game of Thrones*?'."

"Ha! I bet that didn't go down well. Remember when she gave our Rob a black eye for sayin' that? Cracked him in the face with 'er lightsaber."

He didn't call me Dinnerees, he called me Tyrion, and I only did it cos he said it imfont of my friends. Me, Simon, Alliah and Michael Ryder were playing *Star Wars* in the back garden and he kept making a holy show of me. First, he called me a Ewok and hung me upside down by my feet, then he kept … anyway, it's not nice, making a holy show of someone imfront of their friends.

"It wasn't funny, Joe. She could have had his eye out!"

I don't know how easy my mum thinks it is for some-one's eyes to come out, but she says it about everything. Throwing my Frisbee; kicking my shoe off; playing with Robbie's darts…

"Anyway, she said Maddie just stared at her like one of those creepy kids from *The Village of the Damned,* so she panicked again and asked if Trevor was a dragon."

"Jeeze… I'm surprised the poor woman's still breathin'."

"I know. She said Maddie looked at her like she was completely insane; put both hands on her hips and said, 'Don't you know the difference between dragons and dinosaurs? Duh!' Then told her she was 'thick as two short plants', and stomped off! I was part cringing; part trying not to laugh. Where does she get these things? She's like a little old woman at times. Thankfully, they thought it was hilarious – they're still laughing about the 'two short plants' – but I felt bad so I told them to come over around five, and that's why we need to go…"

"We? Why can't you go on your own? I'll stay 'ere an' look after…"

"Because, you always complain that I get the wrong stuff."

"It's friggin' charcoal, love! How 'ard can it be?"

"I'm not sure they sell 'frigging' charcoal. Besides, I'm not lifting boxes of beer. So, if…"

"For Christ sake – when d'ya wanna go?"

***

Honestly, my dad spends all year conplaining 'bout the weather being rubbish and today when it's proply boiling, all he's done is moan. He's moaned about the steering wheel being too hot to touch, about his back being hot and sweaty and how the sun's getting in his eyes, but if he doesn't want the sun in his eyes, he shouldn't leave his sunglasses on the floor where people – *me* – can stand on them.

Anyway, we're here but, why do people like going shopping? It's umbelievably boring, and since I found out you're not allowed to help yourself to the pick 'n' mix, there's no point me even coming. I'm not allowed to push the trolley; swing off the trolley; put anything in it; take anything out of it; get in the way of it *or* walk away from it… and my mum takes hours to choose everything and my dad swears 'bout how much it costs. Honestly, we've been in the shop ages already and we're still in the first bit. Humph. I'm sitting down cos we could be here all day, and – ooh? What's that under the shelf?

"I couldn't give a flyin'…"

"Just, answer me, Joe! One five-litre bottle, or these smaller ones? Sweetheart, get up off the floor please."

AH? It's a fifty pence? I wonder if Trev can reach it with his tail?

"Just tell me what you think!"

"For chrissake, Liz, it's friggin' water! Why don't we just turn the tap on like when I was a kid? It never did me any 'arm."

"That's debatable. Right, we'll get these smaller ones; they're more manageable for… Maddie, get up off the floor, please."

Can't you see I'm busy? Come on, Trev, just a tiny bit further. Think of all the pick 'n' mix we can – OH?

"What about juice, Joe? We'll get apple for – Maddie! Get up off the floor."

I'm trying, but Trev's stuck.

"And we'll get a couple of cartons of – Maddison! Up! Now!"

Come ON, Trev. We're gonna get in trouble if you don't…

"I won't tell you again, Maddison."

Uh-oh? Quiet voice…

"Soz, Trev, but I'm gonna have to pull you extra-OW! *OW!* Ouch! Oopsth! Ohmigod! WATCH OUT, EVERYBODY!"

Well, that wasn't made very well?

"Nice one, princess. What d'you do for an encore?"

I'm not sure what a encore is, but I can't do anything stuck in this stupid trolley. And not the chair part either – the actual trolley – like I'm shopping! And you wouldn't believe how many bottles of Dandylions and Bird-dog landed on me, or how easy old ladies fall over. Honestly, you don't even have to touch them. And it's not my fault she's so deaf she didn't hear me cos I warned everyone to watch out.

"Cheer up, princess. You're lucky she didn't break anythin'."

"God! She only fell a bit! An' she'sth not made of actual glassth! I fell off the shed roof yesterday, spyin' on the new people, and I didn't…"

"You'll get locked up, talkin' to yourself."

Flippin' 'eck? I thought I was just thinking?

"Dad, *pleasthe* can I get out the trolley? It'sth really umcomfy."

"Don't ask me, kiddo, I'm keepin' outta this. Your mum said you 'ave to stay in there, so you'll 'ave to wait till she gets back."

"But, how long will she *be*?"

"Well, I imagine, when the paramedics've gone – so, your guess is as good as mine."

"Well my guessth isth… if she doesthn't hurry up and let me out of here soon I'm gonna phone Childline an' tell them I'm bein' kidnapped in a actual shopping trolley!"

"You're gonna phone, who?"

God's sakes, Maddison? Think quietly, idiot. Ooh? The dragon's coming…

"Not ONE WORD, Maddison. Right, Joe, we need toilet roll. I bought twelve rolls yesterday and I couldn't find any this morning. I don't know where it all went?"

Oops? Me and Trev do. Imfact, we were gonna ask if we could buy white ones this time cos pink mummies look ridiclious, but it's probly not a good time to ask at the moment.

"Do you prefer quilted or–?"

"I prefer you to hurry the fuck up. I'll be wipin' my arse on it, not decoratin' the front room. Just get whatever's cheapest."

"Quilted it is! What do you think of the aloe vera? Do you think it makes any—?"

"I think you're mistakin' me for someone who gives a shit – no pun intended! Just…"

"For God's sake, Joe, do I have to make ALL the decisions in this family?"

"You don't have to but you do. Like decidin' to have a barby – I don't recall bein' consulted on that – but, when it comes to bog roll I'm a bloody authority? Right! Shift your 'ead, princess…"

Ouch! Flippin' 'eck, Dad!

"Be careful, Joe! You could have had her eye…"

"There you go, Liz! Shite goes with white – *sorted*!"

"Yesth!"

"BE QUIET, MADDISON!"

Grumpy dragon. I don't know why we're bothering with a Barbie queue? I don't know why we don't just get my mum to breathe on the flippin' sausages! And how much stuff do we need? Is the whole street coming? I can't hardly move in here for all this…

"Waaaaaah! Meat'sth touchin' me!"

"Be quiet, Maddison, they're only sausages. Lift her out Joe… Joe? We're having a barbecue, not a stag party. How much beer do you need?"

"As much as it takes to get shit-faced. Why?"

"Why do you need to get—?"

"Because, Liz, I don't know these people. What if I don't like this Mike an' whatsername? I'm gonna be trapped in my own garden with you peckin' my 'ead every five minutes, sayin' 'Watch ya bloody language', while I'm cookin' for complete strangers an' pretendin' to be interested in what they've got to say! So, a little somethin' to take the edge off won't go miss. Okay?"

"Wow? Someone got out of bed the wrong side this morning? Okay, but we'll have to get something for Wendy – we can't just give her beer. Get a couple of bottles of Prosecco. Everyone likes…"

"Didn't you tell 'em to bring a bottle?"

"We barely know them, Joe. It would have felt rude."

"Rude? But it's okay for me to fork out… how much is it? SIXTEEN QUID? Fuck me! For sixteen quid, I at least expect a shag."

Message to Maddison: find out what's a shag?

"It's a joke, Liz!"

"Well, you're not funny. Come on, let's head for the – Maddison, put that back! You're not having Cherry Sourz!"

Meh!

★★★

I feel well sorry for my dad. The dragon's been so bossy since we got back that he's hardly had a chance to sit down. First, he mowed the grass. Then he put my paddling pool up. Then he spent ages scraping all the black off the barbecue from last year. Then he went to the shop for cold-sore. Then went back cos my mum doesn't like the one what's got cheese in it. Then he cleaned all the bird poo off the table and chairs – the ones in the garden, not the ones in the house – and now my mum's shouting at him that he's got – what's turrets sindrone? Well, whatever it is, he's got it, apparently – but shouldn't she let him have a lie down if he's not well? I'm gonna help…

"Dad, I've put most of my toysth away and my paddlin' pool'sth full now, so shall I wind the hosthepipe up?"

"It's okay, kiddo, I'll do it. I'll tell you what you can do, though. Go in the house an' get me a can out the fridge. An' make sure your mum's not lookin'."

"Okay, but…"

"Leave your toys, Maddie, I'll tidy them. You get me a can, yeh?"

"Yup!"

Brilliant. I'll get him two if he's gonna tidy up my toys for me. It's not like there's loads left to tidy. Just, my Frisbee; my space hopper; my football; my supersoaker waterblaster; hoola-hoop; lightsabre – I'd forgot I had that till my dad said about it before – rubber duckies; bucket and spade and my *Jurassic Park* snowglobe, but

I've got no idea what that's doing out here? Hmm? No sign of the dragon so far…

"Muuum?"

She's probly practising blowing fire or learning how to fly? Or – flippin' 'eck, these cans are cold? And, how come my hands are all wet? Honestly, they're absolutely soaking. Imfact, I've just had a brilliant idea… and with all the money my dad'll save from it, he might even buy me a Xbox…

"Hey, Dad, guessth what? You know 'stead of buyin' water from the shopsth, why don't we just lick the outside of the cansth instead? Costh…"

"Were you just shouting me, sweetheart?"

"Erm? Nope? I've not even been in the housthe for anythin', have I, Dad?"

"Really, sweetheart? I could have – *never mind*. Robbie and Eggo are coming to the barbecue later, Joe. I was just upstairs with them and they were showing me Eggo's new binoculars. Apparently, they've taken up bird watching."

"Bird watchin'? Bloody weirdos."

"It'll be nice, won't it? Robbie hasn't made an appearance at a family occasion in ages."

Not them two? I think I'll leave my lightsaber out, just in case?

"Anyway, Joe, I'm off to pick up my mum, so I'll call in at the supermarket on the way back for more bread rolls. So, could get the barbecue started? And find the iPod player? And…"

"Give us a minute, love. I've been run off my bloody feet all day!"

"Oh, and it goes without saying – keep an eye on Maddie. I don't want to come back to find her dressed like a zombie or stuck halfway up a tree."

★★★

Well, I'm not dressed like a zombie or stuck up a tree but, oh my goodness... I don't know what to do? My mum's not back and my dad's gone missing and the Barbie queue's proply on fire. My dad put some sausages on just for me then went to get his eggstension cable out of the van, but he's been gone ages now and I can't find Robbie anywhere. So, it's just me and Trev and – Ohmigod? There's actual fire going on the sausages? And what if the garden goes on fire again? I got in loads of trouble last time that... Ohmigoodness! That was a 'normous piece of fire! And it's proply close to the shed, too. I'd better put it out before something bad happens?

Hmm? Well, the fire's out but...

"OHMIGOD! Sweetheart, are you okay?"

"I don't know?"

"I saw the smoke from the bottom of the – where's your dad?"

"He'sth disthappeared. He went to get somethin' out his van an'..."

"Holy shit, Shortshanks! Hahahaha. Look at the state of ya! The whole street's out, lookin' for the fire."

"Robbie, do you know where your dad is?"

"Yeh, he's on his way now. He was in next door's

fixin' the bathroom light. I was in there myself, helpin' Wendy shift some boxes, when I saw all the smoke an'…"

"What the bloody 'ell's goin' on?"

"HOW COULD YOU, JOE? LEAVE OUR SEVEN-YEAR-OLD DAUGHTER ON HER OWN WITH A LIT BARBECUE? Come on, sweetheart, put your waterblaster down and let's get all that nasty soot off you. And as for you, Joe…"

"Oy, Shortshanks. Smile!"

We've had to tell the new people to come a hour later, to make sure my mum and dad have got enough time to have a proper argue. Mind you, my dad's hardly said anything so far, 'cept to tell my mum to stop shouting or she's gonna blow the second Barbie out. He said it was just the fat off the sausages what was on fire – which is normal, apparently – so now thanks to me and my waterblaster, 'everything's p.i.s.s. wet through and he has to start again'. And Nanna's not coming cos she's got a headache – she forgot her keys again so had to climb in through the kitchen window, and cos she was all hot and sweaty, she slipped and banged her head on the tap.

I don't think I've ever seen my mum this cross? Not even when I actually did set the garden on fire. But, I'm sure she won't really divorce my dad for leaving me on my own with the Barbie queue. Least, I hope not? Cos, I don't want to see him just at the weekends like…

"Coo-ey! Anyone home?"

Ooh, they're – ohmigoodness! Why's she so OR-ANGE? And, where's the rest of her dress?

*** ★★★

I can't believe this. Robbie never comes out his bedroom when we have visitors, but today he won't go away. And he's really bugging me, too. When he's not talking to Orange Wendy, which he is most of the time, he's whispering to Eggo about... I wish they'd talk louder? Spit roast? What does...

"Do one, Shorshanks – stop hoverin' round like a bad smell."

"No! It'sth my garden, too."

What does spit roast mean? Well, whatever it is, they want to do one with Orange Wendy, and Eggo said he wouldn't mind trying her back door? But, I did that yesterday and it's just a normal back door so I don't know why he's getting so eggcited?

"Princess, your sausages're ready."

"Thanksth, Dad. D'you like sausagesth, Orange Wendy?"

"I do but – *sorry*, did you just say orange?"

"I bet Wendy loves a big, fat juicy sausage, don't ya, love? Hahaha..."

"Joe! Hahaha. Yes, Maddison, I *do* like sausages."

"An' d'you like chicken nuggetsth, too? They're my favourite."

"Not nuggets, but I do like chicken. What about you, Joe?"

"Oh, aye, I'm a breast man, myself. You can't beat a crackin'..."

"Joe! Hahahaha. You're so..."

What's wrong with them both? Why do they keep laughing about meat?

"Maddison, I was just saying about your dad's tan and how brown he is, and he was telling me that his mum's half Italian."

"*Is she, Dad?* Which half? The top half or the bottom?"

"Hahahaha! That's a classic, that, kiddo. Anyway, you've got a crackin' tan yourself, Wendy. Have you got any Italian in you?"

"No, it's fake tan and…"

"Would you like some? I'm kiddin', love. It's that old joke, isn't it? I couldn't resist."

"… *Oh!* Hahahaha. No – and, *no!* You are cheeky, Joe. Hahahaha."

What's she laughing at now? She really is thick as two short plants. For a start off, why would anyone want to be so orange? And what's so funny about meat? I'll ask Mike…

Mike's well nice. He's already pulled my finger and give me loads of airoplane twizzies, and he knows nearly as much about dinosaurs as Doctor Alan Grant! And, he said I was a very brave girl for putting the fire out, and if I *don't* manage to be good for the whole of the rest of the year – like I have been so far – then he might be able to fix Robbie's old Xbox for me *and* where I spilled sticky on my mum's labtop! And in all that time, he didn't swear once. I think he's my new favourite person, actually…

"Sweetheart, stop saying that! Sorry, Mike."

"But if she'sth not thick as two short plantsth then

203

why doesth she keep laughin' at—?"

"Maddie, would you please go and ask your dad if the rack-of-ribs is ready yet? Oh? That doesn't sound right, does it, Mike? Ribs is ready? You'd say 'ribs are'. But, as it's the rack that's the…"

Never mind that rubbish – so that's what a rack is? A type of food? I didn't know what Robbie and Eggo meant before when they were saying about Orange Wendy's massive…

"And, sweetheart, whilst you're out there, would you ask Robbie and Eggo if they want some?"

"They do, Mum, I heard them say before. They wasth talkin' 'bout Orange Wendy'sth massthive rack an' how they'd love to have a taste of – no, not a taste – a go on it…"

Why's my mum looking at me, all funny?

"… an' somethin' 'bout spit roastht? Ooh, an' Eggo wantsth to go in Orange Wendy'sth back door!"

★★★

Messages to Maddison. Number one; stop calling her 'Orange Wendy' out loud. Number two; next time your mum's looking at you like that it means stop talking. And number three; don't mention spit roast or rackofribs again. Honestly, I don't even know what I said but Robbie's gonna effing kill me when he gets hold of me, and I wish I'd known we were gonna play chasing cos I wouldn't have ate so many sausages. Anyway, least my dad's still talking to me, I think…

"Dad, are you still my friend?"

"Hang on a sec, princess. Can I top your glass up, Wendy? The fizzy shit's gone, but we've got Malibu an'…"

"Goodness, have I drunk both bottles? No wonder I feel tiddly."

"No worries. I got them for you so…"

"He did, Wendy. An' he said, for sixteen quid…"

"All right, Polly Parrott! Put a sock in it!"

"… he *least* eggspectsth a sha— Ow! Whatdidyoudothatfor?"

"Cos, you never know when to shut up!"

Yes, I do, and I was only gonna say about the shag. I asked my mum what one was before, and after she'd finished choking on her penal colada, she said it's a bird what lives on the sea. It's is a bit weird, eggspecting one of them when you buy someone a drink? Whatever, I don't like this stupid Barbie queue anymore. I'm bored of not knowing what everyone's talking about and no one's telling me anything…

"Come on, Trev, let'sth go an' watch *Kung Fu Panda*, an' we can…"

"'Ey, Shortshanks!"

Ugh? What does he want? I'm too full to do running again?

"Check this out, Eggo – she'll go bat-shit crazy – watch!"

No, I won't? I'm too full to go any type of…

"D'YA WANNA BUILD A SNOWMAN?"

Right – that's it! Where's my lightsaber?

"See, Eggo… I might not be able to catch the little

shit, but I said she'd go off 'er 'ead."

"You're so in for it, Robbie!"

"'EY! Be'ave, will ya? Pack it in, knob'ead. Dad, tell her to stop swingin' that…"

"Put the lightsaber down, princess, before you do someone an injury."

But, that's what I'm trying to do?

"I'm gonna kill you, Robbie Blobby!"

"Or, you could just LET IT GO?"

"ARGH! I'M GONNA ABSTHOLUTELY…"

"Sweetheart – Ohmigod, grab her, Joe – she's gone feral!"

"*Noooooooo*… GET *OFF* ME! PUT ME DOWN!"

"OY! Stop kickin' your legs about an' calm the – JESUS H CHRIST! You okay, Wendy, love?"

Erm, who said Wendy could go in my paddling pool without asking? And what's happened to her dress?

"Bloody 'ell, Wendy! You don't get many o' THEM in a pound!"

"Shut up, Joe, and help her out of – what the HELL do you think you're doing, Robbie? DELETE THAT PHOTO! NOW!"

Well, this isn't good. Eggo's gone home, and the new people have gone home, and my mum's actually gone with them! She's gone to get Orange Wendy's dress so she can sew it back together, but mostly she's gone to get away from us. She said my dad and Robbie are drunkard pervs whatever that means, but what have I done? Orange Wendy said it was mostly her fault for being tiddly, and it was only when Spud jumped in my paddling pool after her and shaked himself so hard that one of her eyelashes fell off that she was even slightly bothered... and I did say sorry for kicking her in the back.

Anyway, it's s'posed to be even more boiling tomorrow so I think I'm gonna check my paddling pool. I hope Orange Wendy didn't put too much grass in it cos I hate it when that happens, *and* when insex land in it cos— uh?

"Robbie, what you doin'? Get your head out of my..."

"*ShutyourfaceShortshanks...*"

He'd better not be drinking it? It took flippin' ages to fill. Actually...

"Are you gonna do a sick, Robbie? You are, aren't you? You'd better not do it in my paddlin' pool costh..."

BLEUGH!

★★★

God's sakes! Is it allowed for mums to go on strike? Cos, mine just has! Just cos my dad was asleep on the couch when she got back from Mike and Orange Wendy's, and Robbie was lying with his head in sick in the back garden... oh, yeah, and Spud'd knocked the bin over in the kitchen and was eating all the chicken bones – but, what've I done? I was gonna ask, and if it counts about my Xbox, but I'm not a complete idiot... I'll just ask in the morning when I ask her to get the sick out my paddling pool.

Oh, well, I'd best go to sleep I s'pose, cos I don't want to make her any more grumpy before tomorrow, but if she is still grumpy and on strike I'm just gonna go and live with Rache in the morning...

"Night, Trev!"

"Night, Maddison... *Roooooaaaarr!*"

Goodnight!

The Postlethwaites

Yes! Only three more days then it's the summer holidays. Nearly seven whole weeks of just playing out. And today doesn't count as a school day cos it's sports day. I love sports day... it's like playing out but with your mum and dad watching how good you are, unless you're Alan Evans's mum and dad, that is.

Alan's the youngest in our class and even though he's proply funny, not a lot of people like him. The trouble is, when he gets eggcited, *well*... I'm glad we're not having a obstacle race this year, cos last year Alan went first and weed all the way through the stretchy tunnel and the whole of year one crawled through it! Then he was disqualified from the egg-and-spoon race for eating his egg and he went home crying after that so I didn't get to do the sack race with him, thank goodness. Well, nobody wants puddles in their pumps.

Another good thing about sports day is that we don't have to be at the school field till ten o'clock. But, I'm sure it must be that time now?

"Come on, Trev. Let'sth go and see if they're ready. We don't want to missth the – Ooh?"

"I mean it, Joe, you'll be for the high jump!"

The high jump? Dads don't do the high jump? Even we don't do it till big school?

"I can't believe you're still goin' on about this – it was months ago, Liz! An' how many times have I been to the pub after work? Once? An' we only went to wet the baby's head – it was Larry's first grandkiddie."

"You didn't wet it, Joe, you positively drowned it. Anyway, the bottom line is, you turned up at Maddie's parents' evening half-cut and proceeded to made a holy show of me, so…"

"I wouldn't go that far…"

"You kept calling her teacher, Mrs Jelly!"

I bet Mrs Jolley didn't like that. I have to write lines when I call her that…

"And you would not shut up about the size of the chairs. Your exact words were, 'Jesus H Christ! I feel like Snow-effing-White, sat here'."

I don't think they were his 'xact words cos my dad never says effing?

"I was three-parts pissed, love, an' they were friggin' tiny!"

"Yes, I know; I was sitting on one too, remember. But unlike you, I didn't spend the whole time squirming about complaining that I couldn't get comfortable, then break wind so loudly that it reverberated all around the hall. Everyone was looking, Joe. I was mortified."

"Why? You never did it?"

"*I didn't do it.*"

"I know? That's what I just said? An' it was only a fart, love – we all do 'em."

"Yes, but we don't all choose to do them so publicly."

"I didn't *choose* to do it. It was an accident – I swear."

"I know you do – constantly. You use profanity as a means of punctuation. So, I mean it, Joe, you'd better make a good impression today or you're a dead man."

"All right, keep ya wig on. I told ya – best be'aviour."

"I hope so, because I still haven't forgiven you for the barbecue yet."

"It's been three weeks! How many more times do I 'ave to say I'm sorry?"

"I'll let you know."

Least she's not on strike any more…

"Phoar! You're so sexy when you've got a bag on, Liz. D'you wanna smack my arse an' tell me I've been a very naughty boy?"

WHAT?

"Stop it, Joe. Maddie'll be down any minute."

She already is but she might go back upstairs again cos… that's just weird?

"Come on, Lizzie, it's not my fault you give me the 'orn. It's been three weeks, for fucksake. My balls are burstin' at the seams. Specially lookin' at you in those…"

"Get off, Joe! Is that all you ever think about? Sex?"

"Do bears shit in the woods?"

Polar bears don't?

"You need a cold shower! MADDIE, IT'S TIME TO GO. What are you doing, Joe? You look like Spud, begging for a bone."

"I'm not beggin' for a bone, love, I'm try'na get rid of one."

"Haha. Behave, and put your tongue back in. Okay, *if…* and I mean *if* you behave yourself…"

"Be'ave myself? Haha. You sound like you're talkin' to the kids."

"It feels as though I am, most of the time. You do look hot in those shorts, though. Maybe I'll make the most of you before you go to seed?"

"Cheeky mare! Hahahaha. So, I'm on a promise?"

"I suppose… but I say that with the same confidence that I was able to promise Maddie an Xbox for Christmas… and you only have to last one day!"

★★★

I'm not sure what that was all about? Or, why my dad was winking at my mum all the way to the school playing field – which I don't think's specially good when you're driving – but, least they're in a good mood now. They've been proper grumpy since the Barbie queue but I think it's to do with my dad sleeping in Rache's bed, cos I heard him tell Stefanos Popple Octopus that it's been so long he's started walking funny… *but he seems to be walking okay to me?* I hope so, cos he's running in the dads' race after, and he'd better not make a holy show of me.

"Mums and dads, boys and girls, it's time for the year two running race. Mrs Jolley's class, please line up."

Ooh? That's me. I'm usually the fastest runner in our class so I hope I win when my mum and dad are watching. And I really want to beat Lucy Postlethwaite cos I can't stand her. Nobody can cos she's proper stuck-up and she's mean to everyone. She's already told me that my pumps are rubbish, my shorts are stupid and only babies wear T-shirts with Miss Piggy on them. And Miss Piggy's my favourite – cheeky cow! So, I told her that if my mum and dad weren't watching, I'd kung-fu kick her into the next field, but she must want me to cos...

"You're *never* going to win, Medicine."

"Stop callin' me that, Lucthy, or I'll..."

"Or you'll *what?* Medicine!"

"Okay, children. ON YOUR MARKS. GET SET..."

"Or I'll – *never mind...*"

"GO!"

"Maddie! Over here, sweetheart!"

"Ooh! Ooh! Did you see me, Mum? Look! I've got a cerstificate."

"I think you mean a *certificate*, and yes, sweetheart. Well done."

"Did Trev see me?"

"He did. He was cheering all the..."

"Did YOU see me, Dad?"

"Nice to know I come after Godzilla, but course I did, princess, you were fantastic. First place, 'ey? Give us an 'ug. You were nearly as fast as your mum leggin' it from the peacock."

"Very funny, Joe. Well, let's hope you can run as fast because it's the dads' race soon."

"Yeh, Dad, an' you'd best not be imbarrassthin'."

"Me, embarrassin'? Pot! Kettle! Black!"

Uh?

"So, what's your next race, princess?"

"Erm? Egg and sthpoon? An' I've told Alan that if he doesthn't eat his egg this time, I'll be his partner in the sack race. But he hasth to do a wee first!"

I'm not fussed about winning the egg-and-spoon race cos I don't really get the point? I mean, I might have to run away from a lion one day so I get why we do running. And I might be in my sleeping bag at the time so I get why we do the sack race. And if I ever get kidnapped and tied to a other person then I get the three-legged race. But when will I ever need to run fast with a egg on a spoon? It's ridiclious. Even if I was rescuing a tiny Humpty Dumpty from all the King's horses I wouldn't bother with a spoon? I'd just carry him...

"Mums and dads, boys and girls, it's time for the year two egg-and-spoon race. Mrs Jolley's class, please line up."

Ooh? This is it, now...

"Alan, try not to eat your – did you just nudge me, Lucthy?"

"No, dumbo! And you're definitely not going to win this one, Medicine."

"Shut your cakehole – *ALAN!* Leave the shell alone!"

"Let him eat it if he wants, MEDICINE. He'll only wee himself when he starts running so he may as well get disqualified now."

"Leave him alone, you stupid cow! An' stop callin' me Medicine or it'll be you what getsth disthqualified for eatin' your egg, an' I won't take the shell off!"

"Oh, really? You and whose army?"

"I don't need a – stop pushin' my arm, you stupid idiot! You're gonna make me drop my egg."

"That's the idea, MEDICINE!"

"Okay, children. ON YOUR MARKS."

"Lucthy, stop it! If you push my arm one more time…"

"Stop that, Lucy! GET SET…"

"What are you going to do, MEDICINE? Make me?"

"I'm gonna— ah! You stupid cow. Pick it up or I'll— AH!"

Ohmigod? She's stamped on my actual egg? Right?

"GO! Maddison, stop that! MADDISON!"

"ATTENTION! Would the parents of Lucy Postlethwaite and Maddison McLaren please come to the teachers' station immediately?"

★★★

Stupid Lucy! Why couldn't she have just behaved? Turns out we've both been disqualified, but least my nose isn't bleeding… and it's not like I didn't warn her. And Mrs Jolley heard her calling me Medicine *and* she saw her knock my egg on the floor and stamp on it but 'One need never resort to violence, young lady!' Meh! I never listen to her anyway. D'you know when I first started school and everyone called me Medicine, d'you know what she told me to say? She told me to say, 'sticks and stones may break my bones, but names will never hurt me'. Can you believe that? There's SIX letter Ss in it! They'd have wet themselves laughing before I'd even got to the end. So, I learned how to punch proply and now hardly anybody says it.

"Sweetheart, what have I told you about fighting? I know Lucy started it, but you didn't need to join in. Anyway…"

"'Ey, Liz!"

"Where've you been, Joe? I just had to go to the…"

"You'll never guess what. D'you remember on New Year's Eve when I said I nearly sparked some bloke out over a bag of ice? Yeh, well, the same bloke just had a go at me. Said our Maddie rammed an 'ard boiled egg down his daughter's throat? You should 'ave 'eard him love – 'With the shell orn!' – pompous get! Apparently, she bust the kid's nose too?"

"Yes, I had to go to the teachers' station. Where were you?"

"Talkin' to Ben Eckersley 'bout football."

"What did you say to Frank?"

"Frank? Oh, the nonce? Just that his kid probably deserved it then walked off all dignified."

"I'm not sure she deserved *that*, but by all accounts, she did goad Maddie into doing it."

"Isn't he that bloke off the council, love? The one who thinks he's the dog's bolloc—knees?"

Isn't that the sauce what you eat with basgetty?

"Hahaha. Yes, he does rather think he's the 'bee's knees'…"

Really? Bees have knees?

"…and see, you *can* communicate without swearing. I'm very proud of you."

"Mums and dads, boys and girls, it's time for the dads' race. Will all the dads line up please, and let's make it a clean fight. Hahahaha!"

"Oh, for fuck's sake, Liz – do I *'ave* to?"

"Well, *that* didn't last long. And, yes, you do!"

"Shit! Hold my phone, will ya? I'd better get a blow job for this!"

A blow job? Is that what it's called when you blow on someone to cool them down?

"Okay, dads. ON YOUR MARKS… GET SET… GO!"

***

Wow! Out of the twenty-two dads what started, one fell over just cos the teacher said GO. Three fell over before they'd probly got going. Two were so slow they're probly still running now, and the rest were normal – 'cept for my dad who proper legged it and he won! He actually won! And he definitely does need a blow job now, cos he's lying on the grass, and his face is bright purple, and he's so out of puff he can't breathe…

"Are you okay, Joe? Do you need another minute? Sweetheart, I'm sure he'll recover a lot more quickly if you get off him."

"Yeh, princess! An' stop blowin' in my bloody face, will ya? I'm try'na get my breath back 'ere!"

"But I'm doin' the blow job, Dad. Isth it helpin' you to cool down?"

Uh? What's so funny?

"Mum, I don't think the blow job'sth workin'. I think he probly needsth a ice-cream, instead. An' can I have one asth well? What're you laughin' at?"

"Hahahahaha… I don't know, sweetheart… hahaha-ha… you did make Lucy's nose bleed… hahaha… and you know I don't reward bad behaviour."

What's she laughing at?

"Hahahaha… come on, Liz, I know she bust the kid's nose but Mrs Jelly-Jolley, sorry, said the other kid started it, an' I've always taught her to stick up for herself."

He has.

"I told her, never start a fight but if you 'ave to get involved, make sure you finish it."

He did.

"Involved? She's only seven, Joe. I don't think you should be talking to her like that."

"Why not? Kids are little bastards, scuse my French."

"True. To be honest, I wish I'd had half her feistiness when I was her age, but I wouldn't say boo to a goose.

And where did she learn to punch like that?"

"Our Rob taught 'er."

"*Really?*"

"Yeh. He said he could hear her cryin' in her bedroom one day, so he went in to see what was up…"

I wasn't 'xacly crying!

"… an' she was upset cos this lad in her class kept pickin' on her… Carl somebody or other…"

"Carl Pilling? Yes, that's him, over there."

"Who, him? *Biffa Bacon?* Bloody 'ell, is he only seven? What they feedin' him on – steroids?"

"So, go on, Joe. You were saying?"

"Oh, yeh. Anyway, Rob taught her how to punch – I didn't tell you cos I thought you'd lose your shit – an' he reckons she's the next Nicola Adams."

"Nicola, who?"

"Nicola Adams – the Olympic boxin' champion? *No?* Anyway, he said she's got a crackin' right hook, an' she hasn't come home cryin' since, has she?"

"Actually, I hadn't realised until you pointed it out, but yes, I remember getting a phone call from school. Carl had tied her plait to the back of her chair and when she stood up it snapped her head back, and… *yes*… she knocked one of his front teeth out. I remember now. I was thinking that they come out easily at that age, but I told her off for fighting. But, sometimes I'm not sure whether to chastise her or give her a round of applause."

"Well, why don't we get her an ice cream instead? You don't want her to get angry, love. You won't like her when she's angry."

"Is that from the *Incredible Hulk*?"

"Aye, but she'll be the Incredible Sulk."

"So, she's a little tough nut, huh? Maybe we ought to let her take martial arts classes. She's always asking."

"We'd have our own mini ninja. She'd be like Cato, always poppin' out o'…"

"Who's Cato?"

"You don't know who Cato is?"

"Is she a boxer too?"

"Jeeze, Liz, what planet d'you live on? Come on, princess, let's go an' get you an ice cream."

The queue for the ice-cream man's massive but my dad didn't conplain one bit, just winked at my mum and said how he couldn't wait for later… but, least he's nearly at the front now. Hmm? I wonder if he knows that the massive fat lady what's standing behind him's Lucy's mum? She's absolutely…

"Sweetheart, every time I look at you today you're the wrong way up. I've spent more time talking to your feet than to your face. You'll end up with a headache."

"I won't, Mum – watch! I can nearly walk on my handsth."

"Yes, Maddie, but why can't you sit and make daisy chains like the rest of the girls?"

"Daisthy chainsth are borin'. Besidesth, you can't join the circusth doin' daisthy chainsth."

"I thought you wanted to be a penguin stander-upper? Hahaha. Or a palaeontologist? Anyway, I need the toilet, sweetheart, so you can either come with me or give your dad a hand with the – *bye then!*"

Who's pale Ian Tologist? And I've told my mum I want to look for dinosaurs when I leave school but she never flippin' listens.

"Three 99s, mate."

"Dad, can I have extra rasthpberry on mine, pleasthe? Ooh, look, Trev. A bee. Shall we check if it'sth got kneesth?"

"D'you want sherbet, princess?"

"Yesth pleasthe. Tonsth! Are you sure that'sth a bee, Trev? I'm not so sure?"

"Maddie, put the change in my pocket while I get 'old of these properly, will ya?"

"One sec… I don't think it is a bee, Trev? I think it'sth a WASTHP! AGH, DAD!"

"Stop flappin' about an' calm down."

"But, it'sth chasin me!"

"Keep still an' it'll leave you alone."

"It won't! It'll bite me– AGH! It'sth buzzthin' in my ear!"

"Thanks, mate, pass 'em ere…"

"Daaaaaaaad! It'sth after me! Heeeeeelp!"

"I'm comin', princess. Bloody kids, 'ey? Cheers, mate. Have a nice – SHIT! Er – sorry, love."

Ohmigod! Deirdre Postlethwaite's got three 99s – one with extra raspberry and sherbet – all down the front of her top. My dad turned round with the ice creams and banged right into her, which isn't eggsacly hard cos she's nearly as wide as the ice-cream van…

"Er… sorry about that, love. I didn't see you there."

"ARE YOU TRYING TO BE FUNNY?"

"'EY? What d'you mean?"

"Go away, you stupid wasthp! Dad! Heeeeeeeelp!"

"I think you know very well what I mean – Mr McLaren, isn't it?"

"Hang on, princess… It is, yeh! An' I can promise you, love, I haven't got a bloody clue…"

Flippin' 'eck? The wasp's landed on Deirdre's top! God, she's massive?

"Dad, the wasp'sth on Deirdre. I think it likesth sherbet."

"OH! OH! GET IT ORF! THERE'S A WASP ORN ME!"

"Friggin' 'ell, woman, it's only a bloody wasp! Stop fannyin' about an' I'll knock it off."

Uh-uh? Here comes Lucy's Dad. Honestly, he's so tall and thin, he looks like the actual Stick Man.

"There – it's gone. You can stop…"

"McLAREN! Remove your hands from my wife's breasts, immediately!"

"Er, calm down, Sergeant Major. I was shiftin' a wasp off her, that's all. No need to get all shirty!"

"I'll get 'shirty' with whomsoever I wish. And that's not what it looked like from where I'm standing."

"Well, stand somewhere else then! Come on, princess, let's get back to your mum."

"But, Dad, what about my—?"

"Excuse me! Don't you dare walk away whilst I'm still talking!"

"Hahaha. YOU WHAT? Who d'ya think you're talkin' to?"

"Frank, leave it! I'd prefer you to help me with my bra. It's a Marks' and there's raspberry…"

"Sort your own bra, Deirdre. I think this Neanderthal needs to be taught a lesson."

"Oh, I'm a Neanderthal, am I? Big words comin' from a small-minded prick. Listen, Frank, I'm gonna do you a favour an' walk away cos I don't want your kid to see you flat on your…"

"Oh, no, you're not! NOBODY gropes my wife and gets away with it."

"Gropes your wife? I'm not bein' funny mate, but who the fuck'd wanna grope that? Sorry, love, I didn't mean it like that, but have you seen my Liz? Why the 'ell would I be try'na—?"

"How dare you refer to my wife as 'that'. It's little wonder your daughter's such a thug."

"Oy, knob'head! Say what you want about me but leave my princess out of it! Come on, kiddo, let's leave this idiot to – er, what d'you think ya doin'?"

WHAT? Did he really just push my dad?

"Seriously, Frank, I'm tryin' my best not to put you in a coma 'ere but I'm fast runnin' outta – what the fuck's THAT? Hahaha. Been watchin' the Karate Kid, 'ave we?"

Ohmigod. Stick Man's doing kung fu.

"Yes, McLaren, consider yourself warned. I have a blue belt in judo."

"A blue belt, 'ey? Well, now I'm shittin' myself! Go on, ya big girl. You're makin' a…"

"*Nobody* calls Frank Postlethwaite a big girl and gets away with it. Watch this, Deirdre, this is called, 'The Crane'... Oooooooo*aaaaaaa*..."

This is actually funny. There's quite a lot of people watching now and they're mostly telling my dad to spark him out, whatever that means? But my dad definitely doesn't want to hit him or he'd have done it already. I don't know why Stick Man won't behave? He just keeps doing kung-fu shapes and making weird noises.

"JOE? WHAT's GOING ON? You were supposed to be getting ice cream, not..."

"He did, Mum, but he banged into Deirdre by accident, an' it went all over her top."

"Come on, McLaren... Oooooooo*aaaaaaa*... Chicken, are we? Bwak bwak bwak."

Ohmigod! He's mental!

"Frank, stop pissin' about, will ya? Won't they be missin' you at the home?"

"Are you insinuating that I belong in a mental institution? Ooooooo*aaaaaa*..."

"Er, I think you're doin' a pretty good job of demonstratin' that yourself. Are you ready, love? We'll..."

"And I can see why you'd want to grope my wife's breasts... Ooooaaaaaaaaa... At least she has some! Watch this, Deirdre. This is 'O Soto Gari'. Prepare to be taken down, Mc..."

"Can I, love? Please?"

Yes! McLarens 2 – Postlethwaites 0, and they're the weirdest family ever.

My dad didn't even hit Frank at first, cos while he was standing there like a pink flamenco, balancing on one leg and making his weird kung-fu noises, my dad just knocked his leg from underneath him and it was the best faceplant ever! But, then Frank got up and swinged at my dad and that's when he hit him... but it wasn't proply hard, just enough to make Frank give up and go.

So, that was it really. Two out of three Postlethwaites went home with loo roll shoved up their noses, and the third was crying 'bout how the raspberry sauce'd ruined her good bra. I wonder if my mum feels left out cos she didn't bust Deirdre's nose? Anyway, it seems like my dad's a proper hero cos all the other dads kept coming up saying that they hadn't laughed that much in years, and that it was about time someone put him in his place.

Anyway, I've won a trophy for being the fastest runner in the... hang on a sec...

"ALAN! Come here! Well done, not eatin' your egg or doin' a wee in the sack race. You can lend my trophy till after the summer holidaysth if you want."

"Really, Maddie?"

"Yup! An' don't forget it'sth wear-your-own-clothesth day tomorrow."

"Oh, yes. I'd forgot. Thanks, Maddie. Sorry, my mum's shouting me. See you tomorrow. Bye, Trev!"

"Come on, sweetheart, time to go. Where's your trophy?"

"I've let Alan lend it for not weeing histh pantsth but he'sth gonna give it back after the summer holidaysth."

"Awww! That's very sweet of you. Your dad and I

were just saying that we fancy a McDonald's. What do you think?"

Ooh? Ooh? What did my dad say before?

"Do bearsth shi—?"

"DON'T SAY THAT, MADDISON!"

★★★

I've had a smashing day today. I've watched my dad win a trophy; I've won a trophy; nearly had a ice cream and had a massive McDonald's. I've watched Frank Stick-Man Postlethwaite try to do kung fu and my dad show him that he can't. But best of all, my mum and dad have been in a brilliant mood all day.

Ooh, and I've got a new favourite telly programme, too. It's the funniest thing ever. My dad showed it to me when we got back cos he said it's who Frank reminds him of… and it's called Flowery Twats, about a man called Basil what owns a hotel in Torn Key. Honestly, it's so funny even Robbie came down to watch it, and my dad hardly even noticed that Trev was sitting on his knee. *And* he read me a bedtime story but so fast I could hardly tell what he was saying, 'cept for – did you know the best way to kill a vampire's by putting steak through a harp? How weird's that?

Anyway, I know I'm s'posed to be asleep but I'm not. Imfact, I think I'm gonna say thank you to my mum and dad again. I know they're not asleep cos I can hear them talking and… my dad sounds a bit weird actually? Just let me have a little listen…

"Ah… Liz… yeh, that's it… oh God. That's good."

He must be itchy?

"… sooooooo good. Don't stop…"

Definitely itchy. He always says that when my mum's scratching his back…

"Oh, shit! Oh, fuck! Oh!"

He doesn't normally say THAT?

"Yeh… keep goin'…"

I wonder if she needs any help? He seems to be getting worse?

"Keep goin'… keep goin'… ah, Liz. Nearly… nearly… I'm gonna…"

BANG!

"Shall I help, Mum?"

"OHMIGOD! SWEETHEART! GET OUT!"

"Uuuuuuugh!"

What a weird way to scratch someone's back? I usually just do it sitting up?

"Are you all right, Dad?"

"Just about… Bloody 'ell, Maddie! Learn to soddin' well knock, will ya?"

There's no need to be so cross? I've only come to help?

"I'm tellin' ya, Liz, I'm puttin' a bolt on her door an' I don't care if there IS a friggin' fire."

"Have you been runnin' again, Dad? Isth that why you're so out of puff and your face isth a bit purple?"

"*Er… yeh!* So, if you wouldn't mind buggerin' off for five minutes while I get my breath back."

"Ooh, Mum, why don't you give him a blow job to help cool him down?"

What are they laughing at NOW?

Turns out my dad didn't need a blow job but he did need banging on the back. And my mum, too? It's funny how they both started choking at the 'xact same time? Whatever, I'll say thank you tomorrow, instead.

I'd best go to sleep actually, cos I definitely don't want to be late for school tomorrow. Not when it's wear-your-own-clothes day and I've hidden my zombie dress at the bottom of my bag. Hmm? I wonder if school will mind if I do zombie make-up, too? Put it in your bag, Maddison, just in case….

Goodnight, everybody, and happy summer holidays! See you all soon…

Goodbye!

Guess Who's Back?

We've only been off school for two weeks and I'm already umbelievably bored. I was so looking forward to the summer holidays but there's absolutely nothing to do… and I don't know why my mum thinks tidying my bedroom's something to do cos it's not. Or learning how to do dusting. Or use the stupid hoover. And who wants to read a book when the sun's playing out? And now, just cos I went for a extra long walk to the swings without telling anyone – I did tell someone but apparently Spud doesn't count – I'm not even allowed out of the garden! How mean's that? It was okay yesterday when me and Simon were playing tennis – 'cept now all my balls're in other peoples' gardens and I can't find them – but he's gone on his holidays this morning so there's nobody left to play with!

It's so umfair cos Michael's gone to Myorca with

his mum and dad, and Alliah's gone to Butlings with her mum and dad, and now Simon's gone to Tie Land with his mum and dad, but I'm not going anywhere with anyone cos my dad's got to work. He's putting some new 'lectricity in at school and– oh yeah, we all thought Mrs Jolley was dancing when she plugged the television in on the last day but apparently she was having a 'lectric shock!

Anyway, my dad's off today cos some people sent the wrong stuff so – ooh? I wonder if he'll put the chain back on my bike? I don't see why not. I'll go and ask…

"I'm not bein' miserable, love, it'll be a nightmare, that's all."

Ah? Are we going somewhere?

"You always say that, Joe. You're like a stuck record."

"That's cos it always is!"

"No, it isn't, and it'll be fun…"

"*Fun?* Fun as in, 'I know, Joe, let's take her to the zoo'. That kinda fun?"

The ZOO? But, I thought I wasn't allowed back 'till I'm old enough to drive myself?

"An' this might surprise you, love, but I don't wanna spend all day with half a ton o' sand stuck up the crack o' my arse."

Sand? Are we going to the seaside?

"But, they'll love it, Joe."

"I'm sure they will, but what about me, 'ey? I bloody won't!"

"Why do you always have to be so negative? And what's not to like about the—?"

"What's not to like? Have you got Alzheimer's or somethin'? Besides seagulls dive bombin' you an' shittin' everywhere? An' kids screechin' their bloody 'eads off? It's always blowin' a gale – I get the evil eye off you every time someone fit walks past in a bikini – an' everythin's covered in fuckin' sand!"

"Have you quite finished? All I'm asking you to do is to take them paddling in the sea. You know I don't like it and he still can't swim…"

Still? Trev'll never be able to swim cos his arms aren't long enough?

"… but she said he's got a flotation jacket…"

I didn't? When did I say that?

"And anyway, there's a chance he might just fall asleep. He still has a touch of jet lag…"

What's jet leg when it's at home?

"It's such a shame. The poor thing's spent the last year stuck inside for fear of being eaten by a crocodile…"

HE HAS NOT!

"… and he was just as scared indoors because of the spiders. Elaine said she was actually relieved when Pete announced he was leaving her for '*that floozie*'…"

Elaine? OHMIGOD?

"I never liked that prick! *Fuckin' Elvis?* I look more like…"

"OHMIGOD, MUM, IS MATTHEW BACK?"

"You made me jump then, sweetheart, and don't say 'ohmigod'. Yes, he got back yesterday morn…"

"YEEESTH! Did you HEAR that, Trev? MATTHEW'STH BACK!"

"I think the whole bloody street heard that, princess."

"OHMIGOD! Isth he comin' to the seaside with us, Mum?"

"How did you—? Hahaha. Well, Joe? It would appear the cat's out of the bag."

"I don't s'pose there's an option to shove it back in, is there?"

Who puts cats in bags?

"Okay… I give in! Tell Elaine to get Little Lord Fauntleroy ready, an' we'll…"

"Come on, sweetheart, let's get ready for the beach!"

"Yeeey… Rooaaaar…"

"*Shit!*"

I can't remember being this eggcited in my *life*. Matthew Elvis Chadwick's my very very very best friend, but last year he had to emmygrate to a Stralia cos of his dad's job, so I haven't seen him for nearly a year. It was horrible before he went and we were so upset cos we wouldn't be able to see each other anymore – well, we have been best friends since we were very nearly two – that we decided to dig a tunnel straight through the middle of the world. It was a brilliant idea, but every time I started mine I got told off for ruining the garden, so… anyway, he's back now and we're going to the seaside for the day. This is the best news ever! I can't even remember what I came in here for? Oh, yes – my bike! Bugger that.

★★★

"Budge up, Matthew, your leg'sth on MY side."

"I am budged up, Maddie. I can't budge up any more!"

"But, your leg'sth touchin' mine an' it'sth all hot an'…"

"One more peep about who's on whose side an' I'm turnin' round an' goin' back home! I told you we shoulda put the car seats on either side, Liz. Turn the radio up, love, an' see if you can drown 'em out."

"Just egnore him, Matthew. So, did you really see crocodilesth?"

"Not crocodiles, but I saw an emu. It was just standing in the road."

"In the road? Really? That'sth – what'sth a emu? I've never seen one of them on *Deadly 60*."

"It's like an ostrich, but smaller."

"I've seen a nostrich. Trev fell in with them at the zoo, didn't you, Trev? An' my dad climbed in an' – are you okay, Matthew? Your face is a funny colour."

"Not really. I feel a bit sick."

"A bit sick or a lot sick? Shall I tell my mum?"

"No, don't tell her yet."

"Okay. What else did you see? Did you see any penguinsth? Hey, guessth what I did at the – are you sure you're okay, Matthew? Your face is nearly the same colour as a witch?"

"I just feel a bit sick, that's all. What was you saying about penguins?"

"Oh. Just that I wanted to see what happensth when they– OH, GOD, MUM! Matthew'sth doin' a –*eeeeeuw!*"

Ohmigoodness. Matthew was sick so many times on the way here that he nearly turned inside out, and even with all the windows open the car proply stunk. I'm surprised I didn't join in, actually? Anyway, we're here now, so— ooh, guess what? My dad put the bag of sick on top of the car while he was getting everything out of the boot and a massive white bird flew off with it. I know. It'll get a horrible surprise when it looks inside later…

"Joe, I'm going over to the beach shop to see if they have anything for Matthew, so could you put some sunscreen on the kids? It's in the big yellow bag: factor fifty. I'll be as quick as I can."

Yuk! This sun cream's horrid – it's made the sand stick to me like I'm a actual donut – but least it smells nice after all that sick. And – flippin' 'eck, what's up with Matthew now? Honestly, he's done nothing but cry since we got here. First, cos the wind blew his baseball cap in a puddle, then cos his shoes were covered in sick so he had to walk in his bare feet… and then a insect popped out of the…

"Calm down, Matty, lad, it's only a bit of sand. Just keep cryin' an' it'll rinse itself out."

"Matthew, stop bein' such a cry baby. It'sth only a bit of— ooh, Mum, Matthew'sth cryin'!"

"What's the matter with him, Joe?"

"He'sth got sand in histh eye, Mum."

"Oh, dear. Let me have a look."

"You were quick, love. I think that's the shortest

amount o' time you've ever spent in a shop!"

"I wouldn't call it a shop, exactly – there was barely anything in it! There you go, Matthew, is that better? Now, try these on, sweetie."

Pink flip-flops?

"*Muuuum…*"

"Shush, Maddie."

"Thank you, Auntie Liz. Look, Maddie."

Yup. Girls' shoes. And how come he's got ones what fit?

"Now will you walk on sand, Matthew?"

"Yes, of course. So, what do you want to – MADDIE, WATCH OUT!"

Hahaha. Well, that was a massive surprise! I didn't even get chance to choose what I wanted to do first, cos just as Matthew was asking, two giant dogs ran right into me and knocked me absolutely flying. I think my dad said they were Rot-while-us? Whatever, it was really funny but you should have seen the mess.

First, they wouldn't stop licking me and they were proply slobbery… then they shaked water everywhere and my mum's book got soaking wet… then one of them did a wee on her hambag while the other one dried itself on her Little Mermaid towel… then they had a fight on it and then ran off! Anyway, after my mum'd finished being hysterical and Matthew'd finished hiding behind her, we decided to play football.

It wasn't s'posed to be funny but have you ever seen someone play football in flip-flops? Honestly, Matthew spent more time falling over than kicking the actual ball. Imfact, we were having the best laugh ever till the giant dogs came back and ruined it, cos Matthew ran off screaming so the biggest one chased after him and the other one joined in with me and my dad and popped my flippin' ball! And, can you believe my mum said it saved her the job, cos if it'd hit her in the face one more time she was probly gonna pop it herself. Humph! Anyway, I'm just waiting for Matthew now, but…

"Flippin' 'eck, Matthew, how long doesth it take to eat a ice cream? Hurry up, or it'll be time to go home."

"I'm trying, Maddie, but it's really cold."

"It'sth s'thposed to be cold! If it wasthn't cold it'd just be milk!"

"I know, but I'm eating it as fast as I can. What shall we do when I've finished?"

"Shall we build the world'sth biggest sandcastle? I'll borrow you my bucket an' spade an'…"

"It's okay sweetheart, I've bought him one of his own. And, it's lend, not borrow."

"Okay, you don't need to *lend* mine, Matthe—ooh, Dad, the umbrella'sth blowin' away!"

"See, Liz – I said it was too windy for…"

"Well, don't just look at it, Joe, run after it!"

"Who the bloody 'ell d'you think I am? Usain Bolt? An' what's wrong with your legs all of a sudden?"

"Nothing, but I'm not chasing after it in my bikini. Hurry up, before it blows away!"

"Bloody 'ell! Well, if ya think I'm chasin' after this all afternoon, you can think again!"

Well, he didn't chase after it *all* afternoon, but on the fourth time after it'd blowed into a completely different post code, apparently, he was so cross he put it back in the car. And I don't see the point in coming to the seaside and sitting under a umbrella the whole time? But, my mum won't stop going on cos there's nowhere to sit in the shade.

And, I don't know who said my dad could join in building our sandcastle but he's completely taken over. We were having a fantastic time till he decided we weren't doing it right. And now – it does look good, though?

"'Ey, princess, why don't you an' Matty look for things to decorate it with?"

"D'you mean, like seashellsth an' stuff?"

"Yeh! Anythin' really. Leave Godzilla 'ere, keep away from the sea, an' stay where we can see you."

"Okay. Matthew, come on. Let'sth see what we can find."

"REALLY, Matthew? All girlsth are called Sheila?"

"They're not *called* Sheila, it's what they…"

"Isth your mum called Sheila, now, or isth she still called Elaine?"

"E…"

"I wonder if Mrsth Collinsth is called Sheila? Did you see her in a Stralia?"

"Well, no, Australia's massive and we was in Perth so…"

"Perf? That's a weird name. Mrsth Collinsth livesth in the Pearly Gatesth. Isth that in Perf?"

"I don't know, Maddie, I've never heard of…"

"So, isth your dad never comin' back, Matthew?"

"I don't think so. When we were going – when I was sayin' goodbye – my mum screamed at him that she wouldn't piss on him if he was on fire, and I don't know what that means but it didn't sound very good."

"That'sth swearin', Matthew. It meansth when a man goesth for a wee. Are you bothered if he'sth not comin' back?"

"Erm, yes, but – what's this, Maddie?"

"Let me – ooh! It looksth like one of them banana bubble gumsth from out the machine at the club."

"Bubble gum? It doesn't look like bubble gum to me? What's all that gooey stuff in it?"

"Erm? No idea? But it wasth abstholutely disgusthtin' so just leave it."

"Okay – can we go back now, Maddie? My head's hot."

"How come?"

"The sun's burning my hair."

"I don't think the sun can burn your actual hair, Matthew."

"Feel it, if you don't believe me."

"Flippin' 'eck, it *is* hot. Come on, I'll race you. Last one back stinksth – OOH! A DEAD BIRD!"

We've found loads of intresting stuff for our sandcastle. First, we found a stick with different kinds of shells stuck to it. Then a massive shell – the kind what you can hear the sea in – but after I'd listened to it I gave it to Matthew to have a listen and a crab popped out, so now he won't touch shells, either. And we found loads of plastic bottles and a man's shoe – but we left those cos we didn't think they'd make a very good decoration for our sandcastle. But, the dead bird was the best – its insides looked like it'd been eating millions of noodles and just eggsploded! Matthew wasn't very inpressed but... one sec...

"Mum, feel Matthew'sth hair. It'sth proply on— Who'sth done THAT?"

"Don't look at me, sweetheart, I had nothing to do with it. Dig him up, Joe, before..."

"YOU WERE S'THPOSED TO BE MINDIN' HIM! It'sth not allowed to bury dinosaursth in the sand!"

"Sorry, princess, but he never said anythin' so I just assumed he was enjoyin' it."

"Stop it, Joe!"

"I'm SO not your friend! Mum, will you come with me to the sea, pleasthe? I need to wash the sand off him."

"Your dad'll..."

"NO! I don't trust him! I want you to come. *Pleasthe!* Are you comin', Matthew?"

"No, I don't like the sea."

"Matthew, you're looking awfully red, sweetie. Let me put some more sunscreen on you. You did put sunscreen on them, didn't you, Joe?"

"Course I did. I'm not a total bloody idiot!"

"He did, Mum, he put tonsth on. *Pleasthe* come with me to clean Trev. He'sth got sand in his mouth an' he wantsth a go in the sea."

"Okay... Joe, will you top Matthew up, please? And make sure he puts his new T-shirt on. And his baseball cap should have dried out by now. Come on then, sweetheart, but I'm not going in – I'll stand and watch."

I love the sea. I'd love it more if it tasted of sugar 'stead of salt, but still, it has the best monsters. There's sharks and noctopusses and jellyfishes and...

"Maddie, that's far enough! Come back! You don't want the current to get a hold of you."

"The currant?"

"Yes."

"There'sth CURRANTSTH? In the actual SEA?"

"Yes. Strong ones, too. And if they get a hold of you they can pull you right out. Especially if there's a cross-current. Now, they're *really* dangerous."

No way? Cross currants in the actual sea? That's nearly umbelievable? Wait till I tell Matthew. I mean, if it was my dad telling me then I wouldn't believe him cos he always tells me rubbish, but my mum never tells me stuff what's not true? Apart from maybe Father Christmas? Or, the Easter Bunny? And most probly the Tooth Fairy? But, besides that...

"Come on, sweetheart, time to head back. I think Trevor's clean enough now, don't you?"

"But, we haven't seen a noctopusth yet. Or any sharksth or wall russthesth..."

"Yes, well, you're not going to see those here, sweetheart, and we've been gone at least forty-five minutes. Poor Matthew will be bored on his own."

"O-*kaaay*. Mum, d'you know if Matthew'sth dad'sth ever comin' back?"

"I don't, sweetheart."

"What'sth a fluzee?"

"Hahaha. I'll tell you when you're older."

"I don't like Matthew'sth dad. He'sth alwaysth shoutin' at him an' callin' him a big Jessthie. It'sth not nice that, isth it Mum?"

"No, sweetheart, it's not."

Hmm? I'm sure it wasn't this far to walk on the way here? And I'm sure the floor wasn't like this either? It's all wavy and wet, and it was definitely dry and sandy? And…

"Mum, where'sth all the sea gone?"

"It hasn't gone anywhere, sweetheart – the tide's going out."

"What'sth the—? Ooh, Mum. You know how a Stralia'sth upsthide down? How come the sea doesthn't just fall off the world?"

"Hahaha. It's not upside down, Maddie. It's…"

"How come?"

"Well, because – you know your dad's the best person to answer this, but because the earth's round and it's floating in space, there is no up or down."

"Why?"

"Because – just look at him, sweetheart; your dad. He could fall asleep on a washing – OHMIGOD!"

Why's my mum running like a looney? Is there a peacock on

the— OHMIGOD? Matthew's head looks like a actual tomato.

"JOE! WAKE UP!"

"Friggin' 'ell, Liz, I was fast asleep then. What's the emergency?"

"Look at the colour of Matthew! HE's PURPLE!"

"What d'ya mean he's – *fuck me!*"

"How? You put sunscreen on him?"

"I did – look! I even put more on when you…"

"THIS? You put THIS on him? For God's sake, Joe, can't you read? This is Aftersun!"

"Aftersun? *Shit!* Well, how come our Maddie's all right?"

"Because, I applied more sunscreen after the dogs licked her, plus, she has olive skin…"

Have I? Eeuw? I ate a olive once and it tasted like actual earwax.

"… and she's been out in the sun all summer long. Poor Matthew's barely stepped outside this last year for fear of being eaten."

"Shit! Well… er… he's cooked now."

"You don't say! Well, we can't let Elaine see him like this. He'll have to have a sleepover and hopefully it'll have calmed down by the morning. Come on, let's go. I'm not risking him being out in the sun a minute longer. Pack everything up, Joe, while I smother him in this."

Poor Matthew. So far, he's had a green face, a red face, and – I wonder if there's anything what makes your face go yellow? Cos, then he'd be a actual human traffic light? Anyway, my mum's covered him in all kinds of cream and now we're on our way home. I hope he's not gonna be sick cos it must be horrible not being able to go anywhere without that happening. But – hmm? His face's definitely gone a funny colour again, and...

"OH, GOD, MUM! He'sth doin' it again!"

"It's okay, Matthew, sweetie, I've got you. Just try to aim it in the carrier bag."

"Where the bloody 'ell's it all comin' from, Liz? He's only had an' ice cream!"

★★★

Elaine was made up about Matthew having a sleepover cos she said she'll get miles more done if he's not there. But, not as made up as I am though. I can't believe he's moved back into his old house again – my mum said he would have moved back sooner if it wasn't for the people what were renting it – and when his sunburn's gone and his legs are back to normal, we can play out like we used to.

Anyway, he's all clean and fast asleep in my bed now. He's been there ages cos he was tired and didn't want any tea. Imagine that? I've never been so tired that I didn't want any tea? But, my mum said it's cos he's got too much sun – and jet legs – and he'll be right as rain by the morning. I hope so cos...

"Come on, princess, time for bed. An' 'ey! No pullin' the stopper out the airbed! I'm not fannyin' about with the pump all night."

I'm sure I only pulled it out twice last time? That's hardly all night?

"An' no gettin' outta bed, clodhopper! We can hear you, ya know."

"Okay… Night, Dad."

"Night, princess. Sleep tight an' don't let the bedbugs bite."

"BED BUGS? Maddie, are you awake?"

"Uh? Coursthe I'm awake? I've not even got in bed yet… An' there isn't really bedbugsth, Matthew. How come you're not asthleep?"

"I don't feel well."

"Are you gonna do more sick?"

"No, I just don't feel well. Can I put the light on? Just to check there's no bed bugs."

"Coursthe, it'sth just at the side of you. Hey, Matthew, d'you wanna know somethin' umbelievable? D'you know what my mum told me today? She told me there'sth…"

"I can't find the switch, Maddie."

"It'sth just there. Anyway, my mum told me there-'sth…"

"Where? I can't feel it."

"Just stretch a bit more. Anyway, I wasth tellin' you. My mum said there'sth currantsths what live in the actual sea. An' not just normal currantsth either – crossth onesth! What actually drag you out an' try to kill you!"

"Are you sure?"

"Yup! My mum said!"

"I don't mind currants – ooh, I've found the switch – but I really don't like sultan-aaaas! OW! Mwaaaaaaaaaa!"

244

***

God's sakes! Who falls out of bed when they're seven? And he looks proply funny without his tooth but it was loose anyway, and I don't feel *that* sorry for him cos – can you believe Matthew's Tooth Fairy pays him five whole pounds? I know! I wish I got that much. If I did, I'd knock all mine out and buy my own flippin' Xbox! But we must have very different tooth fairies cos the one what comes to me's well tight! Can you believe, she only gives me 50p? Anyway, he's gone back asleep again, thank goodness, and least I can read since my mum's left the lamp on for him.

Did you know that, besides steak, you can kill vampires with garlic or…

"Maddie, I don't feel well."

Not again?

"Do you want me to get my mum?"

"Yes, please. But, I might be scared on my own."

"Well, your best friend the Tooth Fairy should be here any minute soon – with your five poundsth – so, don't worry costh you won't be!"

"But, what if I'm scared of the Tooth Fairy?"

"Nobody'sth scared of the Tooth Fairy, Matthew. Here, cuddle Trev an' I'll be quick asth I can."

Am I ever gonna get any flippin' sleep to – ooh? Extra-loud shouting?

"FIVE QUID?"

"Keep your voice down, Joe. Yes. That's what he got last time."

"Jesus! He's cost me a bloody fortune, that kid! New

shoes, bucket 'n' spade, T-shirt – I'm gonna have to get the car fumigated – an' now you're tellin' me you want five quid for the Tooth Fairy? An' 'ey, don't let our Maddie know about this or she'll knock the bloody lot out!"

She's already thinking about it, actually…

"The poor boy's spent most of the day vomiting, Joe – not to mention that he has a touch of sunstroke! He'll be gutted if the Tooth Fairy doesn't come."

"Not as gutted as I will be. FIVE…"

How many more times is my dad gonna say that?

"Mum, Matthew doesthn't feel very well, again."

"Okay, sweetheart, I'm coming. I'll be back in a minute, Joe, so, get it out, ready!"

"Hahaha. Steady on, love. I thought you'd never…"

"You know what I mean! Come on, sweetheart, let's go and see to Matthew."

"*Muuuum*… you know when my tooth came out, how come I only got 50p?"

"Not now, sweetheart."

"But, how come I only got—?"

"I said, not now, Maddie. Hello Matthew, I believe you don't feel very – OH!"

Ohmigoodness. You'll never guess what? Matthew's got chicken pots. Actual chicken pots! I thought it was part of his sunburn but my mum said it's definitely chicken pots cos she knows from when Robbie and Rache had them. Apparently, it takes ages to get better from them. *I wonder if I'll catch them?* Anyway, she's given him some medicine and he's gone asleep with – *what if Trev catches them?* Can dinosaurs catch chicken pots? It'll be so umfair if I catch them in the summer holidays, 'stead of being off school with them. And – hang on a sec? I can't hardly concentrate cos – what's my dad laughing at? He sounds like he's gonna die? I'm definitely gonna have to find out…

"Behave, Joe, it's not funny."

"Not funny? It's fuckin' hilarious! He's been back one day, haha… an' we're sendin' him home, hahaha… with a tooth missin'… third degree burns… hahahaha. He's puked himself inside out… hahahahaha. An' chicken pox! HAHAHAHAHAHAHAHAAAA… I can't breathe, Liz!"

I don't think I've ever heard my dad laugh this much?

"You're all heart, Joe."

"An' he never came out the 'ouse for a year cos he was shit scared o' crocs! Hahahaha… here's your fiver, love. Worth every penny!"

"Honestly, have you ever thought of becoming a counsellor? Right, I'll be back in a minute – Tooth Fairy duty – and, Maddison! What are you doing out of bed again? Come with me, young lady. And, I hope you didn't hear any of that."

I heard all of it actually, and what's the point in going back to bed? Every time I try to go to sleep Matthew either falls on the floor, loses his teeth, or gets chicken pots. And my dad's still laughing his head off so loud that I…

"Okay, sweetheart, give Mummy a kiss goodnight."

What, again? That's about six now?

"Muum. So, about the Tooth Fairy? 'Bout, how come she only givesth me—?"

"Goodnight, Maddison."

"But?"

"I said, goodnight!"

Humph. Stupid flippin' tooth fairy!

See you soon, everyone…

Goodnight!

Being Poorly

"Sweetheart, stop scratching!"

"I can't help it, Mum. I'm all itchy."

"You're not itchy, Maddie. It's psychosomatic."

"Cycle, what?"

"Psychosomatic. When your brain tells your body…"

What's a cycle got to do with – ooh, my bike? I've not played on it for two weeks now.

"…but if you think it'll help, I'll put some calamine lotion on you."

I don't think you will! Thanks to chicken pots and cameline lotion, I've spent the last two weeks looking like Peppa flippin' Pig! And, not just normal chicken pots either – Stralian ones! Matthew brought them back with him apparently… as well as a hat with loads of weird things dangling off it and a big kangaroo with a baby one in it, but I'd have preferred a actual crocodile than being poorly for two weeks!

And did you know that every single kangaroo's called Joey, so how do they know which one's which? Cos if someone shouts 'Maddison!' – which they do quite a lot – I know they're shouting at me. But, if a kangeroo's been naughty and its mum shouts 'Joey!' – but in kangaroo language of course – they must all look up and say, 'What?'. It's very comfusing? Anyway, today's gonna be awesome cos…

"See what I mean, sweetheart? While you were busy thinking, you didn't scratch once. What were you thinking about?"

Erm? Cameline lotion; Peppa Pig; chicken pots; Stralian chicken pots; Matthew; crocodiles; funny hats with corks on them; kangaroos; kangeroos called Joey; naughty kangeroos called Joey; kangaroo language; being called Maddison; being naughty and called 'Maddison'! And not being itchy…

"Erm? Nothin' really…"

And now I'm thinking about being itchy again? But, I'm not itchy, I'm cycle – ooh? My bike?

"Mum, you know now I've not got chicken potsth anymore, can I play out on my bike?"

"Yes. Actually, is the basket still on it, Maddie?"

"Erm? Yup!"

It's not, but…

"Then, could you do me a favour? Could you take this tin of fruit cocktail up to Elaine, please? She needs it for the trifle. You did say you wanted trifle, didn't you?"

"Coursthe we want trifle! Who doesthn't want trifle?"

I'm so eggcited for today. My mum felt so bad about

burning Matthew on his first day back that she said when we're better, me, my mum, Matthew, and Elaine could have a welcome home tea party, but without tea. It's gonna be brilliant…

"And remember the rules, Maddison. Trevor is not allowed on your bike!"

"Yup!"

"ALWAYS wear your cycle helmet!"

"Yup!"

"And stay close to the kerb."

"Yup!"

"And don't be long. We need to go…"

"I won't."

Flippin' 'eck! Stop going on.

"And come straight back!"

★★★

Hmm? Well, I have been long – very long, actually – but not at Elaine's. I bet you can't guess where I am. I'll give you three clues. 1. I'm not at home. 2. I'm not at school, and 3. I'm not in the orphanage. Have you guessed yet? I'm in hospital. I know!

I've not been here for ages, not since last year when I was running round playing ghosts with a big white tablecloth on my head and split my head open when I tripped up the kerb. Or the time before that, when I got a green crayon stuck up my nose. Or the time before that, when I got a red crayon stuck up my nose – or was that when I glued my hand to the cooking torch? Whatever,

I've mostly stopped doing stuff like that now. Oh yes, about today. Orange Wendy saw the whole thing.

She said she was driving up the road when I came whizzing towards her on my bike – in the middle of the road and without my cycle helmet on – with Trev in one hand and something in my other – a tin of fruit cocktail, actually – when a little boy ran out in the – A LITTLE BOY? Simon Eckersley's not a little boy? Anyway, she said Simon ran in the road after his football so I steered my bike away from him; crashed into the kerb, summersalted over the handlebars, and the tin of fruit cocktail flew up in the air and landed on my head. All I remember was a man waking me up asking me 'What day is it, Maddison'? Simon's dad, apparently. But, I don't know what day it is normally, never mind when I've just been knocked unconscience! And wouldn't you think he'd ask someone who's *not* having a lovely sleep in the road?

Anyway, cos my head was bleeding a lot and I kept going on about trifle and dinosaurs, he sent Orange Wendy to get my mum and called for a ambalance. Apparently, it's not allowed to move someone if they've proply banged their head… incase it comes off, I suppose? So, then the ambalance turned up and a man shined a light in my eyes then asked how many fingers was he holding up? And, okay, erm… cos I didn't want my mum to shout at me for doing the 'xact opposite of what she said, I *might* have pretended I didn't know the right answer, and so…

"Right, Maddie, I'm going outside to phone your dad again. And while I'm gone, do not mention Trevor!"

"But, it'sth not my fault. All I said wasth, have they found my best friend yet?"

"Yes! Your best friend who was in the accident! Who flew over the handlebars and into someone's garden!"

"But, he DID!"

"I'm not saying he didn't, but what I am saying is that we'd have been home hours ago if you'd thought to mention that he's a plastic dinosaur!"

There's no need to be mean.

"But, they didn't asthk me that. And, I didn't asthk them to send a police car to look for him."

"THREE HOURS you've been under observation for now, Maddie, and there's nothing wrong with you!"

I know! I keep telling them!

"Anyway, I need to call your dad again and I can't get a signal in here, so stay there and don't move, and don't speak to anyone until I get back. Understood? Good! I'll be five minutes!"

Good? I never said anything? Anyway, the police did find Trev in Simon's front garden, and d'you know what they said to my mum when they did? They said there was no one in at home and he's too big to fit through the letterbox, so they've thrown him over the back gate instead! I'm so cross! How dare they do that to Trev. They wouldn't do that with people. Imagine that on the news...

'The little girl what's been missing's ventually turned up. The police said that when they brought her home

there was no one in, so they threw her over the back-gate cos she wouldn't fit through the letterbox.'

God, I'm bored. Why can't I just go home? I don't need a doctor to tell me I've got a bump on my head the size of a cabrees cream egg cos I can feel it for myself. And, ooh? Is that a cake trolley? I'm absolutely starving. No one's give me anything to eat since I've been here and it's been ages since my breakfast. I wonder if... one minute... I'll ask this little girl in the next bed.

"Scusthe me, what'sth your name?"

"Wuby. What's yours?"

"*Wuby*? That'sth a funny name."

"Not Wuby with a W, Wuby with a R."

"Oh! Soz."

Awww. She can't talk proply...

"My name'sth Maddithon. What'sth up with you?"

"I've got to have an opewation. I've bwoke my leg and it didn't fix pwoperly. What's up with you?"

"I'm starvin'!"

"I am too! I was asleep this morning when they came with bweakfast. I'm so hungwy."

"Shall I see if I can find usth somethin' to eat?"

"If it's no twouble."

"Are you kiddin' me? I'm bored and I'm starving and I love exploring..."

"Hey – you what wooks wike Ewsa! Are you goin' for food?"

Flippin' 'eck? Is this room for people who can't talk proply? If so, how come I'm in here?

"Yesth, boy what looksth like Woody out of *Toy Story*. What d'you want?"

"Can you get me some too?"

"AND ME!"

Honest to God, this hospital's rubbish! How are you s'posed to get better when everybody's starving? Not as starving as me though, not enough to go after the actual trolley. I couldn't reach the thing what you press the numbers on to open the door, so I just followed a lady out, but... hmm? I don't like this part of the hospital very much – there's no toys and it smells funny? Ooh? I wonder what's in – OHMIGOD!

It's like a episode off the actual Simpsons! I'm not kidding, the whole room's filled with fast asleep, yellow people! And all their mouths're wide open, just like Mrs Collins's was, right before she went to live in the Pearly Gates. Specially this one? People die in hospital, don't they? I've never seen a actual dead person before but I imagine one looks like this? I could try poking it but – phew, I can see breathing.

I wonder why everybody's yellow? And why've they all got grapes? Are grapes medicine? And if you take grapes off nearly dead people and give them to hungry, alive children, is that stealing? I wish Trev was here; he'd know. But honestly, you wouldn't believe how much food they've got – mind you, nearly dead people probly don't eat very much so they probly won't miss this. And, I'll just lend this pastry thing and these egg butties and – ooh? Chocolate! I've never seen this type before? It's proper tiny but it tastes okay. I'll just have a couple more pieces then – *what's all this funny writing? Eric Jones?*

"Hello, Eric Jonesth! ARE YOU AWAKE?"

Or asleep? Or dead? I'm not really sure? But, seeing as I can't say thank you, I'll draw him a picture instead. And I'm sure this writing's not very inportant cos besides his name, you can't hardly tell what it says.

"There you go, Eric Jonesth. Hope you like dinos-thaursth!"

Actually? I think I'll draw everyone one?

★★★

Brilliant! I bet they'll be well chuffed if any of them ever wakes up. AH? Someone's coming. Leg it, Maddison…

Oh dear? I can't remember which way I came? Did I come this way or – WOW! Stephen Hawkins drives one of these! And, I've seen them at the Lympics, too! They play tennis in them and do racing and stuff and it's proply umbelievable. I wonder what they're doing in a hospital, though? I SO want a go. And it's a really long corridor so I can go proply whizzing. Hurry up, Maddison, before someone comes…

Flippin' 'eck. It's miles harder than it looks on telly, but once you get going it's absolutely brilliant. But… oh, dear, the corridor's running out now and I don't actually know how to stop it, and – Ohmigod? Where did he come from?

"WATCH OUT, MISTER – MOVE OUT OF THE – Oopsth! Soz! Are you okay?"

Well, least I'm back in the children's bit now. Apparently, it's not allowed to ride the wheelchairs in the hospital at that speed, but Doctor Murray was really nice once he'd managed to get up off the floor. He wanted to know what I was doing wandering round the hospital with a bag full of food, so I told him I'd been to the shop and got lost so he brought me back here. He said my mum'd be really missing me but can you believe, she wasn't even here when I got back.

Anyway, everyone was made up with the food, 'cept for the likrish so I ate that myself, but – uh? What's HE doing here?

"There you are, Maddie! Where've you been? Are you okay?"

Maddie? I don't think he's ever called me that before in my life?

"What're you doin' here, Robbie?"

"Mum called an' said you were in hospital. She sounded pretty hysterical so I was worried an' came down. Close your eyes an' hold your hands out – I felt a right tit, walkin' round with…"

"TREVOR! Yey! An' I'm not *in* hosthpital, I'm *at* hosthpital – I'm fine, see! I'm not even in pyjamasth! I fell off my bike an' got knocked unconscience, that'sth all. Feel my head!"

"Holy shit! Feels like you're growin' another one. Is it sore?"

"Not aspecially."

"Come 'ere, nutter."

Ohmigod? Maybe I have got concushions?

"Erm? Robbie? How come you're huggin' me? I thought you don't like me?"

"Course I like you – you tit! You annoy the shit out o' me but who would I argue with if you weren't there? An' seven twelfths of a calendar isn't really a calendar, is it?"

"What d'you – *oh*, hahaha! YESTH! TAKE A PICTURE OF MY BUMP! D'you know where my mum is?"

"She went to sign some papers so you can go home, but they were in the middle o' their tea break so she asked me to come an' keep an eye on ya. Where were ya? Anyway, Eggo gave me a lift 'ere, so he's hangin' on cos Dad's…"

"Yey, Wuby! I can go home!"

"That's bwilliant, Maddithon."

"I know! I hope your leg getsth better soon."

"Thanks, Maddithon, and thanks for the food. I'm weally gwateful."

"No pwobsth. Come on, Wobbie – God, I'm sayin' it now! Come on, Robbie, let'sth go."

Well, they've let me out of the hospital, but if anything strange happens my mum has to take me back straight away. I wish she'd leave me alone though. She keeps feeling my head and asking if I'm okay – she even told me to try and have a sleep, but how am I s'posed to sleep when I know Matthew's coming for a tea party? And, I hope my lump doesn't go down before he gets a chance to feel it cos he'll be well inpressed…

"Crikey, Maddie, that's massive. Were you scared you might die? I would've been."

"Yesth, Matthew, but you're scared of potatoesth!"

"I'm not scared of them at first, just when they start growing arms and legs and stuff."

"Well, no, I wasthn't. I had quite a nice time, actually. I met a girl who said she had somethin' wrong with her leg but really I think she wasth havin' a operation to fix her voice. It wasth a shame costh she couldn't talk proply. She said 'w' instead of 'r'. An' the boy in the next bed said 'w' instead of 'l'. It wasth quite comfusthin' actually…"

"You can't talk properly, Maddie. You say 'th' instead of 's'. People think your name's Maddith…"

"No, they *don't* and yesth I *can*!"

"No, you *can't* and yes they *do*!"

"DON'T!"

"DO!"

"Shut up, Matthew, elsthe I'll get my mum'sth Mr Potato Head an'…"

"Will you two stop arguing! Honestly, Elaine, she cried for *ages* after you left, and…"

"NO, I DIDN'T!"

"Yes, you did, Maddie, and stop shouting!"

"Matthew was the same, Liz. All I heard for months was, 'Maddie this' and 'Maddie that', and now look at them."

"*Awwww*… did you, Matthew?"

"I might've."

"Aww… shall we play Pop-Up Pirate? Simon Eck-ersthley'sth rubbish at it. He stabsth the sword so hard he breaksth it. You're not scared of piratesth, are you?"

"Little bit."

"Well, don't worry cos you won't be scared of this one – he looksth like Mr Bean."

I'm so happy Matthew's back. I mean, I did try playing with other people but mostly they just got on my nerves. Alliah doesn't but she lives miles away, and Michael doesn't, 'cept when he tries to kiss me, and Simon doesn't, but he plays with his big brother mostly… oh, yeah, Pop-Up Pirate. Trev won the most games, then me, then Matthew. Turns out Matthew wasn't scared of the actual pirate, but he jumped out his skin every time it popped up so he wasn't really trying…

"Okay, you two, come and get it – and don't get too used to this, sweetheart. It's not exactly good for you."

"Right, Matthew. We've got chicken nuggetsth and cheesthe stringsth; chicken goojohnsth and onion ringsth; cheesthe with hotdogsth and picklesth on sticksth; cheesthe and pickled onion buttiesth; cockporn chicken and chipsth; Cheesthy Wotsthisth, trifle, and ice-cream smoothiesth. An' when we've ate this we can watch a movie."

"What film did you say we were watching?"

"*King Kong*! It'sth 187 minutesth so we'll get to stay up late."

"What's it about?"

"Actually, it'sth ridiclious. If you landed on a island an' there wasth a giant grillar an' a T-rexth, wouldn't you be more supristhed at seein' the T-rexth? Costh we've got *actual* grillarsth, but besidesth Trev, we haven't got any T-rexesth. So, why'sth everyone intrested in the grillar? Why'sth no one intrested in the T-rex? It doesthn't make any sensthe? But it'sth three hoursth and twenty-one minutesth long, so..."

"Erm... okay..."

I know how long nearly every film is cos I absolutely hate going to bed early. It's the worst thing in the world. So, when I'm allowed to stay up and watch a deevy dee, I just pick the longest one. And, I've pretended to like loads of telly programmes so I can stay up later. *Down Town Abbey* – boring! *Mid Summer's Murder* – boring! And I don't understand the point of *Master Chef* cos it's just people doing cooking, but everyone else loves it and it doesn't finish till nine o' clock. I've even tried being intrested in The News cos my dad watches that all the time, but cos it's just the same programme going round and round and round, after the first-time round, I have to go to – ooh? My dad's home. I bet he can't wait to feel my bump but – *actually, it's my tummy what doesn't feel right at the moment? I think I might have eaten too many pickles?*

"Ey up, princess, I hear you've been in the wars again. Hiyah, Elaine!"

What wars? I fell off my bike, that's all?

"Feel my head, Dad."

"I've always said you needed your head feelin', princess. It's a corker that, kiddo! Let's hope it knocked some sense in. How was it at the 'ospital, Liz – busy?"

"It's always busy, Joe, but it was fine. They said to keep an eye on her, that's all."

"Ha! What's new?"

"Exactly! Are you hungry, Joe? Would you care to join us for this veritable feast?"

"Nah, love. I'll give it a miss if you don't mind. I sickened myself with cheesestrings at dinner."

"Did you really, Dad?"

"Did I 'eck!"

"What are you going to do about food then? Would you like me to make something?"

"Nah, love, it's fine. I'm just gonna watch the end o' the News – see what's happenin' with this Brexit – then I might go the chippy. I've not 'ad a chippy tea in years."

Not Brexit, again? I don't know who he is. Or Donald Trump. That can't really be someone's name, can it? Trump? Well, whatever… my dad's always swearing at the telly when they come on. Them and the football. And the govament. And the pry minister. Specially, the pry minister. He says she's a…

"'Ey Liz, which 'ospital was our Maddie at today cos – WHATTHEFUCK?"

"JOE! I can't apologise enough, Elaine. Joe, *please*…"

"NEVER MIND THAT, LOVE, COME 'ERE! Just, let me rewind it. You know you said we had to keep an eye on her?"

"*Yes*…"

"… and on a lighter note. Earlier today, a local hospital was thrown into temporary chaos when a little girl…"

"OHMIGOD, MADDISON!"
"CRIKEY, MADDIE! YOU'RE ON TELLY!"
"WHAT THE ACTUAL F—?"
"Quiet, Joe! Rewind that."

"…thrown into temporary chaos when a little girl ran amok…"

Erm?

"Operations had to be rescheduled, after several 'nil by mouth' patients were reported to have been fed. According to little Ruby Rockingham, who was awaiting surgery on her leg, 'a little girl called Maddithon'…"

"See, Maddie – I told you people think you're called Maddith…"
"Shush, Mattie love. Rewind that, Joe…"
Flippin' eck? Even Elaine's joining in?

"… a little girl called Maddithon fed her grapes, egg sandwiches and a Cornish pasty. There was also confusion on the dementia ward, where patient records where obliterated by drawings of dinosaurs…"

"OHMIGOD, MADDISON! WHEN THE HELL DID YOU DO ALL THIS?"
I'm never gonna get a – Oooo? My tummy feels funny?

"… and in this CCTV footage, chief physician Doctor Lawrence Murray is seen having a close encounter with an out-of-control wheelchair…"

"WHAT THE HELL, MADDISON?"
Think, Maddison? Say something… quick!
"Honestht, Mum, I don't remember doin' any of it! It must've been the concushionsth!"
Hmm? I think I need the toilet?
"Well, it doesn't seem to have made you any less crafty!"

"This is Moira Lancaster, reporting from…"

I definitely DO need the toilet?
"Right, Maddison! You can start by explaining…"
"I can't, Mum. I need the loo!"
"I'm not falling for THAT! When they said I had to keep an eye on you, Maddie, I never for one minute imagined I'd be doing it via Granada sodding Reports!"
Flippin' 'eck? It's gonna come out? I can't wait…
"Maddie, come back!"
"I can't!"
"COME BACK, RIGHT THIS MINUTE! Joe, go and get her."

★★★

Oh, my goodness – this is the worst thing ever! Who makes chocolate what makes you poo? What kind of a idiot does that? It's called laxytives apparently, and it's for people who are constypasted – I'd actually forgot I'd eaten it till my mum asked me what I'd ate today – oh, and likrish makes you poo, too, apparently, which is *not* good when you've already eaten quite a lot of poo chocolate. At least everyone's finished laughing or shouting at me now, but it took ages cos of all the interruptions.

First, Nanna phoned from Blackpool to say she'd nearly had a heart attack when she saw me on the telly, and isn't Doctor Murray dishy? Then Rache phoned and said the 'xact same thing. Then Ben Eckersley phoned. Then Stefanos Popple Octopuss phoned and he was laughing so loud you could hear him without being on the actual phone. Then Gaz phoned. Then Dave. Then Mike and Orange Wendy came round to see the 'local celebrity' – they were well inpressed with my bump but they didn't stay long cos I couldn't stop going to the loo. Oh, and Robbie downloaded the picture of me what was on the News; the one where I'm whizzing down the corridor in the wheelchair, and that's August sorted, apparently. But, he's a little bit grumpy cos his mates keep texting, asking if they've just seen his kid sister on the news?

I think I'm famous? But being famous isn't anywhere near as much fun as I thought it'd be. For starters, I've got to go back to the hospital in the morning to say sorry to everyone. I've got to say sorry to the yellow people for stealing their food even though my dad said they'll have completely forgot about it by now. Then, I've got to say sorry to Doctor Murray for running him over with the wheelchair. Then, to all the people whose operations I ruined. Oh, and my chances of getting a Xbox are hanging on by a tiny, tiny thread, and if I don't want the thread to break completely, I have to say sorry like I proply mean it. I'd best get practising then…

"I'm sorry!"

No? Sounds too cross? What about?

"I'm sooooo *sorry*…"

Nope? Sounds like I don't really mean it? What about?

"Crossth my heart an' hope to die, if I never tell a…"

"OY, CHUCKY! I'll give you, 'Cross my heart!'. Go to bloody sleep!"

Who's Chucky? And I'm practising being sorry here? There's no need to bang on my— Ooh?

"Dad, I'm *really, really sorry.*"

"I should bloody well think so too!"

Yes – that one! See you all soon, everyone…

Goodnight!

Back to Flippin' School

"Maddie, are you out of bed yet? And don't bother pretending you are, because I'm not stupid!"

You were for most of last year.

"Answer me, Maddison!"

No. I'm trying to finish my dream.

"RIGHT! I'M COMING UP!"

Ugh, I hate school mornings. I hate having to get up when I'm still asleep; get dressed when I'm half asleep; eat my breakfast when I'm falling asleep, and worser still, have my hair pulled to bits cos my mum has to make sure my bunches are level.

"Come on, Maddie! UP! I'll never understand you. For the last seven weeks you've been up at the crack of dawn, and your first day back at school and I can't get you out of bed?"

What is it my dad says? It's not rockets science?

"You don't want to be late on your first day back, do you?"

I don't want to go at all, actually.

"Your dad's taking you this morning… put your arms up. He's left some of his work tools at school… arms down. I've told Elaine he'll be there at half past eight to pick up Matthew… turn around. So, you'd better get a move on… there! Now, pass me your hairbrush."

"Okay, but – OW! You're pulling my hair out!"

"Don't be so dramatic, Maddie. I barely touched you. And you don't want to go to school with wonky bunches, do you?"

Wonky who? Oh, haha… I wasn't listening proply. I thought she meant it was a new person starting school.

"Unfortunately, Robbie finished the cereal last night so you'll have to make do with toast."

I don't care. I'm not even hungry yet.

"So, eat this and…"

"OW! You're pulling my hair!"

"Sorry, sweetheart. There… all done. And don't you look smart? See, that wasn't so bad, was it?"

That's what you think? My shoes are too big. My uniform's horrid. And my bunches are giving me a headache!

"Stay there, sweetheart, I think I'll take a photo for posterity. It's hard to believe that you leave home every morning looking so smart, and come home looking like nobody owns you. Smile – I said smile, Maddie, not grimace."

Stop talking. You're doing my head in!

"That'll have to do."

"Is she nearly ready, Liz? Bloody 'ell, princess, couldn't you find a bigger bag?"

"I told you it was huge, Joe… and I'm referring to her new bag, before you waste your brain cells trying to come up with a wise-crack this early in the morning. I said you could have it on one condition, didn't I, Maddie?"

"Yup! That I don't leave any food in it after school."

"Because?"

"Becausthe, when you leave a orange in your bag for seven weeksth, it turnsth into a actual monster."

It does. Honestly. I proply screamed my head off…

"It wasn't a monster it was mould, and I hope never to see anything like that again."

Me too. I'd completely forgot about emptying my bag when we broke up for the summer holidays, so when my mum told me to get it out ready for going back to school, I put my hand in it and – honest to God, I thought there was a proper monster living in there. It was all green and furry and took up all the space in my bag…

"Now, hurry up, sweetheart – and no fighting with Matthew on the way. You know your dad's grumpy in the mornings…"

Probly cos you never shut up.

"Um… sweetheart, haven't you forgotten something?"

I don't think so? Heelies – yup? A bag of fizzy sweets – yup? Six jam tarts – yup? Drink – yup? And – hello, Trev!

"Where's my kiss?"

"Oh, that! Soz. Mwah. Bye, Mum."

"Bye, sweetheart. Have a nice day!"

Yeah, right? Come on, Trev…

***

Trev's actually been eggspelled from school a few times but that was when we were in Mrs Jolley-Jelly's class… hang on a sec… I'm just gonna take my bunches out cos they're definitely giving me a headache… but we're not in her class any more cos year three has a different teacher. I wonder what she's like? I hope her breath doesn't smell like egg and she likes – ooh? She's here…

"Good morning, children. My name's Miss Spottis-wood and I'll be your teacher this year."

"Good-mor-ning-miss…"

SPOTTISWOOD? I can't say THAT?

"Maddie, you'll never be able to say…"

"Shush, Matthew."

"So, for today's registration, I'd like you to each introduce yourselves…"

What's wrong with her eyes?

"So, who wants to go first? How about you, dear? The one with the unusual hairstyle."

Uh? Carl Pilling's not got a unusual hairstyle?

"She's talkin' to you, Maddie."

"*Me?* But, I haven't got a unusual hairsthtyle? An' she'sth definitely lookin' at…"

"You have – you've only got one bunch in – and one of her eyes is looking at Carl, but the other one's definitely looking at…"

"You! Yes, you, dear! What happened? Did your mum run out of time this morning?"

"Erm? Yup! She oversthlept, so I had to get mysthelf ready."

"Oh! Okay. Would you like to tell me your name, please?"

"Yup. It'sth Maddithon Elizthabeth McLaren."

"*McLaren?* You wouldn't be Rachel's sister, would you?"

Not this again?

"Yup…"

"I can definitely see a resemblance. In all of my years of teaching, I never had a better pupil."

Well, you're gonna be in for a BIG surprise this time.

"And your brother, Robbie – what a character! Do you know, children, he ate seven inches of his wooden ruler when I taught him, and I still have the remaining five inches to this day."

Or, maybe not?

"Well, thank you, Maddison. So, next? How about the boy next to you? The one with the blonde hair and freckles?"

"He'sth called Matthew Elvi…"

"I can say it, Maddie. I'm just Matthew Chadwick and I haven't got a middle…"

"Yesth, you have, Matthew! It'sth…"

"Or, any brothers or sisters. Just, Maddison, who's my very best friend."

"Aww, *thanksth*, Matthew!"

"Yes, thank you, 'just Matthew'. Okay, who's next?

The boy behind you. We'll have you."

"She meanths you, Simon."

"But, she's looking at Lucy?"

"One eye'sth lookin' at Lucthy, but her main eye'sth lookin' at you. Just say your name!"

This is gonna take forever?

Well, besides not being sure whether she's talking to me or not, she's actually really nice. Imfact, she's so nice I might get Trev out of my bag after dinner and intra juice them. I've left the top open so he can see everything and I've told Carl if he touches him I'll shove his head through the school railings again, and so far, he's not tried anything. Probly cos last time I did it, Mrs Jolley-Jelly had to use butter to get his head unstuck and he smelled like toast for ages. But, it's not nice being mean to people and Alan didn't mean to wee near the Harvest Festival baskets…

Anyway, we ventually finished the register, but I hope it's not gonna take us this long every day or we'll never learn anything besides who everybody is, and we know that already. And learning stuff's the only thing I like about school… and if they'd let me learn stuff while I'm talking or singing or running round and eating sweets then I wouldn't mind coming, but it's not allowed to have any fun and the rules don't make sense either. They go mental if you run in the corridor cos it's dangerous apparently, then five minutes later, when we're doing PE, they force us to throw balls and beanbags at each other. And which is more dangerous? Cos, Chloe Barrow's had to go and see the nurse twice when Carl Pilling bust her nose with a beanbag, and one time Alliah got hit in the face so hard with a football that it broke her actual glasses! But, no one's ever had to go and see the nurse cos they ran on the corridor…

"Maddison, dear, are we daydreaming? And, I do hope you're not chewing in class."

Gulp! Not any more.

"Okay, children, are we all finished? Then, crayons down and who'd like to go first? Lucy, I think your hand went up first. Would you like to talk us through your picture?"

"Yes, miss. This is my picture of my favourite day of the holidays. This is me, my mum and dad, and we're smiling our heads off in Disneyworld…"

That's them smiling? I thought they were being murdered to death with giant ping-pong bats?

"… and this is us having our picture taken with Mickey…"

Oh, right? They're Mickey Mouse's ears. Lucy went to see the delighted state of a Merica in the summer holidays and she's never flippin' shut up about it all morning.

"Excellent try, Lucy. Who's next? Simon? Is that correct? Would you like to go next?"

"Yes, miss. This is a picture of my favourite day of the holidays. This is us in Thailand, and we're at Mc-Donald's…"

"McDonald'sth? Flippin' 'eck, Simon, do they have Mc—?"

"Maddison, put your hand up if you want to speak.

And, are you *sure* you're not chewing?"

Gulp! Not any more.

"No, missth – really, Simon? Actual McDonaldsth? In Tie Land?"

"Yes. And it was the best day cos I didn't like Thai food – it's just rice or noodles!"

"TIE food? People eat—?"

"That's enough, Maddison. Would you like to go next?"

"*Not really…*"

"Can I go next, miss?"

"Yes, 'just Matthew'. Tell us about your favourite day."

"Okay, so, this is a picture of me and Maddie at the beach. We built the world's biggest…"

"That can't be your favourite day, Matth…"

"Quiet, Maddison! Continue, Matthew."

"Well, it was my first day back from Australia and I hadn't seen Maddie in nearly a year, so it was the best day ever cos…"

"But, you wasth sick, Matthew? All the way there an' all the way back? *An'* you got burned in the middle."

"Yes, but…"

"Then you lost your tooth an' got chicken potsth! How can that be your favourite—?"

"Maddison, let the poor boy speak! Are you always this talkative? Yes, Lucy?"

"She is, Miss. She never shuts up. Mrs Jolley used to call her Chatty…"

"And are you always so quick to tell tales?"

Always… and if Miss Spottiswood doesn't like tell-tales, I like her even more.

"Maddison, would you like to—oh, good Lord! That's extraordinarily graphic!"

Eggstraw, what? I don't know what that means?

"Erm? Thanksth? It'sth me an' Matthew at the beach, when we found the dead bird…"

"Blimey, Maddie, I wasn't that red!"

"Yesth, you wasth, Matthew. An' this is it'sth gutsth – hey, Simon, you definitely wouldn't like noodlesth if you saw a dead bird – an' that'sth it'sth blood… an' thisth is the sea… an' they're all the crossth currantsth what most probly killed it…"

"Maddison, if I may be so rude as to interrupt?"

You may not.

"This is a picture of your favourite day of the holidays, yes?"

"Yup!"

"So, could you explain the inclusion of the blood-soaked Tyrannosaurus Rex?"

"Oh! Hahahaha! *Coursthe…* Soz, Missth Spottisth-wood. That'sth Trev!"

"Who's Trev?"

I didn't even get chance to tell her who Trev was cos the whole class did, and it's so rude to interrupt someone else's story. Anyway, one-minute he was in my bag minding his own business, then next minute he just magicked himself up onto my desk. Well, she did say she'd very much like to meet him but I don't think she eggspected it to be quite so soon cos she did seem massively surprised… and not just cos I had a T-rex in my bag and he was a lot bigger than she'd eggspected, but when she saw what else was in there…

"So, let me get this straight? You have one bunch in and one bunch out because your mum overslept and you had to get yourself ready?"

"Yesth."

"The only food you could find in the house was jam tarts and sweets?"

"Yesth."

"You've brought roller boots to school because you had to drive yourself here?"

They're not roller boots, they're Heelies, but…

"Yesth."

"And lastly, you didn't realise that 'Cardi Breezers had booze in them'? Is that correct?"

"Yesth."

Ooh? The dinnerbell?

"Come back, Maddison!"

Bugger!

★★★

I think she believed me *mostly*, but she comfyskated everything 'cept Trev… but only cos I promised never to bring him to school with me again – it doesn't count if you've got your fingers crossed, does it? And I wasn't that bothered about the food cos I'd ate most of it, but she'd better give me my Heelies back at home time, else there'll be trouble.

"Okay children – quieten down!"

Quieten? Is that a actual word? Ooh, guess what? We had a competition at dinnertime to see who's had the best accident in the summer holidays, and Lucy Cho came third cos she fell off a very high wall, I came second with concushions, and Stephen Henderson came first cos he got kicked by a billy-goat at the petting zoo and he's still on actual crutches. So, then we had a competition to see who had the best illness and me and Matthew came second with Stralian chicken pots, but Kylie Pinkerton came first cos we all decided that pendysitus is miles worser than chicken pots – and Kylie nearly died!

Anyway, we're doing music now. I never used to like music with Mrs Jolley-Jelly cos she always gave me the same instrument, and what's the point in the triangle? You hardly ever hit the stupid thing, and when you do, it sounds rubbish. But Miss Spottiswood's letting everyone have a try of all the instraments to see who's good at what.

"Alan, take that mallet out of your mouth this instant! Do you want to choke on it?"

"See, Miss! That's why I ALWAYS have the xylo-phone."

"Quiet, Lucy. Excellent work there, Matthew."

"Did you hear that, Matthew? You're eggsellent at the – what'sth it called again?"

"Our Monica, and I'm just blowing it really."

"Well, you're blowin' it really – OW! PACK IT IN, CARL! That'sth where I got concushionsth an' it'sth still proply sore!"

"Carl Pilling. If I have to tell you once more about striking Maddison with your maracas, I'll— Yes, Maddison?"

"I can't make any noisthe come out thisth recorder."

"Try blowing harder, dear."

"I AM blowin' harder but it'sth just bubblin'."

"Bubbling? Pass it here. It's probably got a bit of— *huk… Huk… Huk!*"

"Are you gonna do a sick, Missth Spottisthwood?"

"No, dear… *huk*… just… carry on everyone, I'll be with you in a… *huk*… minute."

It's a shame there was so much gob in the recorder cos I was really enjoying music, but by the time Miss Spottiswood'd finished trying not to do a sick while she emptied it, the bell went. So, now it's our last lesson and we've been doing a picture about our favourite things so Miss Spottiswood can get to know us better. She told us to pick five things what tell her something about us… but I don't know how she's going to get to know Matthew cos I can only tell what three of his things are and I actually know him. I'll just check…

"Isth that a giraffe, Matthew?"

"No! That's my mum."

Oh? Two things – and since when's Elaine had a massive long neck?

"Oh. Right. Soz. But, that'sth me and Trev?"

"Yes. It's really good, isn't it?"

Not really. He's wrote Maddison and Trevor, with big arrows pointing at us.

"Yup. It'sth brilliant! An' I can tell that'sth space – an' they're planetsth…"

"Yes. Jupiter and Saturn. D'you know Jupiter's eleven times bigger than Earth?"

"Yesth, Matthew, costh you go on about space all the flippin' time."

"Do I? Hey, when I was in Australia I could see different stars cos it's a different part of the sky."

"Really? The sky'sth upsthide down asth well? So, how come you didn't fall off?"

"Off the world? Cos of gravity."

"Gravvy tea?"

"Yes. It's what stops you falling off."

"How?"

"Cos, it presses down on you."

"What, REALLY? Is it pressthing down on me now?"
I can't feel anything?

"It's always pressing down on you, Maddie."

"*Alwaysth?* What – even when I'm on the toilet?"

"Yes."

"Even when I'm asthleep?"

"Yes."

"What doesth it look like?"

"Nothing. It's invisible."

"IMVISTHIBLE? How d'you know it'sth there, then?"

"*Cos* – I've drawn other pictures too, Maddie!"

"Flippin' 'eck, I wasth only asthkin'."

I bet they don't fall off cos everyone's got sticky on the bottom of their shoes?

"Maddison and Matthew, less of the chattering please. I don't want to have to separate you."

"But, I've finished, Missth!"

"Really? Let me have a – is that a pig doing martial arts?"

"Yup! It'sth Missth Piggy doin' kung fu."

"And, what's this?"

"Can't you tell? It'sth my housthe on fire with all my family wavin' out the windowsth."

"Oh?"

"It'sth not *alwaysth* on fire. Just, when my brother getsth drunk an' cooksth pizztha."

"Oh? Right!"

"An' that'sth 'Dinosthaursth V Zombiesth', which isth my favourite…"

"It's okay, dear. I literally 'get the picture'. Okay, children, have we all finished? Yes? Then can everybody please wash their brushes and return to their seats."

"Crikey, Maddie, is it home time already?"

"Yup! Come on, Matthew, let'sth hurry up so'sth we can be first out."

"But, what about your Heelies?"

"Oh yeah! Will you wash my brush an' I'll go an' asthk for them?"

"Course."

I've decided, I specially like Miss Spottiswood – she gave me my Heelies and my sweets back and she's even let Trev have a smashing day at – Uh? Where's he gone? He was on my desk when I went to ask for my Heelies?

"Okay, children. I've really enjoyed getting to know you all today, but tomorrow we'll begin with…"

"WHERE'STH TREVOR?"

"Maddison, dear…"

"WHERE ISTH HE, CARL?"

"Maddison, please don't ball your fists…"

"Crikey, Maddie! Look on top of the book…"

"AH! YOU'RE DEAD, CARL PILLIN'!"

He absolutely IS! I'll teach him to paint other people's dinosaurs blue. And I know it was Carl cos he's covered in blue paint but there's absolutely none on his picture. And I heard him whisper to Lucy that next time he'll colour him in red! Poor Trev.

"And remember, children – don't forget to get those forms signed! Okay. Class dismissed!"

"Matthew, hold Trev for me, pleasthe."

"Oh, no, Maddie, what you gonna do? I don't want to get in trouble on the first day back."

"You're not gonna get in trouble, Matthew. Just hold Trev for a few minutesth."

"Okay, but…"

"Right – where isth he?"

"QUICK, MATTHEW – LEG IT! Mrsth Jolley'sth comin'…"

"Oh, good Lord, Carl – not again! WILL SOME-BODY GET THE BUTTER?"

★★★

"...no, Rache, it's your special day so he'll just have to grin and bear it. Listen, Maddie's home now, so speak later... I will, yes... love you, too... okay, bye! Hello sweetheart, Rache said – ohmigod! What on earth do you look like?"

Did she? That's a bit weird?

"What happened to your bunches?"

"Erm? One fell out, so I took the..."

"*Fell out?* And why is your jumper on inside out and back to front? And I suppose they ran out of paper, too?"

"What d'you mean?"

"Your polo shirt's covered in paint. And what's that all over your hands?"

"Erm? What?"

"What do you mean, *what*? They're bright red, Maddison!"

"Oh, yeah! I wonder what that'sth off? I'll just go upstairsth and wash them."

"Okay, but pick your coat up off the floor first, and – look at the state of your shoes! You've had them one day, Maddison. How do you do it?"

"*Well...*"

"One sec, sweetheart, just let me answer the phone. It'll be Rache again. She's really stressed about the wedding. This'll be the sixth call today. Hello, sweetie..."

Phew. I need to get the paint off Trev before my mum sees him and know's he's been to school.

She's got loads of stuff for washing her face so I'm sure she won't mind if I lend some. Hmm? I think this is the stuff what gets make-up off? That should do it? I'll just put loads on to make sure…

"Look at you, Trev! I don't think you've been this clean since I first got you."

I can't actually remember when I first got Trev cos I wasn't even one years old. But my mum remembers it really well, cos she said it was the first time I ever…

"MADDISON!"

"WAAH! I nearly jumped out my *skin*!"

"Good! Because – IS THAT MY CLEANSER? For God's sake, Maddie, is nothing sacred with you? That costs thirty pounds! And that was Mrs Jolley on the phone – the new deputy head – she said she's managed to get most of the red marker pen off Carl's face, but his head's grown since the last time you shoved it through the railings so his ears are rather swollen. What have you got to say, Maddie?"

Well, it's all come off my hands so she should use better soap? No, don't say that, Maddie… Hmm? I'm starving, actually?

"Have we got any Jaffa Cakesth?"

"WHAT? DID YOU REALLY JUST ASK IF WE HAVE ANY—?"

"Bloody 'ell, Liz, I can hear you screechin' from the top o' the driveway. What's up?"

"Sorry, Joe. How come you're home so early?"

"You know me, love, I don't hang about…"

Me neither. Quick, Maddison. Leg it! Or better still, run away. Or maybe just spy from behind the door and see how much trouble you're in first. Cos you do want to watch Horrible Histories in a bit and I'm sure you can smell basgetty and meatballs…

"She did *what*? To that Biffa Bacon kid? Hahaha…"

"It's not funny, Joe. Do you know how Mrs Jolley described her? AUDACIOUS!"

"Calm down, love! Fuckin' 'ell…"

"She's seven years old, Joe. She doesn't even know what audacious means!"

"*And?* Neither do I!"

"And she'd brought…"

"What's all the racket, Shortshanks? What've you done now?"

"Shush, Robbie. I'm trying to hear how much trouble I'm in."

"… Heelies, jam tarts, and a BACARDI SODDING BREEZER!"

"Holy shit! You took booze to school? Legend! Ha-hahaha…"

"Shurrup, Robbie, I'm try'na listen."

"… so she coloured Carl Pilling's face in with a red marker pen, then shoved his head through the school railings – again!"

"Jeeze, Shortshanks. Busy day, huh? What did the prick do this time?"

"Well, first he kept whackin' me on the head with his maracasth, right where I fell off my bike, an' then he pinched Trev an' painted him…"

"You took Suarez to school?"

"Yesth, but that'sth not inportant. I was just givin' Carl a taste of histh own medicine."

"I get *that*, but why shove his 'ead through the bars?"

"To stop him goin' mental! He swinged his bag in

284

the back of Alliah'sth head and knocked her glassesth off costh she said he looked like Red off Angry Birdsth, then he shouted imfront of everyone, 'Least my mum an' dad love me enough to take me on a proper holiday, MEDICINE'! Then he pushed Alan over an' went to kick Matthew – with histh 'mad face' on – so, I just did it."

"How badass are you? What they sayin', Mum 'n' Dad?"

"I don't know costh I'm talkin' to you. Shush! …"

"… stop laughing, Joe, it's not funny. Why don't you ever back me up?"

"Sorry, love, but it is a bit. He's twice her size! Did you ask 'er why she did it?"

"No. Mrs Jolley said that Miss Spottiswood said…"

"Spottiswood? Didn't she teach the other two?"

"Yes, she was Rache's favourite teacher. She really knew how to get the best out of…"

"Didn't she 'ave Pontoon eyes? One sticks an' one twists?"

"She has a lazy eye, Joe, and DON'T let Maddie hear you say that."

Pontoon eyes? What on earth's that?

"Shit. Not another parents' evenin' with her. Remember, Liz? We didn't know which one of us she was talkin' to so we both kept answerin' at the same time?"

"Yes… Anyway, she said Carl Pilling painted Trevor…"

"Trevor? What the fuck's Godzilla doin' at school?"

"I don't know. Did *you* check her bag this morning? *No?* Me neither."

"Shit. We're not back to this again, are we? I thought she'd outgrown it?"

"I guess she thought she'd try her luck with a new teacher. Honestly, I'm at my wit's end."

"'Ey, Shortshanks, she's all right, old Spottiswood."

"I know, Robbie. Hey, guessth what? She told everyone 'bout you eatin' seven inchesth of your ruler. Did you?"

"Haha, *yeh*, I forgot about that."

"Why did you eat wood? You're not a flippin' beaver!"

"There's a massive double entendre in there, Short-shanks, but I'm too hungry to think. D'you know what's for tea?"

"Well, it'sth definitely not wood! *Weirdo!* I'll *never* eat wood."

"Hahahahaha. Trust me – you will when you're older! I'll go 'n' see if tea's ready an' I'll see if I can help you out. Mind out the way…"

Wow? Robbie's being nice to me again?

"So, Joe? What d'you suggest we do?"

"What you askin' me for? Ey up, son!"

"Uh…"

"Jeeze, it's the walkin' dead!"

"What's for tea, Mum?"

"Bloody 'ell. It speaks!"

"Yes, Joe, it has three sentences. What's for tea? I'm going out. And can you lend me twenty quid please? Which roughly translates as, can I *have* twenty pounds because you'll never see it again. Oh, and the response to any question you ask is, 'dunno'. Which doesn't really qualify as a sentence, but…"

"What is this? Pick-on-Robbie day? *Fucksake…*"

"Oy, Softlad – watch ya bloody language! An' how come you weren't in college today?"

"Cos, it's shut – Duh! We don't go back till next week."

"Yeh, well, you'd better finish whatever the hell it is you're doin' this year. What is it, again?"

"Art an' photography."

"What the bloody hell kind of a course is that? An' I mean it, Rob, this is your last year pissin' about at college. If you don't finish this course, you're either out on your arse, or you're comin' to work with me."

"Joe, can we deal with one dysfunctional offspring at a time, please? What about Maddie?"

"D'you know why she did it, Mum?"

"It doesn't matter why she did it…"

"Course, it does! The little shit was takin' the piss out of her, sayin' you didn't love her enough to take her on a proper holiday. Then he kept twattin' 'er on the head where she fell off 'er…"

"ROBBIE! Don't say that word! Did he *really* say that to her?"

"Yeh, in front of everyone. Then he went for little Matty so she stopped him. Nowt wrong wi' that. Anyway, I'm starvin'. I only came down to see if tea's ready. What we 'avin?"

"It's homemade pasta with pork and fennel meatballs, and I found a new recipe for…"

"Sounds good that, love. Are you doin' chips?"

"I'll pretend I didn't hear that. Right, everybody, wash your hands. MADDIE! COME DOWN FOR YOUR…"

"I don't need to wash my handsth, Mum. That stuff'sth really good for gettin'…"

"How did you appear so quickly? Oh, Joe, guess what she used to clean Trevor with? My Chanel cleanser! Anyway, Maddie, your dad and I have decided that…"

"Have we? I don't remember sayin' a bloody word?"

"We've decided that…"

"Hey, Shortshanks, tell Dad what you said before. About when I ate my ruler."

"D'you mean, when I said about eatin' seven inchesth of wood? When I said – what you laughing at, Dad? What'sth he laughin' at, Mum?"

"I have no idea, sweetheart. Joe? Robbie? What's so funny?"

"Hahaha. You don't know what wood is, Mum?"

"Take no notice of them, sweetheart. Nobody wants to eat wood."

"Speak for yourself, love! I would, if I could reach. Hahahaha…"

"What on earth are you talking abo—OH! THAT WOOD! Erm? Who wants parmesan?"

"No ta, Mum, it stinks o' puke. An' your mobile's goin' off again."

★★★

Well, it *was* Rache that time. Honestly, she's completely

hysterical about the wedding. Every morning she phones my mum to tell her about her weird wedding dreams but I've promised I'm not gonna spoil it, and I'm definitely not gonna turn into a zombie and eat all the flippin' guests. Can you believe I actually got warned about doing that?

Anyway, my mum calmed down 'ventually and what she decided is… oops? I can't remember? Whatever, I'd better do as I'm told and go to sleep cos I can't really afford to get in any more trouble today. I mean, it's only fifteen weeks till Christmas and I don't want to completely ruin my chances of getting a Xbox. So… Hmm? What if I say my prayers, to make me be good? Good idea, Maddison.

"Our Father, who'sth art'sth in heaven. Hello be my name."

See you all soon everyone.

Goodnight!

Hens and Chickens

"Sweetheart – *please*. Just – go away! You're driving me insane!"

"But, why can't I come?"

"Maddie, I've told you a million times already. You're not old enough."

"But, what if I put tall shoesth on?"

"Hahaha. I don't think that will help."

"Well, what *will* help?"

"Nothing! You have to be eighteen to…"

"UGH! It'sth NOT FAIR!"

Honestly, I'm so cross. I've been trying for ages to get my mum to change her mind about me going, but – what eggsacly is a hen's party, anyway? I know it's where girls go before they get married, but what's so special that I'm not allowed to go?

She's MY flippin' sister, so how come everyone else

gets to go and not me? Elaine isn't even Rache's friend – imfact she's only my mum's friend cos of me and Matthew – and Adele's going, and she's not even going to the wedding. How annoying's that! Stupid hen's party. And what do hens do at parties, anyway? Actually…

"Mum, what'sth the difference between a chicken an' a hen?"

"Maddie, am I EVER going to finish getting ready?"

How should I know?

"And, I thought I told you to go away."

"I thought you meant go away about hensth' parties, not actual hensth."

"I meant go away, full stop! What did you want to know? The difference between a chicken and a hen?"

"Yesth. Costh, aren't they the same animal?"

"They are."

"So, Rache could have a chicken'sth party, and I could asthk for hen nuggeths?"

"You could, but people would think you were strange. A hen is female, but a chicken can be male or female."

"Like Mrsth Doubtfire?"

"Hahaha… *no!* And how do you know Mrs Doubtfire?"

"Robbie showed me her on YouTube. He said she looksth 'xactly like Matthew'sth nanna, an' she doesth!"

"Well, no, not like Mrs Doubtfire. Okay, for example, you'd say, 'Look at that horse!'"

"OOH! Where?"

"No, there isn't a horse…"

Make your flippin' mind up?

"…but if there was, you'd say horse. Now, if you knew it was a female horse, you could say mare, or if it was a male horse you could say stallion. It's the same with lots of animals, really. We have ewes and rams, but collectively we call them sheep."

"So, what'sth a boy hen called?"

"A male chicken's called a…"

"Bloody 'ell, love, aren't you ready yet? I've cleaned the car, the van, an' mowed the lawns an' you're still goin' at it. An' you look miles better without all that shite on your face. How much're you trowellin' on?"

"First of all, I'm not trowelling it on, and secondly, why do you think you've managed to get so much done? Perhaps, because you haven't spent the last few hours being grilled by a miniature member of the Spanish Inquisition? Honestly, every two seconds, 'BUT, WHY CAN'T I GO TO THE HEN'S PARTY?'"

"Hahaha – *probably!* An' you're not goin', princess, so end of! So, love, what time did you say the transport's comin'? It's just, the match kicks off at five thirty, so I don't know whether I'd be better to record it then watch it after you've gone."

"Well, Elaine and I are the first pick-up, so around six-*ish*."

"I'll record it then. I wonder how much I'll get to see with Tilly Mint, 'ere."

Tilly Mint? I thought it was just me and my dad watching the football?

"I'm sorry, Joe, I know it's a big game, but I had no say in when Rache decided to have her hen do, and I doubt she could care less who or when Liverpool are playing."

"I know – selfish bitch! I'm kiddin', Liz. Princess, promise me when you get married, you'll check the fixture list first."

"ME? I'm NEVER gettin' married. I'm gonna live with you FOR *EVER*!"

"Don't you threaten me, kiddo! You're gettin' married at sixteen, if I 'ave to bloody well pay someone."

"We're *never* gonna leave home, are we, Trev? No, Maddithon, costh we love them too much an' we'd be sad without them… *roaaaaaar*!"

"Aww… isn't that lovely, Joe?"

"Lovely? It's bloody terrifyin'!"

"That'sth not very nice! An' you still never answered my question. What'sth a boy chicken called?"

"What d'ya wanna know that for, princess?"

"Costh of the hen'sth party."

"Aah! I see. It's a cock."

"A COCK?"

"Well done, Joe…"

"Like, cock-a-doodle-do?"

"Yes, sweetheart – exactly like cock-a-doodle-doo. I was going to say cockerel, Joe."

"Why? Who the bloody 'ell calls it a cockerel?"

"So, Mum, when boysth get married do they have COCK partiesth?"

"That's why. No, sweetheart. Boys have a stag do."

"A STAG DO? What'sth a stag?"

"A stag is a male deer."

"A REINDEER? Like, Rudolph?"

"*What?* Yes, I suppose. So, when a man gets married, he has a stag…"

"ISTH JONATHON GETTIN' A REINDEER?"

"WHAT? Joe, please. For God's sake, take her downstairs and out of my way. The transport will be here soon and I'm nowhere near ready."

Humph! I'm nobody's friend. And why d'you have to be eighteen to go to a hen's party? It can't be that grown up cos my mum's wearing big fluffy rabbit's ears and – UH? What's going on? Are we on fire again? I can't smell pizza burning, but a massive fire engine's just stopped in front of our house and – ohmigod? A actual fireman's walking up our drive…

"MUM… DAD… PIZZTHA… I MEAN, FIRE! FIRE, EVERYONE!"

"Calm down, princess, it's not a real fire engine. It's your mum's lift."

"WHAT? My mum'sth goin' to the hen'sth party in a fire engine? But, I want a go in a fire engine…"

"I take it the transport's here, Joe?"

Ohmigod? My mum looks like a movie star?

"I don't know what time I'll be back, Joe, but…"

Jessica Rabbit, actually?

"Friggin' 'ell, Liz. How come you never look like that when I take you out?"

"Because, I'm slightly over-dressed for Nandos or Wetherspoons!"

"You cheeky mare – you're the one who can't be

arsed goin' anywhere! I've asked you loads o' times if you fancy goin' out, but you'd rather stay in an' watch Strictly Come what's-it-called, or Ant an' bloody Dec."

"What can I say, Joe? I'm not much of a drinker. Anyway, as I was saying. I don't know what time I'll be back, but make sure Maddie's in bed by ten."

"She'll be lucky if she lasts that long, love."

"And make sure she cleans her teeth before she goes to bed. And don't let her eat all kinds of…"

"I know how to look after my own daughter, Liz. Go on, go! You're givin' me a boner stood there."

I've never seen my mum look like this before. She's done proper make-up like Rache does, when she sticks extra eyelashes on and everything, and her hair's gone absolutely massive. She looks a bit like Malifisense, actually. 'Cept she's wearing rabbit ears and her dress is a bit rude. And her shoes are so tall she looks like a actual giant.

"An' 'ey – don't do anythin' I wouldn't do!"

"Don't worry, Joe, I have no desire to steal traffic cones and get myself arrested. Give Mummy a kiss, sweetheart. Mwah! And, Maddie, remember what I said?"

"Yup! If I want to go to the Splash Zone tomorrow, I have to be on my very best behaviour. An' do I get good pointsth for my Xboxth, too?"

"I think we'll see how the wedding goes first and then we'll discuss your Xbox. Right. Bye, you two. And, Maddie, be a good girl for your dad."

Well, the good news is, we *can* go to The Chicken Shack for our tea, but the bad news is, we can't go till after this football's finished... but I'm completely starving now, and how much longer's it gonna be? It's been ages already and I don't understand anything what's going on. All I know is, no one's scored a goal yet and the referee's a wanker. That's what you call someone what gets something wrong, apparently, like when Liverpool should've got a penalty and the other team's man should've got sent off.

My dad said he'd make me a butty at half-time but I don't know when that is, and it's probly best not to ask just yet, cos if I ask one more question he's gonna cellar tape my gob shut and he won't take it off till it's time for me to eat. But, I haven't asked that many questions.

Just, how long do they play for? Why are Liverpool called 'The Reds'? Why aren't they wearing red? What does playing away mean? Where do Liverpool play at home? Why are most of them wearing odd colour shoes? Why do they keep spitting on the grass? How come it's allowed to spit on the grass? Why do they fall over so easy? Why did they carry him off? Why did he run straight back on? Is it allowed to run straight back on? Why can't they hit it in the goal? What's a corner? What's offside? What's a wanker? Ooh? I've just thought...

"Dad, what happensth at half-time?"

"Half-time, princess? Well in thirty-five minutes when the ref blows the whistle, the players'll go off to the changin' rooms an' I'll be gettin' the gaffa tape out the van! Does that answer your question?"

Bugger.

Bored. Bored. Bored. Bored. Bored. It must be nearly time now? Course, it seems longer cos of when we had to pause the telly... but, if my dad didn't shout so loud everytime Liverpool nearly scored a goal, then I wouldn't have jumped out my skin and chucked my Ribena all over him, and Spud wouldn't have wagged his tail so hard that he smashed his Liverpool mug... and if Liverpool don't win it's all my fault apparently, cos now he's not wearing his lucky shirt. Meh!

"Jesus, Maddie, stop bloody fidgetin', will ya?"

"But, I'm *booored*. Has it nearly finished yet?"

"If you're bored, why don't you go 'n' ask our Rob if he wants anythin' from The Chicken Shack later?"

Yes. Good idea. And it might be nearly over by then.

I can't believe there's this much fuss over football. I don't understand why my dad loves it so much. Or Robbie? And I thought old people fall over easy but football players fall over if someone just runs past them. Mind you, I'm not surprised with all that gob on the grass – which is absolutely disgusting!

Right, I have to be careful now cos Robbie gets so cross watching the football that he sometimes chucks stuff at his telly...

BANG!

"Robbie, my dad said..."

"Once again, come in, Maddison."

"I *am* in! Oh, what'sth it called again? That thing you're bein'? Startastic?"

"Close enough. What d'ya want?"

"My dad said d'you want anythin' from – are you

watchin' the football too?"

"What's it look like, Einstein? Hang on a sec, there's only a few – SHIT!"

"What'sth up?"

"Full time."

"It'sth finished?"

"Yeh – an' that's ninety minutes of my life I won't get back. Nil friggin' nil – how borin's that? What were ya gonna say? Do I want any what?"

"Oh yeah, d'you want anythin' from The Chicken Shack?"

"Aye, go on then. I'll have a big bucket o' chicken, ta. An' close the door be'ind ya!"

Thank goodness it's finished. Football's okay I s'pose, but mostly it's just men running round, falling over and gobbing on the grass – which wouldn't be so bad if it only lasted a few minutes or if something intresting actually happened, but… one sec…

"Dad, Robbie wantsth a big bucket of chicken, ta."

"Does he, now? Okay, princess, the second half's startin' in a…"

"WHAT? You're KIDDIN'? But, it'sth finished up-stairsth! I'm goin' back up then…"

"Oh, no, you're not! You can stay 'ere, where I can keep my eye on ya!"

"But it'sth BORIN'! An' no one even scoresth a GOAL!"

"OH FOR— what the bloody 'ell did you say that for, Maddie?"

"What? What've I said?"

"So much for bloody recordin' it! Well, that's that ruined!"

"Soz… Doesth that mean we can go to the chicken shop now?"

"I suppose so. Anythin' to shut you up. Right, get your coat on. An' you can leave Godzilla 'ere – we won't be gone that long."

★★★

Flippin' 'eck, it's absolutely boiling in the chicken shop. Imfact, I'm going dizzy I'm so hot. And the queue's flippin' massive, too. But worser still, the man behind us is wearing a Manchester United shirt, and him and my dad've been arguing 'bout football ever since we came in…

"Who – *Giggs*? It's Gerrard, all day…"

"Dad, *pleasthe* can I take my coat off? I'm abstholutely boilin'."

"No, you'll only leave it somewhere. Anyway mate, Liverpool've won five Champions League titles so…"

"But, Dad, I'm *boilin'*!"

"Well, you'll just have to bloody well boil! An' how many 'ave United won? Three, isn't it?"

"But, I can't. I might boil to actual deaf!"

"Don't talk stupid, an' can't you see I'm talkin', princess?"

Yes? But what's more inportant? You talking, or me dying of hot?

"Yeh, well, we'll see how we go on with Klopp, 'ey…"

Clop? Horses go clop? What's that got to do with football?
God's sakes. How much longer in this – Ooh? I've just had a idea?

"Dad, you know if I can't take my coat off?"

"Will you SHUT UP about your BLOODY COAT, Maddie!"

"GOD'STH SAKESTH! Well, will you LEASTHT give me a BLOW JOB, THEN?"

Hmm? Well, that was all a bit weird? I didn't hear what everyone in the queue was laughing at eggsacly, and no one seemed to be able to stop laughing long enough to tell me, but least my dad took my coat off me straight away and him and Mister Manchester seem to be best friends all of a sudden. Imfact, everyone seems to be – yes! At last, it's our turn...

"Who's next?"

"Hiyah, mate. Can I have one extra-large bucket o' chicken; a Cajun meal deal an' – 'ave you decided what you want yet, princess?"

"YUP! Can I have SIXTH HEN NUGGETSTH pleasthe. An' a LARGE COCK PORN COCK!"

"JESUS CHRIST! Sorry mate, she means a large popcorn chicken. How many times, princess? It's pop corn, not..."

"But, I thought it wasth cock? Like a boy chicken?"

"Yeh, well, you know what thought did? Pee'd the bed an' thought he was sweatin'!"

WHAT?

"There you go, sir. I'll just get your sauces."

"Cheers mate. Here, Maddie. Grab hold o' yours, kiddo."

Pea'd the bed? What does that – UH? These aren't chicken nuggets?

"DAD! DAD!"

"Pipe down, princess, there's no need to shout. What?"

"He'sth got mine wrong – LOOK!"

"All right, keep ya wig on! 'EY, MATE! She asked for nuggets, not wings."

I definitely did. It's him what's got it— ooh?

"Hey, Dad – what a MASSTHIVE WANK– *nooooooo*! Don't drag me out! I've not even got my dinner!"

★★★

Well, besides my dad imbarrassing me when he dragged me out before I'd even got my dinner – oh, and locking me in the car while he went back in to get it – and then being specially grumpy cos we had to go back for my coat – I'm having the best night ever! Imfact, I've decided that my mum should go out more often.

My dad's not in the least bit bothered about how much ketchup I eat or how much fizzy pop I drink, and he proply laughed his head off at me doing burp songs. Imfact, he only made me stop when I nearly did a sick out of my nose, but 'Ten Green Bottles' does go on for ages? Then he let me choose a deevy dee so I choosed *Avatar* – 200 minutes! And every time I talked he put a Jaffa Cake in my mouth – and I talked through two whole tubes!

Anyway, it's half past eleven o'clock at night and I'm in bed – with my telly on – I know! Watching *Godzilla* – 140 minutes – and it's a good job it's a extra-long movie cos I'm absolutely wide awake! And I feel a bit eggcited, but I don't know why? I wonder if this is why my mum doesn't let me eat too much sugar? I have had quite a lot.

★★★

Flippin' 'eck. It's quarter past two o'clock in the morning – *Godzilla*'s finished, and I'm still wide-a-flippin'-wake. I've just been downstairs to ask my dad if I could have a drink but he was fast asleep on the couch, and he didn't even notice when I fell off the chair trying to reach the chocolate biscuits. So, now I'm just listening outside Robbie's bedroom door cos he's playing on his Xbox, and it's so funny. He puts his headset on then talks to his friends down the micra phone, but you can't hear them talking, so it sounds like he's talking to himself. Listen. He sounds proper mental…

"'Ave that, ya bastard! Yes! Get in… … … Hahaha. You what? Is she the one with hair extensions an' massive tits? He's talkin' shite, man! No way's he nailed…"

Ooh? Someone's trying to open the front door? I hope it's my mum, and not burglars?

"HE-LLO-O!"

Definitely not burglars. WAY too noisy.

"JOEY, I'M HO-OME— OW! Who left that there? HIC! *Oh, it's the door…*"

OHMIGOD? What's happened to my mum?

"JO-SEPH! WHERE ARE YOOOOOO? THERE YOU… HIC! Are!"

"Bloody 'ell, Liz, keep it down, will ya? Jesus Christ – how much have you 'ad to *drink*?"

"I've had lotsh and lotsh and lotsh and lotsh and hic! And, lotsh…"

"Okay, love, I get the gist. Jeeze, what've you been drinkin' – Absinthe?"

"I've had champagne – *lotsh*! Then we went on to HIC! cocktails HIC! Rache said we could only have one's with sexual HIC! connotationsh. So, I had an Orgasm, which was *very* HIC! nice."

"I bet it was."

"Then HIC! I had a Shlippery HIC! Nipple. Oh, yesh, that reminds HIC! OW! That hurt! This guy wouldn't leave me HIC! alone HIC! so, I pretended to be a lesbian… and Adele's a surprisingly good HIC! kisser."

Uh?

"HIC! I wish these stupid hiccupsh would go away. Would you like to kiss me, Joe?"

"Er… I would, love, but you're makin' my eyes stream."

How? Is she poking them? I can't see.

"*AM I?* Hey, guessh HIC! what else I had? A Long Comfortable Screw Up Against the Wall followed by a Screaming Orgasm. The Screaming Orgasm was my HIC! favourite. *So creamy.* Doesh my voice sound hoarse, Joe? I've been shouting all HIC! NIGHT!"

"Yeh, you sound husky as hell. You're givin' me an 'ard on, love, so stop talkin'…"

"Why? HIC! OW! Ooh, that hurt."

"Cos, you're absolutely shit-faced! Look at the state o' you! You can't even stand up!"

"HIC! *Saysh who?* Hey, I'll tell you something, Joe. I'm so glad I'm not HIC! shingle. Honestly, I didn't shee a shingle guy I hic fancied all night…"

"Ha! I bet they were all quein' up to see you. What state's our Rache in?"

"Trollied. Have you heard that before, Joe? Trollied? I don't HIC! know what it means. Anyway, Jonathon's promised he'll look after her. Hey, Joe, do you want to look after me? We could play doctorsh and nursesh?"

Doctors and nurses? I love playing that?

"Another time 'ey, love? Maybe, when you're a bit more sober?"

"Don't be HIC! boring! *I'll* be the nurshe, and *you* can be the patient, and…"

"You're pissed as a fart, love! It's more likely, I'll be the doctor; or vet – take those bloody rabbit ears off – an' you'll be the patient."

"AN' I'LL BE THE NURSTHE! I'll just get my…"

"ER? WHAT THE BLOODY 'ELL ARE YOU DOIN' UP? It's three in the friggin'…"

"MADDIEEEEEE… MY LITTLE BABY! Aren't you beautiful? Isn't she beautiful, Joe?"

"Yes, Liz, very beautiful – an' outta friggin' bed! Why aren't you asleep, princess?"

"Erm? I wasth… but my mum waked me up bein' noisthy. Are you drunk, Mum?"

"*Noooooo*, HIC! *sweetheart!* Mummy'sh not *drunk!*

Come and give me a kissh. D'you know how much I love you, Maddiepants?"

Maddiepants? Why's she calling me that?

"Have you been a good girl for – HIC – daddy?"

"YUP! I've been on my very best behaviour, so…"

"Come on, princess, I'll take you back to bed. Say goodnight to your mum – not that she'll remember a bloody thing in the mornin'."

She better had! I've been good as gold all night cos she promised to take me and Matthew to The Splash Zone in the morning.

"Night, Mum."

"Night, sweetheart. And hurry back, Joe, I'll be HIC! Waiting."

Waiting for what?

Whatever it was, my dad was in a proper hurry to get back. I think he's scared she'll do 'a Robbie', which is be sick on the carpet then set fire to pizza. Whatever, I'm actually quite tired now, and I don't want to be tired tomorrow for when we go to the – what's all that noise outside my bedroom door? I'll NEVER get to sleep…

"It's all right, son, she's pissed, that's all. Go back to bed."

"I've never seen mum drunk before."

"*Drunk?* She's fuckin' hammered! Why d'you think I'm carryin' her?"

"Dad, watch her head on the…"

"Shit! Sorry, love. But, she'll have bigger problems than a bang on the 'ead tomorrow. She's promised to take our Maddie an' Mattie to The Splash Zone in the mornin'."

"Ha! Like that's happenin'!"

"I know, son. Night."

"Night, Dad."

"Night, Big Ears. No doubt you're earwiggin' through the door as always."

"No, I'm not!"

"Then, how did you manage to 'ear that?"

Oh, yeah? Hmm? I wonder if my dad'll take us to the Splash Zone tomorrow, instead?

"*Daaaaad…*"

"Night, princess. Sweet dreams. An' before you bother askin' – no, I won't take you to…"

"Joe… I don't feel very— *oh, no. I think I'm going to be*– GETMEABUCKET!"

Oh, well, never mind. Actually, I might be too tired to go myself tomorrow. Or, is it today? Imfact, it's so late, I don't know whether to say good morning or… yaaawn, I'm really sleepy now, so, see you at the wedding, everyone…

Goodnight!

The Wedding: Part 1

"No, Maddison, I said you could play out in the street – I didn't mention *anything* about going across to the fields, and if I have to send a search party out looking for you ONE MORE TIME! Honestly, as much as I love you there are times when I could happily strangle you."

Thanks…

"And what are you wittering on about? What bullet-proof vest?"

"The one what'sth got SWAT on the front from when we went to Stefanosth Popple Octopusth'sth copsth and robbersth party."

Flippin' eck? I think that's the hardest sentence I've ever said?

"Oh, that! No, Maddie, you may not take a bullet-proof vest to your sister's wedding. And will you stop calling him Stefanos Poppleoctopus – I'm sick to death of hearing that name! And get a move on – we're already an hour late because of you!"

Is it rude to tell your mum to shut her gob?

"And what part of 'keep yourself clean' didn't you understand?"

I understood all of it… I just didn't manage to do it…

"I didn't even know you could pick blackberries in October."

Well, you know now…

"But, I suppose that's global warming for you. And look at the state of your face. Let me have one last…"

"*Noooo*. It'sth really sore an' I've got no skin left!"

"But, you look demented – like Ronald McDonald crossed with an axe murderer! It had better be gone by tomorrow, Maddie. And look at your hands – could they BE any more stained?"

Hmm? Probly not? They are bright purple…

"Of all the days to rub blackberries into your cheeks, Maddison, why choose the day before your sister's wedding?"

"Costh, I wanted to look like Noddy."

"Well, you don't look anything like Noddy. Now are you SURE you don't want to go to the toilet before we set off?"

Flippin' 'eck? How many more times?

"Posthitive!"

"Okay. Get in the car and ask Robbie to make sure your seatbelt's fastened properly – and make sure you keep it on."

Humph! I don't even want to go to the stupid wedding. Well, I do, but… one sec…

"What you lookin' at, nosthe disthease?"

"What d'ya think, knobchops? Our Rache's gonna be over the feckin' moon when she discovers she's got Pennywise for a bridesmaid."

"Who'sth Pennywisthe?"

"Bloody 'ell, Liz, can't you get any more off? She's friggin' purple!"

"I know, but, barring dermabrasion, I'm afraid that's it. Do you think it'll have faded by tomorrow?"

"I bloody well 'ope so! She looks like the Joker from *The Dark Knight!*"

"Nice one, Dad – best movie psychopath, ever."

"I'm not a flippin' cycle path, an' will everyone stop talkin' 'bout what I – STOP IT, ROBBIE! Mum, tell him! He'sth takin' photosth of me again!"

"Don't, Robbie."

"What? I'm not doin' anythin'!"

"Yesth, you – AH! You've just took a other one. STOP IT!"

"Stop what?"

"IT!"

"Hahaha. That's who Pennywise is. The scary-ass clown from Stephen King's…"

"I do NOT look like a CLOWN!"

"I beg to— SHIT! That hurt, you vicious little midget! She just dead-armed me."

"Well – OW! STOP FLICKIN' ME, ROBBIE!"

"THEN, DON'T PUNCH ME, MADDITHON!"

"FOR FECK'S SAKE – SHUT IT – THE PAIR OF YA! We haven't even got off the bloody driveway yet! An' shift your noggin' out my rear window, block'ead. I can't see a bloody thing."

God's sakes. This is gonna be flippin' torture. I have to sit next to Robbie for over 200 miles, which is gonna take nearly four hours my dad said, all to watch Rache get married in Scotland.

Why couldn't she have got married at home? Why's she going to Jonathon's mum and dad's house to do it? Cos they live in a state near Headinburrow – which is the capital of Scotland case you didn't know – and that's in a whole different country! And it sounds well dangerous cos Rache said I'm absolutely not allowed to wander off once I get to the party or I might get shot. Actually shot! And she's a hundred percent not joking. And who has a party in the back garden where there's people running round with guns? Anyway, there's not enough room to stay at Jonathon's mum and dad's house tonight and my dad's too tight to pay for a hotel, apparently, so we're staying at his auntie's house instead.

She's called Harriet and she lives on a farm, and – oh? Erm? You might want to plug your ears for a minute, actually…

"… an' the one time I want her to come – to separate these two – an' she's galavantin' round the Highlands with that Mavis!"

"Joe, don't talk about my mum like that, and it's not her fault our children are feral. Anyway, she said she should be at Aunt Harriet's around seven, depending on the coach driver."

"Whoop-de-feckin-doo!"

"*Muuuuuum.*"

"Yes, Maddison?"

"I need a wee."

"You're kidding? How many times did I tell you to go before we set off?"

"But, I didn't want to go then."

"But, we've only been driving ten minutes. How far is it to the next services, Joe?"

"'Bout twenty miles. She'll just 'ave to hold it."

"Do you think you can manage that, sweetheart?"

Have I got any choice?

***

I don't know why I always want to go to the toilet as soon as we start driving, but I do. And I don't know why grown-ups think I can go when they tell me to cos I'm not magic. Anyway, we're back driving again and…

"Sweetheart, shall we play I Spy?"

I hate eye spy…

"Would you like to go first?"

Not really…

"Erm? Thisth one'sth easthy. Eye sthpy with my little eye, somethin' beginnin' with c."

"Is that a curly c? Or kicking k?"

"Curly."

"Okay. Is it car?"

"Nope."

"Coat?"

"Nope."

"Cardigan?"

"Nope."

"I've got one, Shortshanks. Clown?"

"NOT FUNNY, ROBBIE!"

"OW! What did I say about punchin' me? *Dick'ead.*"

"What did I say 'bout callin' me a clown, dickhead?"

"Oy! Pack in sayin' dick'ead! Both o' ya!"

They've been guessing for ages now and I can't believe they've not got it. It's SO easy…

"Chair?"

"*Chair?*"

"Car seat, then."

"Nope."

"Can?"

"Nope."

"Coca-Co—?"

"For God's sake, Mum, give in will ya? It's doin' my swede in."

"Mum, doesth sthweed mean head?"

"It does, sweetheart – and okay, we give in. What is it?"

"Cow."

"COW? Where's there a bloody COW in the CAR?"

"It'sth not *in* the car, Dad, it wasth in a field when I spied it."

"What the—? That's not how you play I Spy!"

It's how I play it?

"God, you're a tit, Shortshanks."

"Mum, tell Robbie. He just called me a TIT!"

"Don't call her that, Robbie!"

"Well, she is. Half an hour try'na guess somethin' what's fifteen miles back down the road. Total tit."

"*Shit off, Robbie.*"

"Hahahahahaha. Did you hear that, Mum? She just told me to shit off!"

"NO, I DIDN'T! I didn't, Mum, he'sth makin' it up."

I did, but he wasn't s'posed to hear.

"Will you two SHUT UP! I'm try'na soddin' well drive 'ere! Remember that film, Liz, *Sophie's Choice*? You blubbed all the way through it? Well, now it's your turn – cos if they don't pack it in I'm pullin' over an' you can pick which one you wanna keep."

Hmm? I don't think it'll be me cos…

"Dad, I need the toilet."

"Jesus Christ! What is this, Maddie? A Grand Tour o' the service stations along the M6? How much as she 'ad to drink, love?"

"It'sth not a wee, it'sth a poo, an' it'sth proply comin' out."

"Friggin' nora. Are we ever gonna bloody well get there? You've got two miles to the next services. I'll wait at the entrance. Again!"

★★★

Oh, my goodness – *that* wasn't normal! I've just proply eggsploded.

"Right, princess. That was your last stop. Next time you'll have to shove a plug in it!"

"Isn't she a bit young for a butt plug, Dad? Hahaha…"

"What'sth a–?"

"Never you mind, princess."

It would've been funny if my tummy wasn't hurting so much or – uh-oh? I feel like I want to go again? Hmm? This isn't good? Specially cos my dad's only just got back on the motorway and he's still moaning from the last time…

"She'd better not be plannin' to shit her way up the M6, Liz!"

"I'm sure she's fine now, Joe."

She isn't… imfact…

"Dad! Stop the car!"

"OH FOR – what is it THIS time?"

"I need another poo. My tummy hurtsth."

"ANOTHER ONE? Is she doin' a sponsored crap-a-thon?"

"Stop shouting, Joe. I wonder if it's the blackber-ries?"

"HOW CAN IT BE? SHE'S WEARIN' MOST OF 'EM!"

"I guess that depends how many there were. How many did you eat, sweetheart?"

"Erm? Millionsth… Ooh! It'sth comin' out."

"She'll have to hold it, Liz. It's fifteen miles to the next services."

"But, I *can't!*"

"Well, you'll 'ave to."

"BUT I CAN'T!"

I've never done a poo in a carrier bag at the side of the road before and now I've done three. And it was lucky my face was already red cos it was *well* imbarrassing. And it's not my fault cos I didn't know eating millions of blackberries would give me dire rear.

Anyway, we're ventually here – after six and a half hours! I know! My dad said I should get a medal for being the most annoying person to be stuck in a car with. But, I didn't go to the toilet at *every* service station from our house to Headinburrow, cos one time, well – I'm not deaf, I just didn't hear proply, and I could have swored the lady on the radio said that *One Direction* were at the services after junction two, and not 'The traffic's moving in one direction after the services at junction two'. But, it was the only time I pretended to need the toilet and I didn't mean to go across the bridge and get lost. And what's so bad about rush hour traffic anyway?

Anyway, I could tell when we were getting close to being here cos my mum started giving me loads more instructions. First, the usual ones: mind my manners; don't keep saying 'WHAT?'; keep my voice down; don't be nosy; don't make a holy show of her – like I'm gonna do – *eeeuw, what's that horrible smell?*

"POOH! It abstholutely STINKSTH out here. Sniff up, everyone!"

"Keep your voice down, fog'orn. You'll frighten the pigs."

"Pigsth? What pigsth? IS THIS IT?"

"Keep your bloody voice down!"

"But, it'sth mostly fallen down?"

"It 'asn't, princess, it's just a very old farm'ouse, that's all."

"But half of it'sth on the floor? An' why'sth the door so tiny? You an' Robbie'll…"

"Shush, sweetheart, she's here. Now remember…"

I know! Stop going on! Don't make a holy show of you, blah blah blah…

"Joseph! Alizabeth!"

"OHMIGOD, MUM! Hasth she been pickin' black-berriesth too? Her face isth nearly asth purple asth mine!"

"Keep your voice down, Maddie. Hello, Harriet!"

But, it is. And I don't think she's much taller than me, either?

"Och, ye wee bairns. Leuk at ye all. A misst ye sae muckle!"

"WHAT – OW! You're sthqueezin' my hand, Mum!"

"Yes, and I'll stop squeezing it when you stop shouting. Harriet, how lovely to see you."

"Aye! Ye all tae. Come away ben the hoose. Joseph, if ye'd like tae take ye bags upstairs, A'll stack the kettle on. So, Maddison, hou ar ye after the jerney?"

"WHAT?"

"Maddie, say pardon, not what!"

"A saed, hou ar ye after the jerney?"

"What'sth she sayin', Mum? I can't understand her."

"Don't be rude, Maddie. She asked, how are you after the journey?"

"Oh, right! Well, I had dire rear, didn't I, Mum? I did a poo— OW! You're doin' it again with your nailsth! LOOK! You're makin' marksth in my…"

"SHUT. UP. MADDISON."

Why's she talking like a Dalek?

"I'm so sorry, Harriet. She's had a bit of a rough day."

"Aye, A can see that. What happened tae ye wee face?"

"WEE FACE?"

"MADDISON!"

"Ye fetched yersens a bonnie'n thaur, Alizabeth. She's a wee beauty awrait."

"Mum, I don't know what she'sth sayin'. Can't she talk proply?"

"Maddison, stop it!"

"Stop what?"

"I'm so sorry, Harriet. She's been blackberry picking, and…"

"Guid fegs! They seem tae hae got the better o' ye, ye wee barra."

Absolutely no idea?

"So, who's fer tea?"

This is umbelievable! How am I supposed to understand someone what can't talk proply? And why am I the one what's being rude? She called me wee face! How rude's that? Although, she did say Trev was a fine-looking gentleman – I think – so I don't specially not like her, it's just everytime she talks I get in trouble. *Oh, no? I think she's gonna do it again?*

"So, hen…"

God's sakes? Now she's calling me a HEN!

"Are ye leukin' foward tae the widdin?"

What? Think, Maddison? Widdin – Wedding? Something 'bout the wedding? Are foward wedding? Am I looking forward to the wedding? That's it! Not really…

"Yup."

Phew!

"Harriet, I had a text from my mum before…"

"A text ye say? Is that those wee telephones?"

Ohmigod – she's absessed with wee? I wonder if she's mental? Mind you, most old people are absessed with wee and a little bit mental?

"It is, Harriet. Anyway, she said she'll be here within the next half hour and she's very much looking forward to seeing you again."

I wonder how old she is?

"Aye! A have ne seen her since the last widdin."

Her face looks like when a balloon goes down and it turns all wrinkly. I wonder if that's what's happened? I'll ask…

"Scusthe me, Harriet. Did your head usthed to be milesth bigger?"

"Och, whit's at yer seyin, hen?"

"She'sth doin' it *again*, Mum. Isth it costh she'sth really old that she can't talk proply?"

"Maddison, for God's sake, she's right next to you!"

"Hahaha. Dinnae worry, Alizabeth. Ye ken what they say. Oot o' the mooths o' bairns!"

"BERENTHS? What'sth— stop it, Mum! Let go of me! Where're we goin'?"

"She needs the toilet, Harriet."

"NO, I DON'T! It'sth all gone now."

"Yes, you do, Maddison!"

I think I know if I need the toilet or not, and for the first time in ages, I actually don't!

"We'll be back in a bit, Harriet."

"Och aye. Make yer sens at home, hen. I'll set to the neeps 'n' tatties. A hope yer all hangry."

Angry? Who hopes everyone's angry? She's definitely mental. Aww, it's a proper shame. But I am a little bit angry cos I can't understand a word she says, and every time she talks my mum digs her fingernails in me. I wonder if they have Childline in Scotland? I don't s'pose it matters though cos I probly wouldn't be able to understand them anyway...

"Sweetheart, this must be yours and Robbie's room."

"MINE AN' ROBBIE'STH? I HAVE TO STAY IN A ROOM WITH–?"

"Bloody 'ell, princess, they'll hear you in the Shetlands."

"There you are, Joe – stay put, Maddie – what are you doing up here? Is this our room?"

"Yeh, an' it's fuckin' freezin', love. You could hang meat in it!"

I bet it's more freezing in here cos the flippin' window doesn't shut proply!

"It is on the chilly side – the whole house is! Can you imagine having no central heating? So, what have you been doing up here?"

"Keepin' out the way. I can't understand anythin' she's sayin'."

"She's not that bad. I can make out most of what she says. Anyway, it serves you right for being too tight to pay for a hotel."

"Too tight! This weddin's costin' me an arm an' a leg!"

"Shush! Harriet'll hear you. Where's Robbie?"

Probly, gone outside for a warm?

"He's gone for a smoke, love. I'm thinkin' of startin' myself, just for an excuse to…"

"Well, you're not, you're staying here to help me with Maddie. Honestly, every time she opens her mouth I'm…"

"Mum! It'sth so freezin' in here, I can see my actual breath!"

I can – every time I talk, it's like little ghosts are coming out of me. Ooh? I wonder if it's haunted? I hope so. How cool would that be? Seeing a ghost from a different country. As long as it doesn't speak Scotch though, cos I wouldn't be able to understand what it…

"HO YE! ALIZABETH! YE MA'S HAUR!"

Absolutely ridiclious?

You'll never guess what – Nanna speaks Scotch! She turned up; burst out laughing at me for being mostly purple, then started gabbing to Harriet 'bout her holiday on the coach. She's been driving round Scotland with massive Mavis and honest to God, I don't think my dad's ever been so happy to see her. Me too, actually, cos least Harriet's stopped talking to me.

Hmm? I'm not very inpressed with my present

though – a Scotch boy dolly wearing a funny hat and skirt? I don't really know what to do with it? Whatever, our dinner's ready now but – *oh, dear? I can't see any chicken nuggets or pizza?*

"Dag an, ye all. Whit ye dinnae eat, the pegs will."

"PEGSTH?"

"She means pigs, poppet."

"Oh… *Muuuuum*… I don't like any of thisth!"

"Be quiet, sweetheart."

"What isth it?"

"Och, that's neeps and tatties, hen. It's mashed…"

"NEEPSTH AN' TATTIESTH? Hahaha. What'sth that when it'sth at home?"

"It's spuds 'n' turnip, isn't it, 'arriet?"

"Aye, Joseph! But this is swede…"

"WHAT – STHWEED? I'm not eatin' mashed head!"

"Oy, mouth, dial it down, will ya?"

"Joe, please don't call her that. You don't have to eat it, sweetheart. Sorry, Harriet, do you have anything I could make her a sandwich with, please? She's a bit of a fussy eater."

A fussy eater? How's not wanting to eat a head being a fussy eater?

"Aye! A've a farm full o' pegsth, Alizabeth, an' a dinnae keep 'em as pets!"

"How many've you got, 'arriet?"

Ohmigod? How come I've only just noticed that?

"Och, thaur's aboot fifty-three 'cluding the wee peglets."

It can't be, can it? Can that even happen?

"Bloody 'ell – fifty-three? That's a hell of a lot o' bacon… but don't you get sick o' the smell, 'arriet'? It's proper rank; like sour…"

I'm gonna have to ask?

"Scusthe me, Harriet. Have you alwayths had a beard or did you grow it specially for the—?"

"UPSTAIRS, MADDISON!"

"BUT…"

"NOW!"

"UGH!"

I want to go home! I really don't like it here cos it's not even a proper house. The outside's mostly fallen on the floor and the inside's full of weird stuff. I'm not kidding, Nanna told me off before for playing with something called a mangle – case my fingers got trapped in it – and I don't even know what one of them is? Apparently, it's what they used in the olden days to get water out of clothes, but how am I s'posed to know that? I wasn't alive in the olden days? Then my mum yelled at me for phoning someone in – I think she said India? But I didn't know it was a actual telephone cos I've never seen one like that before, so I was just making the numbers go round then next minute I heard someone talking!

And now I'm in trouble for letting Harriet's dogs in the house, but they weren't that muddy? And besides, who has dogs and doesn't let them in the house? And I only wanted to play with them cos there's absolutely nothing else to do here. For a start off there's no internet and the telly's flippin' ridiclious! Honestly, the front's so tiny you can't hardly see what's on it, but the back's absolutely massive. And worse of all, the toilet isn't even inside the house! Imfact, the only thing I *do* like here's the magic kettle cos, can you believe – it hasn't even got a plug? 'Stead, it works on top of the oven-thing and when it's finished boiling it whistles. It's actual magic! Which is why I've had three cups of tea so far and I absolutely can't stand it...

"Yo, Shortshanks, you look more miserable than me. It's shit' ere, innit?"

"Yup! I'm so bored, Robbie. It'sth like bein' in actual pristhon."

"I know. I'm sure I've been on a school trip to 'ere when I was about ten... '*How we used to live*', or summat like that? I can't even check my Instagram or nothin'."

"Well, leastht my mum doesthn't keep bein' horrible to you."

"Bloody 'ell, am I hallucinatin'? How come you two aren't at each other's throats? What you up to?"

"Usth? Nothin', Dad. We're just bored that'sth all."

"I know, kiddo – you an' me both! It's like livin' in the dark ages. D'ya fancy a pint, son?"

"NO SHIT? There's a pub?"

"Yeh. It's a bit of a trek mind, but if you're up for it?"

"If I'm up for it? *Course*, I'm up for it."

"So am I, Dad – can I come too?"

"Sorry, princess, but your ten years too young an' your mum's on her way up to sort your wig out for tomorrow. You ready then, Rob?"

"I've been ready since we got 'ere. See ya later, Shortshanks. I'll bring ya back some crisps."

★★★

Humph! Stupid wedding! I'd much rather have gone with Spud to stay at Elaine's, or still be driving up the motorway with blackberry dire rear. But, 'stead, I'm in a freezing cold bed; in a freezing cold room; with so far, no ghosts, and I can't go to sleep cos Robbie's doing extra-loud snoring. Well that's one reason, but the main reason I can't sleep's cos my mum's put a million rollers in my hair to make it curly for tomorrow and it's like trying to sleep lying on actual Lego. And I've tried loads of different positions to get comfy but – ooh? Actually, I've just had a idea?

Aaah… why didn't I think of that sooner? That's miles better. NOW I can go to sleep. So, see you in the morning, everyone…

Good McNight!

The Wedding: Part 2

"The bathroom's all yours, Mum, but there's no 'ot water."

"Really? Eesh! Okay, thanks, Robbie. Is Maddie still in bed?"

"Yeh, she's buried under the blankets somewhere. I think she's still asleep."

No, she's not, it's just miles warmer here…

"Well, as much as I'm enjoying the peace and quiet, I'd better wake her."

"Hahaha. On your 'ead be it. Right, I'm goin' outside for a cig."

"I wish you wouldn't – *okay, okay* – I know you're old enough to make your own choices, I just wish you'd make better ones. I'll see you at breakfast – and don't be late! Wakey wakey, Maddie, time to get – OHMIGOD – WHAT THE HELL HAVE YOU DONE?"

Uh? I've not even got up yet?

"I don't believe this, Maddie. You NAUGHTY GIRL!"

UH?

"It wouldn't have been so bad if you'd taken BOTH SIDES OUT!"

Both sides? Oh, my rollersth?

"But, I didn't need…"

"AND your face is still purple."

So's yours…

"Liz, love, what's— BLOODY NORA! Rob, lad, get your camera – this is a classic!"

It can't be that bad? And stop shouting, everybody. I've only just woke up!

"I haven't even brought my curling tongs because– has ANYONE got a signal?"

"Nah – we're in zero bars territory 'ere, love."

"I don't believe this. Joe, run downstairs and ask Harriet if she knows of a hairdresser will you? Tell her it's an emergency."

How can hair be a mergency?

"I just hope to God we can rescue this. Robbie, have you seen what she's done?"

"Hahahahaha. That's epic, Shortshanks!"

"Stand still, while I take the other side out."

"OW! You're pullin' my – ROBBIE, STOP TAKING PICTURESTH OF ME!"

"BE QUIET, MADDISON – OHMIGOD! WHAT ON EARTH do you LOOK LIKE? THIS IS A COMPLETE DISASTER!"

How can hair be a disaster? And stop shouting – you're

giving me a headache!

"Did you know she'd done this, Robbie?"

"Did I balls! She was lyin' under the covers so…"

"Harriet heard you, love. She said don't panic – she's on with it. Hahaha. What the bloody 'ell d'ya look like, princess?"

"Isth it bad, Dad?"

"Bad? Well, from one side you look like Shirley Temple…"

Is that a person or a building?

"… an' from the other, you look like Cousin Itt!"

"Ooh! Is that the one from The Addamsth Family'sth Valuesth? The one what'sth got no face, just hair down-to-the-ground? Hahahahaha, do I *really* look like—?"

"STOP LAUGHING, MADDISON! This is no laughing matter. And from now on in, you're on borrowed time!"

★★★

Well, I've had a horrible morning. First, Harriet made porridge which, no matter how much jam I put in it – *and I put a lot in it* – it still tasted revolting. Then, a lady called Morag turned up with her curly tongues, so I had to sit there for ages with her burning one side of my head and my mum pulling on the other, then Nanna turned up and tried to get the purple off my face and – what's a liar billy-tea? Cos, Nanna said I'm one and I haven't even told any lies yet? And all the while my mum was, '*Rachel this*' and '*Rachel that*' but, what about me? I'm starving hungry, I've got three different kinds of headaches, and now the rollers are back in my hair again to make sure it stays curly till the wedding! All I need now is for Trev to go missing and it'll be the worstest day in my life. And, it's not even half past ten o'clock in the morning!

Least, we're going to Jonathon's mum and dad's house now. I hope it's warm there and I don't get shot? Or that I don't get in trouble for what I did with Nanna's dolly? But Trev didn't have a wedding costume and the dolly hasn't been imvited. Oh, and, the good news is, Harriet's not coming to the actual wedding cos – I can't remember? Something to do with the pigs? So, least my mum won't keep shouting at me all day cos I can't understand her…

"Maddie, come on. What are you faffing about with *now*? What's that in your bag?"

"Erm… promisthe you won't shout, Mum?"

"Why? What have you – ah! Have you vandalised Nanna's dolly?"

Vandal eyes? I don't think so? I've definitely took all it's clothes off and…

"Haha… He looks fantastic, sweetheart. I've never seen a dinosaur in a kilt and busby before. Now, hurry up and get in the car."

Well, I hope I never have to stay at Harriet's farm again. Honestly, we've been driving for over half a hour now and I've only just got warm. And I'm quite cross actually, cos the reason we stayed at Harriet's farm 'stead of Jonathon's mum and dad's house isn't cos there wasn't enough room for us, but cos my mum didn't trust me to – *why are we turning down here? This can't be it?*

"Sweetheart, did you hear me? I said…"

"HOLY SHIT! IS THIS IT?"

"Yes, Robbie…"

"When our Rache said they lived on an estate, I thought she meant an housin' estate, not…"

"Mum, isth this Down Town Abbey?"

"No, sweetheart, this is where they live."

"Jeeze, Mum – I thought it was gonna be proper rough-arsed with her sayin' about guns 'n' shit."

"She was referring to the hunting season, Robbie, not drive-by shootings!"

"How thick're you, son? If you spent more time in the real world, 'stead of playin' on that Xbox 24/7, you'd…"

"24/7? I wish! An' Jon's – normal. I'd never 'ave thought he came from somewhere like this. I hope they're not all toffee-nosed gits."

Ooh? I'd like a nose made out of toffee. I'd never stop picking it.

"What's his mum an' dad like? Are they proper posh?"

"We've only met them a couple of times, Robbie – obviously not here – but Alistair and Margaret are incredibly nice people and I'd like them to think the same about us. So, for one day, do you think it's at all possible for you to behave like a civilised human – ohmigod! What's that smell?"

"Sorry, love – it's all that turnip 'arriet fed me last night. My guts're…"

"*Eeeeeuw!* OPEN THE WINDOWSTH!"

"Ugh – Joe – that's not *human*! You smell like a gas leak! Right, are you all listening? No burping; no breaking wind; no swearing; no getting drunk – that doesn't apply to you Maddison – no making personal comments about people – that specifically does! And, mind your manners! Am I understood?"

"Jesus, Dad. That's rank!"

"I hope you're not including me in any of that, Elizabeth?"

"No, Mum – well, maybe the 'no getting drunk' part. Maddie? Robbie? Joe?"

"Yup!"

"*Fucksake…*"

"I'd best get it all out now then, love…"

THRRRRRRPPPPP…

"MUM! LET ME OUT OF THE CAR!"

"So, Margaret, you've met my mum and dad before, and Nanna, of course. So, this is my brother, Robbie."

"Nice to meet you, Robbie. You're very tall, aren't you? I didn't expect you to be so tall."

"Er? I s'pose? Nice to meet ya."

Thank goodness his mum doesn't talk very Scotch.

"And this is…"

"HELLO MADDISON!"

Flippin' 'eck? What's she so eggcited about?

"We've been so looking forward to meeting you, haven't we, Alistair? And would you look at her dinosaur – *bless!* Where on earth did you get a Bearskin hat and kilt to fit him?"

"Erm? I did vandal eyesth with Nanna'sth dolly. Soz, Nanna!"

"Did you hear that, Alistair? Vandal eyes with Nanna's dolly! Hahaha…"

Alistair hasn't talked yet.

"We've heard so much about you, Maddison, and your sister wasn't exaggerating at all when she said what a beautiful little girl you are. We've seen photos of course, but you're usually covered in something unsavoury. Hahaha. How lovely to finally meet you!"

"Erm… thanksth, your magicstee. How come your housthe is so massthive?"

"Oh, how utterly adorable! There's really no need to curtsey, my dear. Elizabeth, I'm not just saying this, but I don't think I've ever seen a more beautiful child. I mean, look at those dimples! If she were mine, I don't think I'd get anything done."

"You wouldn't have thought that if you'd seen her a couple of hours ago, Margaret – and I don't get anything done, but not because she's…"

"OHMIGOD! Why'sth Rudolph'sth head stickin' out the wall?"

"Don't say ohmigod, Maddie, and it's not Rudolph, it's a stag. Margaret, where shall we put our bags?"

"Sorry, of course. Rachel, dear, would you like to show your parents to their room?"

"Sure. They're in the main guestroom in the west wing, yes?"

"Yes. And Alistair, would you show Robbie and Betty to theirs? Don't look so alarmed, Robbie – you have separate rooms but in the east wing."

East wing? Houses don't have wings? Angels have wings? Or birds? Or Tinkerbell?

"And dear little Maddison, you can come with me. Is that okay, Elizabeth? I thought it would give you more time with the bride-to-be, plus the hairdresser ought to be arriving soon."

"Don't mention hairdressers, Margaret, and are you sure? She can be a bit of a handful."

"Nonsense – hahaha! I had five rambunctious boys, and girls are so different, aren't they?"

"Well…"

"And may I just say – Alistair and I couldn't be happier! Jonathon couldn't have met a more perfect young lady to spend the rest of his life with. She's a credit to you both!"

"Thank you, Margaret. We feel the same about Jonathon."

"Then, this is going to be a truly wonderful day. Now come on, Maddie. Shall we see if Cook's taken the biscuits out of the oven yet?"

Cook? Biscuits? Do bears—?

"And, sweetheart, remember what I said? Behave yourself!"

***

Margaret's proply nuts and sometimes it's like she's never seen a girl – mind you, Jonathon's got four brothers and no sisters, so? Anyway, she's let me eat tons of biscuits and have a play on the piano – till my dad said that if hears Three Blind Mice one more time he'll chop my bloody hands off! And she was even gonna let me slide down the bannister till my mum shouted me that it was time to get ready, which is what I'm about to do now, but…

"Now, Maddie, what I'm about to say is *extremely important*, so I want you to listen very carefully…"

Uh-oh?

"As you know, today's the most important day of Rachel's life and I don't want ANYTHING to spoil it. So – when we get to the church and you see the other bridesmaid, it's called a port wine stain, and it's just a birthmark. Okay?"

A pour wine stain?

"So, you don't need to yell, 'Mum, what's wrong with her face?' halfway through the service. Got it?"

"Yup!"

"And the man in the wheelchair – he's not Stephen Hawking, so there's no need to ask!"

"O-*kaaaay*…"

"Also. The thing in Alistair's ear's called a hearing aid. Jonathon's grandma's ninety-six and, no, she can't stand up properly, and…"

Flippin' 'eck? Is there anyone normal coming to the wedding?

"Oh yes… and the best man, Marlon? You met him at Rache's twenty-first, remember?"

"Yup! The one I thought wasth the actual Predator?"

"Yes – and they're dreadlocks, remember! So, please don't ask him again. Okay, sweetheart, it's time to get ready, and if you so much as BLINK once you've got this dress on, I'll send you to one orphanage and Trevor to another. UNDERSTOOD?"

"Yup!"

"If you do anything to spoil today, Maddie…"

"Like, what?"

"Really? You have to ask? Just be a little less…"

"OHMIGOD! What the flippin' 'eck'sth THAT?"

God's sakes! No wonder I wasn't allowed to see my prizesmaid's dress before today – *it's meant to be a surprise, Maddison* – well, it's not a surprise, it's a shock! Honest to God, I Iook like the dolly what Harriet puts her toilet roll in. It's so imbarrassing and – AH? OHMIGOD?

"Close your mouth, princess – you'll catch flies! What's up? Have you never seen a man in a kilt before? What d'ya reckon 'ey, Liz? We-hey!"

"Stop it, Joe – not everyone wants to see what's under there. And where's Robbie?"

"Upstairs with a right gob on. I don't blame him, mind – you should see his legs, love – like two strands o' spaghetti danglin' from under his kilt. How's our Rache?"

"Nervous! Her train's so long, she keeps tripping over it."

Train? I thought we were going in a car?

"I can't believe it, Liz – in 'alf an hour I'll be givin' her away an'…"

"WHAT – givin' her away? But I thought she wanted to get married?"

"Shush, princess… she won't be a McLaren anymore, love. She'll be Mrs Scott-Reid."

"I know, Joe. I guess she's not our baby any more. Well, are you ready?"

"To give my daughter away? I'll never be ready, love, but, yeh."

Is my dad nearly crying? That's funny? I didn't know there was any football today?

★★★

"Maddie, keep hold of your flowers. And, didn't I tell you not to go in the cemetery? I found them on one of the gravestones."

Oh, that's what that is?

"Mum, isth it allowed to bury someone just costh they fell asleep? Costh that'sth what it said on the stone-thing."

"No, sweetheart, it's not. Now let me see the bottom of your shoes... good! So, do you remember how we practised? You walk behind Rache, very, very..."

"ATISHOO! ATISHOO! Mum, I think the flow-ersth're makin' me... ATISHOO! Sneeze."

"Well, you only have to hold them for a little – she's here! I'm going before I start to cry again, sweetheart. I don't want to set her off."

Set her off? She's not a flippin' firework?

Is it normal for weddings to make people weird? I'm not kidding, everyone keeps crying. Specially the other prizemaid – a little girl called Grace – cos she cried so loud when her mum went to sit down that she's actually gone to sit down with her. And Nanna's cried. And my mum's cried. And, I'm sure my dad nearly cried before, and I've only ever seen him cry about the football… but Robbie said that Liverpool definitely aren't playing today.

"Jeeze, Rache, calm down, love. You're shakin' like a shittin' dog!"

"Hahaha. Trust you to make me laugh, Dad. I haven't heard that expression in…"

"ATISHOO! ATISHOO! ATISHOO! Rache, you look eggsacly like ATISHOO! A princessth."

"Thanks, Madds, so do you. And thank you for being such a good girl today. Margaret's completely smitten. She said she wants to adopt you."

Flippin' 'eck – don't tell my dad that! He's giving you away, and you're the good one.

"ATISHOO! So, Rache, you know after you're married? Won't we be sistersth any more? I don't want you to not be my sister."

"Of course we'll still be sisters, you muppet! Nothing will ever change that. Even when we're really old and wrinkly, you'll still be my crazy, fearless, curiously deranged little sis, and I wouldn't want you any other way."

"*Really?*"

"Really, Madds. Sisters forever."

"For ever an' ever, our men?"

"Forever and ever…"

"AAAAAATISHOO!"

"Amen. Madds, have you got hay fever?"

"What'sth ATISHOO! Hay fever? Ooh, is this the vicar, Rache?"

"Well, now, are we all ready? Rachel? Mr McLaren? Good, then…"

"I'm ready too, thanksth for ATISHOO! Asthkin'."

"Bless you, my child."

MY child? I'm not your child? You're not my dad?

"Erm? Thanksth."

"Ohmigod, Dad. This is it!"

"I know, love. I can't believe my little girl's gettin' married. An' you're as beautiful on the inside as you are out."

Eeeuw? What a weird thing to say to someone when they're just about to get married?

"Ohmigod, Dad – the music!"

"Calm down, love. Just hold on to your old dad an' put one foot in front of the other an' you'll be fine. Are you ready, princess?"

"Yup! An' so'sth Trev!"

Ooh? I know this song…

"HERE COMESTH THE PRIDE…"

"Pipe down, princess!"

"Leave her, Dad. It's funny."

"THIXTY INCHESTH – A-TISHOO! WIDE. Wave to everyone, Trev… HELLOOOO… roooarrr…"

"Hahaha. Where did she learn— ouch! Watch my veil, Madds."

"Stop fannyin' about with Godzilla an' look where your goin'. D'ya wanna break your sister's neck on her weddin' day?"

Why would I want to do THAT?

"Soz, Rache, I didn't mean to... AATISHOO! AATISHOO! Tread on your AAAAAA-TISHOO! GOD'STH SAKESTH! LOOK, DAD! SNOT'STH COME OUT MY ACTUAL NOSTHE!"

Well, it did – and it's not my fault I'm lergic to flowers. And I didn't mean to shout God's sakes in the church, but I was so surprised, it just came out! Well I've never had a whole bunch of Chrisamfamums stuck up my nose before so I didn't eggspect to sneeze so hard it looked like I had a actual icicle growing out of it. Anyway, Nanna's got them now and she's at the opposite end of the bench from me so hopefully I won't do it again but – ooh, the vicar's talking...

> *"In the presence of God, the Father, the Son, and the Holy Spirit, we have come together to witness the marriage of Jonathon and Rachel..."*

Eeeeeeuw? What's that horrible smell?

"Joe, have you—?"

"Sorry, love. Remind me never to eat neeps 'n' tatties again!"

"POOH! IT STINKSTH!"

"Quiet, sweetheart... Joe, couldn't you have just held it in?"

"Jeeze, Dad, have you dropped your arse again?"

"THAT'STH DISTHG..."

"Shut up, Maddison! Have you got any sweets, Joe, to keep her quiet?"

"I'll give her one o' these. This'll keep her busy for a while."

"First, I am required to ask, that if any of these persons here present, knows of any lawful impediment to this marriage, they must declare it now."

"Oh, God! Give her a couple!"

"What you doin'? I don't like..."

"Keep your bloody voice down! You're havin' it whether you like it or not. So, open your gob – stick it in – an' suck it!"

"I'm sure you've said that to me before now, Joe."

God, this is so boring. I wish the vicar'd make his mind up. One minute he's telling us to stand up, then sit down, then stand up again – it's like the worstest game of Simon Says cos you can't be out! And the songs are absolutely rubbish! Rache likes McFly so why didn't she choose some of theirs? Or the kicking song? Everyone joins in with that? But, 'stead she's choosed to sing about amazing Grace – which must be about the other prizemaid – but she wasn't in the least bit amazing cos she cried and then ran off?

Actually, I don't think my family's made any noise 'cept to tell me to stop asking if it's nearly finished yet, but, how much longer can it be?

"Do you, Jonathon Alistair Cameron Scott-Reid, take Rachel Jane McLaren, to be your lawful wedded..."

"AH! Did he just say Rache wasth awful?!"

"Shush! Give her another one, Joe."

"I would, if I could fit any more in!"

Well, you can't – and this vicar's got to be the most boring man in the world. All he's talked about so far is Jesus! It's not even Jesus' wedding but he's mentioned him miles more than Jonathon and Rache. And did you know Jesus is everywhere? I know! He's here now, apparently, but he definitely wasn't imvited to the wedding so I'm sure there won't be enough food? Ooh, Rache's gonna talk...

"And now, Rachel, repeat after me. I give you this ring, as a sign of our love."

"I give you this ring, as a sign of our love."

"With my body, I thee honour."

"With my body, I thee honour."

"All that I have, I give to thee."

"All that I have, I give to thee."

"According to God's holy law."

"According to God's holy law."

"In the presence of God, and before this congregation, Jonathon and Rachel have given their consent, and made their marriage vows to each other. They have declared their marriage by the joining of hands, and by the giving and receiving of rings. Therefore, I now pronounce you, husband and..."

"*BuuuuuUUUUUURRRRRP!* OHMIGOD! Sorry, Jesthusth! That'sth three foodsth what make me do massive great burpsth! Applesth, pepper mintsth and cumcubersth!"

"Ahem – wife!"

I'm not my mum's friend. Fancy saying I ruin everything. And, how's it my fault? I didn't want to eat the pepper mints in the first place! And I didn't do it on purpose – it just came out, and it was lucky I didn't do a sick, actually. And how's saying 'ohmigod' being naughty? My mum says it all the flippin' time.

Anyway, we're outside the church now, waiting for Jonathon and Rache to come out, but why does everything take so long at weddings? I wish they'd hurry up cos I'm proply bored and I just want to go to the party.

"Sweetheart, stop kicking stones or you'll ruin your shoes."

"Well, how much *longer* are they gonna be?"

"They'll be out any second now. Have you got your confetti ready?"

"Yup!"

Hmm? It's strange cos I normally get told off for throwing stuff at people but my mum's told me that I absolutely have to throw it – it's all cumfetty's for, apparently? It's a bit of a weird thing to do if you ask me but...

"They're on their way out now, sweetheart. Doesn't she look beautiful? And don't they look happy together?"

"Yup. *Muuuum...*"

"Get ready, Maddie..."

"Okay, but…"

"After three, sweetheart. 1 – 2 – 3. Congratul—
OHMIGOD, MADDIE – NOT LIKE THAT! You're
supposed to take it out of the box!"

Well, I didn't know cos I've never throwed cumfetty
before so she should give better instructions. But Rache
said it didn't hurt that much; she was just massively
surprised that's all, and now that her eye's stopped
watering we can finally go to the party. I wonder if we'll
play musical chairs? Or pass the—?

"Oy, birdbrain, where d'ya think you're goin'? It's
this way for the photos. An' do me a favour, 'ey? Try not
to injure anyone this time."

***

SIXTEEN TIMES I got shouted at doing the photos.
Probly more actually, cos I didn't start counting straight
away. Once, for having my finger up my nose but a actual
fly flew up it. Once, for asking Alistair if he's proply deaf
but I don't think he heard me. Once, for telling amazing
Grace that my face looked like hers yesterday after I'd
rubbed blackberries in it. Once, for asking the man in
the wheelchair if he knows Steven Hawkins. Once, for
asking Marlon if he knows the actual Predator. Twice,
for going bozz-eyed. Once, for doing a cartwheel and
kicking the vicar in the back, and the rest for messing
about and getting dirty. But least we're at the party now,
even if it *is* the boringest one ever.

I'm not kidding, the best bit's the actual tent! It's even got a first name – Marky! And it's absolutely massive. I didn't know you could get tents this big 'cept for at the circus, but we're definitely not at the circus cos all we've done so far's eat some boring roast dinner in it! Then, Marlon talked for ages. Then Alistair talked and it turns out he's quite Scotch. Then my dad talked and he was really funny. Then my mum stood up and mostly just cried so she sat back down again. Then just when I thought all the boring stuff'd finished, the weirdest thing happened.

I could hear this noise coming from somewhere and it got louder and louder and louder, then next minute a man walked in dressed eggsacly like Nanna's dolly – how weird's that? And, he was making a horrible noise.

First, I thought he was carrying a upside-down animal and he was blowing in one of it's legs, but have you heard of the bad pipes? Honestly, they're so noisy you wouldn't believe. But, even more umbelieveable, halfway through some girls turned up and started jumping in the air like Scotch kangaroos – my dad said it's called 'The Eyeland Fling' – and they looked absolutely mental! Imfact, I'm beginning to think all Scotch people are mental? And what if it's catching? What if Rache turns into one?

Anyway, then a man came on the micra phone and said it was time for the first dance, and next minute my dad was on stage singing the Wetwetwet song while Rache and Jonathon danced. And all that took *hours*. I was so bored, I decided to have a taste of other people's drinks to see if I liked them or not, and so far I've decided:

Rachel: Shampain… good bubbles but tastes horrible

Robbie: Beer… tastes like sprouts

Nanna: Portont lemon… absolutely disgusting

Margaret: Bay Leaves… only nice at first

Mum: Mallyboo with pineapples… lovely

Dad: Wiskee… absolutely revolting… then my mum saw me about to try a old ladies drink what looked like tomato soup, so now I'm stuck on a chair and I'm not allowed off it even if the tent goes on fire! Humph! Ooh, here's Rache…

"Mum, can I borrow Maddie for a bit?"

Can you borrow people?

"Jon's nephew's really bored, so I thought she might like to talk to him."

"Okay, but, Rache…"

"I know – keep my eye on her. Come on, Madds. He's really nice… that's him, over by the chocolate fountain."

What? There's a chocolate fountain? How come I didn't see – WOW!

"Scusthe me, Jonathon'sth…"

"HAHAHAHA…"

What the flippin' 'eck's he laughing at? Cheeky pig.

"Do you know you've got chocolate – like – all over your face?"

"No, but I've just had a go of the fountain."

"I'd never have guessed – you're meant to eat it, not snorkel in it. Aren't you the one who did the enormous burp in the church?"

"Yup! It wasth a accident though. What'sth your name?"

"Ewan. What's yours?"

You-an? That's a weird name?

"My name'sth Maddithon. How old are you?"

"Twelve. How old are you?"

"Eleven."

"ELEVEN? Are you sure? You're a bit small for eleven."

"Coursthe, I'm sure! I'm just small, that'sth all. An', it'sth rude to make persthonable commentsth 'bout someone'sth 'peerance."

"Sorry. Who's your friend?"

"Trev? He'sth my besthtest friend."

"Bestest?"

"I mean best!"

"Bit weird that, your best friend's a plastic dinosaur. Hey, have you seen the stag?"

"Ah! Did you go to the stag'sth party?"

"What? I'm talking about the stag in the woods."

"Oh! The type what'sth like a reindeer?"

"Yes. Do you want to see it?"

"Coursthe I want to see it but we'll have to wait till no onesth lookin'. Not costh I'm not eleven, but costh I'm not allowed to get my prizemaid'sth dressth dirty."

"It's a bit late for that! You probably shouldn't have wiped your face on it. So, Rachel's your sister? I think we're related then – Jonathon's my uncle."

"Really? So, are we – QUICK! She'sth not lookin'! Leg it!"

"It'sth a bit dark, You-an'. How will we see where we're goin'?"

"Haven't you got a torch on your mobile?"

"Erm? *Coursthe* I've got a mobile, an' it'sth got a well good torch, but I've forgot it."

"Okay, share mine. Just watch where you're going. It's this way."

"Will we get shot?"

"They don't hunt in the dark, idiot! Are you SURE you're eleven?"

"YESTH! STOP ASTHKIN'!"

"Keep your voice down or you'll spook it. It was just over here. Can you see anything?"

"Nope."

"Me neither. Just be quiet and wait."

"D'you think it might be scared of the light?"

"Maybe. I'll turn it off."

"WOW!"

"*Quiet!* You'll scare it away."

"Soz, but, look at all the starsth. They've got milesth more in Scotland."

"*What?* Hey! Look… next to the biggest tree. Can you see it?"

"Wow! Yesth. D'you think we can go closer?"

"Best not to; it'll probably run. Isn't it awesome?"

"Yesth… doesth it ever go in the housthe?"

"Hahaha. I don't think so. Why?"

"Costh one of itsth friendsth' headsth is stickin' out the wall. Just imagine if— bugger! It'sth movin'. Shall we follow it?"

346

"We'd never be able to keep up. Anyway, we'd best go back. My Grandad goes – son of a bitch!"

Some of a bitch?

"What'sth up?"

"My phone's dead. I hope you can see in the dark."

"Erm? Well, I don't really like carrotsth but I'm sure I'll be fine."

★★★

"Ohmigoodnessth, You-an! D'you think they'll notice we were gone?"

"Probably."

"Princess, is that—? SHE'S 'ERE, LIZ – I'VE FOUND 'ER! Where the bloody 'ell 'ave you been? Christ on a bike – it's Worzel Gummidge!"

Worzel what?

"SWEETHEART! Thank God you're— OHMI-GOD! What happened to your dress? You look like you've been dragged through a hedge backwards."

Nearly. I walked through one forwards, actually.

"RACHE! She's over here! Just wait till Rache sees what you've done to your dress."

"Where did you find her, Mum? Is she – hahahaha-haha. Perfect!"

What?

"Oh Madds, you little superstar!"

WHAT?

"Rache, love, are you pissed?"

"No, Dad. It's just… every time Jon and I come to

visit, the first thing Margaret and Alistair ask is, 'What's Maddie done now'? They think she's *hilarious*. Honestly, when I told them about her knocking a penguin out at the zoo, I thought they were going to die laughing. I told them, it wouldn't be Maddie if she doesn't look like a train wreck by the end of the night so they've been waiting for it. I thought she was going to make a liar out of me… Come here, you little nutter. What happened?"

"I saw the stag, Rache, in the woodsth. You-an said about usth goin' but then his phone stopped workin' so we had to come back in the dark. An' we got a bit lost. An' I couldn't climb over the hedge in my prizemaid'sth dressth so I walked through it, instead. Have I got sticksth in my hair?"

"Yes. Hahahaha. Look, Dad, she looks like Medusa."

"I'll bloody Medusa 'er!"

"Come on, Madds. Let's find Margaret and show her your dress."

See, I said Rache never shouts. Anyway, Margaret was in the house talking to Nanna and the bad pipes man, and when I told her that I hadn't been dragged through a hedge backwards – why does everyone think that? – that I walked through one forwards instead, she laughed so much that other people came to listen. And, suddenly there was loads of people listening to Rache talking 'bout my accidents. And when she told them about me taking my rollers out last night, a lady called Pelenope laughed so much some volley-vont went down the wrong hole and she nearly choked to deaf!

Anyway, after that we all went to do dancing, and even Robbie and my dad joined in. They were doing Scotch dancing with Nanna – and she only fell over twice before Robbie took her to sit back down cos she's had a skimful of portont lemon, apparently. So, then my dad sat down so it was just me, my mum and Rache… and the deejay played loads of Abba songs for us then even Margaret joined in.

But I can tell it's time to finish now cos we've already done the Spelling Song *and* the song about Eileen – ooh, and the Five Hundred Miles Song, too. I'd never heard that one before, but it's already my new second favourite, after…

"De de – de de de. De de – de de de…"

YES! The Kicking Song! I've got to go now sorry, cos this is my absolute favourite, and I can't talk and kick at the same time, so…

"DAD! Look how high my leg – OOPSTH! Soz, Margaret! Don't worry, Dad, I'll find my shoe after it'sth finished."

Goodnight everybody! See you all soon, and…

Goodbye!

Happy Halloween!

"Did you have a good day at school, sweetheart?"

"Yup. Mum, guessth what? Connor Pinkerton fell over in the playground at dinnertime an' there wasth so much blood, Mrsth Hutton had to put her head imbetween her kneesth so she didn't faint! It wasth *well* excitin' – like he'd done it on purposthe for Halloween. Oh, an' Lucthy'sth got nitsth so you have to check my head. Can I get my costume on now?"

"Er, Hello, sweetheart… I missed you, too. Lucy's got nits?"

"Yup! But, Missth Spottisthwood said you only get them if your hair'sth clean, so it'sth probly best if I don't wash mine till *least* after Christm…"

"Nice try, Maddie! Pass me your lunchbox – thank you. Okay, hang your coat up and put your shoes and bag away, and *then* we'll think about Halloween."

Okay, but I've been thinking 'bout it all day?

I like Halloween nearly more than I like Christmas. I know you don't get presents but you do get millions of sweets, and best of all, you get to look scary while you're eating them. And looking scary's quite inportant, cos when me and Matthew knocked on people's doors in the summer holidays and asked for sweets, quite a lot of them told us to go away. But, the main reason I love Halloween is cos it's all to do with witches.

Witches are awesome. They have fantastic clothes, and they fly on broomsticks, and live in houses made of actual sweets. And, if they catch you eating their house, they cook you in a oven like in Hamsel and Gretel. I know! I've never seen a *actual* witch before cos I'm not allowed in the woods but – ooh? One sec…

"Mum, you know after we've done trick or treat, can we go watchin' doggin' in the—?"

"WHAAAT!"

"Carl Pillin' said he'sth not doin' trick or treat this year costh it'sth for babies, so 'stead, he'sth goin' with his big brother, watchin' doggin' in the woodsth. I love dogsth, don't I, Mum? So, can we—?"

"NO, WE CANNOT! And, I don't want to hear another word on the subject!"

God's sakes, I was only asking 'bout dogs. There's no need to bite my flippin' head off…

"And, remember the deal, sweetheart? You have to eat something sensible before you…"

"But, WHY? That just takesth up ROOM!"

"I've made chicken with pasta, and once you've eaten

it, you can start getting ready."

"Humph! Is thisth it?"

"It is."

"I'll do it now, then."

"Do it? You make it sound like a chore."

"What'sth a chore?"

"A tedious task."

"What'sth tediousth?"

"Tedious? Something that is dull or boring…"

Like eating chicken pasta when it's Halloween?

"…and don't talk with your mouth full, it's very rude."

Well, stop talking to me then.

"*Buuuurp* – scusthe me – FINISHED!"

"Finished? Ohmigod, you have? How? You've barely stopped talking? Okay, come and see what your dad made for you last night."

"Ooh? What?"

"It's in the front hall. I thought you might have seen it on your way in. Look – isn't Daddy clever?"

"Ah, a pumkin man! He'sth awesthome – specially the sick! Is that all it'sth seedsth?"

"It is."

"I'm gonna call him Wendy costh they're nearly the 'xact same colour."

"Maddie, Wendy isn't orange, she's…"

She's Orange Wendy.

"…she's… she just uses the sunbeds a lot. Right, come on. Let's get you ready."

I'm so eggcited cos this year I'm being The Corpse

Prize. It was Rache's idea, after I ruined my prizemaid's dress, and…

"Maddie, sit still if you want me to do a good job."

"I *AM*! Put tonsth of white on, Mum."

"I know what I'm doing, sweetheart."

"An' do tonsth of stitchesth."

"There aren't any stitches in the picture, Maddie."

"I know but do them anyway. An' will you do the black bitsth really black? An'…"

"I can't do anything, if you don't stop talking."

"O-*kaaay*… … … … Mum, what time doesth it go—?"

"STOP TALKING!"

Humph! I was only gonna ask what time it goes dark cos that's when Matthew's coming. He's coming as a pumkin man this year, which is a bit boring, but last year he didn't even do Halloween in a Stralia…

"Okay, sweetheart – all done. Go and look in the…"

"Flippin' 'eck, that'sth brilliant! I thought you wasth rubbish at doin' make-up?"

"I only said that because Rache loved doing it. Who do you think did hers, when she was little?"

I can't imagine Rache being little?

"Now, let's get your dress on then I'll backcomb your hair."

"And will you make me look mental?"

"I can't see that being a problem!"

I look absolutely brilliant. I can't believe my mum's so good at doing – ooh, someone's coming down our path…

"Mum, Matthew'sth here. Can I ansthwer the door pleasthe?"

"Yes, sweetheart, but don't scare him before he's even…"

"WAAAAAAAAAAGH!"

"Aaaargh! MADDIE! You frightened me half to death! You look well scary."

"Aww, thanksth, Matthew. You don't."

"Really?"

"Nope! No witchesth'll be scared of you. You'll probly get eaten by a…"

"Sweetheart! Hi, Elaine – don't say things like that, Maddie. And I think you look very scary, Matthew. Right, are we all ready?"

"YESTH! OOH! OOH! CAN WE GO TO—?"

"Maddie, calm down. I don't know about you, Elaine, but I'm predicting a headache."

I love trick or treat. I love eating sweets, and I love playing tricks, and I love dressing up like a witch or a devil or a zombie – and it's the only time I get to play out in the dark. The only bad thing is, I wish we could go on our own – I don't see why my mum and Elaine have to come with us? Specially, cos my dad said that if anyone ever did run off with me they'd bring me back after five minutes cos I'd do their head in – so, it's not even dangerous?

"Right. Where would you like to go first, Matthew?"

"He wantsth to go to – OW, Matthew! That'sth three timesth you've banged into me, an' we haven't even knocked on anybody'sth door yet! Can't you see?"

"Not really – this head's too big so the eye holes keep moving round to the side."

"Why didn't you just glue it to your head, then?"

"Erm? I don't think my mum would let me do that, Maddie."

"Coursthe she's not gonna let you, Matthew, you just do it then say it wasth a accident. Are you ready now?"

"I think…"

BANG BANG BANG BANG BANG BANG

"SWEETHEART!"

"What?"

"Knock quietly."

"But then she won't be able to – Ooh! She'sth comin'! SHE'STH – TRICK OR TREAT!"

"Heavens above – is that Maddison? Don't you look fantastic? And, Trevor, too. Hi, Liz!"

"Hi, Wendy. Sorry about the door. You've met Elaine, haven't you? I thought so. And this is little Matthew, underneath the pumpkin head."

Hurry up. I haven't got all day.

"He's quite shy, aren't you, hun? Say hello to…"

Bugger this. It'll be nearly bomfire night by the time Elaine's finished talking…

"Have you got any sweetsth, Orange Wendy?"

"Sweetheart, stop saying that! And, where are your manners?"

I don't know where they are actually? Are they in my head?

"Soz. What sweetsth have you got… *pleasthe*?"

"I'm sorry, Wendy, she's a bit hyper."

"Don't worry, Liz. I remember what it was like to be seven on Hallow…"

"Really? Costh that wasth, like – agesth ago!"

"Hahaha. I'm only thirty-two, Maddie, I'm not that old."

"I think you'll find you are."

"Maddison!"

"*What?*"

"Hahaha. Liz, it's okay. Look, Maddie. Mike hollowed out a pumpkin so I could fill it full of…"

"ISTH THAT IT? JUST TANGERINESTH?"

"MADDISON! I'm going to kill her, Wendy. I'm so sorry."

"Stop apologising, Liz. There are sweets at the bottom, Maddie, but look, I've carved little pumpkin faces into the…"

"Oh, yeah. Look, Matthew, little tangerine pumkin men. That'sth well cool. Why don't you do that, Mum? I'd probly definitely eat a…"

"Maddison. Just. Pick. A. Tange-rine."

"Why're you talkin' like that again, Mum? You sound like a actual dalek."

"Because – for God's sake, Maddison, just pick a tangerine! Whatever you do, Wendy, don't have kids!"

"Ooh? D'you know if you do have a baby, Wendy, will it be the same colour orange asth–?"

"HAPPY HALLOWEEN, WENDY!"

Why's my mum shouting?

"Say goodnight, Maddison."

"Uh? Goodnight, Maddithon? That'sth why I called my pumkin man Wendy, isn't it Mum? Costh he'sth the 'xact same colour as – stop draggin' me – I'm gonna drop Trev!"

I hope Matthew's having a nice time? But the only thing he likes about Halloween's the free sweets, and he can't really eat any of them at the moment, cos – I can't believe he didn't notice that his pumkin head's got no mouth? What a idiot! And when I posted some jelly spiders through his eye-holes before he went completely hysterical, so I'm not gonna bother trying to post these fizzy ghosts. Ooh?

"Matthew, I've found a cobweb. Will you eat cobwebsth?"

"Eeuw, no!"

"But, cobwebsth aren't…"

"Maddie, don't! *Stop it!* You're making sherbet go in my eyes."

"Maddie, leave him alone and stop posting sweets through his eye sockets! Sorry, Elaine, what did you say? Is Rache back from her honeymoon yet? She is and they had a wonderful time. Just imagine it – two weeks in the Maldives – for a wedding present! All that Joe and I got from his parents was a measuring jug and three Pyrex dishes off his mum, and his dad got himself arrested the night before for being drunk and disorderly so he didn't even make it!"

"I know, it's a – Matthew, look where you're going, hun!"

"He can't, Elaine. He can't see. He keepsth bangin' into

lamb poststh costh his eye holesth are round the side. Turn it round, Matthew, so the head'sth facin' the right way."

"I can't see, Maddie. Will you do it?"

"Yesth, just watch the – OOH! Lamb post! Did that hurt?"

"Not really. I can't feel anything with this pumpkin head on."

"Good – costh, if we have to stop doin' trick or treat costh you've got concushionsth I'll – Mum, can we go down thisth one on our own?"

"Yes, we'll wait here at the top. And don't…"

BANG! BANG! BANG! BANG! BANG! BANG! BANG! BANG!

"MADDISON!"

"ANSWER THE FLIPPIN' DOOR! Join in, Matthew."

"No! You're gonna break it, Maddie."

"You can't break a door just by knockin' on it – they must be deaf? Shall I – OOH! TRICK OR TREAT!"

"Well, aren't you a sight for sore eyes?"

"UH? Who'sth got sore eyesth? An' have you got any sweetsth, pleasthe?"

"I most certainly have. Would you like to come inside? My husband can't come to the door easily because…"

"MUM, THE LADY SAID…"

"Yes, I heard what she said, Maddie! Go on!"

"My mum said it'sth okay. Will we get more sweetsth for comin' in?"

"Hahaha. Maybe. Just, be careful of the – oh, dear – the step."

"Flippin' 'eck, Matthew – what you doin' on the floor? Get up, silly Billy!"

"Is he okay?"

"He'sth fine – he doesthn't feel anythin' costh of his pumkin head."

"Well, this is my husband, Robert. Look, Bob, look how cute they…"

"Hello, Robert. My brother'sth called Robert. What'sth wrong with your legsth?"

"Maddie, don't say that."

"Robert's been in a wheelchair since…"

"I had a go of a wheelchair when I wasth at hosthpital, didn't I, Matthew? I went whizzin' like they do in the Lympicsth. Did you do the Lympicsth, Robert?"

"He didn't, no. He's a bit old for the…"

"How old are you?"

"He's sixty…"

"Can't he talk? Is he like Stephen Hawkinsth? My brother lovesth Stephen Hawkinsth."

"Of course he can talk. Say something, Bob."

"The. Entire. Universe. Is…"

"HAHAHAHA. That'sth a well good inpression. Isthn't Robert funny, Matthew? Matthew, your head'sth on sidewaysth again. Let me fixth it."

"I like your outfit. Are you the Bride of Dracula?"

"I'm bein' the Corpsthe Prize, silly. Can we have some sweetsth, pleasthe?"

"Of course, the Corpse Prize, would you like to take some?"

"Yesth, pleasthe."

"And you, Matthew the Pumpkin Man? Are you having a happy Halloween?"

Happy? Who wants to be happy on Halloween? I want to meet zombies and fight witches.

"He'sth too shy to talk, aren't you, Matthew? Bye, Robert Hawkinsth! Hope you don't get killed by witchesth. Bye, nice lady, and thanksth for the sweetsth. Wasthn't Robert nice, Matthew?"

"I CAN'T SEE!"

★★★

You wouldn't believe how many sweets me and Matthew've got. And we would've got more if Elaine hadn't kept slowing us down taking Matthew's pumkin head off checking him for bumps every five minutes. And, I wouldn't mind but…

"Okay, kids, make this the last one. Our feet are freezing!"

"BUT, MUM?"

"Maddison, stop shouting! Why can't you be more like Matthew?"

What? Walking round with my head on sideways and falling over everything?

"We'll wait on the corner for you. And, Maddison, do NOT batter the door down!"

BANG! BANG! BANG!

"Ooh! That'sth quick, Matthew. Someone'sth comin'. TRICK OR—?"

"Neither! Bugger off!"

That's not very nice?

"Okay, but, have you got any sweetsth firstht?"

"Do I look like I've got money for soddin' sweets?"

How should I know?

"Sling yer 'ook!"

Sling my hook? I'm the Corpse Prize, not a flippin' pirate!

"Well, what about cake?"

"What about it?!"

"Have you—?"

SLAM!

Well, he's the rudest man in the world, and I should know cos he said nearly the same thing to me when I went carols singing last Christmas.

"That'sth deffo trick, don't you think, Matthew?"

"Er? I suppose so, but… Maddie, what you doing?"

"Shush."

"But, what are you doing?"

"Postin' dog poo through his letter box, what'sth it look like? But my arm'sth a bit stuck. Hold it open an'…"

"DOG POO?"

"SHUSH! Yesth, Matthew. Robbie told me about it, so I got a bag of Spud'sth out the bin."

"You got *potatoes* out the bin? But you know I'm scared of…"

"Not potatoesth, idiot! Spud, our dog. A bag of his poo."

"*Eeeeeeeuw…* Have you been carrying poo round?"

"No, Trev hasth. It wasth in his pumkin lantern."

"Oh!"

"My brother said that when him an' Eggo used to do trick or treat if someone didn't give them any sweetsth, they'd set fire to a bag of dog poo; leave it on the front step; knock on the door an' then leg it. An' when the persthon answered the door they'd see the fire so they'd stamp on it an' get dog poo all over their slippersth. But, I'm not allowed matchesth, so I'm just gonna post it through his…"

"What the fuck d'you think you're DOIN'?!"

"WHAAAH! LEG IT!"

★★★

I don't believe this? It's so umfair to be in trouble for doing tricks on Halloween, cos isn't that the whole point? And, I bet you Matthew's not in trouble and it was his fault we got caught. He's such a idiot! He couldn't see where he was going cos his eye-holes were round the side, so 'stead of running away like a normal person, he ran straight into the man's house! Umbelievable! I was half-way up the street before I realised, and that was only cos I heard him screaming. Honestly, he can't even run away proply. Anyway, my dad's finished shouting at me, and he's nearly finished shouting at Robbie, so…

"What the bloody 'ell were you thinkin', Softlad? Tellin' her to post dog shit through someone's letter-box?"

"*Fuck sake*, Dad, I didn't tell 'er to do it. She asked me for a good trick so…"

"Yeh, well, your mum's just had a right ding dong

with that miserable shit on the end house, so I'd make myself scarce if I were you."

Knock! Knock!

"Ooh! Can I answer it, Dad? *Pleasthe*?"

"Go on then, but…"

"I'm answerin' the door – nobody get it! Happy Hallo— WOW!"

I think it's a actual witch?

"Isth that a costume, or your normal clothesth?"

"*Costume?*"

"Where'sth your hat?"

"My hat?"

"Yesth, your witchesth hat."

"Sorry?"

"I've never met a actual witch before. How old are you?"

"I'm not a witch."

"Isth that your normal face?"

"What do you mean, my normal face? Of course, it's my…"

"An' your normal hair?"

"Yes. Is…"

"An' your normal clothesth?"

"YES. Is…"

"So, you ARE a actual witch."

"For God's sake, I'm not a witch! You must be Maddison. Is Robbie in?"

Robbie?

"Well, my dad'sth shoutin' at him at the moment, but who shall I say wantsth him?"

"Tell him it's Andromeda."

"Ann Dromeda? That's a rubbish name for a witch. Okay, one sec – ROBBIE, THERE'STH A WITCH AT THE DOOR FOR YOU CALLED ANN DROMEDA, AN' SHE'STH PROPLY…"

"Do one, Shortshanks! Sorry about 'er, Andy. I told you what she's like. Come in."

★★★

Humph! Apparently, she's not a witch she's a goff – but I don't know how you're s'posed to tell the difference? She looks eggsacly how I imagined a witch would look – 'cept I didn't eggspect they'd have earrings in their face or in their tongues, either? But, if she's not a witch then why's she brought chocolate brownies? I spied them in her bag before – when Trev was checking for witches' knees – and everyone knows witches catch children with cake, so…

"Sweetheart, listen. Nanna's just been on the phone. She's had a bit of a to-do with some trick or treaters so daddy and I are going to nip up and check she's okay. Robbie's going to look after you until we get back, but we won't be long, so…"

"Isth she okay?"

"She's fine. She was on the toilet so she couldn't answer the door, so…"

"Are you ready, Liz? *Friggin' gnomes*! I don't see why it can't wait till tomorrow. What harm's gonna come to 'em on the shed roof?"

"Because, it's very windy outside and she's worried that they'll blow off. She's had them years and – what are you laughing at, sweetheart?"

"What d'you think she's laughin' at, 'ey? Fartin' gnomes, princess?"

"Hahahaha. Yup!"

I wonder what witches laugh at? Ann Dromeda's been laughing her head off in Robbie's room and – I wonder if they'll let me join in? I know I'm s'posed to stay put, but I've never played with a actual witch before. And, it *is* Halloween. I'll go and – ooh?

"It'll be fine, Andy. It's only ten minutes to the shop."

"But, what about your little sister?"

"Mum's put a DVD on for 'er so she won't even notice we're gone."

"Are you sure? She's a bit young to leave on her own."

"She'll be fine with Spud. Trust me. We'll be back before you know it."

"Okay. I must have dropped them at the bus stop and I can only smoke menthol."

"Come on – before she notices we're gone."

Well, I WAS watching *Goosebumps*, but… hmm?

"Are you sure it's okay for us to come in here, Trev? An' you're sure it'sth okay to have a go on his Xboxth while he'sth – OOH? BROWNIESTH!"

I'm sure they won't miss one?

★★★

"HAHAHAHAHA. Do it again, Spud. You're so – ooh! They're back. Hahaha. Why aren't I hiding, Trev? Hahahaha…"

"God, Rob, it's *freezing* out there."

"Don't worry, Andy, I'll keep you warm. So, it's between *The Wolf of Wall Street* or WHAT THE ACTUAL FUCK?!"

"Robbieeeeeeeee. Hahahahahaha…"

"WHAT THE?"

"Shit, Rob – the brownies! Oh, my God. How many did she eat?"

"Fuck knows? There's only six left. How many's that?"

"Enough. You'll have to tell your mum."

"Yeh, right. Imagine that conversation? ''Ey, Mum, guess what? Our Maddie's off 'er tits on hash brownies. Really, Robbie? An' how did she manage that? Oh, didn't I say? I left 'er on 'er own while I nipped to the shop for some fags!"

"What'sth hash, Robbie? Isth the room movin'?"

"Rob, what are we going to do?"

"Fuck knows! We could keep her 'ere till she mongs out."

"How old is she?"

"Seven."

"I'm not, I'm nearly eight. Robbie, isth the room movin'?"

"Shit! Shit! Shit!"

"Listen, Rob, I know it's not ideal but I'm ninety-nine per cent sure you can't OD on weed, so why don't we keep her here till she falls asleep then put her in bed? I'm sure she'll be fine and your mum'll never know."

"D'ya reckon? How d'you feel, Shortshanks?"

"Can I have some more cake, pleasthe? Hahaha. Cake'sth a funny word. Cake. Cake. Cake. Cake. CAKE. CAKE! CAAAAAKE! Hahahahahaha – keep sayin' cake, Robbie. It'sth *well* funny."

"For fuck's sake, she's proper bombed!"

"Should you be swearing like that in front of her, Rob? She's only – is that the front door?"

"ROBBIE! We're back!"

"Robbie, what'sth the difference between hash BROWNSTH, an' hash BROWNIESTH?"

"SHIT – ER?"

"Is Maddie in with you, Robbie? She's not in her room."

"What shall I say, Andy?"

"What can you—?"

"I'M IN HERE, MUM. I'VE BEEN EATIN' WITCHESTH..."

"Put a sock in it, Shortshanks! She's in 'ere, Mum, an' she's fine."

"Aww, how lovely! Can I come in? Hello, Andromeda, nice to meet you. I'm Liz, Robbie's mum. Come on, sweetheart, time for bed."

"I don't feel very well, Mum. I've eaten witchesth poisthon."

"I'm not surprised you don't feel well – you've consumed enough sugar tonight to keep an ant colony going for years. You look exhausted, sweetheart. Do you want me to carry you next door?"

"*Yesth, pleasthe. I'm very… very… sthleepy…*"

"It's all the excitement. Say goodnight to Robbie and Andromeda."

"Night, Ann Dromeda, an' thanksth for the browniesth… *yaaaaaaawn.*"

"Have you had a lovely Halloween, sweetheart?"

"Yesth… Ann'sth a rubbish name for a witch, isn't it, Mum?"

"It is, sweetheart. Hop into bed."

"I liked her browniesth, but the poisthon'sth made me soooo tired."

"Yes, I can see. Here, let me fluff your pillow up… and here's Trevor. Goodnight, sweetheart. Give Mummy a big kiss. Love you, infinity."

"I love you, imfinity, too… *yaaawn*… I ate lotsth of them, Mum."

"Lots of what?"

"Witchesth browniesth… Mum, what'sth the difference between hash brownsth an' hash browniesth?"

"WHAT?"

"Costh, I ate… *yaaaawn*…"

"HASH? OHMIGOD – ROBBIE!"

"Mum – you jumped me awake then. Hahahahaha. Happy Hallow-*zzzzzzz.*"

Stupid, Stupid Ballet!

This is gonna be the worst day ever. It shouldn't be allowed for your mum and dad to go to school just so the teachers can snitch on you. Stupid parents' evening. Fancy telling my mum and dad that my work's good – I'm very clever, apparently – but I have way too much energy, I never stop talking, and I mess about in class. And just cos all of that's true…

"Liz, love, have you seen those pies I brought back from last night's gig?"

Oh, yeah, my dad's started doing shows with his band again, and last night he played at someone's birthday party so me and my mum went with him. It was fantastic cos they had three different kinds of pizza AND a enormous chocolate birthday cake, and there was so much food left over that they gave us some to take home with us.

I've ate the cake already and…

"The mini meat ones, Joe? I haven't – no. Robbie's your best bet. Now, sweetheart, should Mummy call for the doctor? And should I tell him that my beautiful little daughter doesn't want to go to ballet class today, so she's covered her face in talcum powder then pressed her forehead up against the radiator… for how long, Maddie?"

God's sakes? How does she know that?

"If you want to fake illness, sweetheart, look in the mirror first. You have a considerable amount of talcum powder in your eyebrows and eyelashes, and radiator stripes across your forehead. You look like a cross between a Pierrot clown and Bagpuss."

"What'sth a pea row clown?"

"It doesn't matter. Now, get a move on because you're going whether you like it or not. You've only got yourself to blame, sweetheart."

Well, I'm definitely blaming it mostly on my teachers?

This is so umfair! Saturday's easy my favourite day of the week cos I don't have to go to school today or the next day either – but, humph! I can't wait till I'm a grown-up and I don't have to do stuff I don't want, cos you'll never believe what my mum's decided. She's decided that I've got to do something what'll use up my energy and make me calm down so she's forcing me to go to actual ballet. ACTUAL BALLET? I know?

I don't want to go to ballet, I want to go to kung fu, but she said it's bad enough having to apologise cos I posted dog poo through someone's letter box, never mind cos I've kicked someone in the middle of next week! And, how do you do that? I wouldn't mind finding out, but – ooh! She's coming.

"Sweetheart, are you—? Maddie, do they look right to you?"

I don't know? I don't know how ballet tights're supposed to look?

"The seams are meant to run down the back of your legs not the front! Take them off and turn them around and I'll be back in a minute."

Honestly, ballet's miles harder than I thought and I haven't even left the flippin' house yet. For starters, I've got no idea how they do these tights? Three times I lied them on the floor then put my legs in them, but every time I stood up, they were on the wrong way round? In the end my mum was so cross she did them for me. And I wasn't doing it on purpose – I really was that stupid! And – ugh! This leotard-thing keeps going up my bum! And she's pulled my hair so tight it's made my eyebrows go up – like when I get a surprise – which is definitely giving me a headache.

"I'm sorry you're having to make do with Rache's old hand-me-downs today, but we'll go to *En Pointe* next week and get you everything you need. It's been a while since I've…"

"But, I don't *want* to go today. I've got a abstholutely *terrible*…"

"I'm not listening, sweeheart, so you may as well stop there."

"But, my head might eggsthplode!"

"Then, I guess you'll be a YouTube sensation."

"But, what if it goesth all over the—?"

"Enough! You're going, and that's that!"

This is a disaster? I think I'm actually going?

I've tried being poorly but she's just egnored me and she proply bursted out laughing when I said I wanted to tidy my room. I even tried to waggle my tooth looser but she said I'm going even if they all fall out! Well, if I have to go I'm taking some things with me, so... *hmm? I'm gonna need a bigger bag?*

"Maddie, it's time for you to – hold on a minute. Give Trevor, here."

"But, I won't know anybody there!"

"No, but you soon will. It'll be good, sweetheart – you'll make some new friends."

"But, I don't want any new friendsth. I've got Matthew and Alliah and Simon and Michael. And, Alan and Lucy Cho…"

"Hand him over, Maddie! You're not taking a dinosaur to ballet class – they'll think you have a screw loose!"

"BUT – *bugger*."

"EXCUSE ME, WHAT DID YOU SAY?"

"I said, *bug hair*."

"I'm not deaf, Maddison – get in the car, now! And you can straighten your face while you're at it."

Meh.

I'm so umbelievably cross. Just cos Rache used to do ballet and she was proply good, doesn't mean that I will be. And what about when it's summer? I'm not doing ballet when I could be playing out! Well, she might be able to force me to go but she can't make me try. I'll just be absolutely rubbish on purpose…

★★★

"Elizabeth, dahling! How lovely to see you!"

Ohmigod? How weird's SHE?

"How long has it been? Six years? And, how is the lovely Rachel?"

"Actually, Miss Dew…"

Actually, missed you? That's rubbish cos Rache's never even mentioned her?

"… she's just got back from her honeymoon. So, Miss Dew…"

"Call me Daphne."

"Okay. Well, this is Maddison. Say hello, Maddie."

"Hello, Daphne."

"It's 'Miss Dew' to the students, dear. So, are you ready for your first lesson?"

Not in the slightest, Daphne…

"Erm?"

"Okay, dear, take your coat off and hang it on this peg, then if you'd like to pop your shoes on…"

Pop my shoes on? How? These laces are absolutely ridiclious?

"So, the honeymoon, Elizabeth? Where did they go?"

"The Maldives – absolute paradise!"

"Isn't it, just! Poor thing, coming back to a wintery November. I was so disappointed she chose not to further

her training – such a beautiful dancer, so I have high hopes for young Maddison, here."

Well, I wouldn't bother cos young Maddison can't even put her own shoes on…

"ARGH! God'sth sakesth! How're you s'thposed to do these stupid–?"

"Sweetheart, don't say that! And, not like that – you wind the ribbons up your legs – don't tie them in a bow."

"Well, I don't know, I've never done them be…"

"Lower your voice and stop making a scene."

"I'm NOT – I'm just SAYIN'!"

"Well, say it quietly."

"Are you staying, Elizabeth?"

"I can't, unfortunately. I've promised my mum that I'll take her to the hairdressers this afternoon, but I'll be here every Saturday, from next week on."

Erm, I don't think you will?

"Joe will pick her up. Do you remember Joe?"

"I do, yes. Well, I shall see you next week, Elizabeth. Are you ready, Maddison? Would you like to follow me into class?"

Not in the slightest, Daphne.

"Bye, sweetheart."

"Meh!"

Right!

"And, one and two and three and four, and, stretch and two and three and – Maddison, dear – I said, point your feet! No, not AT them? POINT them!"

"What d'you mean, Daphne?"

"Miss Dew!"

Why's she sayin' she's missed me? I haven't even been anywhere?

"Watch! Stretch *through* those arches and – that's it! What a beautiful instep you have."

What's one of them?

"And *plié*… keep your heels on the floor and, Sophie, dear, remember to tuck your tail in."

"OHMIGOD – WHO'STH GOT A TAIL?"

"And you, Maddison. Tuck your tail in."

"WHO, ME? I've not got a tail? I'm not a flippin' dog!"

"Your tailbone, dear."

"My, WHAT?"

"Don't stick your bottom out."

Why didn't she just say that?

"Perfect. Excellent posture. Don't forget to drop those shoulders…"

Drop my shoulders?

"Copy me, Maddison – YES! Excellent deportment."

She keeps saying eggcellent. I hope she's just being nice.

"And, *rest*."

Thank goodness for that? I don't s'pose it was all that—?

"Turn to face the barre. We'll have *Battement tendu* in first, second and third positions."

What – MORE? But my legs're killing and that's not even proper English? I've had enough…

"Where are you going, Maddison?"

"I need a wee, Daphne!"

"I need the toilet, 'Miss Dew'."

"You need one too? Are you comin'?"

"No… just… go… and hurry back!"

I don't think so?

I don't really need a wee but it's proply mental in there. Honestly, she's just making words up. And, it's inpossible to remember everything all at the same time. Point my feet; don't stick my bum out; keep my shoulders down; keep my back straight; pull my knees up – I didn't even know they were down? Keep my tongue in; stop pulling my leotard out my bum; stop pulling faces in the mirror, on and on and on. Oh, and the lady what's playing the piano – Miss Arkwright – she's *easy* the oldest person I've ever seen. Honestly, she looks like she'd die if you just said 'Boo' to her in a very quiet voice.

I can't believe people actually like this? It's worse than actual torture? And course, you're not allowed to talk in class so I can't imagine I'll be allowed to eat my mini meat pies what my dad brought back last night? I'll just have to eat them here, instead? It should be nearly over by then and… *mmm? These're well nice?*

"There you are, Maddison. I was beginning to think you'd fallen down the toilet."

Why didn't I think of that?

"What's that in your mouth, dear?

"Erm… *IcantreallytalkrightnowDaphnecosth…*"

I've got one and a half meat pies in my mouth and they're absolutely delic…

"GOOD GRIEF! Is that PASTRY?"

Flippin' 'eck? Even Matthew's not scared of pastry?

"Yesth. D'you want a bite?"

"HEAVENS, NO! And, it's rude to talk with your mouth full, dear."

Then don't talk to me when I'm in the middle of eating? And it's a pie not a flippin' tranchella! It won't kill you!

"Take my advice, Maddison. If you want to be a ballet dancer, steer well clear of pastry."

"But I don't want to be a ballet dancer, I want to go to kung fu, but my mum's completely forced me to come here, instead."

"Oh? Well, there's nothing quite like honesty. Come on, dear, back to class."

But, I've got a other two pies left to eat?

"Right, girls – everybody into the centre of the room. We'll have *Pas de Chat*, starting with the right leg first and – put that pie in the bin, Maddison. There's no eating in class."

No chance? I'm not wasting it?

"AH! Goodness gracious me! How is that even possible?"

Easy, really? You just open your mouth dead wide and – NOO? What's SHE doing here?

"Miss, sorry I'm late, miss. It wasn't my fault."

"It's okay, Lucy."

"Daddy's car wouldn't – MADDISON! What are YOU doing here?"

Eating a pie in one go, if you must know?

"Okay girls. We'll have *Pas de Chat*…"

She's doing it again? I'm gonna have to ask?

"Scusthe me, Daphne, but are you talkin' in a made-up language?"

"It's Miss Dew, Maddison. My name's Miss Dew."

"Oh? I thought you wasth sayin' 'missthed you'. Soz, Daph!"

"I – I give in! Okay, girls, don't forget, we have our exams in two weeks so…"

"EGGTHAMSTH? I'm NOT doin' THEM!"

★★★

"Maddison, will you please pay attention and stop pulling faces in the mirror."

God's sakes, this is worse than school? Least, I understand what Miss Spottiswood's saying, even if I'm not always sure who she's saying it to? And doing sums doesn't make my legs hurt!

I think you have to be a idiot to like ballet, and I'm not a idiot so – humph! Surely, it can't go on for that much longer? I hope not, cos I'm actually quite dizzy from all the spinning and…

"Okay girls, next week we'll really knuckle down for those exams… So, let me see some beautifully extended curtsies, and…"

"Thank-you-Miss-Arkwright…"

Am I s'posed to be joining in?

"And-thank-you-Miss-Dew."

"Thank you, girls. Class dismissed!"

Well, least I've got six whole days to make plans for being

poorly next Saturday cos there's no way I'm doing that again. I can't wait to get home and tell Trev how rubbish ballet is and… hmm? What are they all nosying at?

"I can't believe she's *that bad*, Lucy. And, really? Her name's actually Medicine?"

"Yes… and she is… honest to God… and her family's really poor… see, she hasn't even got new ballet shoes!"

"Are you talkin' 'bout me, Lucthy?"

"AND she's got nits!"

"I HAVE *NOT! YOU* WASTH THE ONE WHAT CATCHED…"

"My daddy said I'm not allowed to play with her cos she's common."

"Yeah, well, your dad'sth a knobhead, so who caresth?"

"No, he's not! Anyway, he said you're all CHAVS!"

What's a chav?

"So? Takesth one to know one."

"And your dad'll probably end up in prison FOR MURDER!"

"I mean it, Lucthy, if you don't shut your cakehole, I'll…"

"Tell your dad to murder me?"

"I can manage that by mysthelf but I don't want to…"

"And, no wonder you're so FAT, MEDICINE! How many pies is that now?"

★★★

One less than I'd eggspected, actually, and Lucy hasn't got a cakehole any more cos it's stuffed full of pie!

Anyway, it's all gone quiet now cos their mums and dads came to pick them up ages ago and the next class's gone in already, so it's just me on my own now and I'm getting proply bored. I wish my dad'd hurry up? He was s'posed to be here ages ago but… actually, I'm gonna go outside and wait. It's only a little bit raining and least it doesn't smell of sweaty – OOH? SWINGS!

"Hmm? Well, it'sth not *your* fault your dad'sth forgot about you, isth it, Maddithon? No! And, you have to do *something* while you're waiting for him to remember about you, don't you, Maddithon? Yesth!"

I'm not sure about the roundabout, though? There's two big boys on it and I'm not sure if they're nice or—?

"Oy! Tinkerbell! Talkin' to yerself, are ya?"

"Nope."

"What's in ya bag?"

"What'sth it got to do with you, nosthe disthease? Ballet stuff, if you musht know."

"Oooo-*eee*-ooo… Ballet, 'ey? You gonna do a dance for us?"

"Nope!"

"Got anythin' interestin' in ya bag?"

"Nope!"

"Let's 'ave a look!"

"Get lostht, idiotsth!"

"Hahaha… 'ave y'eard 'er, Ste? She's got a right attitude. Give us ya bag, Tink."

"NO!"

"Grab it off 'er, Ste. Hahahahaha…"

"GIVE IT BACK!"

"Hahahaha… Catch!"

"STOP IT!"

"Temper, temper, ya narky little…"

"GIVE ME MY BAG BACK! *NOW!*"

"Or what, Tink? You gonna whistle Captain Hook? Or Peter Pan?"

"Captain Hook'sth Tinkerbell'sth enemy, stupid. GIVE ME BACK MY BAG! RIGHT!"

"Hahaha… Argh – *FUCKIN' 'ELL – Aaaaaargh.*"

"Shit, Ste, you okay, bud?"

"Not really… … … She's crushed me fuckin' ball-bag… I can't breathe."

"She didn't 'alf boot ya one. Random, that?"

"Are you gonna give me my bag back now, or do I have to—?"

"Here, ya little fucker – get it yerself!"

"AH! SOME OF A BITCH! YOU BLOODY STUPID BUGGERSTH!"

God's sakes! How am I gonna get that?

★★★

I think my dad's actually forgot about me, cos I've been sitting on the roundabout for ages now, and I'm freezing cold, soaking wet, and covered in bits of tree. I was gonna go back to the ballet school but – at last!

"DAD! Where've you *been*?"

"Never mind, where've I been? What the bloody 'ell's 'appened to you? You okay, princess?"

"Yesth, but some big boysth took my bag off me

an' wouldn't give it back so I kicked one of them in his boy'sth bits an' his friend threw it up in the tree. An' when I climbed up to get it, I got my hair stuck in some twigsth, and when I tried to untangle it, my foot slipped and I fell out. I'm not hurt though, just a bit muddy, that'sth all."

"Okay, take a breath, kiddo – an' a BIT? I've seen hippos with less mud on 'em! How old were these boys?"

"I don't know – big – an' they wasth filmin' me, too!"

"Really? Well, if you see 'em, princess, you point 'em out, okay?"

"Yup!"

"An' I'll wring their feckin' necks! Come on, let's get you in the warm. Listen, your mum's gonna go ballistic if she sees you like this."

"What d'you mean?"

"Well, if she finds out I forgot you she'll probably – no, she'll definitely divorce me – an' when she sees the state o' you, well, our Rache never came home lookin' like a mud-baked hippo. So, how's about we make a deal?"

"Cool!"

"How's about, I'll phone your mum an' say we're goin' out for a bit, then we'll find a laundrette an' stick your clothes in – go for a Maccy D's – then you can put your clean clothes back on and she won't be any the wiser. Deal?"

"Deal! An' can we go to the toy shop asthwell? They've got massthive dinosthaur kitesth."

"Hahaha. Don't milk it, princess!"

Are you kidding me? I only fell out a tree what I wasn't

supposed to be in. YOU forgot to pick me up cos you were too busy watching football!

★★★

"Maddie, pass us your kite an' I'll stick it in the boot, an' not a word to your mum, d'you hear me? If she finds out you've been walkin' round town wearin' nothin' but my coat all afternoon, she'll hit the bloody roof!"

"I won't say anythin'. Promisthe."

"What? Like when it was her fortieth an' every other word was party?"

"I won't, Dad... Dad, why d'you think Lucthy'sth alwaysth horrible to me?"

"Why? She's probably jealous, kiddo. Let's face it, when she fell out the ugly tree, she broke every bloody branch on the way down!"

"The ugly tree? THAT'STH THEM DAD! THE BIG BOYSTH!"

"What, them two? By the recyclin' bins? Stay 'ere, princess, I won't be a minute."

★★★

"Liz..."

"Mum! We're back!"

"Hello, sweetheart, how did it – why are your tights on back to front? Did you take them off and put them back on again?"

Flippin' 'eck? She notices EVERYTHING!

"Erm? Yesth. When I went to the toilet."

"Why on earth would you take your tights off to—?"

"All right, Sherlock, leave the poor kid alone. Here, I got you some…"

"Ohmigod! What's happened?"

"What d'ya mean, what's 'appened? Nothin's 'appened. Can't I buy my wife a bunch of flowers with-out—?"

"I don't know, Joe. Can you?"

"Course I can. Everythin's fine, love."

"It isth, Mum. Look! I've got no mud on me!"

"What do you mean, no mud?"

"Liz! Your phone's goin' off."

"Yes, it'll be Rache, she's dying to know how Maddie got on. How did it go, sweetheart? Just let me answer it, one sec – Hi, Rache! Oh, hello, Miss Dew…"

Oh?

"Yes… yes… Oh, dear, no. No, they don't get on at all… Yes… *she didn't*… Ohmigod! I'm so sorry… Sorry, could you say that again?… Are you sure? Yes, goodbye, Miss Dew… You too, and once again, I'm sorry… okay, bye… yes, bye – JOSEPH! MADDISON!"

Joseph? I'll deffo let my dad go first?

Honest to God, besides the time I got lost in the Traffords Centre and accidently broke the hescalator by turning it into just stairs, my mum finds out…

"Maddison, come here!"

Uh-oh. Here we go…

"Did you or did you not ram a mini meat pie down Lucy Postlethwaite's throat?"

Did.

"So, that's where my pies went, you little tea leaf."

"Never mind your sodding pies, Joe – why didn't you pick her up on time?"

"Er? Is that your phone again, love?"

"Yes, and stay there, you two – Hi Rache, one sec, sweetie – you two are an absolute disgrace! Oh, just your dad and Maddison... How did she get on? I'll give you three guesses? No... No... It's worse than that – she's banned! Well, not banned but... I know!"

Eggsellent work, Maddison.

"But, Rache... I know... but that's tantamount to sending a drug addict on an errand to a crack house! Of course, I've heard of a crack house..."

I haven't? What's one of them? And, who's Tantamouse?

"But, she's lethal enough as it is. No, I haven't, why? What? WHAT? You're kidding? How in the name of God did that happen? I suppose so... you're right... oh, God, what am I letting myself in for?"

What?

"Okay, Rache, speak soon, love you too. Bye! RIGHT! Firstly, Maddison, why is there a video on Facebook of you kicking a teenager in the testicles? And, secondly – who taught you to use language like that?"

★★★

What happened is, when my dad went over to shout at the big boys they were watching the video of me, so my dad made them send it to him, then he sent it to Robbie and told him to put it on Facebook to make a holy show of them so they don't do it again. It's just a shame he didn't watch it right to the end though, cos my mum was *well cross* about me swearing. And, fancy asking me who taught me to use language like that. So, now my dad and Robbie are quite cross with me too. But, it's easy the most likes I've ever had, and you'll never guess what? I'm finally being allowed to go to kung fu! How brilliant's that? I can't wait to learn how to kick someone in the middle of next week, and I'll be nails just like Miss Piggy!

"Hey, Dad, watch me do this. HIY-YAH!"

"Watch what your doin', numbnuts – an' mind the bloody mirror! We've already had seven years' bad luck since your mum's waters broke with you – we don't want any more addin' to the sentence."

Charming! Actually, I'd better start practising if I want to win a gold medal at the Lympics cos…

Uh? Why's my mum sniffing me?

"Sweetheart – that's strange? Joe, why do Maddie's clothes smell of lavender fabric conditioner?"

I told him, you don't put the WHOLE bottle in…

"Because, since the wedding I've been using an eco-friendly, hypoallergenic one, and it's odourless."

"Oh? Right? Have you, love? Er, *well* – SHIT – watch what ya doin' – they're bloody sharp, them thorns!"

"THOSE THORNS!"

Aww, that's a shame? She's completely ruining her flowers…

"AND, GOOD! I KNEW you wouldn't buy me flowers for no reason."

Oh, well? I think I'll start practising my kung fu moves...

"So, Joe? What happened? You may as well tell me now because I'll find out one way or another..."

Humph! I'm going outside to practice. It's too flippin' shouty in here and I definitely don't want to smash anything this close to Christmas, cos I don't want to completely ruin my chances of getting a Xbox, so...

See you soon, everyone...

Good – Hi-YAH! – bye!

The Nativity

"Sweetheart, what's today's date?"

"Erm? Well, it'sth twelve daysth till my birthday, an' thirteen daysth till Christmasth, so…"

"So, it's December the twelfth, right?"

"Erm? I think so."

"So, how come there's only one chocolate left in your Advent calendar?"

Ooh? Did I miss one?

"Liz, love. What time's this thing today?"

"The Nativity? Two o'clock."

"Right. An' do I *'ave* to come? I'm try'na get as many hours in at work so we can have a crackin' Christmas, an' Larry's about as much use as a chocolate teapot at the …"

"A CHOCOLATE TEAPOT? Can I have one of those?"

"Shush, sweetheart, and yes, Joe, you do! You hardly ever come to any of her school things and she really wants you to."

I do, cos it's gonna be brilliant...

"All right, Liz, don't gimme the death stare. You'd better be good this afternoon, kiddo. Your mum says you've got the starrin' role."

"But, I've not. It'sth abstholutely rubbish! I haven't even got a..."

"Take no notice of her, Joe. She's just in a grump cos they won't let Trevor be in it. Which reminds me. Bag check! Let me see... good girl."

"Right, love, give us a kiss – you too, princess. See you later."

"Bye, Joe... hurry up, Maddie, and get in the car. We've got to pick Matthew up and I don't want to be late for the dentist... Robbie, we're going! Don't forget, you're in college at nine-thirty!"

***

Today's gonna be fantastic cos... just cos Miss Spottiswood won't *let* Trev be in the Nativity doesn't mean he's not gonna be... cos Mrs Jolley wouldn't let him be in last year's when we did the *Wizard of Oz*, but he was Toto for at least five minutes before she noticed.

I loved last year's cos I was the Wicked Witch of the West, with a broomstick and a green face and *everything*. But this year, can you believe that I haven't even got a costume? I know. And, how can the best part not have a costume? It's so umfair.

Lucy 'pie-face' Postlethwaite's being Mary cos her dad said so. Simon Eckersley's being Joseph cos his mum's sewing all the costumes. Carl Pilling's being King Herod cos he's the only one who's head's big enough to fit the crown. Stephen Henderson's the Star of Bethlehem cos he's the tallest in the class. Matthew, Chloe, and Thomas are being the Three Wise Men, which is ridiclious cos one of them's a girl! Michael Ryder's being the Angel Gabriel cos his dad's made the flying rope. Connor Pinkerton's being the front half of the donkey and Kylie Pinkerton's being the back, cos they're twins and they can practise at home. And, Alan's being the innkeeper cos Miss Spottiswood said that, least if he wets his pants this year it'll just go in the straw, and not like last year when it ran all the way down the Yellow Brick Road and onto Dorothy's ruby slippers. And, everyone else gets to be a shepherd or a angel or animals with fantastic costumes… and me? Who do I get to be? The flippin' n'rator! How rubbish is that? And, I have to be on stage the whole time, with tons of lines to say, and I have to do it all in my school uniform. Honestly, I can't even have a flippin' tea towel on my head or anything…

Miss Spottiswood said I'm being the n'rator cos I'm the best reader in year three, cos I wouldn't need a micra phone if I was playing at Albert's Hall, and cos she knows I won't run off the stage crying. But it doesn't matter what the teachers say cos I've decided to do my own plans. Imfact, I did my first one last night, when me, Trev, and one of my fancy-dress costumes went to

Matthew's house for tea, but only me came back. Well, Elaine never checks Matthew's bag. So, last night was the first time Trev's ever had a sleepover all by himself...

"Maddison! Matthew! Stop dawdling on the corridor!"

"Yesth, Mrsth Jolley..."

Bossy cow...

"Okay, Matthew, have you got everythin'?"

"Yes."

"Where'sth Trev? Let me – Trev! I've really missthed you. Now you stay there like a good dinosthaur... Can you remember the plansth, Matthew?"

"Yes. I have to..."

"Ooh, the bell! Come on, we can talk about them in classth."

We've been practising the Nativity all morning, and besides Chloe Barrow bursting into tears everytime she has to say 'Meh', no one's been aspecially rubbish. And, what is Meh? I know what gold is and Frank Instine, but Meh? And what rubbish presents to give a baby? What can a baby do with gold? Or a massive monster? Poor Jesus. No wonder he died of being cross. And, d'you know who else was cross before – Miss Spottiswood.

Deirdre Postlethwaite's sewed millions of seaquims on Lucy's Mary costume and now she's so sparkly you can't hardly look at her! Miss Spottiswood said it's s'posed to be the Nativity not The Grand Old Opry, whatever that is, and as far as she remembers, Dolly Parton wasn't present at Jesus' birth. But, she was even crosser with one of the shepherds cos he brought a tea towel what said, 'Keep calm and do the f*cking dishes'…

Anyway, we've just practised the last song, so it's nearly time for dinner.

"Thank you, children, and thank you, Maddison, for that ear-splitting rendition of 'Little Jesus Sweetly Sleep'…"

You're welcome.

"I believe the little Lord Jesus would have had considerable difficulty sleeping through that cacophony. Remember, Maddison – volume isn't everything! Now, do we all know our lines? Alan, don't forget it's 'there's no *room* in the inn, not womb. And, Michael, it's the Lord, not the lard! We're not frying chips, dear! Okay. Any questions? Yes, Maddison?"

"What'sth a fur gin?"

"And, I want everybody back from dinner, straight after the bell. Class dismissed!"

Uh?

★★★

Well, me and Matthew are completely starving now. We were so busy doing plans at dinnertime that we didn't have time for any actual dinner, but we think it's gonna be so good we'll probly be able to go for a McDonald's after it's finished. So, the first part's going smashing, though I am quite hot in here, and I hope my tummy doesn't rumble too loud before the big surprise, cos if Miss Spottiswood hears it then everything'll be – ooh?

"Okay, children – QUIET, EVERYONE! Now, hands up – not yet, Matthew, it's not a stick-up – hands up, any shepherds wearing unsecured tea towels? Miss Steadman, could you—?"

"MISS! MISS! Something terrible's happened!"

"Good Lord! What is it, Kylie?"

"Someone's pulled the head off the Baby Jesus!"

"Someone's *what*?"

"Jesus' head's come off and we can't find it anywhere! WHAT ARE WE GONNA—?"

"Calm down, Kylie. Right, own up – who pulled the head off Lucy's Tiny Tears?"

Well, I did actually, but I can't really own up right now cos…

"Come on. Somebody must know something! It's the Nativity, for goodness sake – not John the blooming Baptist!"

Who's John the blooming—?

"Take over, Miss Steadman, I'll get to the bottom of this. And, where's Maddison?"

She's in the music cupboard at the side of the stage, actually, and she would've brought a different costume if she'd known it was gonna be this hot cos it's flippin' *boiling* in here! Mind you, I have been hiding for quite a long time now. And, I know it's not nice to pull the head off Lucy's Tiny Tears but it'll easy go back on again, cos I used to pull the head off mine all the time to fill it up with water quicker and it went back on every single time. And, if Miss Spottiswood even *tries* to shout at me for doing it, I've wrote a list of all the things what Lucy's done to Trev so she won't have any legs to stand on, and I'll put its head back on straight after we've finished.

"Does anyone know where Maddison is? I thought it was unusually quiet. Has anyone seen – yes, Matthew?"

"She's gone to the toilet, miss. She said she thinks she's caught dire rear."

Brilliant! Just like we practised…

"Oh, okay, so, who's brought the reserve?"

"I have, miss. He's…"

"Matthew, didn't I say that Stuart Minion would make a highly unsuitable baby Jesus?"

"You *did* say that Miss Spottiswood, but then you said yes, anything to shut Maddie up…"

She did. And why isn't Stuart very Jesusy? Just, cos he's got one eye in the middle of his forehead?

"… and you said that he probably wouldn't be needed anyway."

"Did I really? Okay, Matthew, place it in the crib. What is the world coming to, Miss Steadman?"

"I know, Miss Spottiswood, but I'm sure nobody will notice. However, it is almost two and there's no sign of Maddison. We can't start without her."

"Actually, we can. She's not on for the opening song."

"Of course."

"So, if you could 'curtain up', Miss Steadman, and I'll go and fetch her. She's probably up to no good somewhere."

AH? What a cheek?

★★★

"So, mums and dads, I give you our year three's performance of… The Nativity!"

"Si-i-lent night"

"Miss Steadman!"

"Ho-o-ly night"

"Pssst! Miss Steadman!"

"Yes, Miss Spottiswood?"

"All is calm"

"I can't find her!"

"All is bright"

"What?"

"Round yon fur-ur-gin, mother and…"

"I can't find her, you'll have to do it!"

"Holy imfant, so tender and…"

Oh, no, she won't…

BANG!

"STHLEEP IN HEAVENLY PEA-EASTH – HIYAH, MUM! STHLEEP IN HEAVENLY PEAAAAAASTH."

"Oh, good Lord! What is she *wearing*?"

"A SWAT vest, Christmas hat, grenade belt and machine gun, Miss Spottiswood."

"TODAY WE'RE GONNA TELL A STORY WHAT CHANGED THE WHOOOLE WORLD!"

"I thought so – I'm going to get fired."

"THISTH ISTH THE STORY OF THE FIRSTHT CHRISTMASTH…"

It's going really good so far. Miss Spottiswood did try to get me off the stage, but everyone was laughing so much

– and she couldn't catch me anyway – so, she ventually gave up and left me. Then my dad turned up and when he saw me he bursted out laughing, right in the middle of a sad bit. It wasn't meant to be a sad bit, but one of the shepherd's stood on the Star of Bethlehem's dress by accident and he fell off the edge of the stage. Then, after he'd finished crying and Miss Spottiswood'd tried to bend his star back into the right shape, we carried on singing 'Star of Wonder'. 'Cept, he didn't look like the Star of Bethlehem any more, he looked more like a wonky Teletubbie. And now it's coming up to the big surprise…

"An' The Three Wisthe Men arrived at the stablesth, bringin' gold, Frank Instine, and Meh!"

"We-are-The-Three-Wise-Men-what-followed-the-star-to-Bethly-hem."

"We've-brought-these-gifts-for-the-baby-Jesus. Can-we-see-him-please?"

"Yes. He's-in-his-crib. What-gifts-did-you-bring?"

"I-brought-him-some-gold."

"Thank-you-wise-man!"

"I-brought-him-some-frankin– hahahaha, look who's in the…"

"Shush, Thomas."

Thanks, Matthew…

"And-I've-brought-him-some-MAAARGH! Oh? Haha. It's okay, it's only…"

"BEE HOLE! THE MAGNIFICTHENT BABY JESUSTH! ROAAR!"

Stick THAT in your pipe and smoke it, Lucy flippin' Postleth…

"MADDISON ELIZABETH McLAREN! Remove that dinosaur from the crib, this instant!"

It's not up to you, Mrs Jolley-Jelly. You're not my teacher.

"And, SEE ME, after school!"

Bugger! Where did he come from? Cos, it's definitely up to him…

★★★

I can't believe I have to see the flippin' headmaster? I'll be late for my McDonald's and everything! Least, my dad's here and he's nowhere near as cross as my mum. Imfact, he said it's the best laugh he's had all year. I wish my mum thought the same thing though. 'Stead, she's all… ooops, she's talking again…

"What I don't understand, Maddison, is why?"

"Why, what?"

"The SWAT costume? Why?"

"Costh I thought you'd be well crossth if I wore my zombie dressth to do The Nativity."

"But wearing a SWAT vest's okay? And why pull the head off Lucy's Tiny Tears?"

"Costh when Missth Spottisthwood wasth choosin' who wasth gonna be the baby Jesusth, she said Trev wasth too ugly then made a really mean song up about him. Then she said I wasth only the n'rater costh we didn't have enough money to make me a costume, so…"

"Mr and Mrs McLaren, could you come in, please."

"Of course. Wait here, Maddie. And no listening through the door."

"Friggin' 'ell, Liz, it's like bein' back at school all over again."

"Not for me, it's not. This is the first time I've ever been called into the principal's office and I'm forty years old!"

"How the fuck did you manage that? I had my own speck, I was in there that often."

"Close the door and take a seat, Mr and Mrs McLaren."

"Thank you, Mr Tickle. First, may I…"

"Mr Tickle? Hahahaha. Sorry, mate, but fancy havin' a Mr. Man for an 'eadmaster."

That's what we all say…

"Take a seat please, Mr McLaren."

"Thank Christ for that. I feel like Gulliver, sittin' on those little kiddie chairs."

"Er… yes! Quite! So, about Maddison."

"Whattabout 'er?"

"Well, Mr McLaren, we've had an official complaint from Mr Postlethwaite…"

"Who, that prick? What's up with him now?"

"He claims that his daughter has endured psychological trauma, due to the decapitation…"

"Psychological bollocks, more like!"

"JOE!"

"Yes, Mr McLaren. Which leaves me no other option than to suspend Maddison, pending an enquiry."

"ENQUIRY? Are you 'avin a laugh?"

"Now, I am aware that Maddison has presented Miss Spottiswood with a list of occasions where she claims that Lucy has been, and I quote, 'mean to Trevor'…"

"That friggin' dinosaur, Liz! I'm…"

"Mr McLaren, *please*. And as extensive as that list is, as Mr Postlethwaite rightly pointed out, 'Trevor' is not a pupil at this school and therefore has no business attending it."

"*You what?* Is this a wind-up?"

"I beg your pardon?"

"You're pullin' my plonker, right?"

"JOE!"

"So, she pulled a doll's head off? So, what? It's hardly an 'angin' offence – an' it's back on now, isn't it?"

Yes, thanks to my dad…

"Fuckin' nonce couldn't even put a doll's head back on!"

"JOE!"

"An' how come all the other kids got to dress up an' our Maddie didn't?"

"Well, Mr Mc…"

"I'll tell you why! Cos, that snot-nosed bastard has way too much say in what goes on in this school. Fuckin' Mary? If his kid was any more wooden, she'd be a fuckin' spoon!"

"Calm down, Mr McLaren…"

"She looked like Dolly pissin' Parton! It's supposed to be the Nativity not The Grand Ole bloody Opry!"

"JOE!"

That's 'xactly what Miss Spottiswood said, but without all the swearing.

"Do you 'ave any idea how many times our Maddie's come home upset cos o' that spiteful little… cos, she's told our Maddie that she's common an' we don't love her cos we haven't bought 'er the latest friggin' gadget. She's seven for f-God's sake! When I was seven, all I had was a catapult an' an imaginary friend. I mean, who gives a seven-year-old an iPad Pro? They're seven hundred quid! An' we're supposed to buy our Maddie one so she doesn't get the piss ripped out of 'er?"

"Mr McLaren…"

"I haven't finished yet! She's a little shit-stirrer that Lucy, tellin' people Maddie's got nits, or mange, or some other shite. I usually keep out o' school stuff but not this time. So, you can tell that arrogant prick, Postlethwaite, that if he's got a problem to sort it out with me, an' to leave my princess out of it! CAPICHE?"

"Ahem… right… well…"

"Come on, love… *fuckin' Postlethwaite*… At least our Maddie doesn't go cryin' to the 'eadmaster when things don't go her way. Say goodbye, love – we're done 'ere!"

OH! MY! GOD!

"Let go of my arm, Joe. GOODBYE, MR TICKLE! Joe, have you been drinking? He'll report you to the school board!"

I hate it when they whisper…

"Will he bollocks, report me. I'm tellin' ya, love, he's got his hand so far up Postlethwaite's arse he could take his tonsils out from the inside! An' he knows it!"

"*Joe?*"

"What, love?"

"Is it weird that I feel… *you know*…hahaha…"

"You what? You're kiddin' me, right? Hahaha. I'll text you next time someone grinds my gears. But, seriously, love… suspendin' her for pullin' a doll's head off?"

"It does seem a tad severe."

"Remember when I picked her up from ballet a few weeks ago… I never told you at the time cos you had a massive bag-on, plus, I couldn't get a word in edgeways… but she asked me, 'Why's Lucy horrible to me all the time?'. D'you know what she said to her in front of all the other kiddies – besides the usual shite – that we're common chavs an' I'll end up in prison for murder. That's why she rammed the pie down her throat, to shut 'er up."

"What a HORRIBLE thing to say. Sweetheart, come here…"

"So, 'ow d'ya fancy a Maccy D's, princess?"

Is this really happening?

"Joe, this is sending out very mixed messages."

Stop whispering again. I have to hold my breath to be able to hear.

"Look, Liz, besides takin' Godzilla to school, which technically she didn't… let me finish… what exactly did she do wrong? They wouldn't give her a costume, which is pretty shitty if you ask me, so she used her initiative and brought her own. Nobody complained. Everyone thought it was funny as…"

"Yes, but…"

"So, she wiped out Lucy's doll an' shoved Godzilla

in the crib, which again she didn't…"

"Yes, Joe, but she did pull the head off it."

"So? It's a bloody doll, love. Jeeze, I remember my first nativity. Two o' the angels had a proper punch up cos one of 'em said the other one's line, then halfway through his speech, King Herod put his hand down his strides an' pulled out a massive great turd!"

"OHMIGOD! Hahahaha…"

"An' you know our Maddie, Liz. She wouldn't do anythin' like that without good reason, even if it is a bit skewed."

"No, she – sweetheart? Why's your face a funny colour? Are you holding your breath?"

"Yup! I was practisin' for if I ever drowned."

"Weird child…"

"An' I'll tell you what, love. Never mind pullin' her doll's head off. If that'd been me on the receivin' end of all her bullshit, I'd have twatted the little…"

"OKAY! We'll take her to McDonald's!"

***

Honest to God, if my mum tells me one more time that she's not rewarding me for bad behaviour I'm gonna squirt ketchup in her face. It's bad enough here in McDonald's, but least I can escape… but now we're gonna drive round looking at all the Christmas lights, so I'm gonna be trapped in the car and…

"An' 'ey, princess, I wanna word with you. Stop drawin' dinosaurs on the car windows! I'm not kiddin',

Liz, I started the car this mornin' then sorted the sat nav…"

Why? I only drawed them in the condysation? It's not like I used a flippin' crayon or anything? And I only drew a couple…

"… an' when I looked up, love, it was like bein' in Jurassic Park. I'm not kiddin' – dinosaurs everywhere! So, I gets the cloth to clean 'em off, not realisin' it was covered in sherbet, an' it went all over the windscreen! I coulda bloody…"

"One sec, Joe. Sweetheart, I've just recieved a text from school. They said that on reflection, they've rescinded your suspension and will be expecting you bright and early in the morning. That's excellent news, isn't it?"

What's the opposite of eggsellent?

"And now you'll be able to go to the school Christmas – ooh, my phone. One sec, it's Nanna. Hi, Mum, where've you been? I tried calling your mobile several times but… you were what? Ohmigod! Are you okay?"

"What'sth up with Nanna?"

"But, you're okay now?"

I wondered why she wasn't at my nativity.

"Yes, of course. I don't know why you didn't just ask him in the first place!"

"What the bloody 'ell's she done now?"

"Hang on, Mum… She's fallen out of the loft trying to get her Christmas decorations down."

"She's what? Hahahaha."

"Isth she okay, Mum?"

"She is, sweetheart. Nothing's broken other than a

box of baubles. Okay, Mum, we'll be there as soon as we can."

★★★

Poor Nanna. Least my dad got all the rest down for her, even if he was laughing the whole time. He said it's not a good idea to drink that amount of eggnogs then climb in the loft. But, guess what? She had a other Advent calendar for me, and even though it tasted like it'd gone off a bit, I'm up to the fifteenth of December already. Anyway, we're gonna try to look at all the Christmas lights again and... I can't believe there's only a few days left before I get my Xbox. And can you believe how good I've been all year? Imfact, I might have been so good that I get extra games. Ooh, one sec...

"Mum, that'sth the place where I do kung fu!"

"I know, sweetheart, and I promise I'll come to watch you soon."

"Oh yeh, I forgot to tell you, love. The guy said can we 'ave a word with 'er about calmin' the fuck down – preferably before she kills someone – but, other than that, she's shit hot!"

Yes! I'm definitely gonna get a Xbox in thirteen days time. I'm not sure how I'm gonna manage to wait that long though, cos I'm completely, absolutely and ridicliously eggcited, already. But, I've got to go now cos...

"Mum! Look at that one! Why can't we have a massthive Father Christmasth on our roof?"

"Don't start, Maddie."

"I'm not startin', I'm just asthkin' a – LOOK AT ALL THEM FAIRY LIGHTSTH! Can we have some more on our housthe?"

"Sure, princess, if you wanna pay for 'em... an' for all the extra leccy they use... an' if you're gonna put 'em up."

Fantastic, but, hmm? I don't think I've got any pocket money left? Oh, well, I'll just have to go carols singing again... but I definitely won't bother going to Mr Dog Poo's house this time cos he never gives me anything so it's just a waste of voice. Anyway...

See you all soon, everyone...

Ohmigod, I'm SO eggcited...

Byeeeeeeee!

Happy Christmas Eve-Birthday!

"Erm? Thanksth, Nanna. I've alwaysth wanted my own game of Junior Bingo."

Junior Bingo? Is she mental?

"I'm so glad you like it, poppet."

"Erm… I do, but, I'm probly gonna open my chemisthtry set first, costh…"

"Good Lord! Which idiot bought you a chemistry set?"

"I'll give you one guess, Mum. Robbie! And you're not playing with that now, sweetheart. I'd rather you blew the house up after Christmas, if it's all the same with you."

"Oh… okay."

"Okay? Is that it? No arguing?"

"I'm eight now, Mum. I'm all growed up!"

"All grown up, and I know. I can't believe my baby's eight. Time goes so fast…"

No, it doesn't. It's taken me ages to be eight.

"Imagine how I feel, Elizabeth. My little baby's forty! And, if you think time goes fast now, just wait until you're my age. One minute you're playing kiss-catch in the playground, then before you know it, you're pushing up the daisies."

Pushing up the daisies? Ooh? My dad's back...

"Ey up, princess, how's the birthday girl? Where d'ya want this turkey, love?"

"Just plonk it in the kitchen, Joe, I'll see to it in a minute. What took you so long?"

"I was in next door's. Mike shouted me in cos they had a coupla pressies for our Maddie, an' cos you're not drinkin' tonight, I had a cheeky one with 'em. But, we can get taxis, love, it's not too late to..."

"No, Joe, it's fine. I don't want a hangover on Christmas morning and Jonathon's more than happy to drive."

"Dad, shall I go an' say thank you to them?"

"Gordon Bennet! You're volunteerin' to say thank you? Is this my princess, or an alien swapsie?"

"It'sth me, Dad, but I'm all growed up."

"Ah – I see! Well, they've gone pickin' Wendy's dad up, kiddo. He's stayin' with 'em over Christmas, Liz, an' he's a right rum bugger accordin' to Mike. Oh, yeh, they've invited us round Boxing Night, but I said I'd speak to the boss first."

"I thought you wasth the bossth, Dad?"

"I bloody wish! What d'you say, love?"

"Yes. It should be okay."

"Just okay? Don't get too excited, will ya?"

"Sorry, Joe, I'm a bit tired, that's all."

"I hope you're not comin' down with that flu bug, love. Larry's still on his arse with it."

"No, Joe, I don't feel fluey, just…"

"Dad, what doesth pushin' up daisiesth mean?"

"Ha! Let me guess? The Grim Reaper's been on about 'er favourite subject again?"

"Don't call my mum that, Joe."

"It's okay, Elizabeth, you should hear some of the names I have for him. Now, if it's all the same, I'd like to go for a lie down before we go out to dinner."

What, again? But, she was asleep when we went to pick her up? And who sleeps in the day, besides vampires?

"I was out with Mavis again last night, and I'm a bit long in the tooth to be burning the candle at both ends."

Ah? Vampires've got long teeth – and don't they burn candles too?

"Before you go, Betty, I 'ave to ring the restaurant to confirm the order for later, so is yours still the prawn cocktail an' fillet steak?"

"It is, Joe, and remember to tell them no garlic! You know how I hate garlic."

Don't vampires die from garlic?

"Er, they don't need that much detail, Betty, just what ya…"

"And, I want my steak bloody or I shall send it back. Am I okay to go now?"

She wants it bloody?

"Nanna, are you a actual vampire?"

"A vampire? No, poppet. Whatever made you say that?"

"Costh you're alwaysth asthleep in the day, you've got long teeth an' you like blood an' hate garlic."

"Hahaha, that's so— what do you mean, *long teeth*?"

"So, that'sth why my dad saysth you're a pain in the neck."

"*Princess* – I never said that, Betty!"

"Of course, you didn't, Joe. Well, I'm off for forty winks. Can someone wake me when it starts to go dark, please? That should give me ample time to get ready."

And she gets up when it's gone dark? Hmm?

"Sweetheart, could you tidy some of your presents away, please? At least so we can see some of the carpet? And before you start…"

"Yup!"

"Goodness me. I could really get used to this 'no arguing' business, Joe. Couldn't you?"

"I'll believe it when it lasts."

"I've told you, I'm all growed up."

"Well, sweetheart, you can start by saying 'all grown up'! Now, chop, chop. We can't have the birthday girl being late for her own celebration."

No, we can't but it's ages off yet… and the birthday girl's had a smashing birthday so far.

First, Alliah dropped my presents off when she was on her way to the airport – she's gone to see her nanna for Christmas, what lives in Bangledesh! Then, Ben Eckersley dropped my presents off cos Simon's in bed with the flew. *Awww!* Then Jonathon and Rache turned up and had a fantastic surprise for me and Matthew – they took us to the cinema to watch a movie, then to The

Smoothie Bar for a chocolate milkshake, and then we went to The Farm Shop to pick up my mum's Christmas order and had a play with some bunnies while we were there. But we had to come home after that cos Matthew's staying at his auntie's house in Wales, tonight, and Elaine doesn't like driving in the dark…

"Madds, are you coming to watch *The Grinch*? And mum said you can open the Christmas chocolates now, so…"

"COMING!"

★★★

"How cute does she look in those furry boots, Mum? With her skinny jeans too?"

"I know, Rache, and that matching gillet's gorgeous. Where did you find them? Honestly, it's the first time I haven't had a stand-up argument with her over what she's going to wear – probably since she first learned to talk."

"They were online. I've had them weeks now, and I've been dying for her to try them on."

I'm not a flippin' dress-up dolly but they are brilliant. Imfact, they're the first clothes someone's choosed for me what I actually like. Mostly, cos these furry boots make the bottom half of my legs look like Chewbacker's off *Star Wars*, and this furry jacket-thing makes me look like a monster with no arms. Even Robbie said I look fantastic – like Sussquashed, which is a complimence, apparently…

"Er, I know it's your birthday, princess, but get Godzilla off the table, will ya? An' tuck your elbows in while you're eatin' – you look like you're try'na take off!"

"Take off?"

"He means your elbows, Shortshanks. You look like an aeroplane with 'em stickin' out."

"This lamb's gorgeous, Liz. What's your fish like?"

"Absolutely delicious! The sea bass is cooked to perfection and the fondant potatoes are to die for. Would you like a taste, Joe?"

"Nah, you're all right, love. What's yours like, Rache?"

"Yoursth looksth abstholutely disgusthtin', Rache! What isth it?"

"Hahaha, thanks, Madds. They're called Langoustines."

"Longer steamsth?"

"Would you like to try one?"

Try one? I don't even want to sit in the same room as one?

Honest to God, when it turned up I thought she'd ordered a plate of pink monsters cos it didn't look anything like food… but that's cos all the outside stuff was still on them. And d'you know what the outside stuff was? It's head, body, and legs! I know! And by the time Jonathon'd pulled them off there was hardly anything left on Rache's plate, so she'll probly be starving later – but, least hers was actually cooked. Nanna's steak had so much blood coming out of it that I had to move to the opposite end of the table, but it's just as bad at this end cos Jonathon's eating a actual duck! Imfact, there's only me and Robbie what's normal…

"How are your chicken goujons, sweetheart?"

Well, besides all this other stuff they've put on my plate…

"They're lovely, Mum."

"And how's your burger, Robbie?"

"Er? Nice, once you pick all the green shit off."

"Robbie, have some decorum, please. Joe, are you going to do the toast?"

"I am, love. Okay, everyone, well, Christ knows 'ow but she's survived another year – just the one trip to A&E, 'ey, Liz? Which is a whoppin' improvement on previous years. D'you know, princess, there was a time when you'd had that many accidents or shoved somethin' where you shouldn't, that I had my own parkin' space at the 'ospital!"

"And, at the doctor's, too, Dad – she was *always* in there! Hahaha. Remember the time you took me to see Doctor Aziz, Mum, because I had really bad period pains?"

"Shit, Rache. I'm try'na eat 'ere!"

"Behave, Rob! Wait until you hear this, Jon. I was a bit embarrassed so Mum came in with me, and Madds was with us, of course… and do you remember, Mum? She kept pulling on his stethoscope and asking him 'what does it do'?"

"Yes, and he told her it helped him hear things better…"

"And, bearing in mind, Jon; mum had a major crush on Doctor Aziz…"

"Did she now? First I've heard of it?"

"I didn't have a crush on him, Joe, I thought he had

412

a nice bedside manner, that's all."

"Steady on, love – go easy in front o' the kids!"

"You know what I mean."

"Anyway, Jon. Doctor Aziz asked me what the matter was, and before I'd even had chance to answer, Maddie grabbed hold of his stethoscope and yelled down the end of it, 'I've not done a poo for three days!' The poor guy nearly had a heart attack, didn't he, Mum? I'll never forget the look on his face, hahahaha… I think she blew his ear-drums out. Then, after he'd calmed down and asked her why, she told him she'd eaten most of the money out of her moneybox…"

"And she had, Jonathon! I checked when I got home and she'd eaten £2.57 in change! I had to take her to the hospital for Xrays, and every time she went to the loo we had to search through her…"

"All right, love, people're tryin' to eat! Where was I? Oh, yeh… so it's been an okay year. One trip to A&E…"

"Two trips actually, Joe. What about the next day, when we had to go back to apologise?"

"Oh, yeh… two trips to A&E. But we 'aven't been called to the school…"

"No, but that's because on two occasions we were already there – and when she shoved Carl's head through the railings it was her first day back and I think they just felt sorry for me!"

"Okay, love, calm down. So, besides…"

"And she killed two fish, made a TV appearance *and* got herself banned from ballet!"

"And bingo! Hahaha…"

Nanna!

"What do you mean, bingo?"

"Oy! Am I ever gonna finish this bloody toast? Raise your glasses to our little…"

"And what about the salmon, Joe? Have you forgotten about that? AND she knocked a penguin out at the zoo!"

Flippin' eck? Maybe I haven't got a Xbox?

"Yeh, but, besides all that…"

"And what about the two old ladies? The paramedics had to be called out to one of them, and I doubt the other one will ever feel safe on a public toilet again!"

The one at the pizza place? But that was Trev? And it was his fault about the other one too. If he hadn't got stuck under the shelf at the supermarket then…

"Bloody 'ell, Liz, 'ave you finished? We're gonna be 'ere all day. To our Maddie! She might have the odd screw loose but we wouldn't swap her for a big clock!"

"A BIG COCK?"

"Clean your ears out, princess. I said a big clock!"

"HA! I'd swap 'er for a bag o' fresh air, Dad!"

"An' I'd swap you, son, for one with an 'ole in it. Happy Birthday, kiddo – to Maddison!"

"TO MADDISON! CHEERS!"

"Thanksth, everyone. Cheersth, Nanna."

"Cheers, poppet!"

Ohmigod…

"Nanna, what'sth that your doin' cheersth with?"

"This, poppet? It's called a Bloody Mary."

"A BLOODY MARY! What the flippin' 'eck's that?"

Absolutely disgusting, that's what it is! It's made from vodcar; tomatoes mixed with wuster sores, and blood! I know. Who drinks tomatoes? And what on earth's wuster sores? And is drinking blood even allowed? I can't believe no one's said anything?

"'Ey, love, 'ave you seen the time? It's comin' up to twenty past seven."

"Ooh, sweetheart, this time eight years ago, I was in agony over you!"

Not THIS again?

"Honestly, Jonathon, I bent down to take the turkey out of the fridge and my waters broke all over the kitchen floor…"

I still don't know what that means, break water? Cos I've managed to break most things but I've got no idea how you break that?

"So, I shouted Joe, who… and I'm not making this up… told me to cross my legs and keep breathing while he watched the end of *Only Fools and Horses*! Can you believe that? And, it wasn't even half-way though."

"Yeh, but it was the Christmas special, love."

"That you'd seen a million times before!"

"Yeh, but how was I supposed to know she'd be out not long after it finished? You took ages knockin' the other two out…"

"Ohmigod, Dad. Knocking us out? Please tell me you'll be a tad more poetic, Jon, when we have kids."

And you were dead surprised cos I wasn't s'posed to come out for at least a other two weeks…

"And, I was so surprised, Jonathon, because she

wasn't due for at least a fortnight…"

But, you was dead glad I came out cos…

"But, once she was born and I knew everything was fine, I was so relieved to get her out. She never kept still, did she, Joe? You were convinced she was the next Steven Gerrard; her kick was so powerful. But, we weren't prepared at all, were we? I hadn't even packed a bag. Because Rache was born on time and Robbie was really late, it never entered my head that you'd be early, sweetheart."

I know! You tell me the same thing every year. And now, how you went mental at my dad for being drunk…

"Yeh, Liz, an' you proper fell out with me cos I'd had a few scoops an' couldn't drive you to the 'ospital… but it was Christmas Eve, for Chrissake! I was havin' a quiet festive tipple, laughin' my head off at Del Boy an' Rodders, then next thing you're screetchin' like a barn owl that your waters've broke an' can I take over from you peelin' the bloody sprouts! The last thing I was expectin' that night was the Little Lord Whatthefuck to make an early appearance. I'd've been less surprised if Father Christmas'd dropped down the chimney, an' we haven't even got one!"

"So, how doesth he bring all the presentsth then, Dad?"

"Oh… er… *he…*"

I know he's not real.

"So, Jonathon, I ended up having my baby on the kitchen floor! It was the worst nativity scene imagineable."

"It wasn't that bad, love… but every time I tried to

move you, you proper kicked off."

"Yes, Joe. Because, by that time I just wanted to punch you in the face, and have you ever tried to stand up with a baby on it's way out? Honestly, Jonathon, I checked the Guinness Book of Records for the fastest delivery time afterwards, and she wasn't far off."

"D'you remember the Three Wise Paramedics, love? Standing on newspaper on the kitchen floor… hahaha. You screamin' that the next time I want sex to 'Ask the soddin' Trotters', an' Robbie and Rache yellin' every five seconds, 'Can we come in yet?'"

"Yes, Dad, but it was traumatic, wasn't it, Rob? One minute we we're upstairs drinking hot chocolate with marshmallows and watching *Home Alone*; then next minute we're in the dining room, listening to our mum screaming her head off on the kitchen floor. And, I'd turned fourteen, remember. I wanted to help."

"You probably would have been more use, Rache. He had one eye on me and one eye on the TV, Jonathon, then just as Maddie's head popped out I heard, 'Eff me! Woollies is closing!'"

"What'sth Woolliesth?"

"It was a chain store, sweetheart."

A chain store? No wonder it was closing if that's all it sold? And now 'bout how noisy I was…

"Yeh, but, when the rest of her popped out – Jesus Christ! I asked 'em if they could shove her back in, she was so bloody loud."

"It was deafening though, wasn't it, Joe? You used to call her 'Audrey', after the plant in the *Little Shop of*

Horrors, remember? Feed me!"

And, I wasn't a bit like the other two…

"And, she wasn't at all like the other two, Jonathon. Rache was so quiet I used to forget I had her. She'd just lie there watching the world go by, happy as Larry…"

"Or, Stefanosth Popple Octopusth. Hahaha…"

"Not *again*, Maddie. And, you, Robbie. You arrived three weeks late…"

"No surprise there, 'ey Flash!"

"… and then pretty much slept until you were three. We used to think there was something wrong with you."

"There was, love, an' there still is. It's called lazy shite-uss."

"Very funny, Dad. An' I'm not lazy, I'm chilled."

"Chilled? If you were any more chilled we'd have to feckin' defrost you!"

"Leave him, Joe… but you, sweetheart, you were anything but! I'll never forget the first time you walked. I was absolutely astonished, Jonathon. My mum'd won Trevor in a raffle and intended to give him to Robbie…"

"Yeh, son, if you'd've had him back then, he'd o' been in the bin years ago."

"Don't listhen, Trev!"

"Anyway, Jonathon, I'd put him on the coffee table waiting for Robbie to get home from school, but Maddie saw him; shrieked her head off; waddled right up to him and grabbed hold of his tail. I just stood there, open-mouthed! And then she started bashing him on the coffee table, which had a glass top at the time…"

"Not for long, 'ey, princess?"

"Anyway, I tried to get him off her but she *wouldn't* let go, and every time I said 'let go', she just said 'E OR', which sounded like Trevor, and that's how he got his name."

And, I wasn't even ten months old…

"And, you were only nine months old. I didn't know babies could walk that early. Anyway, thirty minutes later the glass top was in pieces and Joe had to come home from work early to get the safety gates out of the loft."

"Yeh, an' nothin's been the same since. Thank Christ that's all over with, 'ey. You're all growed up now, aren't ya, kiddo?"

"Yup!"

"It was lovely though, Joe, when they were little…"

"Lovely? It was a bloody nightmare. Specially, with this one."

I wonder what's wrong with Nanna? She keeps scratching…

"Nanna, are you itchy?"

"I am, poppet. It's this necklace Mavis bought me."

"Sorry to interrupt, Betty, but I'm spittin' feathers 'ere. More drinks, anyone?"

"Go on then, Joseph, if you're twisting my arm, I'll have a port and lemon this time."

"What about you, princess? D'ya want another Shirley Temple?"

Shirley Temple, again? But, I thought it was either a building or something to do with hair?

"Make that two, Joe. I'm all coffee'd out."

"I'll have another prosecco, please, Dad… and Jon's fine for now, aren't you, sweetie?"

"I'll have another pint, Dad… an' will you go to the

bar for 'em? It's miles quicker than…"

"What d'ya think I am, Softlad? A fuckin' octopuss?"

"JOE! And there are such things as trays."

"It'sth okay, Mum, I've heard swearing before, and now I'm eight, I might start doin' some mysthelf…"

"What d'ya mean, start, Shortshanks? You wanna hear 'er, Mum, when you're not there!"

"Oh, really, Maddison?"

Erm? Ooh! Nanna's scratching again…

"Why'sth Nanna itchy?"

"I must be allergic to the metal, poppet. See, it's a beautiful silver…"

OHMIGOD? Nanna's got the shape of a cross burned on her! She really IS a vampire.

"I thought it was silver but it must be nickel because of my allergy…"

Think, Maddison? What gets rid of being a vampire?

"It's such a shame…"

I know silver bullets kills them? Or, is that weird wolfs?

"'Ey, Liz, remember before when Maddie asked if your mum was Dracula? Look! She's been burned by a cross. Hahaha…"

Ooh? I remember? Something 'bout putting steak on your heart? But, I can't do that cos she's ate it already?

"Are you sure you're not Dracula, Betty? You always look like death warmed up."

Ooh? I remember? Holey water! But, how do you make holes in water?

"If I *were* a vampire, Joseph, I wouldn't bite you. I prefer my meat young and fresh!"

So, let me think? She sleeps in the day and wakes up when it's dark? She said about having long teeth? She hates garlic but eats and drinks blood? She's lergic to crosses and my dad says she's a pain in the neck? Yup! Definitely a vampire…

"Hey, Elizabeth, I'll tell you who I wouldn't mind a bite of. Who's that actor? The one who plays the grey wizard in Lord of the whatssits?"

"Sir Ian Mckellen?"

Gandalf?

"That's him!"

"Er – Nan."

"Yes, Robbie?"

"You do know he's gay, don't ya?"

"IS HE REALLY? Well, I never! I still wouldn't mind a bite of him though. He's got the look of the…"

"Oy, Flash, are ya comin' to the bar, or what?"

"Yeh…"

I can't let Nanna bite Gandalf – she'll go to actual jail? Do it now, Maddison. Make her go back to normal before she…

"Er… sit back down, princess. No one invited you."

No chance… I'm on a inportant mission…

"He's got such a twinkle in his eye, don't you think, Elizab— OHMYGIDDYGOODGOD!"

"MADDISON?"

"Have you stopped being Draclia, Nanna?"

"Well, *that* was unexpected!"

Ohmigod – Jonathon just talked!

God's sakes, it was only a jug of water, and most of the ice cubes'd melted by then so it couldn't have been *that* cold.

And, how am I supposed to know it's Holy Water from a church? I was only trying to save her from going to jail.

Anyway, now that I've eggsplained why I did it and everyone's finished laughing at me, we're gonna order our afters. It's the main thing I come for cos they're brilliant here... so, I can't decide between stiffy tocky pudding with ice cream? Or chocolate brownies with ice cream? But I've gone off brownies quite a bit since Halloween... or just a ice cream Sunday with loads of...

"Earth calling Maddison. Have you decided yet, sweetheart?"

"Yesth! Pleasthe can I have the ice—?"

"And a large chocolate sundae with extra everything, please."

"'Ey, Mum, when did Mrs Collins kick the bucket?"

"Quiet, Robbie!"

"Hahaha. What doesth kick the bucket mean?"

"Nothing, sweetheart."

"She must be dead well over a year now..."

"*Robbie, shut...*"

"DEAD! Mrsth Collinsth isth dead? But, you said she'd gone to live in a Stralia, Mum."

"I... she..."

"Isth she *really* dead?"

"She is, sweetheart. I didn't want to upset you so..."

"Nice one, Softlad. What the bloody 'ell did ya say that for?"

"I was just try'na remember, that's all – cos o' the time she came here with us – an' I didn't know she didn't know."

I *didn't* know! And, I was so upset when I thought

she'd gone without saying goodbye to me cos I thought she didn't like me anymore, but I'm not so upset now cos dead people don't have any choice…

"Mrs Collins always used to say that you were the only thing keeping her going, sweetheart, but then one day, I guess she couldn't keep going any more."

"So, what did she die of?"

"A shortage o' breath!"

"Really, Dad? So, what'sth Pearly Gatesth?"

"I'll tell you what it is – miserable bloody talk! She's eight not eighty an' it's only four hours off Christmas! 'Ey, princess, d'ya reckon Father Christmas'll—?"

"Bring me a Xboxth? Well, I know he'sth not actually real – soz, Mum – so if I haven't got one, then it'sth not really Father Christm— OOH! ICE CREAM!"

I don't see how I can't *not* have got one, though? I mean, I have been on my very best behaviour all year. And, I know I've had a couple of little accidents but nothing really bad, and like my dad said, we've only had to phone for a ambalance once this year, which is miles less than all the other years, and we haven't had to call the fire brigade, the police or the… one sec…

"Aaargh!"

"Bloody 'ell, kiddo, you made short work o' that. It didn't even touch the sides!"

"I know… *aargh!*"

"What's up?"

"Brain freezthe. Aah! It killsth, Dad!"

"Well, that'll teach you to shovel it in so fast."

No, it won't. I do it every time.

"An' don't you have to 'ave a brain to get brain freeze?"

"I have got a brain!"

"Yeh, but it's not screwed in right."

"So, Dad, will you be pushing the sofa up against the living-room door tonight?"

"Too bloody right! We don't wanna repeat o' 2012, Rache."

"No, we don't. Listen to this, Jon. She came downstairs about three thirty in the morning…"

"Yesth, but I asthked Nanna *first*!"

"Who was half-cut on sherry and eggnog…"

"I have no recollection of this, Jonathon, but according to Maddie I said yes, so at half-four in the morning she woke the whole house up crashing her new bike into the patio doors! Do you remember, Joseph? You thought we were being burgled, so you flew downstairs and…"

"Bloody 'ell, *yeh*! She'd left the lid off one of her new jigsaws at the bottom o' the stairs, an' I came tear-arsin' down; stood in it, an' went arse over tit!"

"Hahaha… yes, Joe, and by the time I arrived on the scene you were splayed out in the hallway with Maddie standing over you, dressed in her Harry Potter cape and glasses; waving her wand and shouting 'Reparo'!"

"Yeh. An' cos I'd sprained my ankle an' I was limpin' all day, she had a right gob on cos she wouldn't 'ave it that we hadn't bought 'er a wonky wand."

"An' I wasth covered in glitter and paint, wasthn't I, Mum?"

"You were, sweetheart, you looked like a Christmas tree bauble. And you'd eaten almost a whole tub of sweets, so, yes, Rache, we will be blocking the living-room door again this year."

"Where was I when all that 'appened? I wondered why you'd started doin' that, Mum."

"You, Robbie, slept through the lot!"

"Was that the year I got totally shit-faced an' threw up out my bedroom window?"

"It was – straight onto the flat roof, Jonathon, and Spud jumped out and started eating it!"

"Yeh, an' I nearly fell off the bloody roof, tryin' to get him back in!"

"Dumb dog. What does he wanna eat puke for?"

"Eeeeeeeuw… Spud'sth ate sick?"

"Aye, princess, an' it's not the worse thing he's eaten. When he was a puppy he used to regularly eat his own sh…"

"Joe! What is it with this family? Why does every conversation end up with us talking about breaking wind? Or going to the toilet? Or being—?"

"Hang on a sec, love. CAN I GET THE BILL PLEASE, MATE? An' 'ey, princess, well done! Besides, 'vampire-gate' – are you nearly dry now, Betty?"

"Yes, Joseph. Thankfully the lion's share went in my face."

"You've managed to be'ave yourself all night."

"I've told you, Dad, I'm all growed up!"

"Madds, promise me you'll never do that. What would we have to talk about?"

"'Ey, Shortshanks, check it out! I think you're gonna get serenaded again."

Not again? They do it every year and it's well imbarrassing. It wouldn't be so bad if they could actually sing or if they didn't keep telling my mum about how cute I am. Which I'm not!

"Pleasthe, can we go now, Mum?"

"We can, sweetheart, just let your dad settle the bill. And, Joe, don't forget to leave them a decent tip."

"All right, love. Giz a chance, will ya!"

"Because the food was excellent as always…"

Hurry up, everyone – they're coming?

"Come on, Trev. Let'sth leg it outside before they start singin'."

"…and the service was absolutely-OHMIGOD-MADDISON!"

Uh? How did that happen? Well, least they don't have to clear the table now cos everything's on the floor…

"What were you sayin', love? Leave 'em a decent tip?"

"I didn't mean THAT! You, and your big mouth!"

"'EY? What've I DONE?"

"Congratulating her on behaving herself while we're still in the restaurant!"

Aaah? So, that's how it's happened? The label off the tablecloth's got stuck on Trev's tail?

"You, what?! Don't go blamin' me! You're the one said she could bring Godzilla!"

"HAAAPPY BIRTHDAY TO YOU. HAPPY BIRTHDAY TO YOU. HAPPY BIRTHDAY DEAR…"

"JESUS H CHRIST – I can't hear myself THINK!"

"Happy birthday to you. Hip Hip Hooray…"

"Robbie, tell everyone to stop shoutin'! It wasth a accident!"

"What? Like you, Shortshanks?"

"OY, SOFTLAD! STOP TELLIN' HER SHE WAS A BLOODY ACCIDENT!"

Do something Christmassy, Maddison?

"OH! JINGLE BELLSTH, JINGLE BELLSTH, JINGLE ALL THE…"

"Be quiet, Maddison!"

"You all be quiet! It'sth my flippin' birthday!"

"'Ey, Shortshanks!"

"What?"

"SMILE!"

★★★

Well, I hope Robbie's got a new phone for Christmas cos I really am brilliant at kung fu, and I think I might've just broke that one? But, the lady whose dinner it landed in said it was okay cos accidents happen all the time, and she'd had enough anyway, and my mum did a specially good job of cleaning all the gravy off her glasses. But, I've told Robbie I'm sick to deaf of him taking photos of me when I'm all covered in stuff…

Anyway, we're home now and we're watching the *Muppet's Christmas Carol*, which is my favourite

Christmas film ever, and when it's finished my mum's gonna read me *The Night Before Christmas* once I'm in bed. But, I'll never sleep, I'm so eggcited…

"*'Happy Christmas to all, and to all a good night!'* Okay, sweetheart, remember, no coming out of your room in the morning, not until either your dad or I come to get you."

"Okay, but, what time can I start makin' noisthe?"

"You can't, now give Mummy a kiss. Mwah! Love you, sweetheart. Night, God-bless."

"Sweet dreamsth, Mum… Night, God-blessth."

Ooh! Ooh! Only nine hours till I can play with my Xbox. I wonder what games I'll get with it? But, what if I don't get one? I can't see how?

"What d'you think, Trev? D'you think we'll get a Xboxth?"

"*ROOOAAARRRRRR!* I think we'll definitely get one, Maddi…"

"Stop roaring, Maddie, and go to sleep!"

"It wasthn't me, it wasth Trev!"

"Well, tell Trev to stop roaring and go to sleep, too. Father Christmas will be here soon."

No, he won't. But, just in case…

Merry nearly Christmas everybody and… *Rooooaaaaar…*

Goodnight!

We Wish You a
Merry Christmas...

SIX o' FLIPPIN' CLOCK? How can they still be
asleep? Have they forgot that there's presents to open?
I've been waiting ages for someone to come and get
me. Imfact, I've already eaten most of what was in my
stocking; jumped on my bed and been accidently noisy
on purpose, but so far, no one's even woke up to tell me
to go back to sleep.

If they don't wake up soon, Christmas'll be nearly
– ooh, that's weird? Spud's barking his head off? He
doesn't normally bark when everyone's in bed? And, he's
proply barking, too. How can they not wake up? And –
AH? What if it's burglars after our Christmas presents?
Okay, so, I know my mum said I have to stay in my
bedroom till someone comes to get me but someone's

got to imvestigate? And seeing as I'm the only one what's awake…

"Come on, Trev, let'sth see what'sth up with him."

He's going proply mental… like when the postman comes or…

"Spud, stop barkin'! What'sth up with you? Aww… d'you want to go in the kitchen? Are you thirsty? I wonder which stupid idiot left the door shut? There you – NOOOO! SPUD, NO! HELP, EVERYONE – COME QUICK! THERE'STH A ACTUAL CAT IN THE KITCHEN!"

Well, they're all awake now! And I'm never gonna drink booze when I'm a grown-up cos besides that I hate doing a sick *and* having a headache, it turns you into a absolute idiot. Robbie came home from the pub in the middle of the night and went outside to do smoking, but he left the patio doors wide open and a cat ran in the house. And cos he was too drunk to chase it, he shut the door on it and then went to bed. Least, he didn't decide to burn pizza but still… the kitchen looks like a massive twister came to visit, stead of a pussy cat, and my dad's arms are so scratched he looks like he had a fight with a actual tiger.

Anyway, now Nanna's finished having a nearly heart attack, and my dad's finished washing blood off his arms and shouting at Robbie, and my mum's brushed all the broken glass up and made everyone a brew, and Rache's finished bossing Jonathon round and washing her face we can finally open the presents. I'm so eggcited, I might do a actual wee!

"Dad, *pleasthe* can I do the countdown now?"

"I…"

"54321OPENTHEPRESENTSTH!"

Ooh? Which one's my Xbox?

"All right, princess, calm down. Here, this one's yours. It's off your nan."

"Ooh? Ooh? What isth it?"

"How the bloody 'ell should I know? Open it an' find out… Christ, Liz, I thought the cat was feral – look at the speed she's rippin' into it!"

I'd be speedier if it wasn't for all this cellar tape? Why do grown-ups put so much on?

"Yesth! A dinosthaur onesthie! Can I put it on now, Mum? Can I?"

"Yes, sweetheart. Come here and I'll…"

"I can do it mysthelf!"

"Okay – *sorry* – I forgot you're 'all growed up'. Erm, that's the wrong way around, Maddie. I'm fairly sure the tail's meant to be at the back."

"Oopsth! Stupid idiot, Maddithon. Hahaha. I'm silly, aren't I, Mum? Ta-dah! How cool do I look? Thanksth, Nanna. Look, Trev – we're twinsth!"

"You're welcome, poppet. Just be careful where you're going with that tail. I didn't think it through properly, did I, Elizabeth? That's definitely an accident waiting to happen."

Everything's a accident waiting to happen, 'ccording to Nanna?

"Here's another one for you, princess. An' this is for you, Rache."

I can't see anything what's shaped like a Xbox? But it could be at the back I s'pose?

"Ooh! Look what I got, Mum. It'sth a 'lectric shock game! Thanksth, Robbie, it'sth…"

"Bloody 'ell, Soft-shite! What the 'ell did you buy 'er that for?"

"Why not? It'll be fun…"

"Yeh, well, we'll see how much fun it is next time you come home shit-faced an' make a balls-up, cos I'll be attachin' yours to it!"

"An' a 'Merry Christmas' to you, Ebeneezer!"

"Maddie, poppet, this one's off Mike and Wendy."

"Ooh, let me see! I wonder what it– Oh? Oh, no – don't look, Trev! Someone cover histh eyesth."

"Can't he do it 'imself, Shortshanks?"

"Coursthe not, idiot – histh armsth aren't long enough."

"What is it, sweetheart? Is it another dinosaur?"

"Yup! It'sth a stegosthaurusth."

"Hahaha. A what, Shortshanks? A stego what?"

"A stegosth – oh! Not funny, Robbie. I don't want a other dinosthaur, Mum, I only want Trev. Can it just be a ormanent?"

"Yeh, Shortshanks, whatever. Okay everyone, the moment you've all been waitin' for. Here's one for Mum an' Dad… an' one for you, Nan… an' you, Rache. An' as requested, one for Margaret an' Alistair. So, I give you The McLaren Christmas Calendar – enjoy!"

I wish they'd all stop laughing at pictures of me and concentrate on opening the presents...

"Hahahahaha. Oh, Madds, look at you in June! Was that when she put the barbecue out with that massive watergun-thing, Mum? So funny! She looks like a sooty Ghostbuster..."

"Yes, Rache. My personal favourite though I didn't think so at the time, is October. The montage of your wedding."

"I know, Mum. I can't believe I missed all of this. Ohmigod, Madds, the indignity of it all! And look at the colour of your face..."

Great! Me, having a poo in a carrier bag with a purple, blackberry face...

"At least it was a posh carrier bag, Mum, so there wouldn't have been any holes in it – ohmigod! I never got to see this. Hahaha... you look... hahahaha..."

Great! Me, with one side of my hair like Shirley Temple and the other side like Cousin Itt...

"I remember this, though. Worzel Gummidge! Hahaha. This is fantastic, Rob. You have to do this every year."

No, he flippin' well doesn't. I'm sick to deaf of him taking photos of me...

"No sweat, Rache – I intend to! Check out April. She's in the bin with pepperoni stuck to 'er grid."

"What made you climb in the bin, Madds?"

"Costh, he hid my Easter egg in there."

"Rob, that's cruel! Which is your favourite, Dad?"

"Deffo the front cover. The one of her holdin'

Godzilla in the air, waist high in the fishpond. She looks like the Statue o' Liberty after a zombie invasion. 'Ey, princess, at least you only killed two fish this year…"

Yes, but there's still time to kill one brother! And, where's my flippin' Xbox?

"SCUSTHE ME! Can everyone just stop doin' thisth an' open more presentsth?"

"Keep your wig on, kiddo… 'ere, open this."

"Ooh? Ooh? What is it? I'm so eggcited in case it'sth – Oh? Erm? Who'sth thisth off?"

"What is it, sweetheart?"

"I don't really know?"

"Oh, Madds, that's off Margaret and Alistair. It's a bouncy castle… and don't blame me, Mum. I only mentioned to Margaret how she's forever jumping on her bed and next minute she'd ordered it. I think she forgets that not everyone lives in a Manor."

"Well, next time can you tell her that she loves cooking and the oven's on the blink? Hahaha…"

"You can tell her yourself if you accept her invitation for New Year's Eve. Do you like it, Madds?"

"Coursthe, I like it. It'sth just – never mind! Can I blow it up now, Mum?"

"No, you blooming well can't!"

"But if you take my lambshade off it'll easy fit in my bedroom."

"I don't care, Maddie – you're not having a bouncy castle in your bedroom. There's nowhere near enough room in there, and knowing you, after one bounce you'll come straight through the living room ceiling. Here,

434

open this off Mummy and Daddy."

Hmm? It's a bit big for a Xbox?

"So, what do you think, Mum? Are you gonna come up for New Year?"

"Maybe… it just depends on your dad and whether he can be bothered driving…"

A DESK? How's that a present? I think I'm gonna do a cry.

"Do you like it, sweetheart? Now you've got somewhere to do your homework."

Great! An' I s'pose there's plenty of room in my bedroom for a stupid desk!

There's no way I've got a Xbox now cos I've got loads of presents off my mum and dad already. I've got a desk – not great. A proper kung fu suit – great, but I'm not allowed to wear it in the house cos I'll kick things, apparently. A new coat cos I melted my last one with a sparkler on bomfire night. I didn't *want* a new coat but…

"Madds, you haven't opened ours yet. Will you pass it to her, Jon?"

"Sure. Merry Christmas, Maddie."

"Thanksth, Jonathon."

It's quite heavy and almost the right shape? I wonder? AH!

"A labtop? Thanksth! I can't believe you got me a actual labtop. Wow!"

"I'm glad you like it, Madds. Don't worry, Mum, it's more of a learning tool – she can't go online with it properly… and you can do your schoolwork on it too, sweetie."

Will everyone stop talking about school and…

"Okay, Liz, that's it, I think? All done for another year. What d'you think of your camera, son?"

"It's shit hot, Dad! I've been lookin' at these GoPros for a while now. How did ya know?"

"We do listen to you on occassion, son. What about you, Rache?"

"I can't believe it, Dad. I can't believe I'm actually going to see Adele!"

Erm? What about my—?

"Right, then. Hands up, who's for bacon sarnies? I'll do it, love, you've got enough to do with the Christmas dinner."

Don't cry yet, Maddison…

"So, that's everyone except … *princess*? Hello! Is there anybody there?"

I was sure I'd been good enough? I don't know what I did wrong?

"Oy, princess, who knitted your face an' dropped a stitch? D'you wanna bacon sarnie or what?"

Not really. I'm too busy trying my best not to do a cry…

"Sweetheart, are you okay?"

"Erm? Coursthe, Mum. I wasth just thinkin'…"

"Thinking, what?"

I was thinking, how come I didn't get a Xbox?

"Don't be tight, Liz – she's nearly in bloody tears! 'Ey, princess, look what I just found. It's off Godzilla."

Uh? Trev's got me a present? Surely, he can't have got me a Xbox? He doesn't get enough pocket money?

"'Ere – open it!"

Oh? It looks like a deevy dee? But – UH?

"What's the matter, sweetheart? Don't you like it?"

"Well, I think you've got comfusthed costh…"

"Poppet, would you be a good girl for Nanna? Fetch my handbag out of the dining room, please."

Erm? Can't you see, I'm a bit busy at the moment, Nanna?

"I will, but…"

"Now, please. I need my tablets."

"But can't I just – *okaaay*."

"There's a good girl."

Humph! Well, I can't have been that much of a good girl cos I didn't get a Xbox and I've been on my very best behaviour all year. How good do I have to be? And Nanna's not gonna die if she waits one more minute for her – *ooh? What's that next to her hambag?*

"To our dear little Maddithon. Merry Christmasth, sweetheart. Love you, imfinity. Mum and…"

NO WAY? OHMIGOD? It looks like it could be… oh, please, please, please let it be a… ohmigod-ohmigod-ohmigod…

"YESTH! OHMIGOD! EVERYONE, COME AN' SEE! I'VE GOT A XBOXTH!"

"Hahahaha. Your little face, sweetheart, when you thought you hadn't got one."

"YESTH! YESTH! YESTH! YESTH! YEEEEE…"

"Calm down, princess, an' watch what you're doin' with your tail. The house's taken enough of an hammerin', what, with that bloody cat!"

"'Ey, Shortshanks, no excuse for touchin' mine, now."

"Hahahaha. You might wanna rephrase that, son."

"Thisth isth the BESTESTHT Christmasth, EVER!"

"All right, Tiny Tim! Pipe down, will ya? We're not all deaf!"

"Soz. D'you like Xboxesth, Rache?"

"Not really, Madds. I only tried playing on one once. Do you remember, Rob?"

"Hahaha. Yeh! Every time you saw a zombie, you shit yourself an' dropped the controller."

"I did. Anyway, I don't know about you lot but I'm starving. Mum, you go and sit down and we'll sort this. Rob, will you set Maddie's Xbox up, please? Dad, you get the bacon on… and Nan and I will get everything else ready. Oh, and Jon, come with me, you're on brew duty. Grab the Baileys, will you? McLaren Christmas coffees, coming up!"

Well, besides having a little bit of a sore throat from screaming 'I got a Xbox' about a million times already, this is the bestest day ever!

After we'd finished our breakfast I talked to Matthew on the phone for a bit, and he's definitely coming back in time for Mike and Orange Wendy's party tomorrow. Then I accidently knocked the Christmas tree over with my onsie tail, so my mum said I could put my kung fu suit on, but no kicking… but then I accidently kung fu kicked Robbie cos he put a photo of me all tangled up in the Christmas tree on Facebook. So, now I'm wearing my zombie dress but I think it's a bit too small? Good job I got money of Auntie Ailish for Christmas cos I'm definitely gonna need a bigger one…

"Oy, Shortshanks, your Xbox's workin' now, an' you're up to fifty-two likes on FaceTube!"

★★★

Wow, it's weird having my own Xbox. I keep eggspecting someone to come in and shout at me for playing on it, though Robbie did shout at me for trying to borrow his 'Gram Feft Auto' game before – and he said I'll ventually get used to my hands not feeling like my own, or maybe don't play on it for so long? So, I'm gonna stop for a bit now and see what's going on…

"Hello, sweetheart, I was just about to come and get you. It's nearly time for dinner and we haven't seen much of you at all today."

Nearly time for dinner? How long have I – oh my goodness? I can't believe it's nearly three o' clock? No wonder my hands feel weird? I've been playing on my Xbox for nearly *four hours*! It's proply awesome though, so…

"'Ey up, princess. If we'd known it was gonna keep you this quiet we'd have bought you one years ago, wouldn't we, Liz?"

"Maybe… and I hope you haven't been eating too much rubbish, sweetheart. You'd better still have room for your Christmas dinner."

I have got room, but… I don't know why I look forward to Christmas dinner cos I really don't like most of it. I don't like turkey, sprouts or colly flowers… or the yellow carrot things what taste like weird potatoes…

"Quiet everyone, she's starting!"

Who's starting?

Oh, flippin eck, Nanna – not The Queen, again? Why can't she talk to us on a different day? Why does she have to do it at Christmas? I wouldn't mind, but it's umbelievably boring, and she's so posh it's hard to tell what she's saying. But Nanna absolutely loves her – she's always going on about how fantastic she looks and how wonderful she is, but she's just a very old lady in a very funny hat – or sometimes a crown – what mostly looks so cross that she wants to kill people!

"Oh, Elizabeth, doesn't she look regal?"

"Well, she is the Queen, Mum. Sweetheart, move Trevor off the table, please. I need all the room I can get."

"I wonder how many outfits she owns?"

"I have no idea – Robbie, love, put these parsnips next to the roasties."

Parsnips! That's what the yellow carrot things are called…

"I hope *I* look that good when I'm ninety. Isn't she marvellous for her age, Elizabeth?"

"Yes, Mum. Move your elbows, sweetheart. I'll put these next to you."

"Yesth! Pigsth in blanketsth."

"She must have fantastic genes, mustn't she?"

"Yes, Mum. Joe, love, will you see to the bubbly, please?"

The Queen doesn't wear jeans. Old people never wear jeans.

"She didn't attend church this morning, did she? I hope she's okay. Do you know what's—?"

"I don't *know*, and I don't *care*! Sorry, Mum, I'm a bit busy at the minute. Rache, can you bring the gravy through, please? Okay, has everyone got a drink? Maddie, would you like a taste of Nanna's Spumante?"

Spew WHAT? I'm not drinking sick on Christmas Day?

"Erm, no thanksth, Mum, I'll just have fizzy – ooh, The Queen'sth gone!"

"Switch the TV off please, Joe, and I'll put some Christmas music on."

"My pleasure – an' 'ey, love, this looks bloody gorgeous."

"Thanks, Joe... Okay everybody, time to pull your crackers."

"Mum, pull crackersth with me!"

"Okay, sweetheart... pull... pull... clever girl!"

"Yesth! D'you want the hat, Mum? Hey, everyone! What'sth Good King Wenth – I can't say that – what'sth that man'sth favourite pizztha? D'you give in? One what'sth deep pan cristhp an' even. Hahaha! Dad. Pull crackersth with me."

"Aren't you crackers enough, princess? Okay... pull... pull... well done, kiddo!"

"Yesth! D'you want the hat, Dad? Hey, everyone, this one'sth brilliant. What d'you call a one-eye dinosthaur? D'you give in? A 'do-you-think-he-saw-usth'! Hahahaha..."

"Jeeze, Shortshanks, that's got more cheese than the cauliflower sauce. Come round 'ere an' pull mine."

"Rob, son, you might wanna re-phrase..."

"Dad, stop bein' such a perv!"

"What'sth a perv?"

"Nothin', Shortshanks. Grab hold an' pull… don't even bother, Dad!"

"Robbie, you're pullin' too hard. You're pullin' me over."

"I'm hardly doin' anythin', Shortshanks. Pull 'arder!"

"I am. I'm pullin' my abstholute– WHOA! OH! Oh! *Oh!* Oopsth! Soz, everyone. What d'you call a blind reindeer? D'you give in? A no-eyed deer! HAHAHA."

I don't get it?

Have you heard of The Donimoes Effect? I just have. It's when one donimoe falls over and knocks all the others over too, 'cept, 'stead of donimoes it was actual people. Stupid Robbie. Fancy letting go when I was pulling my absolute hardest, so it's actually his fault that Jonathon's covered in gravy.

Anyway, my mum said that, so long as I eat two sprouts and two mouths of brockally with colly flowers and cheese, I can eat what I want. So, I've ate millions of pigs with blankets, and so far, six Yorkshire puddings; four roasties and some stuffing. But, the best bit was the red jam. We don't normally have jam with roast dinner, but it tasted so nice that I've…

"Maddie, just because you have an Xbox doesn't mean that I can't take it off you…"

I never thought of that?

"… so, eat your broccoli! Joe, would you pass the cranberry sauce, please?"

"You'll have a job, love. She's ate the bloody lot!"

"*Oh, Maddison!*"

"What?"

"A whole jar of cranberry sauce? What did you do that for?"

Well, first, cos it made my sprouts taste a bit less revolting, and second, cos Christmas afters are actually quite disgusting. It's the only cake in the world I don't like and the only pudding in the world I don't like and the custard's the wrong colour with booze in! Imfact, everything's got booze in it at Christmas – even the mint spies! And, the other day when I was at Nanna's I pressed the squirty-cream squirter in my mouth and nearly did a sick! *I don't know who Tia Maria is but she makes the horriblest squirty cream?* And the pudding's absolutely horrid! Imfact, it's so horrid, my mum puts actual money in it to get us to eat it, but I don't care how much money she puts in, I'm still not eating that. Mind you, I'm hardly surprised it's horrid, cos if she poured booze all over chicken nuggets then set fire to them, I probly wouldn't like them either?

Anyway, everyone's nearly finished eating their dinner so we've decided that after we've had our afters, if I'm quiet while everyone has forty winks, when they all wake up we can play games. I love playing games. Imfact, after being off school for two weeks and getting presents and chocolate and fizzy pop and sweets – ooh, and all the decorations and stuff – playing games is the best thing about Christmas. And, I can't wait to play the 'lectric shock game cos I'm deffo gonna win at that. I always win games where you have to be the quickest at something, but that's probly cos I'm the only one what's not usually drunk…

★★★

"Argh! Shittin' 'ell, that hurt! Hahaha…"

"Don't be such a wuss, Joe. And I thought with you being an electrician you'd be used to the occasional shock? It can't be that bad, surely?"

"This might surprise you, love, but we don't play Russian roulette with the leccie at work. An' if it can't be that bad, why don't you have a go?"

"Yes, Mum. I'm more than happy to swap."

"It's okay, Rache. I'm more than happy to…"

"Argh! Shit-a-brick, that's…"

"Robbie! Right, that's enough. Put this away and we'll play 'Who am I?'."

"But I've not had a 'lectric shock an' neither'sth Jonathon or Rache!"

"It's okay, Madds, I really don't want to get electro-cuted! Shall I wake Nan? She likes playing 'Who am I?'."

"Yes, Rache – you wake my mum and I'll get some nibbles. Sweetheart, can you get the pens and the post-its out of the office, please? More drinks, anyone?"

★★★

"Okay, princess, you go first."

"Yesth! Who wrote mine?"

"I did, Shortshanks."

"Right. Am I a persthon?"

"Yes."

"Am I a girl?"

"Yes."

"Am I magic?"

"Yes."

"Am I Elstha from *Frozthen*?"

"Bloody 'ell, princess, how d'ya guess that?"

"Easthy peasthy. Robbie wrote it, so I just guessthed someone who'd bug me. Nanna'sth turn! I wrote your one, Nanna."

"Okay, poppet. Am I a person?"

"Yesth."

"How old am I?"

Not again?

"Nanna, you can only ask yesth or no questionsth, remember."

"Oh, yes – am I a girl?"

"Yesth."

"Am I on the telly?"

"Yesth."

"What programme am I in?"

"Bloody 'ell, Betty, how's that a yes or no question?"

"Oh, yes, sorry. Am I magic?"

"Nanna, you can't just asthk my questionsth but, yesth."

"I AM? Oh? What kind of magic do I do?"

"OH, FOR – yes or no, Betty!"

"Yes or no, what? Oh, I see, sorry! So, I'm a girl who's magic and off the telly. I give in."

"Nanna, you can't give in yet. Asthk more questionsth."

"Okay. What colour hair have I got?"

"Friggin' 'ell, Betty – YES or NO!"

"Calm down, Joseph, it's only a game. Hmm? Let me think? Am I Debbie McGee?"

"Who'sth Debbie Ma—?"

"OH, FOR F—"

"There's no need to shout, Joseph. It was only a guess."

"Yeh, a bloody stupid one! How the 'ell would our Maddie know who Debbie McGee is?"

"Well, I don't know any female magicians."

"She's not a bloody magician! Jeeze, this is gonna take all night. D'you wanna clue?"

"Go on, then."

"Think of 'arry Potter."

"AM I HARRY POTTER?"

"JESUS H CHRIST! What planet are you on? YOU'RE HERMIONE FRIGGIN' GRANGER!"

I didn't know she had a middle name?

"Who?"

WHO? How can Nanna not know who Hermione Granger is? I think my dad's right when he said she's from a other planet. Anyway, we've had to stop for a bit cos Jonathon doesn't feel very well. He's got a sore throat and a headache and he feels shivery and hot at the same time. Nanna said it might be the flew cos there's a lot of it about apparently, so he's gone upstairs for a lie down. I think I'll go and see if he's okay, actually. I really like Jonathon, even if he doesn't talk much.

"Can I come in, Rache? Aww, it'sth a shame, isthn't it? ARE YOU NOT WELL, JONATHON?"

"Shhh, Madds, he's poorly, not deaf! Do me a favour, sweetie. Go get the thermometer please, so I can check his temperature."

"YUP! Back in a sec!"

Poor Jonathon. Fancy being poorly on Christmas Day. Mind you, when I was three I had measles on my birthday *and* on Christmas, and he said it's just a cold so it's not that bad. It's weird isn't it – measuring how hot you are to see if you're not well? Cos I'm usually boiling in summer but I feel absolutely fine. One sec...

"Will thisth one do, Rache? I don't know where the other one isth."

"Hahahaha. This isn't a – OHMIGOD! Where did you get this?"

"Out my nursthe'sth bag..."

"Yes, but before your nurse's bag? Where did you find it?"

"Sweetheart, are you in here? Come on out and leave Rache and – Oh. I – um? I wasn't going to say anything until after..."

"OHMIGOD! THAT's why you haven't been drinking!"

"What'sth up?"

"OH! MY! GOD!"

"WHAT'STH UP?"

"OH MY – AND THAT'S WHY YOU'VE BEEN TIRED! OHMIGOD!"

"Jesusth hatesth Christht – will someone tell me

what'sth the matter?"

"Bloody 'ell, you lot, what's with all the OHMI-GODs? We can hear you from downstairs. Come on, princess, leave the poor bloke to 'ave a lie down. What's up, Rache? You look like you've just seen the gas bill?"

"Um... I think *you're* the one who's going to need a lie down, Dad. Come on, Madds, let's leave them to it. Ohmigod!"

Leave them to what? What's going on? If somebody doesn't tell me soon, I'm gonna go absolutely...

"JESUS-H-CHRIST-ALL-FRIGGIN'-MIGHTY – NOT ANOTHER ONE!"

Well, that doesn't sound very Christmassy? And a other one, what?

★★★

OHMIGOD! OH. MY. GOD. Even I'm doing it now but – I can't believe it? My mum's having a other baby! I know! I definitely don't remember asking for THAT for Christmas?

I'm not sure if it's a good thing – but it's turning up in July anyway, my mum said. I heard her telling my dad that she's not sure how it happened but she thinks it's when we were at Rache's wedding. But how d'you get a baby in you without noticing? Mind you, she was a bit drunk by the end? So, that's a other reason I'm never gonna drink booze when I'm a grown-up cos I don't want anyone putting a baby in me when I'm too drunk to notice. I mean, what if you don't want one?

What are you s'posed to do with it? Whoever does that, they should definitely ask first.

Anyway, I think my dad's calmed down a little bit now. And Nanna. And Robbie. And Rache. But, I'm the one what should be most bothered cos I'm gonna be its big sister. And, what if it touches my Xbox? Or, tries to play with Trev? And what if it goes in my bedroom without asking? Or tries to join in with me and Matthew? Or, bugs me? Or... hmm?

"Dad."

"What, kiddo?"

"You know when the new baby comesth, will I still be your princessth?"

"You'll always be my princess, kiddo. Always."

"Well, what will you call it, then?"

"Jesus Christ..."

I don't think you can call a baby that?

"...I'm not sure I'm cut out for this again, Liz. All that squarkin' an' shitty nappies – an' wakin' up before we've even gone to sleep..."

How do you do that?

"... an' goin' to work with puke all down me – friggin' 'ell – we've only just got rid o' one an' now another one's on it's way."

"Mum, Margaret's on the phone. I told her you were a bit busy at the moment, so she said to wish you a Merry Christmas and have you decided whether you're coming up for Hogmanay yet? What should I say?"

Hog man what?

"What do you think, Joe?"

"I'LL BE FIFTY-ONE WHEN IT STARTS SCHOOL!"

Yes! Guess where we're going for New Year's Eve? I've just found out that Scotch people don't call it New Year they call it hog-money – *they really can't talk proply?* – but Rache said they have the bestest parties in the world.

But – who cares about that now? It's still Christmas Day and my mum's put some chicken nuggets in the oven and now we're gonna have a disco.

"Madds, are you coming to dance with me?"

"Yup, one sec…"

So, besides the baby bit, this is the best day ever. And so what if it's horrible? We can always do what my dad said and give it to some gypsies, or stick it in the wardrobe till it's eighteen – and, least I know what to do with my spare dinosaur now.

"Come on, Madds – it's your favourite next! I've put 'Gangnam Style' on for you."

It's not my favourite cos that's The Kicking Song, but it's definitely one of my favourites. Ooh, it's starting so I've got to go now. So, I hope you all have a fantastic time and see you on New Years Eve. Merry flippin' Christmas everyone!

"COMIN' RACHE!"

Goodbye…

And a Happy New Year!

"Elizabeth, welcome back! How lovely, you could make it."

"Hi, Margaret. It's lovely to be back… and thank you for inviting us."

"What do you mean, inviting you? You're family now, dear."

"Sorry to interrupt you both but I'm desperate for the loo. Is it this way, Margaret?"

"It is, Betty – just through there, second on your left. Hahaha. Someone's in a hurry. So, how was the journey? Not too bad, I hope?"

"You know us, Margaret – eventful as always! Joe and Robbie won't be a minute. They're just giving the back of the car a bit of a wipe over."

"A wipe over? Good heavens, what happened? By the way, dear, I hope you didn't mind me inviting Maddie to come up earlier with Jonathon and Rachel, but Rachel mentioned that her dad was a little shell-shocked so I thought it might help you both to have some time alone. A new baby's a lot to take in… but, of course, we've *loved* having her here."

"Not at all, Margaret – it was really thoughtful of you – and to be honest, I was actually quite relieved when you rang. We'd barely had time to talk on Christmas night and Joe was still in shock Boxing Day, then at night we were at our next-door neighbour's party so…"

"Yes, Maddie said. Did they manage to get the curry stain out of the carpet?"

"No, not yet, they're waiting for something to come off the internet. Did she tell you that she spat it all over their *cream carpet* and it's only been down for six months? But I did tell Wendy she wouldn't like it. Anyway, the next morning I'd been talking to Joe; trying my best to reassure him – he's really panicking about having to go through it all again at his age. And just as he was starting to come around to the idea we heard an almighty bang coming from the kitchen, so the pair of us shot through thinking we'd left the gas on or something, and she'd only decided to see what would happen if you put an egg in the microwave. And not just one, Margaret – FOUR! You've never seen such a mess in your life! They practically blew the door off. So, for the first half hour I was glad to see the back of her, before she did anything else to put him off."

Charming… but if she'd let me have my chemistry set like I asked, I wouldn't have had to make up my own eggsperiments. Ooh? Hahaha. Egg speriments! D'you get it? Anyway, I didn't think THAT would happen. Honest to God, I got the fright of my actual life! And, my mum wasn't kidding when she said about the mess cos it was actually umbelievable.

"Good heavens! Well, I can assure you she hasn't done anything like *that* since she's been here."

I haven't, but since me and Trev've been here we've done lots of things we've never done before. Like when Alistair took us for a ride in the jeep to look for the stag. It was just like in Jurassic Park, 'cept the T-rex was already in the car with us. And I've been for a ride on a horse but that was just boring cos the lady wouldn't let go of its lead, and who wants to ride round slowly in a circle for ages when you could definitely hop faster? And last of all, Margaret's been teaching me to play the piano. I'm absolutely rubbish at it but not as rubbish as Trev, cos he can't even play Three Blind Mice proply, never mind Chop Sticks. Anyway, I missed my mum and dad loads so I'm specially glad – ooh? I s'pose I should go down and say hello?

"*Wheeeeeeeeeeeeeee!* Hiyah, Mum! I missthed you *millionsth*. Did you missth—?"

"Sweetheart, who said you could do that?!"

"It'sth okay, Maggie said it'sth allowed for me to slide down the – MATTHEW! What're YOU doin' here? An' why're you covered in sick?"

"My mum's got the the flu, so…"

"I've missed you SO MUCH, sweetheart! The house has been like a ghost town without you. Give me a great big hug and kiss!"

"I missthed you – OW, MUM! You're squashin' me!"

"Ey up, Margaret, where should I put all this? Bloody puke monster!"

"DAAAAD! Did you missth me?"

"Like an 'ole in the 'ead! I'm kiddin', princess, give us a hug! How's she been, Margaret?"

"Good as gold, haven't you, dear?"

"I have, yesth! Maggie letsth me slide down the bannister ALL THE TIME…"

"I'm sorry, Elizabeth, I said she could try it the once."

"It's okay, Margaret, trust me, she'd have done it anyway. And, who said you could call her Maggie, sweetheart?"

"SHE did! An' she letsth me jump on the bed."

"*Really?* And, who's SHE?"

"Soz. An' she even let me…"

"One sec, Shortshanks. Margaret, where shall I put these bags?"

"Oh, hello, Robbie. You're all in the same rooms as last time if that's okay. Now come away into the drawing room, you must all be thirsty after the journey. Tea? Coffee?"

"Could I have a tea, please, Margaret? I've completely gone off coffee."

"Of course, Elizabeth. And for you, Robbie? And, you, Joe? Or would you two prefer something stronger?"

"I wouldn't say no to a whisky, Margaret."

"You're in Scotland, Joe. It would be rude not to!"

"Same 'ere, Margaret, thanks. 'Ey, Shortshanks, did you ask if that girl's comin' tonight?"

"The one what you wasth snoggin' at the weddin'? I forgot, soz. But, You-an'sth comin' an' that'sth his sister, so…"

"Hahaha… his name's Ewan, not You an, ya divvy. As in, 'Ewan McGregor'."

"Isth he comin' to the party?"

"I wish! No, dipshit. Ewan McGregor, outta Trainspottin'. It's a film!"

"Have I seen it?"

"I doubt it. It's about drugs 'n' shit…"

What a weird thing to make a film about?

"… best film ever. It was set in Edinburgh, actually… 'ave you seen Jon an' our Rache anywhere?"

"Yup! Rache'sth still in the bath an' Jonathon'sth in Marky, playin'…"

"In, who?"

"Not, who, idiot – what! Marky! The massthive tent. God, Robbie, don't you know—?"

"It's called a marquee, dumbass! So, don't go callin' me an idiot when it's you who doesn't know what your're talkin' about. Right, I'm offski – an' 'ey, knobchops, it's been quiet without ya – an' not necessarily in a good way. Nice work with the eggs, by the way, but if ya really wanna get yourself chucked out, check out YouTube for Diet Coke an' Mentos!"

Diet coke and—?

"Maddie, you're wanted in the room with the piano

in it. Margaret wants you to show your mum and dad what you've learned."

"Okay... how come you never said you wasth comin', Matthew?"

"It was a surprise."

"It'sth a fantastic surprise. Are you all right now? You still don't look normal."

"I'm okay now we've stopped moving, but I was sick most of the way here. Your dad was going mental. I heard him tell your mum that he's gonna drug me on the way back. What does that mean?"

"Robbie wasth just talkin' about drugsth an' he said they're awesome."

"But, I don't want them, Maddie. I've heard they're dangerous! D'you think he'll really do it?"

How come everyone's talking 'bout drugs today? I'm not really sure what drugs are, but they can't be that bad – not if Carl's big brother sells them at school? Not our school, the big school, but surely they wouldn't let him do it if it was dangerous?

"My dad? Coursthe not! Nearly every day he saysth he'sth gonna send me to the orphanage but I'm still here."

"Yes, but I was sick all down his back while he was driving."

"Oh – then he might!"

"Anyway, your mum said I should have a sleep, so I don't fall asleep at the party. Are you gonna have a sleep?"

"A sleep in the DAY? Are you mental? I'm milesth too eggcited about the party an' – ooh? Shush, Matthew! Can you hear bangin'?"

"Not really, Maddie…"

"Shush! Listen!"

★★★

Poor Nanna! She was locked in the toilet for *least* twenty minutes before I found her, but she was miles more upset cos no one'd noticed she was actually missing. But she proply cheered up when she heard me playing the piano – mind you, everyone did – and I wished I *did* have boxing gloves on like my dad said, cos I would've punched him with them, he was pulling his face so much. He said he'd rather have his teeth out without Anna's thetic than listen to me murder Chop Sticks, and how mean's that?

Anyway, it's time to get ready for the party now and least I won't look like a toilet-roll dolly this time. Guess why? My mum's bought me a new zombie dress off the Internet and it's even better than my last one. It looks 'xacly like Alice in Wonderland's dress, 'cept it's all covered in blood, but the best thing is, Trev's got a costume as the White Rabbit! My mum made him some rabbit ears and… one sec… God's sakes? I've got my hair stuck in the flippin' zip. I'll have to ask my mum to get me un – *ooh? What's going on?*

"Hahaha – JOE! Get away from me! Haven't you done enough damage already?"

"Yeh, but, Christ knows 'ow? I can't remember gettin' to the end once without the human contraceptive burstin' in an' ruinin' it…"

Ooh? That's what he calls me?

"…never mind gettin' off at Edge Hill, love – I barely get out the bloody station! Come on, wop 'em out. They're the only things keepin' me goin' at the moment. Remember when you were preggers with our Rache? Talk about 'from small acorns'…"

"GET OFF, JOE! And I thought you said you didn't like big ones?"

Big whats?

"I don't particularly. I mean, I prefer fun-size Mars Bars, but every now an' again, I don't mind a biggun."

Ooh? Chocolate?

"You and me, both! Hahaha…"

What's she talking about? She never eats Mars Bars?

"Touché, Bizzy Lizzy. So, you don't mind a big one, huh?"

Me too. I much prefer the big ones, cos the mini ones are only two bites…

"Well, I've got a really big one for ya, love!"

Ooh? There'll deffo be some left for me?

"Put it away, Joe, I'm not interested. Hahaha…"

Ooh? Even MORE for me?

"Joe, behave! Hahaha…"

"Come on, Bizzy Lizzy, wrap your chops round this. 'Ey, they come in handy these kilts, don't they? No messin' about with…"

"Get it away from me, Joe. I told you – I'm not interested!"

Well, if my mum doesn't want it then I'll deffo have it…

BANG!

"I'll eat it, Dad, I love big WHAAAAH!"
"BUGGER OFF, WILL YA? See what I mean?"

★★★

Well, we're finally at the party, but I've decided to do some of my own revolutions this year, and the first one I've decided is, I'm never going in my mum and dad's room, ever again. And, who's Jonno Groats? Cos, apparently, I yelled so loud even he must've heard me. Anyway, I can't believe how many people are here? There's even more than at the wedding.

The bad pipes man's back making his horrible noise, but the Scotch people and Nanna seem to love it. And the band's back too, and at midnight we're gonna have a massive fireworks display, with music and everything...

"'Ey, Shortshanks, I believe you caught the old man at it before..."

What old man?

"...randy git! He needs to pack it in! An' who wears a kilt in this weather?"

Oh, the bad pipes man? And, he does need to pack it in cos he's giving me a headache...

"Can you believe, some of 'em go commando?"

"What'sth commando?"

"No boxies."

"No underpantsth? That'sth well rude! Why?"

"Er... don't ya know? That's how ya tell if they're Scottish or not."

"Are you jokin' me?"

"I'm tellin' ya, if you wanna know if someone's Scottish or not just pull up their kilt an' check if they're wearin' undercrackers. Everyone does it."

"No way!"

"Way! Why else d'you think they wear 'em?"

"Honestht to God?"

"Honest to God."

"Crossth your heart an' hope to die?"

"That, too."

"Pinky sthwear."

"Be'ave, ya muppet – 'ow gullible are you? Right, I'm off to the bar to make a serious dent in it. Giz a shout if ya see whatsername."

"Sweetheart, would you like to come with me and get something to eat?"

"Isth it the hogsth roastht now, Mum?"

"It is, sweetheart. Silly question, but, are you hungry?"

"Yup! I'm starvin'! Isth that why it'sth called hog-money, Mum? Costh of the—?"

"No, sweetheart. It's Hogmanay, not hog money. Hey, I believe you've been playing cards with Jonathon's brothers while you've been here. Rache said you practically wiped them out."

"I did! I won nearly two whole poundsth, Mum, an' I didn't cheat once! Honestht to God!"

"I'll believe you. So, were all of his brothers there?"

"Yup, but not all of the time. I specially liked Adrian an' histh wife… erm? Erm?"

"Fiona?"

"Yup – Feeowner! Me an' Rache had a game of Trivia Persutesth with them, an' we had nearly all our cheesesth and they only had their pink— WHAT THE FUG'STH THAT?"

"OHMIGOD! Who the hell told you you could say THAT?"

★★★

Humph! Nobody told me I could say it, but it's what Adrian said yesterday when Feeowner showed him the picture what she'd just drawn of his face. And, first, I thought he'd said the eff word, but he said he didn't say the eff word he said fugg, and fugg's absolutely not swearing. Anyway, I'm not bothered about being shouted at cos I'm too upset to care.

Who puts a pig on a stick then cooks it? Well, I'm never eating meat again and I don't care if it *is* bacon butties. Imfact, I might just be a veggytablearian – *'cept, you absolutely hate veggytables, Maddison?* So, it's just chicken nuggets from now on? Ooh, Margaret's on the stage with the bad pipes man and she's waving me to come up...

"Maddie, dear, how would you like to draw the raffle tickets?"

"Erm? Not really? Besidesth, I haven't got any pencilsth."

"Hahahaha! No, dear! I mean pull a ticket out of the drum then read out the number. Do you think you can manage that?"

"YUP!"

"Come on up then – that's it. Now, you stand there and…"

Wow, it's weird being up on the stage? I can see everything from here and – *why's my mum looking at me, all worried? I hope she's alright?*

"MUM, LOOK AT ME! I'M ON THE STAGE!"

"Maddie, could you pass the microphone here, please? Thank you…

Okay, ladies and gentlemen, before we all get a little worse for wear, I thought now would be a good time to draw the raffle…"

Why does the bad pipes man keep smiling at me?

"… so, could everybody get their tickets ready, please?"

Oh, no, he's gonna talk?

"Ee, she's a canny lass, Margaret. A reet bobby dazzla!"

Makes no sense? Definitely Scotch?

"Isn't she! This is Maddison, Rachel's sister."

"Give ower. Y'a kiddin' me?"

That's not Scotch? I still can't tell what he's saying but…

"Well, a divent naa that. Y'alreet pet?"

Imfact, he sounds like that lady what's sometimes on the Ex Factor? The really pretty one what's always got a different last name?

"Maddie, dear, are you ready?"

"Yesth, Maggie. Hello, everyone, it'sth me! I'm doin' the – soz, one sec! I can't hold everythin' all at the same time…"

I wonder if he'll hold Trev for me?

"Scusthe me… SCUSTHE ME… SCUSTHE ME!"

Flippin' 'eck? Is he deaf?

"OY, YOU – RANDY GIT! Can you hold my dinosthaur, pleasthe?"

"Hahahaha. Wey aye, lass. Pass him owor heur."

WHAT? That's definitely not Scotch? What did Robbie say to do if you want to know if someone's Scotch? Oh, yes…

"Thanksth. An' can I just…"

"HOWAY MAN! Wot d'ya think yas DEEYUHN?"

"OH! Definitely not Scotch! Hello, Spiderman!"

I'm gonna kill Robbie and I don't care *what* he says – he absolutely did tell me that the bad pipes man's name's Randy Git, and that if you want to know if someone's Scotch or not, just pull-up their skirt.

Well, he's not Randy Git he's Callum, apparently, and he's from Geordie, wherever that is? Anyway, now everyone's stopped laughing, I think we're ready to start again…

"Okay, ladies and gentlemen, apologies for the delay. Elizabeth, take your head out of your hands, dear. Callum, as with everybody, found the mix-up hilarious… and if anyone's stuck for a Christmas present next year, well, we now know that he's a fan of Spiderman! Hahaha.

So, if we're ready to continue? Over to you, Maddison."

"Thanksth, Maggie. Okay, the first one'sth – hang on a sec. Ooh? I know this one. Two little ducksth. It'sth twenty-two! QUACK! QUACK! I'M DOIN' BINGO, NANNA!"

"Thanks, Maddie. So, that's third prize; the home cinema system… ticket number zero zero two two… Joseph! Hahaha. I can promise everyone, there's been no cheating here."

"YESTH! WE'VE WON ONE, MUM! WE'VE WON A PRIZE!"

"Yes, dearie, you have, and I'm sure you'll all be delighted with it. Okay, over to…"

"Okay, next one'sth – can it go in my bedroom, Mum? – okay, a duck, a fat lady, an' a doctor'sth ordersth. That's a hard one, Maggie!"

"Hahaha… So, that's second prize; the fifty-year-old single malt, ticket number… pass the ticket, Maddie… zero two eight nine. ZERO TWO – and we have a winner at the back. Marlon, come and collect your prize, please… and, for the last one back to Maddie."

"Thanksth – I bet you're dead glad we didn't win fifty yearsth old booze, aren't you, Dad? Costh it'sth probly gone off! Okay, the last one'sth – ooh? Ooh! I know this one, too!

Least, Bingo with Nanna wasn't a complete waste of time?

"DINNER FOR TWO – IT'STH SIXTHTY-NINE!"

I'm not sure what I've done eggsacly but my mum's still hiding in the toilets and even Rache can't get her to come out! But, it can't be that bad when people laugh, can it? Anyway, we've won a fantastic prize and…

"Oy, princess, your mum's finally agreed to come out the toilets, so bloody be'ave yourself. D'you hear me?"

YES! Flippin' 'eck! Why do grown-ups only ask if I can hear them when they're shouting? Why don't they ask me when they're talking normal? Cos, that's most probly when I – ooh, she's here…

"Honestly, Maddison, I've never been so embarrassed in all my life! The raffle was bad enough, but what on earth made you lift Callum's kilt up like that?"

Robbie's so dead…

"Costh…"

"I don't want to hear it, Maddie, I just want you to sit there and behave yourself. Am I understood?"

"Yup!"

I do understand, I just don't want to do it. I don't want to spend the rest of the year sitting on a chair when I could be having fun. I wonder if?

"Mum, if I promise to be good, can I go and play with Matthew? Matthew never doesth anything naughty so I'll…"

"Just go, Maddie! I'm too tired to argue…"

Ohmigod – that was quick? And I've had a well good idea?

"Matthew, d'you want to play a brilliant game?"

"Yes. What is it?"

***

"Crikey, Maddie. That was mental!"

"I know. How many did you do, Matthew?"

"I only did seven then someone kicked me in the head."

"Seven'sth brilliant! I only did five costh a man blew off under the table, right in my face."

"*Eeeeeeuw!*"

"I know! It wasth disthgustin', imfact, it stunk so bad I had to leave! Come on, let'sth sit down an' watch."

"Are you sure it's not dangerous, Maddie?"

"Coursthe not! It'sth perfekly safe."

"'Ey up, princess… er, is it me, or d'you look like you've been up to no good?"

"Me? I've not been up to anythin', have I, Matthew?"

"Erm?"

"Good! Cos your mum's – Bloody 'ell, Liz! Did you see that fella over there? He just stood up an' face-planted the floor!"

"I know, Joe. How much has he had to – ohmigod, there goes another one? What's happening? Oh, my – why's everyone falling over?"

"Hahahaha. Jeeze, Liz, look at 'em all. Hahahahaha – what the?"

"OH, GOOD GOD! WHAT'S HAPPENING?"

The Shoelace game's what's happening…

"This is crazy, Joe! That's Adrian – the one who just fell face-first into his Cranachan."

"Hahahaha – what the fuck's Cranachan?"

"You're eating it! Maddie, please God, tell me that

you didn't have anything to do with this?"

D'you mean, did I crawl under the tables and tie people's shoelaces together? Erm? Time to not be here…

"No! Crossth my heart!"

Oops, sorry for telling lies, Jesus, but I've got my fingers crossed so it doesn't actually count.

"Come on, Matthew… I didn't do anythin', Mum, but we're gonna do dancin' with Rache, now. Isth that okay?"

"I suppose. So long as you are 'doing dancing'. And if I find out you had anything to do with those poor people falling – come back, Maddison. I HAVEN'T FINISHED YET!"

Yes, you have…

"Hey, Matthew, have you ever seen a actual stag?"

"No, and I don't want to. They've got massive antlers and – I'm still scared about the drugs, Maddie. What if—?"

"Stop bein' such a scardey-cat, Matthew, my dad won't do anythin'! Imfact, if you don't believe me, there'sth Rache. Asthk her. Rache… Rache… RACHE… RAAAACHE!"

Is everyone deaf tonight? And who's that weird man she's talking to?

"Scusthe me, mister, can I just talk to my—?"

"Madds! I do apologise, Lady Amberford. This is my little sister, Maddison, and her best friend Matthew. Say hello to Lady Amberford, Madds."

"Erm? Hello… Rache, will you tell Matthew that my dad won't force him to do drugsth costh he'sth proply terrified and – are you sure you're not a man?"

"AH! Goodbye, Lady Amberford. Say goodbye, Maddison… Ohmigod, Madds – you have NO FILTER!"

"What'sth one of them? An' soz, Rache, but…"

"You can't just say what you see!"

You can if you're playing Dingbats?

"Sorry, Rache. I don't like it when you shout at me."

"I'm not shouting, I'm – apology accepted, but you have to learn not to blurt things out, sweetie. There's such a thing as tact. And what on earth are you talking about drugs for?"

"Costh, Matthew said my dad'sth gonna give him drugsth on the way home."

"Travel-sick pills! Now, are you gonna come and dance with me before you offend anybody else? Scottish country dancing's the best. I'm so hopeless, I spend more time picking myself up off the floor than actually dancing, and I laugh so much, I can't breathe."

"But, you're a brilliant dancer, Rache."

"Not at this!"

***

She wasn't kidding either – Scottish dancing's crazy – specially when you don't know any of the steps. Imfact, it was so dangerous I had to put Trev down! It wasn't bad at first when it was just me and Rache, but then Nanna joined in and it was a absolute disaster! She kept going the wrong way and banging into people, and one time she banged into Callum so hard that she went proply flying, and by the time she'd managed to get up, she'd laughed so much she'd done some actual wee! I know! But, they've gone for a sit down now cos they're all out of puff…

I wonder how old you are when you start running out of puff? Cos, I've still got loads left and… one sec…

"Matthew, where've you been?"

"Outside with your dad. He was showing me all the stars."

"There's miles more in Scotland, aren't there?"

"Not really. Your dad said you can see more cos there's no streetlights here… it's called light palution when they make it too bright to see all the stars."

"Really? Shall we go outside an' look? I'm all hot and sweaty and – ooh? I wonder if we'll see weird wolfsth? Or Scotch ghoststh? Or the Lot Lessth Monst—?"

"DON'T SAY THAT, MADDIE!"

"Soz… let'sth go this way. Flippin' 'eck, it'sth freezin' out here, isthn't it? I can see my breath an' everythin'."

"I know. It was weird being in Australia cos it was sunny all the time. Even on Christmas Day."

"REALLY?"

"Really!"

"That'sth one of my favourite thingsth from this year, Matthew, that you came back to live in – ooh! What'sth that?"

"WHERE?"

"*Shhh! Whisthper. I can hear talking comin' from inside that horse'sth housthe.*"

"Talking? I can't hear any…"

"Shhh! Whisthper! You must be able to hear – ohmigod, it'sth Robbie with a girl."

And what a WEIRD thing to say?

"A GIRL?"

"Flippin' 'eck, Matthew! WHISTHPER!"

"WHO'S THERE?"

"I TOLD you to whisthper, Matthew!"

"If that's you, Shortshanks, I'll…"

"QUICK! LEG IT! And watch out for the poo!"

Well now I'm out of puff thanks to Matthew and his big loud gob – honestly, I don't know how many times I told him to whisper? Anyway, thanks to him, I didn't get to hear the end of what Robbie was saying to the girl, but I can't believe anyone'd want to do that. I mean…

"Maddie, your dad's shouting you."

"Oh! Okay. You asthk my mum to get the horsthe poo off your shoesth, and I'll see what he wantsth."

I wonder what I've done now? I don't remember doing anything, but…

"Here she is… Princess, I was just tellin' everyone about when you ate the blackberries the day before the weddin'…"

Phew! I haven't done anything…

"Tell 'em what you did, when you couldn't get to sleep."

"D'you mean, my rollersth?"

"Yeh. Listen to this everyone."

"Okay, but… would you lick a cat, Dad?"

"'Ey? What kind of a question's THAT? See what I

'ave to put up with, Nick. This is Ewan's dad, princess."

"I know, I've been playin' cardsth with him. But, would you, Dad? Lick a actual cat?"

"Why would anyone lick a cat, princess?"

"Well, Robbie wantsth to."

"What ARE you goin' on about?"

"Robbie said it to the girl!"

"WHAT BLOODY GIRL?"

"THE GIRL IN THE HORSE'STH HOUSE! I think it'sth Ewan'sth sister. Well, he didn't say cat eggsacly, he said pussthy, but it'sth the 'xact same…"

"Come on, princess – that's enough o' that! Bye, everyone!"

"DAD, PUT ME DOWN! I'M NOT A FLIPPIN' BABY!"

"All right, kiddo, an' don't mention babies. Let's go find your…"

"Hey, Maddie!"

Oh, no! How imbarrassing…

"Erm? Hello, Ewan."

"Why are you dressed like *Alice in Wonderland*? And, why's your dad carrying you?"

"I know my dad'sth carryin' me but… I am eleven, really!"

I can't believe he's made such a show of me? And Ewan's *never* gonna believe I'm eleven now…

"Ladies and gentlemen… just a reminder. The fireworks are due to start in ten minutes. That's ten minutes!"

Flippin' 'eck? Is there only ten minutes left of this year?

"D'you wanna get on my shoulders, kiddo, an' I'll carry you down to the fireworks?"

"Yup! Hey, Dad, d'you know in ten minutesth I'll be TEN next year, and I've only just finished being seven!"

"Is that so? I don't even wanna think about how old I'll…"

"Forty-seven! Flippin' 'eck, that'sth nearly as old as Nanna!"

"Cheers for that, princess. So, what's been your favourite things about this year?"

"Well… Matthew coming back from a Stralia. An' Rache and Jonathon'sth wedding. An' learning kung fu and – ooh, you winning the dad'sth race at sportsth day! An' Trev bein' the baby Jesusth…"

"Let's not talk about that, 'ey, princess. Hahahaha…"

"Okay. Robbie being nice to me when he thought I might've died. And getting a new baby brother or sister – I think? But best of all, I GOT A XBOXTH! Oopsth! Pardon me!"

"Did you just crack one off on the back o' my neck?"

"YUP! Hahahahahahaha."

"Ladies and gentlemen… The fireworks are due to start in five minutes. That's five minutes!"

Only five minutes left? Least this time when I sing 'Old Lang's Eyes' I won't be soaking wet and covered in fish poo! That definitely wasn't good… Hmn? Not good things about this year? Killing two fish: that was horrid.

Nearly killing a penguin at the zoo: even more horrid. Getting chicken pots in the summer holidays – thank you, Matthew! Being sick, standing in poo and getting grounded all the time. Finding out Mrs Collins didn't really go to a Stralia, she went to heaven instead... but the worst thing? Well, I'll never eat so many blackberries all in one go again, cos having dire rear when you have to drive all the way to Scotland isn't good... specially when your brother's taking pictures the whole time.

"Here, Liz, grab her – the mingin' monkey's just cracked a corker, right on the back o' my neck."

"Sweetheart!"

"Mum?"

"Yes, Maddie?"

"I love you."

"Awww... I love you too. What made you say that?"

"Costh you smell lovely, an' you are lovely, an'..."

"Aww, what a sweet thing to – RACHE! WE'RE OVER HERE!"

"We're into the last minute of 2016..."

"Hey, there you all are. Come on, let's hold hands."

"Where'sth Jonathon, Rache?"

"Losing badly in a shots competition with his brothers. I've told him if he's ill tomorrow – which he will be – I'll have zero sympathy for him. Come on, Mattie, hold my hand, sweetie. Big Ben's about to chime!"

What, Big Ben again? Is he following us?

"Give me a hug, Madds. OOH! 10 – 9 – 8 –"

"MUM! DAD! HOLD MY HANDSTH! 5 – 4 – 3 – 2 – 1 – HAPPY NEW YEAR! OHMIGOD! Look at all the fireworksth, Mum! OHMI…

Should old equatorsth be forgot, an' never brought to mine
Should older quaintness be forgot, for old lang'sth eyesth
FOR OLD LANG'STH EYESTH, MY DEAR;
FOR OLD LANG'STH EYESTH
WE'LL BREAK A CUP OF TIZER, YUP!
FOR THE SNAKESTH OFF OLD LANG'STH
EYESTH… HAPPY NEW YEAR EVERY-
BODY!"

"Happy New Year, sweetheart! Gosh, those fire-works *are* loud."

"I know, Mum. They're brilliant."

I can't believe it's the new year again? I wonder if I'll be good as gold again this year? Last year's probly the goodest I've ever – OHMIGOD – Nanna's snogging Callum! That's not normal? Anyway, I hope you don't mind but I'm gonna go now cos it's definitely gonna be the…

De de – de de de – de de – de de de

It is! It's The Kicking Song, and I've never done it outside before…

"Mum, watch me. See how high my leg goesth now!"

"Stop 'er, Liz, she's havin' kung f— An' there it goes!"

"DAD! PICK ME UP! I'VE LOST MY SHOE!"

"What's new, princess? I'm thinkin' of openin' a one-legged shoe shop, it happens that often!"

Well, maybe if you buyed me ones what fit?

"Dad! Shortshanks! Get in the picture... OKAY, EVERYONE, SAY CHEESE! Nice one!"

"Happy New Year, Robbie!"

"You too, Shortshanks!"

"Matthew, Happy New Year!"

"Happy New Year to you, Maddie, and Trev, of course!"

And a Happy New Year to you!

But I've definitely got to go now cos it's gonna be my new favourite song next, and I can't walk 500 miles without my other shoe, so...

"Maddie, here – that lady gave it to me. She said it landed on her head, hahaha...."

"Yesth! My shoe! Thanksth, Matthew, just in time..."

"Crikey – why's everyone going crazy?"

"Why? It'sth the 500 MILESTH SONG, that'sth why! It'sth only the best song ever! Just copy me, Matthew, an' let'sth be the first people this year to go ABSTHOLUTELY MENTAAAAL!"

"MADDISON, CALM DOWN!"

No chance...

See you next year everyone, and don't forget about your revolutions in the morning...

This is Maddison saying... Happy 2017 and...

Goodnight!